The Weight of Small Things

The Weight *of* Small Things

JULIE LANCASTER

MIRROR BOOKS

First published by Mirror Books in 2020

Mirror Books is part of Reach plc
10 Lower Thames Street
London EC3R 6EN

www.mirrorbooks.co.uk

ISBN 978-1-913406-18-9

Typeset by Danny Lyle

Printed and bound in Great Britain by
CPI Group (UK) Ltd, Croydon, CR0 4YY

A CIP catalogue record for this book is available from the British Library.

1 3 5 7 9 10 8 6 4 2

Cover credit: iStock

For Margaret

Part One

Broken

Chapter One

Arctic Red

1988

Frankie Appleton was counting gates.

Heavy rain was flicking forward-slashes onto the car windscreen and the botanical temperature inside the car was steaming up the glass like a curtain but she was soon able to find a rhythm.

Wipe the glass, count the gate.

Wipe the glass, count the gate.

As the glimpsed gates sped by, wrought-iron, double-hinged, Buxton, lattice, Frankie's fingers grazed the slip of paper in her coat pocket, a sentence from the magazine *Garden Gates – A Definitive Guide*:

'*A gate is the first thing that a visitor sees and its appearance gives an indication of what lies beyond it, providing either a positive or negative first impression.*'

She didn't just like counting gates. She liked designing them too.

She'd written the quote in red felt-tip pen on her bedroom wall, behind a Madonna poster – the 'Angel' one, where she's wrapped in a blue towel, or maybe it's a blue dressing gown. She could never quite decide which. As with most things, one day it was one thing, the next day another.

It was also glued onto the eight shoebox lids beneath her bed, the boxes housing hundreds of pencil sketches of gates, all named after rivers, because, like rivers, gates led elsewhere too. Some were named after famous rivers like the Nile and the Danube, others after lesser-known rivers such as the Yellowknife and the Arctic Red.

Fellow gate-enthusiast David Miller, author of her most treasured book *The Grandeur of Gates* and a graduate of the Academy of Fine Arts in Florence agreed:

'*A gate is the ultimate link between you and what lies ahead and both functionality and aesthetic appeal are of equal importance.*'

His gate designs were some of the most innovative and inspirational that Frankie had ever seen; so much so that she'd spent three days last summer composing a fourteen-page letter to him.

She was yet to receive a reply. But she hadn't given up hope. Designing gates took patience, letter-writing, similarly so. And he was no doubt extremely busy. There were so many neglected gates to renovate, so many empty spaces to fill. Their paths would cross one day, she was sure of it, but there was no time to think about exactly when that might be because her current favourite gate was a mere five gates away. Distance for Frankie was always measured in gates.

She quietly counted down, building up the tension like they did when announcing Miss World: 4 . . . 3 . . . 2 . . . 1 . . . *And the winner is . . .*

7, Darwin Crescent was a long-limbed four-storey redbrick townhouse that bowed and swayed like a drunken sailor. Without the support of the two properties either side of it, each gripping an elbow, it would have been swallowed up like saltwater long ago. Frankie liked the thought of buildings supporting each other, cheering each other on, always being there when you were a little the worse for wear.

The gate, however, required no such support, the wood hardy and dense, the violet varnish shimmering beneath a blistering summer sun, sometimes with a hint of citrus lime, other times an apricot glaze. Even in winter it welcomed the heaviest of snow, retaining its sturdiness and its shape, never buckling under the extra weight. You could still tell that it was a gate. Frankie liked that. Everything should live up to expectation. A gate should always look like a gate.

Today, silver sparks were ricocheting angrily off the tearstained wood. But even during the worst downpour it still fulfilled all the demands that were made of it, the dark timber glistening like tinsel, the rainwater trickling down the bevelled grooves like un-soothed tears running into the gutter.

Frankie stopped counting gates. She was nearly home. Ellie was chatting to her mother about the type of dog that she desperately wanted (really furry). She'd already given this fictitious dog a name, Ringo Starr, after her favourite Beatle, regardless of whether it was male or female. She'd heard them have the same conversation many times. Ellie would promise to feed it twice a day and take it for three-hour walks, 'cross my heart and hope to die'. Her mother would promise to think about it.

That was as far as they ever got, promising and thinking, promising to think. Crossing hearts and dying. Her mother was still grappling with the Beatles obsession. 'It seems such an unusual fixation for a nine-year-old girl who spends hours in her bedroom making dresses for her dolls out of old pairs of 15-denier tights and who still watches *Rainbow*,' she would explain to Frankie. People often spoke to Frankie as if she was an adult when she still wanted to be a child. But sadly on this occasion she could offer no insight. She was similarly perplexed, although for an entirely different reason. Everybody knew that Paul was the best Beatle.

The car purred gently at the traffic lights and the windscreen wipers squeaked in a hypnotising game of cat-and-mouse. Frankie sat cradling the two slices of birthday cake that Ellie's mother had wrapped in a yellow napkin and pressed into her hands. The package felt hot on her lap, like sunshine melting. The traffic lights finally turned green on the thirty-first squeak.

Ellie craned her neck towards the backseat, her glasses magnifying her eyes so many times that her eyes seemed bigger than her face. She was nothing but eye, a giant questioning eye, an optical illusion.

'Are you still coming to Alton Towers on Saturday?' she asked Frankie. 'Liam Lewis says the Corkscrew's awesome.'

Frankie turned away from the melting sunshine and the gates now sailing by uncounted.

'I'm not sure. Mum's a bit under the weather.'

What did that even mean? Weren't they all under the weather? Still, that's what everybody said and Frankie had always found it a conveniently evasive and vague response.

'I'm sorry to hear that, Frankie,' Ellie's mother said. 'Is there anything you need?'

'No thank you, Mrs Barlow.'

Frankie didn't elaborate; being 'under the weather' allowed you to forgo the small print of an ailment, imagined or otherwise. Besides, her mother would never forgive her for 'airing their dirty laundry in public', even though it was something that her mother did on a daily basis, showing everyone her underwear while she was still wearing it.

They drove through another set of traffic lights ('They're always digging something up,' Mrs Barlow complained, her fingers impatiently tapping the steering wheel), which took eighty-three squeaks (a new record) to change to green, and then Frankie closed her eyes, visualising the rest of the journey behind closed eyelids – the four lefts, the three rights, the two roundabouts, the six potholes and the two zebra crossings – plotting it all on a map inside her head, her fingernail following the spiral contours, the world condensed beneath a fleshy fingertip.

She flatly refused to visualise the two gates on Hillside Drive, though; could barely breathe when she had to go past them. They were hideous. Thank goodness David Miller would never see them.

She timed it perfectly. When she next opened her eyes they were pulling up in front of an equally hideous wooden gate, the paint peeling off it like a damp plaster that can no longer protect the wound beneath it.

Frankie had begged her mother to buy a new gate, but her mother had told her not to be ridiculous, they didn't have money for gate repairs. A new gate was the least of their worries, she'd said – what did it matter if it didn't close properly? It would be easier to walk through. And then her mother had held a palm up to her forehead as if her thoughts were spilling out onto the floor and she was trying to catch them before they scattered everywhere.

Frankie didn't want to be the cause of her mother's thoughts spilling everywhere, but how else would they keep the bad things out, how else would they stay safe? Her mother just didn't understand the importance of a resilient gate.

Deciding to purchase the necessary materials herself, Frankie began collecting loose coins in a pickled-onion jar that no matter how many times she washed still smelled of pickled onions. Currently, she had eight pounds and twenty-five pence and a cent and a peseta that she'd found on the pavement outside Woolworths, and that had taken seven months to collect.

Perhaps she could do a sponsored swim, although she'd have to learn to swim first. She spent the majority of her school swimming lessons hiding in the changing rooms inking verrucas onto the soles of her feet because she was scared of drowning.

Sharon Jackson had nearly drowned at the start of the autumn term when her armbands had unexpectedly deflated and none of the teachers had even noticed. Robin Bloor, who'd only completed his first full length of the baths the week before, had had to drag her to the steps flailing and gulping like a fish. And even though Martin Sargeant was suspected of deliberately deflating them – he kept a box of drawing pins in his blazer pocket – Frankie still thought it entirely possible that things could deflate all on their own.

Perhaps washing cars would be less hazardous, and there was a sponge and a bucket in the pantry so there'd be no start-up costs. Only elbow grease would be required and she had plenty of that. Or a delivery service. People always wanted things delivered: newspapers, letters, babies . . .

Ever hopeful of securing the additional funding needed, she would spread her DIY catalogues and pamphlets across the bed and either add something new to her designs or erase what had once been there and start again. It was a continual process, searching for the perfect gate, and the secret was to never accept what was already there but to look beyond the expected, beyond the landscape, beyond the ordinary. Nobody, apart from David Miller, quite realised the effort or the financial commitment involved.

Frankie got out of the car and thanked Mrs Barlow for the lift home. Ellie was still waving as they pulled away, her features now blurred by the running rain, and then they turned right at the bottom of the road and disappeared. Frankie kicked open the garden gate with her foot, she never liked to touch it, and walked towards the front door.

She suddenly hesitated, wondering what would be waiting for her on the other side of the door. Would her mother be out of bed? Would she be happy to see her? If the day was black (there were only black days and blacker days) then her mother would be on her hands and knees trying to scoop her thoughts back up off the living room carpet with a dustpan and brush, the carpet swirls making it that much harder. She didn't want to think about the possibility of it being a blacker day.

She took a deep breath and unzipped her rucksack. Ellie always made fun of her rucksack, said that she must walk around with 'everything but the kitchen sink' inside it because it was always so heavy, but it only really contained the things that she considered essential, the things that she needed access to at all times: a notepad with at least forty blank pages, two pens in case one ran out, a pencil, a rubber, a ruler, David Miller's book and a copy of the letter that she'd sent him, a chocolate bar – usually a Mars bar, because the fridge was often empty and the cupboards full of other things – a local map that she'd picked up at the bus station, a photograph of her mother with tomato-red lips and far too many teeth and, most importantly, a front-door key.

She didn't mention the pickled-onion jar that she now had to carry around with her as well. Even though she'd written 'GATE FUND MONEY' on it in angry capital letters and hidden it inside a vase on a shelf in her bedroom, there was one pound and eighty three pence missing from it. She'd checked it four times just to be sure, disappointed that her mother hadn't at least left an IOU.

Unlocking the front door, she stepped inside. The hallway was as dark as liquorice, the rooms either side of it silent and chilly. Normally, the central heating would hiss and the water pipes whistle and the house would yawn and stretch; you could hear it breathing, especially at night. But today it sat quietly, watching and waiting. She checked for her mother's camel coat. It was hanging from one of the coat hooks.

Frankie had locked herself in the bathroom and refused to come out when she'd first seen her mother wearing it. Through the bathroom door her mother had assured her that 'the camel would only have been made into a coat when it was very, very old and about to die or even already dead,' *and*, she'd said, as if this was the most exciting part, 'having spent a long and happy life ferrying people across hot deserts, it's the camel that's now being ferried, only to town and back and the weather isn't as good, but still. Isn't that wonderful?' Hardly wonderful, but it had made Frankie feel a little less queasy.

She closed the front door and went into the kitchen, placing the squashed yellow napkin on the kitchen table. She hadn't realised that she'd been clenching her fist and the crumpled napkin now reminded her of the tiny yellow bird that she'd once caught her mother stamping on in the backyard. She hadn't dared ask her whether it had already been dead (like the camel, *and*, if it had been dead, then why was she stamping on it?) or whether she'd killed it by stamping on it. Her eyes were like pebbles.

When she'd gone back inside Frankie had carefully cupped the lifeless bird that was as flat as a pressed flower inside her pinafore dress and buried it beneath a patch of daisies. She was sorry that the bird had been yellow and not brown. Being yellow made you stand out. It made you noticeable. Later, she noticed blood on the sole of her mother's left shoe and a small yellow feather on the yard brush and she wondered if there'd been other yellow birds, other things that she didn't know.

She quickly blinked the image away, remembered instead the grey half-moons beneath her mother's eyes that morning that had been slowly sliding down her cheeks. She'd been wearing her customary red lipstick, but instead of looking like her younger self she'd looked like a circus clown. All Frankie wanted was for her to look like herself, but she imagined that her mother had forgotten who that was.

Blood-red picket-fencing ran along her lip line, as if her lips had been stitched together and she'd had to cut through the stitches with scissors to speak, and she must have forgotten to blot her lips with a tissue because she left a second pair of rosebud red lips on Frankie's right cheek when she kissed her goodbye. Frankie couldn't bring herself to wipe them away. It would have been like wiping her mother away. And so she'd gone to Ellie's birthday party with one rosebud red cheek and one white unloved cheek and nobody had spat on a handkerchief and tried to remove the traces of her mother.

There were two mugs in the kitchen sink. Frankie wondered if her mother was 'entertaining'. She picked up the one that wasn't smudged with lipstick. It smelled of whiskey and Nescafé. Sylvia didn't drink whiskey. And Stan wasn't expected back for another two weeks, although he often liked to surprise them, her mother's pale and unready face shooing her upstairs. She shuddered. She hated Stan. So many times she'd tried to tell her mother just how much she hated him, which was the most that she'd ever hated anybody, but then she would catch sight of her mother's trembling fingers in the hall mirror as she was clipping back her hair, the fluttering, shallow breaths as she sat nervously biting her fingernails, and she couldn't do it.

She didn't want the half-moons to become full moons. And it probably wouldn't have made any difference anyway. Apparently, her mother didn't need 'the approval of a fucking nine-year-old'.

And so he continued to manoeuvre her mother away from her with his garlic-fried breath and his frostbitten stare. She'd hoped that he'd drift quietly away like the others, but unfortunately he seemed to be inching his way ever closer, bringing her conciliatory childish bribes that he thought might pacify her and buy him more time with her mother (obviously unaware that her approval wasn't necessary); things that other people had discarded, and for good reason: a *Beano* comic that smelled of Campbell's mushroom soup, a plastic beaded necklace with a broken clasp, sticky, glittery hairslides, a naked Sindy doll with no arms, things that she suspected he'd stolen from another child's hands or dustbin finds that he'd decided to recycle.

'People throw away a lot of perfectly useable things that just need a good wipe,' she'd overheard him telling her mother. She wondered if this included her mother.

Frankie could barely disguise her contempt and often threw his 'gifts' straight into the bin while he was still waiting for a 'thank you' (her mother would fish them back out again and tell her not to be so ungrateful).

A diary that he left outside her bedroom door belonged to 'Diana Copeland, aged 12', according to the inside cover, and entries for the whole of September had been completed (none of them particularly riveting) – *lunch today was cod in parsley sauce, the slimiest fish ever; Nigel Fenton is a massive cry baby, I barely touched him; a woman who wasn't Mum was in Dad's car today* – and she hated him for stealing something so personal. She wanted to return it, she'd already read too much, but there was no one by that name at any of the local schools. She'd called them all pretending to be Diana's mother (and then Nigel Fenton's mother). The diary was the only thing that she ever kept in the hope that she could one day return it.

She wondered what Christmas would be like this year. Normally, her mother would be barefoot in the kitchen with a dusting of flour in her hair humming 'Silent Night', the silver baubles dangling from the artificial tree branches like Pat Butcher's earrings. There'd be a bottle of Le Jardin perfume or a C&A cardigan and a pair of slippers to unwrap, followed by the Queen's speech and *It's a Wonderful Life* and then, later, repeats of *The Morecambe and Wise Christmas Special* and a Quality Street orange creme or caramel swirl. It was the same each year, like the programme listings in the Christmas *TV Times*, but that was what her mother liked most – the familiarity, the uneaten toffee fingers rolling around the tin at the end of the night.

By Boxing Day morning, however, it was as if the previous day had been a different Christmas or another family's celebrations. The tree would be Norwegian green again and back in its box, the turkey carcass unceremoniously tossed into the pedal bin, and her mother would be lying in bed, curiously intrigued by the spider cracks in the ceiling that were apparently 'the size of Yellowstone canyons'. Frankie hoped that Stan was planning to spend Christmas elsewhere. She didn't want him ruining the only nice memories that she had of her mother.

She carefully unfolded the napkin and slid what wasn't still stuck to it onto a plate. It was carnage, a bloodbath of buttercream and strawberry jam. She tried not to think about the tiny canary-yellow bird buried in the back garden, the slightly raised earth not noticeable at all now, but like the bird, her mother still hadn't stirred.

Canaries were once used by coalminers as early-warning systems, she'd recently learned. She'd immediately raised her hand and told Mr Thomas, her teacher, that it was a cruel practice and could she please be excused from the lesson. But he'd said that human life must always come before that of an inferior species and no, she couldn't be excused. Furious, she'd broken her pencil rubber in half, pushed the two halves into her ears, and reproduced the Celtic knot gate accent that she'd seen that morning on her way to school in the back of her science book instead. Not all humans deserved prior warning of imminent death. Mr Thomas obviously hadn't met Stan. And the canary-yellow bird in their backyard couldn't alert any of them to potential dangers any more.

She couldn't remember seeing Stan's car in the street, a rusty metallic grey Volvo with leopard-print seat covers and a reclining backseat, a car that you didn't forget in a hurry, a car that you were lucky to escape from alive. But perhaps he'd walked or hitched a ride. He often parked streets away, as if he didn't want anybody to know where he was, didn't want to be held accountable for what might happen when he got there. She decided to wait a little longer just in case.

If she ever interrupted him, often accidentally, he would go white with rage, never red like normal people, and wait until her mother was out of earshot before roughly pinching her arm and cursing under his breath and telling her to '*never, ever, do that again, you sanctimonious little shit*'. She always tried to hold his gaze, pretended to know what words like 'sanctimonious' meant (it didn't sound particularly complimentary), but would have to rush to the toilet the minute he let go of her, her bladder never quite as fearless.

She wondered what colour he would go if he was being stabbed. Orange, she imagined, like tangerine peel. She silently listed all the different ways that he might die and the different colours that he might turn as he lay dying.

She sighed and went into the sitting room. The curtains were still drawn. She pulled them open to let in the day, but the day was so dark that all it did was let in more darkness. The room had been tidied, she noticed, the ashtrays emptied and the wine glasses cleared away. The coffee table smelled of lemon furniture polish. Frankie generally did all the housework, but sometimes it would have to wait if she had homework to finish or gates to design. And this morning she'd been busy wrapping Ellie's birthday presents.

Fortunately, with the dusting done, she would be able to catch up on her reading. She was halfway through *136 Ornate Garden Gates* by Penny and Gilbert Jones and was planning to read *The Perfect Gate for the Perfect Space* by Carl Franks next.

She was looking forward to building a gate that Stan could never get through – the Stan-Repellent, she would call it. She was running out of rivers.

The house was eerily quiet apart from a clock ticking (she couldn't tell which one). Her mother had a huge collection of clocks, although many of them no longer worked, and those that did work were either too fast or too slow. One of them, a glass-domed anniversary clock, didn't tick at all, the minute hand rotating in a sullen silence.

Growing increasingly impatient, she collected what she'd salvaged of the birthday cake and went upstairs to wake her mother. When she got to the top of the stairs she noticed that her mother's bedroom door was open. She could see a sliver of room, a corner of bed. Her mother always kept the door closed because she hated the thought of somebody spying on her. She didn't consider staring into the neighbour's houses from the bedroom window for hours at a time spying. That was apparently 'showing a neighbourly interest'.

She also didn't like anyone going into her bedroom when she wasn't there, although there was nothing much to see. Frankie had looked. Anything of interest was hidden in a less conspicuous corner of the house. But she did like trying on her mother's shoes and putting on her lipstick.

Frankie wished that they didn't have doors at all so that everything could be easily seen. She always dreaded what might be behind them. She took another deep breath and pushed open the bedroom door, preparing herself for a 'get the fuck out' and a spinning gin bottle. There was neither.

She saw her mother's slippers first, fluffy pink bedroom mules that had all sorts of matter stuck to them, swinging gently to and fro, on the wrong feet. And then when Frankie looked up she saw the rest of her hanging from the ceiling. Her eyes weren't any colour at all, they were colourless, like pearl barley, but she still seemed to be searching for all those lost thoughts still stuck to the carpet swirls or maybe she was wondering why her slippers were on the wrong feet and there were three baked beans stuck to the matted fur. That seemed more likely.

Frankie had wanted to tell her about the one-eyed magician and the rabbit that wouldn't come out of the hat and the trampoline that no one could bounce on because Ellie's father had had to leave before he could finish assembling it and Rachel Collins pinning the donkey's tail onto Lydia Thompson's 'Bros' bomber jacket instead of on the donkey. Lydia's mother had had to come and collect her because she wouldn't stop crying about the tiny, barely noticeable, pinprick in her jacket.

But instead the plate slid from her hand and she wondered who would eat the second slice of cake now.

Chapter Two

So Many Reasons Why

(she couldn't be an astronaut)

1979

'Hurry up, Peg, it's like being in the Mediterranean, I've just seen a—'

The rest of the sentence was swallowed up by a swooping seagull, so Peggy had no idea what Ed had just seen – a stingray, a message in a bottle, a corpse that had been weighted down with bricks? She hoped that it wasn't something as mundane as a plastic fork or a string of seaweed.

What she *was* certain of however was that Southport could in no way be deemed comparable to the south of France. As far as she was aware Ed hadn't even been to the Mediterranean, so comparing it to the Côte d'Azur or the Amalfi coastline when it was probably more reminiscent of a bank holiday Skegness was certainly wishful to say the least, although in fairness things were often improved by your imagination (when you weren't imagining the worst).

Her bare feet left a trail of size-five footprints across the oven-hot sand as she made her way towards the water's edge, but by the time she'd reached the shoreline he'd already disappeared. Which was a blessing really. The water looked far too cold; she certainly had no intention of swimming in it. Whatever Ed might think, it was hardly St-Tropez. It was definitely Southport. And nobody's imagination could convince her otherwise, no matter how vivid it might be.

A small boy in red swimming trunks stood shivering beside her.

'Do you think it's cold?' he asked her, his teeth chattering along with his trembling body.

'It's probably warmer than it looks,' she lied.

'It doesn't look very warm.'

'No, it doesn't,' she conceded.

The boy hesitated and then, scooping up his clothes, rejoined his parents.

Unfolding a beach towel Peggy watched the tide playfully swallow Ed up and in the next breath spit him back out again and then she slotted Bob Dylan's *Blood on the Tracks* into the cassette player (the first track appropriately titled 'Tangled up in Blue'), but the lyrics were drowned out by the thrashing waves. And then the tape itself became tangled so she had to pull a pen out of her handbag, insert it into one of the spools and manually rewind it. The tape gathered in a nest of knots on her lap, the silver inscription on the pen shimmering maliciously.

It was the personalised Paper Mate ballpoint pen that Ed, a stranger who she'd turned to in the queue, had handed to her at the second of Bob Dylan's six London Earls Court concerts so that Bob Dylan could sign her bra. She'd brazenly lifted up the 'Lay Lady Lay' T-shirt that she was wearing so that the bra could be signed more easily, and then kept the pen. It had been an eighteenth birthday gift and wished him a *Happy Anniversary, love Leslie & Sheila* ('whoever the hell they are', Ed had said) instead of a *Happy 18th Birthday, love Mum and Dad*, so it was hardly of sentimental value.

Ed later told her that the manager of Timpson's had insisted that that was the inscription requested and refused their request for a refund even though birth certificates and marriage certificates were produced and a formal complaint forwarded to their head office in Wythenshawe. It was even featured on *That's Life* in a segment warning of the dangers of letting retailers engrave precious heirlooms, with various examples of spelling mistakes produced as evidence: '*Nappy First Birthday*', '*Congratulations on Your Law Decree*', '*My Harp Belongs to You*'.

Peggy, however, liked to think the mistake serendipitous because if there had been a refund then there would have been no pen for her to borrow and they wouldn't now be renting a one-bedroom flat above a florist. And it was an anniversary of sorts, the anniversary of their first meeting, although admittedly at the time she'd been planning her Malibu beach wedding to Bob Dylan and editing an eight-page wedding special for the September issue of *Harper's Bazaar*, until she later noticed a willowy brunette being ushered into his dressing room and realised why he'd been in such a hurry to sign her left breast.

She buried the pen (a permanent reminder that, at five foot three, she was anything but 'willowy') in the sand and, the cassette tape now ruined, angrily began flicking through the *Creative Living* magazine that Ed had been reading on the train. Ed was a temporary administrative assistant for an architectural design company, although according to Ian Stubbs, the managing director of the company, photocopying and filing duties were far too menial a task for someone like Ed who was *most definitely* Going Places, even though he could never quite pinpoint exactly where those places might be.

'"Homes by Appleton Architects: Investing in Your Future" – just imagine it, Peg,' Ed would say, with the enthusiasm of some born-again Christian being interviewed on *Panorama*. (Peggy was deeply suspicious of anyone who claimed to be able to change their entire belief system overnight. She was sure that spiritual and emotional enlightenment didn't come that easily. Mostly, in her experience, it didn't come at all; the coveting of things that you don't have tending to make any kind of spiritual metamorphosis unlikely.)

Undeterred by her scepticism, however, he would regularly bring home armfuls of cardboard boxes filled with those born-again, spirit-levelled dreams, spreading them across the dining table like tarot cards, project-managing them into existence until there was no room for her or any dreams that she might have had. Instead, the table was littered with more practical concerns: aluminium window frames and loft insulation, roof tiles and plasterboard, how to plumb a sink, how to light a hallway.

He would ask her why she couldn't (or wouldn't) grasp these dreams of his and hold them in her hands, try them on for size. Doing something for the first time shouldn't be a reason not to. There's a first time for everything. But she'd been fooled like that before – having aspirations that were unexpectedly washed away before you could dip a toe in the water.

'But why do your dreams have to be so big, so ambitious? Aren't we happy as we are?' she once asked him, increasingly afraid that this particular dream would sweep him away completely and she wouldn't know where to start looking for him.

'There's nothing wrong with having dreams – and the bigger the better. Ask Martin Luther King,' was his pious reply.

She couldn't ask Martin Luther King because he wasn't there to ask, and he'd been a civil rights activist, he was allowed to dream big. He'd had supporters who expected nothing less. Ed was on a twelve-month temporary contract and idolised Richard Branson. His dream was the Abba version, mediocre floor plans unfurling like forest fire across a cluttered and chaotic dining table. And even though Peggy never normally swore, everything soon became 'fuck this' and 'fuck that' and finally, 'fuck you', her tongue swollen with an unleashed, simmering venom that only a swear word could quench, until they were barely speaking at all and the tension between them seem to hiss and burn like the scorched tarmac outside.

A few weeks after their trip to Southport Ed came home waving a sheet of paper in the air as if he'd won first prize in a competition, having apparently forgotten that they weren't speaking, that it was too hot to be waving anything in the air unless it was to cool it. At least it wasn't another cardboard box full of pipe dreams, she remembered thinking. There were so many boxes in the flat that it seemed as if they'd only just moved in.

His cheeks were flushed and he smelled of Stella (the beer *and* the barmaid, Stella Evans, who regularly doused herself in Yardley's 'Intrigue', although there was no one less intriguing).

'How's Stella?' Peggy asked.

He didn't reply.

'I've found the perfect piece of land to build on, Peg. Why don't you come and see for yourself?' he pleaded.

'You're drunk,' she chided. 'We'll discuss it in the morning.'

They didn't have conversations any more. They just pecked at each other hurtfully, like woodpeckers on bark, clipped, terse sentences that never led anywhere.

The following morning she adamantly refused to discuss anything remotely dream-related. Whatever she might have said, she stubbornly did the opposite. The two slices of bread that she'd placed in the toaster snapped into the air, much like her mood, as she watched him pause in the doorway, no doubt wondering what had happened to the woman who'd once pulled up her T-shirt in front of a queue of strangers so that Bob Dylan could sign her bra and then refused to return his pen because Bob Dylan had touched it.

Peggy threw the toast away without buttering it. She wondered if the willowy brunette who'd followed Bob Dylan into his dressing room was always stubbing her toe on cardboard boxes. She suspected not. Frustrated, she began to clear the dining table. She needed to see it again. She couldn't let its teak finish elude her any longer. She was tired of using cardboard boxes as coffee tables.

As she was arranging various specification documents and upcoming auction dates into neat piles she noticed the sheet of paper that he'd been waving at her the night before – '*twelve acres of land for sale behind a disused quarry*'. How on earth could they afford twelve acres of land? And how many houses was he planning to build? Was he stealing from his employer? Had he robbed a bank?

So many unanswered questions and the more time that passed, the less she seemed to understand. But a person's dreams were important, she knew that, and it didn't always matter that they weren't your dreams or that they were too big.

As she was moving some of the boxes into the bedroom, the doorbell rang. Two uniformed police officers were standing in the hallway, Jessica from the florist's shop downstairs hovering awkwardly behind them.

Peggy remembered first meeting Jessica. She was wrapping ribbon around a birthday bouquet of carnations, chrysanthemums and roses – the only three flowers that she sold. She flatly refused to stock anything more seasonal such as tulips or lilies or sprigs of mistletoe. Sometimes you can have too much choice she would say, the more choice you have, the more difficult your decision. And I haven't got all day, she complained, as if three types of flower was still two types too many.

And they all die in the end anyway, Jessica had added, resignedly. Peggy had wondered why she sold flowers at all. Their transient nature seemed to be a disappointment to her.

'Mrs Appleton?' the younger police officer asked.

'Yes?'

Peggy didn't correct him. She wasn't married. But she didn't mind that people often assumed that she was. In fact, she encouraged their assumptions. Perhaps she should wear her mother's wedding ring, make the unofficial official.

Peggy's mother had given up all hope of ever having children and when she discovered that she was pregnant and not, as she'd initially believed, menopausal, she'd found it extremely difficult to re-embrace the idea again. Ultimately, she was prescribed a course of antidepressants to provide some semblance of normality. She contracted a rare blood disorder shortly after the birth and died when Peggy was five. Her father died three months later. He didn't even glance over his shoulder to say goodbye he was so intent on following his wife. Peggy often wondered if she'd killed them both, if she should never have been born at all.

Especially when she became a foster child, one vowel away from being a festering child, something unwanted languishing in a corner somewhere, her life a convoluted genealogical nightmare as she was deposited on the doorsteps of the McCalls (don't call us, we'll call you), the Whites, the Shaws (very sure, thank you), the Millers, the Healeys, the Wrights (who were the most wrong), and finally the Hills – a whole estate of surnames (two were actually on the same estate).

An audience of faces would ask her the same uninterested questions in a variety of regional and overseas accents. She rarely remembered their Christian names, only their surnames – one size fits all – and sometimes only their accents or the shape that their lips made as they were waving goodbye. No doubt they similarly erased her from their lives as soon as they'd closed the front door. What was her name, the miserable one, the one who never spoke? Penelope, Pamela, Paula?

She'd actually overheard Mrs Miller pleading with a social worker over the telephone, 'I really can't keep her any longer. We had an agreement. And she's such a depressing child, isn't she? Is she mute? She just keeps staring into space.' They didn't even try to hide their displeasure and instead of a fostering success, she remained a festering disappointment, a lingering smell behind the sofa cushions, but thankfully not forever, as they tried to forget that she was there.

And of course nobody wanted to keep her. Something more permanent? No, I'm afraid not. Do you have any newborns? They didn't want fully fledged five-year-olds with their own thoughts and tantrums. They wanted adorable blue-eyed, two-week-old infants with fat pink cheeks and Shirley Temple curls who they could shape into children of their own like clay pots, children who would answer when spoken to and slip undetected into family portraits.

Politely perched on puckered candy-striped cotton bed sheets and frayed candlewick bedspreads, Peggy would wait for a freckled, wrinkled or frowning face to open the bedroom door and announce the arrival of the social worker, and the island raft that she'd been desperately clinging onto began to splinter into so many different pieces that she didn't know which of them belonged to her any more and she was never in one place long enough to find out.

It was while she was in emergency accommodation 'between families' sitting in the administrative office of the local government Child Services Department that she decided she didn't want to be Peggy any more. Mr Wright had started sitting on the bed with her when Mrs Wright was out shopping. He'd given her a doll, a doll that he said was just like her. She buried it in the back garden a few days later with a note that said 'please leave me as you find me, he must never know that I'm here' because he'd said that it was just like her and she didn't want him anywhere near it.

Most days she wished that she was the one buried in their back garden, not the doll, which *had* looked uncannily like her, the same pink T-shirt and denim skirt that she always wore, the same untameable hair. There was even a mole on its left cheek in exactly the same place. When she rubbed at it, it blackened her fingers.

It was as if Mr Wright had made her smaller, squashed her between his hefty palms until she was small enough to fit inside his pocket and not be seen. Perhaps she and the doll could swap places for a few days so that she could sleep with her eyes closed while the doll pretended to be her, although she wasn't sure what other things might surface if she did that. And it wasn't fair to let someone else suffer just because they could close their eyes and you couldn't.

And then she would wonder if she wasn't already buried in their back garden and the doll was the one with bruises all over its arms and too many secrets to keep. But if the doll was her, then who was she?

Aaron, the social worker assigned to her case, was tapping a black biro against his teeth. He seemed alarmed. Peggy was The Child Who Never Spoke, a case that nobody else wanted. He thought that he must have imagined the sound of her – he'd worked nearly sixty-three hours this week, it was exhausting living other people's lives – and returned to his case notes. He hoped that he wasn't hearing voices again. A gerbil had lost three of its legs last time.

Peggy tried again, but her voice sounded strangely distant, as if it was trapped inside a glass jar. She hadn't heard it in such a long time and it was like learning to talk all over again, even though she couldn't remember the first time that she'd ever tried to say something.

'I don't want to be Peggy any more,' she repeated, a little louder this time.

She really was talking. Her lips were moving. Aaron was relieved. He really didn't want Barry coming back. Monica, he could tolerate, she was actually quite agreeable – she'd been deeply upset about the gerbil – but not Barry.

Aaron wasn't fond of small talk or childish riddles, although both were inevitable when dealing with children.

'But you are Peggy,' he informed her matter-of-factly, removing the biro from between his teeth and beginning to write with it – not 'she *can* speak' or 'Peggy doesn't want to be Peggy'; he was actually writing, 'I'm not listening, Barry. I'm busy.'

'Well I want to be Devon now.'

She'd been thinking about this name change for some time and had settled on Devon because it was the colour of new sandals and summer holidays, neither of which she'd ever had. And she liked the sound of it, how it felt on her tongue, Devon Moon. She could be anything with a name like that: an actress, an ice skater, an astronaut (the clue was in the name); anything at all.

'Your name's Peggy. It's who you are. It's in all the paperwork. And you'll still be Peggy, even with a different name. And isn't Devon a county rather than a girl's name? I'd have to speak to the head of the division and Mr Davies really hasn't got time for non-urgent requests such as name changes. He wouldn't appreciate all the work involved in renaming you. You do understand that, don't you?'

So many reasons why she couldn't be an astronaut when her name suggested otherwise.

She studied the smear of black ink in the corner of his mouth. It sat there like a moth, eavesdropping.

'You don't have to change the paperwork. I just want to be called Devon.'

Aaron sighed. Changing Peggy's name was hardly a priority, whereas placing her with a family was. And no family wanted a sullen, uncommunicative child like Peggy. Or Meredith, the flea-bitten, one-eyed panda that she carried with her everywhere, part of a past that she couldn't let go of. They wanted the improved and updated version, the panda still in its packaging, still having both of its eyes. He wondered what had happened to the missing eye. *Gouged out with a penknife by a sadomasochist, I expect*, he heard Barry say.

He stared at Peggy slash Devon, her legs swinging back and forth beneath the chair like scissors, her eyes stretched wide.

What harm can it do? Monica whispered in his left ear.

'I'm not promising anything, but I'll see what I can do.'

There, that wasn't so hard, was it?

Aaron's office was always like winter, Devon thought; it gave her goose pimples, even in summer. The chaffinches would be chirping and Billie Holiday would be singing 'East of the Sun (and West of the Moon)' and she'd sit there shivering while Aaron hid record sleeves beneath his files and assumed that nobody was listening, but she was always listening, always ready to cross any road. But maybe that was because she'd had to cross so many of them.

Once, when Mr Davies's secretary, Thelma, had popped her head round the door looking for Eleanor Matthews, Aaron had lifted the stylus off the record so quickly that he scratched the vinyl. She'd never seen him so angry. He seemed to behave differently in front of Devon. 'It's fucking ruined,' he snarled when the crown of Thelma's head had gone, holding the record up to the light so that he could better see the scratch, forgetting that she was still listening. And then he sat down and wrote the word 'shit' over and over again in his notepad with a biro, his breathing ragged and sharp.

He was always writing things down (normally not swear words). Even when she wasn't saying anything, he was writing it down, spreading lies about her (or were the lies hers?). She wondered who saw all of these lies, or 'case notes' as he liked to call them; sentences that described her without even knowing her, written in somebody else's handwriting; Aaron's view of her. One day she hoped to put her own scratched record straight and tell her side of the story.

When he'd filled three pages of his notepad with the word 'shit' he looked across at her and said, 'So, Peggy – sorry, Devon – let's find you a new family,' as if Billie Holiday was still spinning and unspoiled and finding a family was the easiest thing in the world.

It wasn't. Family implied two parents, two children, ideally a boy and a girl, aunts, uncles, cousins, generations, ancestors . . . but sometimes family was just you; there were no branches leading to other branches because those other branches kept snapping off.

She'd once asked Aaron if she could stay at a hotel instead, but he told her that the council budget didn't stretch that far and a hotel couldn't possibly provide the stability that a foster home could. She disagreed. A hotel could provide everything that a foster home could. They were practically identical. In fact she thought that hotels might be a little more accommodating, a little more forgiving. They certainly wouldn't sit next to you on the bed or wash your panda without asking, as Mrs Healey had done while she'd been sitting on the pavement squashing ants with a twig.

Aaron removed his glasses and pinched the bridge of his nose. He seemed tired. Of her? Probably. Most people tired of her eventually. And if she wasn't framed inside his glasses any more, was she even there? She couldn't be sure. It seemed like she was sitting opposite a different person when he didn't have his glasses on.

'Do you have parents?' Devon asked him.

The moth was back, this time on a front tooth. He looked like he'd been fighting.

'Doesn't everybody?'

'No, not everybody.'

'You had parents once,' he reminded her.

She didn't answer.

The last family that Aaron ever parcelled her up for were the Hills. She stood on their doorstep wrapped in ribbons and bows and a new winter coat and was mortified when he introduced her, almost apologetically, as 'Peggy, but she likes to be called Devon,' as if she couldn't decide who she wanted to be, as if she was being particularly obstinate about it. She wasn't Peggy. She was Devon. She had no past any more. Isn't that what they all wanted? Even Meredith was gone. She'd dropped her in a litter bin on her way to school because since she'd been washed, she didn't smell like her mother any more.

But now, thanks to Aaron, she sounded as crazy as Crazy Olive who walked around town in laddered stockings telling everybody that Tony Bennett was planning to eat them and Mario Lanza owned a casino on Neptune where you could play blackjack with Doris Day on Thursdays.

Aaron nudged her inside, even though she wanted to stay on the doorstep in her new winter coat where it was easier to breathe, and it wasn't as if she'd been dropped into a dark and inescapable hollow with no rope ladder. Mrs Hill was dressed in Easter yellow, smiling. Mr Hill wore wool and shook her hand. An aviary of birds sat on shelves and walls watching events unfold, porcelain wrens, acrylic starlings, matchstick doves, all kinds of birds made out of all kinds of things, a place for everything. She wondered where her place would be. She could see a green velvet armchair with tassels by the fireplace and thought that she might like to sit in that.

Just as she was imagining herself sinking into the mint velvet cushions the sharp slap of an icy breeze drifted in through an open window and the valleys of soft green disappeared. She pulled her coat tighter. She was rushing ahead of herself. Things could still fall apart. She should know that by now.

When Aaron next visited she noticed that her file seemed slimmer. He was now able to balance it easily on one leg, the Peggy crossed out and the name DEVON added in capital letters as if she was a travel brochure.

'Devon seems to suit you,' he told her. 'A new name, a new beginning. If only everything was that simple.'

His gaze fell on the ship's bell clock on the mantelpiece and stayed there for an unusually long time.

She wondered if she might receive a rosette or a trophy this time; or a pat on the back like her father used to give her (she kept forgetting that he was Peggy's father, not hers). Maybe even a hug. She thought that she might like a hug the most. It had been a long time since anybody had hugged her (besides Mr Wright, but that didn't count).

Although, disappointingly, the green velvet armchair wasn't as comfortable as it looked.

While Cynthia Hill collected birds, Bernard, her husband, collected clocks. He would go from room to room late at night winding them up. There were fifty-two clocks in the house – she'd counted them the day she arrived, severely sleep-deprived due to the disruptive ticking inside every room; a ticking that ultimately made its way inside her own head, the fifty-third clock.

There was never a moment when something wasn't ticking, and each clock had its own specific trademark tick: the grandfather clock in the front room that nobody ever sat in (*adagio*), the cuckoo clock above the kitchen table that never failed to startle you (*allegro*), the pendulum clock at the bottom of the stairs that often skipped three 'tocks' in a row.

She was like a doctor with a stethoscope, a paramedic checking for a pulse, a majorette in a marching band, time never standing still, always moving forward. And it was as if there was never enough time, even though there was far too much of it, Bernard routinely winding up clocks each night making everything beat so much faster, particularly the ticking inside her head.

And then Bernard's Morris Minor hit a sycamore tree on the corner of Pool Dam and the ticking stopped. Cynthia had been in the passenger seat and she died at the scene. Bernard broke his jaw. The wrong way round somehow, the wrong person. Bernard had no interest in winding up clocks after that. But thankfully by then she was sixteen and was Peggy again.

'I'm afraid there's been an accident,' the older, balding police officer continued.

If only she hadn't tidied the dining table that morning; if only she hadn't swept all of Ed's dreams away, boxed them up and moved them into the bedroom, she remembered thinking. If only.

This wasn't how it was meant to be at all.

The fluttering inside her stomach felt like a thousand trapped butterflies, like she'd swallowed a glassful of caterpillars at breakfast along with some of the glass. When she looked down she noticed that she was bleeding, a trail of blood slithering down her right thigh towards her calf.

Daphne, she thought suddenly, the name popping into her head from nowhere. The doll Mr Wright had given her – she'd called her Daphne.

Chapter Three

The Cent and the Peseta

1988

The journey to Frankie's grandmother's home was like a second funeral procession, in transit to yet another place that she'd rather not have been heading to. Although, unlike the driver of the funeral hearse, this driver, who'd introduced himself as Uncle Stewart but who could have been anybody, seemed incapable of travelling at anything less than eighty miles per hour, according to the speedometer that Frankie was nervously monitoring. It was fortunate that she wasn't in a gate-counting mood because she wouldn't have been able to keep count anyway, the outside world racing by in a Ferrari-style, tearstained blur.

She was already missing Ellie, who'd started crying the moment 'Uncle Stewart' had fastened Frankie's seatbelt, the extendable lead of a chocolate brown Labrador wrapped in three eights around her ankles. She'd overheard Ellie's mother telling Ellie's father that now might be a good time to get a dog, to fill the space that Frankie was going to leave, as if she wasn't important enough to be replaced by a human being.

Ellie's father had even bought Ellie a necklace, a letter 'E' on a silver chain, as if it was Ellie's world that had been sliced open. Ellie told her that they'd asked social services if Frankie could live with them but a court had ruled that she be placed with a relative and her mother had apparently cried for a whole week.

It didn't look as if Mrs Barlow had been crying for a whole week. Her mascara hadn't run at all. It was Mr Barlow who had the reddest eyes and Frankie hardly knew him, had barely said two words to him. He'd passed her on the doorstep once when she was coming home from school and when she'd asked her mother why Ellie's father had been there, she'd told her that he'd called to repair the upstairs dripping tap. She asked her mother why he hadn't been wearing his blue overalls and her mother said that he'd been on his way to a meeting. When Frankie went into the bathroom the tap was still dripping.

Sometimes he would pull up alongside her in his van and ask her if she wanted a lift, but she often shook her head and said no, thank you (admittedly that was three words, but three very short words). He made her nervous. She never knew what to say to him. And if she was in the passenger seat then she would have to say something. She always hoped that there was somebody else sitting in the passenger seat, so that he never stopped. And sometimes there was and he didn't.

The last time he'd offered her a lift his black moustache had been glistening with tiny pearls of sweat that kept dripping onto his collar, and he'd seemed short of breath, but she could hear the smile in his voice even though she couldn't see it on his face. She thought of the upstairs tap that was still dripping. Should she mention it? But that would be too many words. She didn't think that she'd be able to say a full sentence. She shook her head.

Inside Uncle Stewart's car, the tears in her eyes bubbled like hot lava. She blinked them away. Why had nobody thought to buy *her* anything? She was the one who'd been orphaned. Although she didn't need an 'F' around her neck to remind her who she was; she was reminded of that fact every day. And why did nobody ever ask her what *she* wanted to do? Why were all these life-changing decisions made without her?

It was too hot in the car so she asked if she could open a window. Uncle Stewart, or whoever he was, nodded. And then she stared blankly into the distance, towards a small patch of sky that was much bluer than the rest.

Over the past few weeks the weather had mirrored her sombre mood, but today the sun was like an unpeeled orange. Frankie thought it inappropriate that the sun should shine like a fruit bowl so soon after her mother's funeral. But then she remembered that she hated her mother, a woman who'd had no qualms about letting strange men fasten her daughter's seatbelt with their fat sausage fingers and drive her to God Knows Where. And she didn't want her anger to fill up the inside of the car until it was impossible to breathe and the empty space that had once held her heart was stretched even wider so she took forty-three deep breaths and closed her eyes.

If she did still have a heart then it certainly wasn't whole. It was probably sitting in two pieces inside her chest, like the two slices of birthday cake that she'd scraped up off the carpet and thrown against the bedroom wall.

As the sponge cake was slithering down the lavender-striped bedroom wall Frankie had tried to pull her mother down, but she was too heavy. She only managed to separate her from her slippers and loosen her skirt which made her look worse, like she hadn't dressed herself properly. She quickly picked up the slippers and placed them on the correct feet and then sprinted back down the stairs, screaming. Derek Price, one of the neighbours, was washing his car in the driveway. She couldn't speak. She couldn't say the words. She could only howl and point towards the bedroom window.

He dropped the wet rag that he was holding into the bucket of soapy water by his feet and rushed into the house, using their telephone to call for an ambulance, although it was far too late for an ambulance by then. The police were also alerted, but it was equally unlikely that they would be needed either. It was like arriving at a party when everybody had already left.

When the ambulance arrived, Frankie was lying on the front lawn coughing up slivers of blackcurrant jelly and pools of vanilla custard, her tears running diagonally towards one of her ears. She wanted to stay like that forever, on her side facing the hedge, so that she never saw anything but privet ever again, and she told the paramedics to fuck off when they tried to move her. She didn't want to be moved. And she didn't want them there. She didn't want anyone there except Derek Price who, she told them, had been really helpful and was the only person allowed to talk to her.

If she didn't discuss it with anyone else then perhaps none of this would be real.

Eventually, when she was too exhausted to resist and Derek Price had run out of comforting things to say and stopped asking her if she liked dolls (she didn't), a police officer was able to manoeuvre her into the warmth of a parked police car, but as soon as he turned away to speak to a colleague she slipped past him and ran back into the house. Her mother was still hanging from the bedroom ceiling and two paramedics were studying her as if she was a museum exhibit that they didn't quite know how to display.

'Don't just stand there, get her fucking down,' Frankie screamed at them before locking herself in the bathroom.

She lay on the chequered lino, now covered in muddy boot prints, staring at the dusty lampshade, wondering who would have wanted to kill her mother. She would never have climbed up there by herself. It must have been Stan. He was the only other person with a key. She should search the house for evidence, before somebody tampered with it, before somebody trod all over it and squashed it into the carpet. Her mother was always telling her that the police were incompetent and not to be trusted, always coercing people into admitting to things that they hadn't done, ruining their lives.

She would often cite her Jamaican friend Marjorie who, on her seventeenth birthday, was arrested for soliciting outside a nightclub. She was queuing outside, waiting to go in, the same as everybody else, when a passing police car stopped and two police officers got out and ordered her into the back of the car. She was held in a police cell overnight where she was beaten and punched so hard in the stomach that she lost the baby that she didn't know she was carrying.

After fourteen hours she admitted that she'd been soliciting just so that she could go to the toilet and wipe the blood away. Ironically, she did turn to prostitution a few months later, when her parents had disowned her, her boyfriend had gone back to Jamaica and she'd lost her job as a dental hygienist.

'I saw her once outside the police station,' Frankie's mother told her. 'She didn't recognise me and told me to piss off. That same afternoon she attacked an assistant chief constable with a syringe. I think she's in a psychiatric hospital now. She would have probably been married with two children and her own dental practice by now if it wasn't for those racist bastards.'

As if corroborating her mother's mistrust of the police force, one of the police officers later found the words 'something brief and joyous with nibbles and wine' written on the back of a receipt and assumed that it was a handwritten funeral plan, a suicide note of sorts, which was ridiculous. Her mother was the least joyous person she knew and it wasn't even in her handwriting. It made Frankie wonder if the police really were as incompetent and dishonest as her mother had always maintained, and who they might frame for her murder if they did believe it to be foul play. She wished that she hadn't touched her mother's slippers. There might have been incriminating fingerprints on them.

Someone was knocking on the bathroom door, could they please use the toilet, 'it's a matter of urgency'. *And this wasn't?* She reluctantly unlocked the door and ran into her bedroom without looking up. She needed to throw something. She picked up a stapler and hurled it at the wall. It made a satisfying dent in the plaster. She then slammed a paperweight into the dressing-table mirror. The glass cracked, splitting her reflection in two. And then the toilet flushed and she was able to scream without anyone hearing her.

The pencil sketches were next. She tipped them out of the shoeboxes, ripping them in half and then half again, and then she scattered them around the room like oversized confetti. She had no use for them now. The perfect gate didn't exist and now that her mother was gone, now that she'd spilled out onto the pavement outside, Frankie didn't care whether there were gates or no gates. She had to move quickly. Mrs Barlow would be arriving shortly.

She crammed two sweatshirts, a pair of jeans, some clean underwear and a book on bereavement that she'd stolen from John Menzies, and had been planning to give to her mother, into her rucksack. She thought that they wouldn't mind, particularly now that there'd been a second death in the family, and it was only four pounds ninety-nine, And then she zipped one of her mother's lipsticks into a side pocket. She almost forgot the gate-fund money and had to rush back upstairs.

She handed the money to a homeless man outside Freeman Hardy Willis the day after the funeral, the one with the hungry-looking dog and the black feather in his cap who she thought was called Brian. At first he was reluctant to accept it, seemed suspicious of her motives, but she persisted until he finally agreed, suggesting that his dog might like some dog food. He fished out the cent and the peseta and handed them back to her.

Worried when he didn't use the coins to feed his dog as she'd tentatively suggested, choosing instead to spend them in the off licence across the road, Frankie returned ten minutes later with two tins of Pedigree Chum and, pointedly glaring at him, set them down by the dog's paws together with a can opener.

Tellingly, Stan didn't attend the funeral. Frankie was relieved. He was the last person that she wanted to see there. He would have ruined the service with his white rage and his clenched fists and his eyes like graphite. But she would need to find him soon, before he disappeared completely. He needed to be punished for what he'd done.

She briefly considered asking her mother's friend, Sylvia, where he lived when he didn't live with them. Sylvia was standing by the graveside in a silk headscarf and sunglasses, looking like Alexis Carrington, but she'd been drinking. Derek Price was gripping her arm so tightly that he was leaving red thumbprints on her skin.

So instead she went over to the bench by the church doors and studied the five creases in each of her leather shoes while she waited for Mrs Barlow.

Uncle Stewart sniffed loudly and fidgeted in his seat. Thankfully, he'd slowed down, having narrowly avoided hitting a cyclist, and an army of slate-grey buildings were now marching briskly alongside them. She couldn't even see the sky any more.

'Nearly there,' he told her.

Frankie said nothing. She was too depressed to speak. She was looking at the boarded-up windows, the broken windows that hadn't yet been boarded up, the betting shops, the launderettes, the

Jamaican food stores, the Vietnamese cafés, the men with tattooed daggers on their forearms sitting on walls wondering whether to stab you as you weighed pears and sipped green tea. She was the blue that the sky should have been.

The car pulled into the forecourt of a dilapidated block of flats. Frankie looked up at the crumbling grey tower block and was suddenly gripped by an alarming thought. What if 'Uncle Stewart' was actually one of Stan's relatives or friends and she'd been driven here to be silenced? She wondered whether to run while she still could, but she really wanted to go to the toilet and she also felt that it was important for Stan to know that she wasn't scared of him (she was terrified). So she let his accomplice pull her rucksack from the boot of the car and followed him towards the entrance, wondering what she would say when she finally came face to face with her mother's murderer.

She hoped that he at least lived on the ground floor. She didn't particularly want to be pushed out of a ten-storey window.

He led her through a concrete underpass to the right of the building, past some rundown garages. There was a Nike trainer hanging from some scaffolding opposite a row of metal bins. It looked new.

'Where's the gate?' she whispered forlornly. 'There's no gate.'

'What's that about gates?' Stan's accomplice asked.

'There aren't any,' she repeated. Her knees wouldn't stop shaking. 'There are plenty of doors, though.'

But you can't see behind doors.

She immediately regretted donating all her DIY manuals to Oxfam. You can never underestimate the importance of a resilient gate, especially in a place like this, a place where she was obviously destined to die like her mother.

A teenage girl with purple hair was pushing a dirty pram towards them. Frankie hoped that there wasn't a dirty child inside it.

'Hi, Stew. How's it going?' she asked.

'Good. You?' he replied.

She assumed that Stew was short for Stewart, but he could be a different Stewart. He guided Frankie towards the lifts before she could glance inside the pram. There was an 'Out of Order' sign on the lift doors so they had to use the stairs, walking in single file up the narrowest of staircases catering for the largest number of people.

Frankie hoped that they weren't treading on or in anything life-threatening. She didn't want to die before discovering the truth. At one point she thought that she may have trodden on a syringe, but on closer inspection she saw that it was a green felt-tip pen. She bent down and popped it into her coat pocket. It might prove useful.

There was every size of penis imaginable, and some unimaginable, decorating the walls, and none of them looked like the ones in the magazines that Ellie's father kept in a metal toolbox on a garage shelf or the ink ones in her human biology textbooks, but thankfully the lighting was so poor that you could pretend you hadn't noticed them even though your nose was only centimetres away.

Fifteen floors later, as she nervously waited for Stan to pull her inside and string her up like her mother, they were greeted by a woman with no teeth. Frankie hoped that it was her grandmother. It was. There was a letter addressed to Brenda Appleton on a console table by the door.

'Goodness, you're so tall now,' her grandmother exclaimed.

'I'm actually quite small for my age. Could you please take me back to Ellie's after I've used the toilet?'

Suddenly, she couldn't imagine living anywhere that didn't have a gate that she could close, a gate that would keep the outside out.

'How about a glass of milk first?'

Frankie shrugged and stepped inside. The front door slammed shut behind her.

'He's coming back, isn't he?'

'Of course, but I'm not sure when.'

'Could you call him please to find out? We'll need to leave before it gets dark.'

She felt so dizzy. She couldn't possibly look out of the window to see which way he'd gone. How did people ever sleep up here where you can see the exact spot where the land falls away and the sea begins?

'Would you like a slice of Madeira cake?' her grandmother asked.

'I don't eat cake,' Frankie told her.

'What about a biscuit?'

'I suppose I could manage a biscuit.'

'Didn't you want to use the toilet?'

'I just want to go home.'

She didn't want to venture any further inside in case the sky wrapped itself around her and she couldn't breathe. She drank the glass of milk that her grandmother handed to her and ate three of the five malted milks (old-people biscuits). Her eyelids felt so heavy. Perhaps she should close them. Just for a few minutes. She sat cross-legged on the floor and rested her head against the door.

When she opened them again it was dark outside and she was lying on the sofa. She was relieved it was dark. She wouldn't be able to see how high up she really was. Her grandmother was sitting next to her, but there was no sign of Uncle Stewart.

'Where's Uncle Stewart? Did you call him?'

'Why don't you brush your teeth and we'll talk about it in the morning?'

Too exhausted to protest, Frankie slid along the outer wall towards the bathroom and then sat on the toilet seat and cried. As she was wiping her nose on toilet paper she realised that she'd forgotten her toothbrush. She owned so few things and yet had somehow managed to remember barely any of them. Grief did that to you, she supposed – made you forget the small things, the ordinary things, the things that don't really matter.

When she'd finally stopped crying she splashed her face with a jet of cold water and reached for the tube of Colgate toothpaste that was sitting on a shelf above the sink, squeezing a little onto the tip of her index finger and smearing it across the surfaces of her teeth. They didn't feel any cleaner. She wondered why her grandmother had toothpaste when she didn't have any teeth.

She wished that Marcel was there so that they could go walking; she always felt less anxious after a walk with Marcel. He was French and always wore shorts. Her mother didn't like him. She said that Frankie was too old to have imaginary friends and talking to yourself was the first sign of madness, but Frankie *wasn't* talking to herself, she was talking to Marcel, and he was real to her. She knew his favourite dessert (crème brûlée), his mother's name (Francine) and how he liked to spend his mornings watching the pink flamingos in Le Parc Zoologique de Paris.

She carried a notebook in her rucksack entitled 'Les Promenades avec Marcel' where she listed all the gates that they'd seen while out walking. But she hadn't seen him since Walk No. 205 and the Cream Feather-Edge Side Gate, when an unusually thin Father Christmas had been sitting on a huge toy drum outside McDonald's with a hessian sack full of colourful plastic. Frankie had heard one child ask if that was where Santa lived, inside McDonald's, and Thin Santa had nodded.

This had annoyed Marcel. Thin Santa , who should have been Fat Santa, had already been ignoring him (she'd tried to explain that it wasn't Santa's fault that he couldn't see him and perhaps his doctor had suggested he diet for health reasons) and now he'd lied by saying that Santa lived in McDonald's. Everybody knew that he slept on a mattress behind Woolworths with three of his reindeer.

In a rage Marcel had sprinted off behind the Methodist chapel towards the nameless woods that the locals referred to as the Dark All Day Woods. Frankie couldn't keep up and although she spent all afternoon peering behind tree trunks and beneath rocks, Marcel never crawled out from under one and he hadn't been back since, which was highly unusual. They shared a packet of Jammie Dodgers most days.

There was a framed photograph above the bathroom toilet of two young boys in school uniforms, their fringes falling over their eyes like napkins. She wondered which boy was her father. Her mother always refused to discuss her father. It was as if he'd never existed, had been a figment of her mother's imagination, like Marcel. Frankie didn't know if he'd suffered from allergies or what size shoes he'd worn or if he'd liked baked beans (Ellie hated baked beans. She said that it was like swallowing bullets, dying from the inside out), information that would have been useful to know for her 'My Family' homework. There was nothing else left to say about her mother.

It didn't stop Frankie from trying to elicit information though, especially when Stan was there. It was worth all the leg slaps just to see the look on his face. And she often made the most outrageous claims: my father built Buckingham Palace; my father went to school with Paul Newman; my father spoke fourteen languages and invented polystyrene. All lies, of course. But she enjoyed tormenting him.

She did want to go to the toilet now, but preferably without an audience (all four eyes were looking directly at her), so before lifting up the toilet seat she switched off the light. It would be good practice for if she ever went blind. It seemed like something that might happen to her if the last few years were anything to go by.

'Is that my father in the bathroom?' she asked her grandmother afterwards, as if he was still alive and running a hot bath.

She was hoping for a more detailed response this time.

'It is. Did your mother tell you that he was planning to build a house?'

Frankie shook her head.

'I was going to build a gate,' she whispered sadly, realising that she still didn't know whether her father was the boy on the left or the boy on the right.

Chapter Four

Rock, Paper, Scissors

1979

Peggy had barely moved since being informed of Ed's death, adamantly refusing to let the magnitude of it sink in. She still kept expecting him to walk through the door, another Louis Taylor auction catalogue in his hands, his cheeks flushed with lunchtime wine, his head swimming with possibilities. She'd tried to absorb the details of the accident, to concentrate, but the words had become more and more jumbled the further they'd travelled; unremarkable, meaningless words when delivered singly: quarry, limestone, fall – an alternative version of rock, paper, scissors perhaps – but when attached to other words, when parts of actual sentences, they'd assumed a far more sinister significance, become a far more deadly game.

Jessica was sitting beside her on the sofa. She told her that Brenda, Ed's mother, would be arriving soon. She'd found her number in the address book by the telephone. The two police officers had left – a fight had broken out in the precinct – leaving

Peggy to grapple with something that she couldn't begin to unpick with someone who she barely knew.

Brenda finally arrived two hours later, her own grief still raw and unmanaged, but instead of being greeted by a sobbing, hysterical Peggy, she was met by an unnervingly composed and business-like Peggy, a Peggy who was sitting rigidly on a dining chair smiling sweetly at her, wondering if she had enough eggs to make an omelette and thanking Jessica for the flowers as she was leaving. There were no flowers.

But there was a damp patch on the carpet underneath the chair, the area markedly darker than the rest. As she was helping Peggy up, Brenda noticed water trickling down Peggy's legs, bloodstains the size of footprints on the back of her dress. She propped her against the wall by some cardboard boxes and telephoned for an ambulance.

Peggy knew that there was somebody there, but she didn't know who it could possibly be if it wasn't Ed, and she was tired of leaning against the wall so she let herself slide onto the carpet and form a lazy 'L' shape instead. Where were her slippers? And why were her feet wet?

'My slippers,' she yelled at the wall opposite. 'I want my slippers.'

The baby that nobody, not even her, had known existed, was born in the ambulance on the way to hospital, a male paramedic with one blue eye and one brown eye, who was midway through his first shift and looked more pregnant than she did, ceremoniously cutting the cord as if he was opening a village fete. He didn't look old enough to be delivering babies and Peggy became particularly disconcerted by his non-matching irises. It was like watching David Bowie reach for the forceps when he should have been on stage.

When the paramedic had told her to push she'd tightly crossed her legs and stubbornly refused. The baby's on its way. You need to start pushing. What baby? Your baby. And then, to add salt to an already infected wound, while the child was being rushed to the neonatal intensive care unit, Peggy was being wheeled into theatre because they couldn't stem the bleeding.

Instead of being left alone to mourn Ed she was now undergoing emergency surgery to repair a tear and remove un-expelled placental tissue.

She felt deceived. She felt as if this baby had been hiding from her deliberately, hiding from all of them, and it made her fearful, having carried something inside her that she didn't even know she'd been carrying.

'She's certainly a fighter,' remarked one of the nurses, as she was checking Peggy's stitches.

Didn't she know it? She was the one with the battle scars, the one who had barely survived.

Peggy ignored her while Brenda sat nodding her head. She was rolling a green grape around in her hand as if it was a loose rosary bead.

'I had no idea you were pregnant,' Brenda said.

'Neither did I.'

It wasn't part of the dream. It wasn't asphalt or copper piping or the head office of Appleton Enterprises, how may I help you?

You wouldn't know that you were on a maternity ward at all if it didn't say so above the door, Peggy thought. There were no cribs, no crying. You could be having a kidney removed instead of a child.

Except that she hadn't thought it, she'd actually said it out loud.

'Hardly a kidney. Have you thought of a name yet?' Brenda asked her.

Peggy sighed. What did it have to do with her? Five hours ago she hadn't even known she was pregnant. But she played along.

'Gene – Selfish Gene,' she suggested.

'I'm not sure that's actually a name.'

'Anything can be a name. I could call her Asbestos, if I wanted to.'

She watched Brenda squash the green grape between her fingers and then carefully wrap it in a tissue and place it inside her handbag.

Just then a nurse walked by singing a Frankie Valli and the Four Seasons song, 'Who Loves You'.

Who, indeed?

'Frankie. You can call it Frankie.'

'Isn't that a boy's name?'

'I don't think so.'

She really didn't care. It could have had two heads like some babies did and she would simply have replied, 'Has it?' She hoped that Brenda had a spare room. Perhaps she could keep it in her handbag if not, wrap it in a tissue and forget all about it. She kept everything else in there. Or maybe it would die like Ed had died, before anyone could say, 'Hello, Frankie,' and she wouldn't have to think about it any more.

'Frankie it is, then,' Brenda reluctantly agreed.

Unfortunately for Peggy, Brenda seemed unwilling to keep Frankie on a more permanent basis when Peggy broached the subject.

'A child's place is with its mother,' she insisted. 'Ed would want Frankie to stay with you. You know he would.'

Ed wasn't around to ask, she reminded her, so his opinion was purely academic. It was emotional blackmail, and she told Brenda so. But still Brenda insisted. She was too old to care for a child full-time. Of course she would help out as much as she could, but a more permanent arrangement was simply out of the question. Peggy had stopped listening. She was already considering alternative solutions. Perhaps she could abandon the child in the hospital toilets as she was leaving.

After lowering Frankie into the carrycot that Brenda had purchased on her behalf under the supervision of Sally, one of the midwives – who had to keep reminding Peggy to support the head, she wasn't a rugby ball – she made her way to the ladies' toilets, being careful to avoid the staff on the reception desk. But everybody, it seemed, wanted a glimpse of Frankie before she left: a ward sister, one of the canteen assistants, a man who'd come to repair a vending machine . . .

Why did people think that they could suddenly start a conversation with you now that you had a child, people who would normally have walked straight past you without bothering to look up? And not all newborn babies were 'beautiful'. Frankie certainly wasn't and there were several more on the ward that looked like they'd been turned inside out and left in the sun too long.

Christine, the woman who'd been in the bed next to Peggy and whose child had been stillborn, was wandering around the reception area in her dressing gown. She seemed to be looking for something and peered longingly at Frankie. Peggy asked her if she'd like to keep her, but she stared at her blankly, not seeming to take Peggy's offer seriously, so Peggy tried again, but the woman became agitated and walked away.

When she finally reached the toilets after several more interruptions, the outer door was wedged open and a 'Caution Wet Floor' sign was blocking the entrance. She left and took a taxi home. She didn't want to be arrested for leaving a child in a toilet cubicle inside the hospital where she'd just given birth and people remembering her being there. Perhaps she'd try again with Christine when she was feeling more responsive.

The flat felt so small that she didn't want to close the front door. She left Frankie screaming on the landing while she went inside and viciously kicked each of the cardboard boxes until her toes throbbed, reducing them to a bulldozed wasteland. Then she swept the pillars of leaflets on the dining table onto the carpet. She was unbearably angry. Unfortunately, of course, anger has to be tidied up again afterwards, although she was stepping on creased sheets of paper days later.

'That's what I think of your fucking dreams,' she screamed at the carpet.

If it wasn't for those dreams Ed wouldn't have been scaling treacherous quarry walls. He wouldn't have lost his footing. He wouldn't have smashed his delusional head against a jagged rock.

'I hope you and your dreams are fucking satisfied,' she wailed at the ceiling.

Frankie wailed with her.

And that became the pattern of their days, one or both of them wailing at some point during the day. A tiny hole in a sock or a trail of vomit on a bonnet ribbon or four hours of continual crying for no apparent reason (Frankie's *and* hers) would bring everything to a sudden standstill, and Peggy would have to sit completely still for several hours, until the tumultuous crashing inside her head became less tumultuous. It was as if heavy furniture was being dragged across her scalp, solid oak sideboards, antique china cabinets, the ottomans and folding tables featured in Brenda's Kays catalogue.

Ed would then slip through unannounced. She'd notice the property leaflets still pinned to the walls, the band T-shirts under her pillow, the Clash *London Calling*, the Rolling Stones Tour of the Americas '75, the Who *Who's Next*. She had the roll of film inside Ed's camera developed, all pictures of her, looking far too happy, far too content. It had only been a matter of time before that amount of happiness turned into something catastrophic. Nobody should be that happy. Why were there no photographs of Ed? Why was he always behind the camera lens, always shrinking her into more manageable spoonfuls? Where the fuck was he?

She turned the flat upside down searching for him behind skirting boards and picture rails, beneath the bed, under the carpet where things often got swept, but there was no trace of him. Even the demolished cardboard boxes just to the left and right of her could have belonged to anybody. Stella Evans's perfume, the estate agent flyers, Frankie – especially Frankie, who assaulted her ears and flooded her eyes daily – felt like other people's stories, anecdotes that she'd borrowed. They didn't feel like they were part of *her* life.

Brenda continued to visit. Peggy liked to think that it was to check on her own welfare, but she suspected that she only came to fawn over Frankie, to gaze at her and remember her son. *She* didn't want to care for her, but she still expected Peggy to. Peggy got tired of answering the same questions. *It's just a cold. Yes, she's sleeping. No, she isn't too hot. Yes, she looks just like Ed.* She wanted to tell Brenda that *she* was the one who had a permanent cold, who couldn't sleep, who was always too hot, but she knew that *she* didn't matter (she wasn't Ed *or* Frankie), so she simply nodded and waited for her to leave.

Until the furniture inside Peggy's head began to leave actual drag marks across the floorboards and Peggy realised that it couldn't be Ed moving it because he wasn't there. He wasn't behind the kitchen wall wedged between two water pipes. He wasn't trapped inside the wardrobe mirror. He wasn't crouching in the eaves, waiting for her to fall asleep. And she couldn't spend any more time searching for him. It looked like she'd been burgled.

She ran around the flat gathering up the lever arch files and the cardboard skyscrapers that had been flattened with her feet, tore down the laminated photocopies of parapets and balustrades and the typewritten addresses of local builders' merchants and she carried it all outside, dropping what was left of Ed's aspirations on the communal lawn so that the rain could wash it all away like it did everything else. She then rushed back inside to collect his shirts and his ties, his suits and his shoes, and when she threw it all down it was as if Ed was still wearing them, trying to wriggle free.

Trying to get up off that quarry floor.

She could hear Frankie screaming inside the flat, competing with the rain that was hitting the dustbin lid like a slew of golf balls, crying for the sake of crying, and she wished more than anything that the Bob Dylan concert had been sold out and she'd been unable to get a ticket.

She'd spent the past few weeks following Stella Evans, convinced that she was in some way to blame for Ed's death, plying him with alcohol until he couldn't walk, couldn't scale limestone quarries safely. She'd told her as much. But Stella had said that she was a barmaid, not a nursery school teacher. And anyway, he'd only had three pints. It wasn't her fault if he couldn't hold his liquor. Peggy slapped her across the face, but it was Frankie who started crying, and a police officer called to caution Peggy later that same day for 'assault occasioning bodily harm' (s.47 of the Offences Against the Person Act). But she wouldn't be deterred. Stella Evans was to blame for Ed's death and she would prove it.

Some time later she woke with a sharp stabbing pain in her chest. Her eyes felt like burning coals. She tried to stand up but her head wouldn't stop spinning so she had to lie down again. Her hands were shaking and her pulse was erratic, the unsettling haphazard rhythm similar to the ticking of the pendulum clock at the bottom of Bernard Hill's stairs that either struggled to keep up or raced on ahead. She had no idea what day it was and her clothes smelled damp. All she could remember were hailstones the size of golf balls smashing against her skull and Ed splintering into a thousand tiny individual flecks, like a human mosaic, and then fire tongs seared her eyes shut again.

When she prised her eyes open again she was somewhere else. Something blue was pressing something opaque into her left arm.

She thought she saw Ed in the splash of blue and the clear liquid and then he vanished. This seemed to go on indefinitely, Ed splashing, her eyes closing, until eventually the blue of a nurse and the plastic of a syringe bled into focus and she realised that she was in hospital and it was a lifeguard in hospital scrubs pulling her out of the icy Southport waters that she'd been swimming in.

Brenda was standing beside the bed looking concerned. She told her how worried she'd been, how if she hadn't heard Frankie crying she doesn't know what would have happened. But she's safe now. They both are. Peggy wondered if she was supposed to feel grateful. When Frankie wasn't there Ed would sometimes swim ashore, although recently it was mostly Frankie, not Ed, who crawled ashore. It seemed that once you had a child you were never free of it.

While sitting in reception waiting to be discharged she asked Brenda if she could keep Frankie a while longer. She still felt quite weak. She thought that Brenda would appreciate the opportunity to spend more time with her only grandchild, but each day like clockwork she would bring Frankie back to the flat and Peggy would be expected to hold her, awkwardly mostly, never quite knowing which part of her to grasp, never wanting to grasp any part of her, and inevitably Frankie would start crying, wailing for no reason. Or perhaps she had every reason.

Peggy felt trapped inside her own flat. She felt like a deer in a headlight. Everybody knew where to find her. Perhaps she should change the locks. Perhaps she should quietly close the front door behind her and walk away. She glanced down at Frankie squirming and gurgling in her arms (making the beguiling sounds that only a baby can), already sensing the sad truth that her own mother didn't want her, didn't particularly like her, and then she suddenly stopped crying, just like that, like a tap had been turned off, and her lips curled into a tiny triumphant smile. Peggy felt wary of this ability she seemed to have of rearranging her emotions at the click of a finger: palm upwards, happy; palm downwards, sad.

'Look, she's smiling at you,' Brenda exclaimed excitedly, although it seemed to Peggy that she was actually smirking at her. *Guess who's back?* she imagined her taunting.

She was officially back a few weeks later. Brenda couldn't cope. Neither could Peggy. But nobody seemed particularly interested. Most weeks Peggy contemplated leaving Frankie in a church doorway or on the top deck of a double-decker bus, but would ultimately change her mind at the last minute. She'd still find her way back somehow. She was quite manipulative for an eleven-month-old child. And it wasn't like losing a glove. She wished she could remember Christine's surname.

She'd considered placing her on the adoption register, although the intrusive questions and excessive paperwork that that would entail was an obvious disincentive and, having spent much of her own childhood being observed under a microscope and passed around like a parcel, she couldn't bring herself to do that to Frankie. She still wanted her child to belong to somebody, just not to her. So instead she wrote a letter of complaint to the landlord of The Swan regarding Stella Evans's failure to provide an adequate duty of care to her customers. It had taken her five days to compose two hundred words and she was still waiting for a response.

She visited her GP to obtain a prescription for anti-anxiety pills which he willingly prescribed: 'Parents deceased, partner deceased, single parent, I don't see why not.' He was more concerned about the newly elected prime minister.

'A female prime minister, for heaven's sake – what's the world coming to?' he asked her incredulously.

Its senses, Peggy thought. She was relieved that there would finally be a woman in charge. They were usually the ones left holding the baby.

She flipped open the spiral notepad that she kept under the sink behind the Windolene, the notepad that her GP had suggested she keep to record her thoughts. She hadn't realised that she'd had so many of them. There were pages and pages of entries, the writing an eclectic mix of taut capital letters and an unruly manic scrawl, as if it was the work of two people. Towards the end it was barely decipherable, both styles merging into one, both voices indistinguishable.

> 25 September
> Today I stood outside The Swan and didn't move for seventeen minutes.
>
> Interesting side note: to avoid colliding with the low beams I suggest adopting a praying stance, although the uneven floor is so disorientating that even though you appear to be walking towards one person, you inevitably arrive at the elbow of another, A LITTLE like LIFE I suppose.

The next few pages had been ripped out.

Had *she* done that or had somebody been inside the flat?

4 October

'It's hiding the poisonous piece of placenta that they can't find,' I told the anaesthetist. 'It's trying to KILL me.'

But he pretended not to hear me or assumed that I was referring to the placenta killing me rather than my own child.

27 December

I'm sitting in the wardrobe with the door closed. It's the only place I feel safe. Yesterday I saw a pair of lips belonging to GOD KNOWS who framed in the brass letterbox.

I couldn't hear what they were saying, but I imagined them pressed against the cool metal wishing me DEAD.

22 March

A doctor is lifting Frankie's fat limbs into the air and then lowering them gently back down again. He lingers over an unsightly rash and a tiny yellow bruise, troubled by their PRESENCE.

28 May

They've formed an alliance, the two of them, a spider's web of SECRETS. I see them whispering at mealtimes, the high chair their conspiratorial headquarters.

3 June
'What are you doing?' Brenda snapped, sternly.

What was I doing? I wasn't entirely sure. 'I'm holding my daughter,' I tried to say, but the words wouldn't stay in my mouth. They were too slippery.

A red palm was gripping Frankie's fleshy right arm, a pink thumbprint pressing down on her neck. Was that *my* palm, *my* thumb?

6 August
A doctor is shining a torch in my eyes while Brenda hovers in the doorway.

He asks me so many questions that I can't be sure whether I've answered them in the correct order.

Like the Two Ronnies' 'Mastermind' sketch.

'What is Bernard Manning famous for?

That is the question.

Who is the present archbishop of Canterbury?

He's a fat man who tells blue jokes.'

He leaves a prescription on the bedside table.

I wonder if he's trying to POISON me. I haven't seen him before.

He isn't the GP who doesn't believe in an illness that he can't see.

23 August
A runway of red brake lights, one pair of EYES behind another.

24 August
He's WATCHING me. He knows I know. I spoke to one of the receptionists yesterday and asked to speak to Ian Stubbs, but she said that she didn't know an 'Ian Stubbs', nor an 'Ed Appleton'. I know what they're doing. They're pretending that he never worked there, that they weren't the ones who put the ideas that killed him inside his head. When I left, I saw Ian Stubbs watching me from an upstairs window.

I don't know when I'll be able to write again.

There are far too many brake lights.

Peggy threw the notepad across the room. Why would she want to be reminded of these things? And why on earth would her doctor suggest that she write them down? It was like the ramblings of a madwoman. Was it even her handwriting? She wondered when she'd last slept. She couldn't remember. Her head felt like it was made of sandpaper, like there were insects that couldn't get out running around inside it. She needed them to stop moving.

She balanced six bottles of paracetamol and a bottle of Plymouth gin on the arm of the sofa, wishing that she'd saved one of the cardboard boxes so that there was somewhere to put a glass, and glanced across at Frankie who was unusually quiet in the corner. Finally she seemed to understand that she wasn't the centre of the universe after all.

Staring into the darkness beyond the window, Peggy wondered how long it would take for her to die.

Chapter Five

A Fifteenth-Floor Birdcage

1988

Frankie had no idea where she was. But it definitely wasn't her bedroom. It was much smaller and there were birds on all four walls, nondescript acorn-brown garden birds in pen and ink, trapped and still. She didn't like being so close to so many birds whether they were still or not, the same bird replicated a hundred times or more.

And then she remembered. She remembered that her mother was dead and that she was now sitting in the sky, alongside the clouds, surrounded by the same brown bird. She didn't want to open the curtains. She didn't want to feel like she was in an aeroplane that was never going to land. What happened when it was windy – did the building move? Did it wave at other buildings it knew?

She calculated that there were fourteen other bedrooms beneath her – she was sleeping in the world's tallest bunk bed! – and then not wanting to think about bodies piled on top of other bodies, or being in the *Guinness Book of Records* for the wrong reasons, she got out of bed and crawled along the carpet towards the door. She was already dressed. She'd slept in her clothes in case she had to evacuate the building during the night due to a fire or gunshots or strong winds. She felt that any might be a possibility. She crouched down lower. She didn't want to lose her grip and slip through an open window. The floor felt really uneven.

Her grandmother was sitting on the sofa, flicking through a photo album.

'Did you sleep?' she asked her.

Frankie shrugged. She felt like crying again. The curtains were open to the right of her and she could see a ragged cloud that was as dirty as a dishcloth, even though she was trying not to look. She moved away from the window and clung to the nearest wall like the birds in the bedroom that had thousands of wings but still couldn't fly.

'You're perfectly safe, Frankie.'

'But it's too high. It isn't normal. And there's no gate. Anything could happen. Anyone could walk in. A fully functioning gate with a working latch and a familiar squeak is an essential requirement for all homes.'

'Doors keep things out too.'

Frankie sighed. It was like talking to her mother.

'It isn't the same. The placement of a gate between a door and the pavement provides increased security and is in the interests of all homeowners.'

'I see.'

'I don't think you do. Nobody ever understands. Our gate had only one hinge and was riddled with woodlice and look what happened. Something got inside.'

Neither of them spoke for twenty-seven breaths. Frankie counted them to distract herself from the cloudy dishcloth outside.

And then on the twenty-eighth breath her grandmother said, 'I was just looking at some photographs of your father.'

Frankie inched her way over to the sofa, still on her hands and knees. She felt dizzy. It wasn't natural being this close to the sky, boxing people up like this. She peered over the sofa arm at the stranger who looked a little like her, the boy on the right, smiling back at her.

Her grandmother peeled back the cellophane and removed one of the photographs from the album, her father wearing a checked shirt and cowboy boots beside a red sports car. He was nineteen, according to the pencilled note on the reverse of the photograph.

'Perhaps you'd like to keep this one.'

Frankie nodded and, tucking it beneath her armpit, she slid back along the wall towards the bedroom and propped it against the one of her mother, but they seemed so dissimilar, despite the splashes of red and the unnatural smiles. She'd thought that they would blend together seamlessly like jigsaw pieces, but her mother didn't look at all comfortable next to her father.

She wondered if identical picture frames might help because it was important that they complemented each other, like salt and pepper and egg and cress. Currently, they looked as if they were from two completely different sandwiches. She wondered if they were together now. She liked to think so. She hoped that her mother had finally forgiven her father for dying and that he'd been able to find her, because Frankie wasn't sure that she would have been easy to find. It had been challenging enough trying to determine the shape of her when she'd still been alive.

Mostly, Frankie was left alone during those first few days at her grandmother's. She was able to sit undisturbed among the garden birds for hours at a time, interrupted only at mealtimes, which enabled her to allocate a set amount of time to 'uninterrupted crying' three times a day, mid-morning, late afternoon and last thing at night. She would allow herself to cry for a full fifteen minutes each time and then she would stop. By the fourth day she'd realised that Uncle Stewart wasn't coming back.

Very occasionally she would crawl over to the bedroom window and, still on her knees, peel back the curtain and peer outside. It always made her head spin. People looked like ants beneath her. She tried to determine the finer details, but her eyes refused to stretch fifteen floors. She thought she saw the girl with purple hair who Uncle Stewart had spoken to, but it could have been anyone. When she looked again she couldn't see anything purple.

Deciding to address her concerns in a more practical manner, she began to record daily descriptive accounts of what was happening beneath her: the number of people present, the time of day, whether there were workmen on the premises, postal delivery schedules . . . as many particulars as she could establish in as brief amount of time as possible. If there wasn't a gate, then she would need to be extra-vigilant in identifying *all* possible risk factors.

Four minutes of long-distance squinting at blurry figures and white delivery vans soon became seven minutes, which soon became eighteen minutes and then a record twenty-nine minutes. And sometimes during this period the scheduled crying sessions lasted only seven minutes or two and a half minutes, sometimes only twice a day, and some days she didn't cry at all, and then she would worry that her mother was getting further than fifteen floors away, becoming even smaller than the ant people beneath her. But forgetting seemed to be so much easier than remembering.

A letter arrived from Ellie on a day when the only colour that she could see was elephant-grey and she'd already cried a record five times and it was still only noon.

'*Ringo Starr is so big now, you wouldn't recognise him, and he keeps licking my face, which makes Mummy cross because she says that you should never let dogs lick your face because it's extremely unhygienic and you might catch rabies, but he's soooo cute. I shall love him forever.*'

Frankie considered her reply: '*I can't see the colour purple any more and I'm living in the sky and sleeping in a birdcage*', although she did have some ingenious suggestions on how to stop Ringo Starr licking Ellie's face (karate chops and belly tickling).

Ellie was apparently now sitting next to Sadie Adams at school ('*she smells like porridge*') so Frankie had been replaced by another human being after all, even if she did smell like breakfast. Before the letter there had been only Ringo Starr to be jealous of, but now there was Sadie Adams too.

Frankie wondered whether she'd ever be able to sit next to anybody who wasn't her grandmother ever again. Venturing outside was becoming an almost impossible task. Perhaps if she kept a record of everybody who entered and left the building and completed several security checks of the outlying area beforehand, it might be less impossible. But even then she wasn't sure whether she'd actually be able to step outside because the sky was so big and the roads too narrow and they were opening up and closing in on her a little more each day.

She reread the last two sentences at the bottom of Ellie's letter. '*Mummy says that you've been very brave. She hopes that you are still being brave.*' Frankie didn't feel particularly brave, but she would be able to see so much more on the ground floor.

So, encouraged by Mrs Barlow's words, she told her grandmother that she was going to get some fresh air, although how fresh the air might be was debatable, and opened the front door. Fluorescent strip lighting buzzed overhead and a corridor of doors stretched ahead of her. She didn't want to contemplate what might be behind those doors. That was a whole other level of anxiety. She took a deep breath and stepped into the narrow corridor. Not having a gate was unsettling. Being so close to other people's front doors was unnerving. And she didn't like not being able to see outside from a safe distance should she need to. What would happen if there *was* a fire, an intruder? Where would they all go, how would they all see? She still slept in her clothes, just in case.

The lifts were still out of order, although she wouldn't have used them if they had been working, she didn't want to get trapped inside one. She slowly walked towards the stairwell. She felt dizzy almost immediately and had to flatten herself against the wall before descending the stairs.

A gate would have made things so much easier: they structured your thinking, packaged it neatly away, although, admittedly, their mechanisms did sometimes prevent people from reaching you. They shrank your circle of friends, narrowed your life, squared it off and gave it sharp corners and defined edges. Frankie hadn't really considered this before in any depth, how her mother may have survived if there'd been no gate at all, if more people had been able to reach her.

Suddenly, her world began to sway and it couldn't only be attributed to vertigo and a sloping floor. How often had she endorsed the benefits of a resilient garden gate? Had she been mistaken? Had she been misguided in her quest to thwart all outsiders from entering their home while at the same time imprisoning her mother inside it?

She reeled slightly as she stood wrestling with this new dilemma. A postman stepped past her, a glove of letters in his hand. She wasn't expecting him for another forty-two minutes and his presence alarmed her. She would have to amend today's spreadsheet before doing anything else. She ran back upstairs and didn't stop running until she was back inside the open birdcage and wallpapered to the walls.

Being brave wasn't going to be easy, but what worried her more was the fact that she was beginning to question the requirement of a gate at all, beginning to wonder whether a residence really did need one. Was keeping things out in fact more destructive than letting things in? But did a gate not do both? Did it not let you in *and* keep you out when necessary? She was exhausted. After she'd amended the postal delivery worksheet, she lay on the bed and tried to access the 'not thinking about anything' portion of her brain until she finally fell asleep.

It was several days before she was able to summon up the courage to leave the flat again, although the decision was ultimately made for her. Her grandmother had a chest infection and needed some cough medicine. She decided that this time she would do it quickly, like pulling off a plaster, in the hope that it hurt less. She kept her head down and made it as far as the garages without breathing at all.

She couldn't remember which way they'd driven to get there, left or right, or what landmarks or shops they'd passed on the way. Heads or tails? She decided to turn right (tails). It was colder than she'd imagined and busier than she'd expected, footsteps swerving impatiently round her, gusts of wind jabbing at her from behind because she wasn't walking quickly enough.

After what seemed like hours, but was probably only ten minutes, she noticed a newsagent and went inside to purchase a bottle of Buttercup cough syrup. On the way back she thought that she heard footsteps behind her. It had suddenly become much quieter. Whenever she quickened her pace, the footsteps did too. Whenever she slowed down, so did the footsteps. She didn't dare look round to see who it was, but she was a fast runner. She could easily outrun them, which is what she did. She was wheezing and breathless by the time she got back, coughing and spluttering like her grandmother.

At the entrance to the flats she briefly glanced behind her, but there was nobody there, not even Marcel, but he didn't have her new address so it wouldn't have been him.

Chapter Six

Nobody's Guinea Pig

1980

The fluorescent strip lighting was casting sepia shadows on the ward walls, ageing them by decades. Peggy sighed as she rolled her head towards the window, the chalk-on-blackboard pain in her temples rolling with it. Normally, hospital stays felt like weekends away, but today it was like being trapped in the 1940s.

She rubbed at the unsightly red rash on her arms, the only evidence of a death that didn't appear to have happened. Why was she still here? Or maybe she *had* died and for her the afterlife was an extended stay in a hospital bed.

A nurse suddenly appeared beside her bed, brandishing a thermometer. Enraged, Peggy yelled at her to leave her alone, she was nobody's guinea pig. When she wouldn't leave, Peggy threw a glass at her, which smashed against a passing tea trolley, narrowly missing both the nurse and an auxiliary who'd fortunately bent down to retrieve a packet of bourbon biscuits. A doctor rushed over and before Peggy could gauge what was happening, the bourbons and the Glenn Miller Orchestra had drifted quietly away again.

On her second day in purgatory, her fury at not being dead had been replaced with lightheaded indifference. A doctor was standing at the foot of the bed, staring at her with his left eye. The right eye was looking at something else, each eye seemingly interested in a different thing. She supposed that you absorbed more when both eyes weren't fixated on one thing and it was no doubt easier to deflect something being hurled in your direction if you could see round corners while still looking straight ahead.

'That was quite a show you put on yesterday, Peggy. How are you feeling today? Better, I hope. We replaced the glass with a plastic beaker from the children's ward just in case.'

Of course she didn't feel better. She should have been dead.

She followed his wandering eye. It seemed to be lingering on one of the student nurses.

'Your daughter's coming to see you today,' he informed her brightly.

She said nothing.

Perhaps if she stayed silent then she'd be as good as dead.

But after he'd lectured her on the dangers of mixing over-the-counter medication with alcohol (when it had been her intention to do just that) and warned her that next time she might not be quite so lucky, she began to wonder if it had been fortunate that Jessica had been stocktaking and had heard Frankie crying and alerted the police. What if this wasn't how she was meant to die? And Frankie was the one who'd saved her. She couldn't quite grasp this new development so had to push it to one side to examine later.

Brenda and Frankie were celebrating when Peggy's eyes opened for the third time – not the news that she was still alive, but Frankie's first birthday, although any cause for celebration on the anniversary of Ed falling to his death was somewhat untimely. She'd often wondered whether Frankie would be the one dead if Ed had survived. Had Ed died so that Frankie could live? It seemed that a contract on one of their lives had been signed without her consent.

There was a chocolate sponge cake decorated with Smarties sitting on one of the chairs like a third visitor, a single candyfloss-pink candle planted like a flag in the middle of it, which the ward sister had said that they couldn't light due to hospital health and safety regulations. Brenda passed Peggy a generous fifth on a pink serviette. She left it on her lap, untouched. It felt as heavy as a rock.

Frankie was babbling away merrily on Brenda's lap, streaks of chocolate smeared across her cheeks. Peggy suddenly felt guilty. None of this was Frankie's fault – she was just a child. *She* was the one who needed to change. Well, not change exactly, nobody ever changed completely, parts of you still remained, but she could certainly make more of an effort, conceal the more disagreeable parts. She wished Frankie a happy birthday, but she was too preoccupied playing with the clasp on Brenda's purse to look up, hadn't even noticed that Peggy was there.

A few days later Peggy was assigned a behavioural therapist and discharged on the understanding that non-compliance with the terms of her discharge (weekly therapy sessions for a minimum period of three months) would result in re-admittance to the psychiatric unit. She felt like she was being sentenced for being ill.

Expecting a man to be seated behind the desk (the 'Dr' giving no indication as to gender) she was startled to be greeted by a woman (Margaret Thatcher had really started something) asking her to 'take a seat'. Doctor Ingalls. Like a character in *Little House on the Prairie*.

Peggy hoped that she wasn't going to stretch another tearful bow across a violin string the way that Laura and Mary always did, find another loose thread to keep pulling at.

But to her considerable surprise, she wasn't at all daunted by the prospect of unburdening herself in what she imagined would be an unenlightening and superficial manner. It had been a long time since she'd spoken to anybody at length or discussed anyone other than Frankie.

'Tell me what brings you here today,' Doctor Ingalls began.

It's one of the conditions of my hospital release, Peggy wanted to say. *As you well know.*

Instead she said, 'My fiancé' – she was about to say 'husband', but thought that Doctor Ingalls might seek official confirmation of her marital status, although fiancé wasn't strictly true either – 'died on the day that our daughter, Frankie, was born. I'm sure it's perfectly normal to be feeling a little "out of sorts" under the circumstances.'

Why was she using her telephone voice?

'I'm not sure that being "out of sorts" is quite the same as having suicidal tendencies,' Doctor Ingalls argued, but Peggy continued to play down the seriousness of the situation.

'Hardly "tendencies" – it was just the once. And I'm feeling much better now.'

But then this woman who she barely knew and who should have been a man began to exact answers to questions from her that she didn't know she knew: her foster father's clocks, her foster mother's birds, Billie Holiday, Daphne (although when she next asked her about Daphne, Peggy denied ever mentioning her. 'But if there's no Daphne, then where are you?' Doctor Ingalls had asked her, cryptically. 'Oh, I'm buried in a different garden,' Peggy replied. 'You'll never find me.'), things that she really didn't want to talk about, things that she *wouldn't* talk about. But it was too late. She was apparently already discussing them.

And life was far simpler when you didn't have to answer probing questions, when you didn't have to participate or 'help yourself' to tissues. What had happened to the cordial, benign conversation that she'd been planning to have?

'Well, I think that concludes our first session, Peggy. Shall we say the same time next week?'

There seemed no reprieve. What more was she expected to say? She'd said it all, her whole life condensed into fifty short minutes. Should she start inventing things? Should she drip-feed her tiny amounts of everything to keep her entertained? She'd watched the earth being raked over behind the desk, something that should be written down so that it wasn't forgotten, and it had made her head spin. Whatever was Dr Ingalls writing down? She desperately wanted to know what was being written about her.

Aaron, the social worker, was always writing things down; even when she insisted that it was a secret, he would write it down – make it everything, and then do nothing – but she pretended that it didn't matter and instead tried to remember which words to grasp and hold on to and which ones to safely let go of, so that like Daphne, the truth could remain buried.

Brenda rarely visited now. She'd spent so long keeping Peggy afloat that there'd been no outlet for her own grief, which had now culminated in a spate of ongoing illnesses. She was currently recovering from a second bout of shingles. A social worker was now making regular impromptu visits instead, a woman who wore her hair in plaits as thick as loaves but who wasn't German or called Inge.

Thankfully, however, Christmas was only two and a half weeks away, so Peggy was able to focus her energies on mince-pie ingredients and plastic baubles. But then John Lennon was shot and killed on 8 December and she couldn't do anything at all that day. Like Ed, he was everywhere even though he was dead, the same retelling of events broadcast on every news channel until it was all she could think about. She didn't realise that being shot outside a Central Park apartment could be retold in so many different ways, turned into so many assorted headlines, affect the scheduling of so many television programmes that she'd been looking forward to watching.

Every song on the radio was written by him, co-written by him, sung by him or inspired by him. Every phase of his life (Aunt Mimi, his first wife Cynthia, his son Julian, the Yoko years) was re-examined and analysed until it felt like you'd met him, like you'd stood beside him at every crossroad, at every wrong turn.

And since she was still mostly alternating between grief stages three and four, some days a seven, other days a one, it resurrected

Ed again, made it seem like only yesterday that he'd died, so much so that she couldn't possibly celebrate Christmas without him, couldn't bear the thought of being trapped inside those seven stages of grief indefinitely.

Were there degrees of grief? Peggy wondered, the grief you feel proportional to the length of time that you've known someone. Should her grief be less than that of a widow(er) who was married for forty years? Or was a person's grief as big or as small as it needed to be? Hers certainly felt enormous. Often, it felt too big.

On Christmas morning, the world still reeling from John Lennon's death, still trying to articulate the enormity of it, Peggy gave Frankie a roll of reindeer wrapping paper to play with and spent the rest of the day in bed with the curtains closed.

The wrapping paper lay scattered across the carpet like torn slivers of venison when she woke the next morning. It felt like the end of everything.

Chapter Seven

Marie's New Shoes

1979

'If anyone asks, I was here all morning.'

Geoff barely looked up from his invoices as Stella unbuttoned her coat and began wiping down tabletops and straightening chairs. But she knew that he'd heard her. He never missed a detail, knew exactly how many twenty-pound notes there were in the till at any one time and what one person had been saying about another. Which she'd always thought unusual. The men she knew rarely noticed anything unless it was naked.

'Been meeting that mystery man of yours again?' he asked her.

'You know you're the only man in my life.'

Geoff's cheeks coloured slightly. He told her that he was going upstairs to sort through some receipts – could she hold the fort?

Didn't she always?

As he was making his way upstairs, she had to abandon the Mr Sheen and run to the toilet. She'd been feeling nauseous all morning. She heard him pause on the staircase, his ears as sharp as his eyes, before locking the toilet door and lifting the lid.

Robbie arrived as she was wiping her chin on a tea towel.

'Everything all right?'

'You're late again.'

'Only ten minutes, could be worse. Is the old man in?'

'He's upstairs.' Or halfway up the stairs, listening. 'A couple of barrels need changing and we're low on Britvics.'

He said something that she didn't quite catch and then disappeared down the cellar steps. Geoff was sleeping with Robbie's mother, Rita, hence the presence of Robbie for a few hours each week, although he seemed to increase the workload rather than reduce it. Two minutes later she heard banging coming from the cellar, whether from the physical exertion of barrel-changing or Robbie's quick temper she couldn't be sure, but she wasn't hopeful that the Britvics would arrive intact.

Terry Campbell, one of the regulars, had once told her that the pub was haunted by a previous landlady who liked to pour herself a drink down there every now and then and put on some tap shoes. Stella thought that highly unlikely – surely there were less damp places for ghosts to tap dance. She'd have spent her days haunting Camber Sands or, if she could still use her passport, the Italian Riviera.

She would happily have locked Robbie in there, though. She wasn't in the mood for babysitting. Yesterday he'd poured a cider instead of a lager and short-changed someone by fifty pence, then broken four beer glasses and mislaid the darts – all in the space of ten minutes. And she had more than enough problems of her own. Each time the door opened she expected to see a policeman heading towards her, a policeman wanting to have a quiet word, wanting to know where she'd been that morning, Geoff listening on the staircase.

At two thirty she told Robbie that she was going to clean the toilets, they smelled of vomit – mostly hers – and, after squirting some supermarket bleach down them, she opened a window and lit a cigarette. After five or six puffs she remembered that she shouldn't be smoking and flushed the cigarette away. She wondered who would be the father of her child now. She didn't want to be a single parent. She didn't want her child to be entitled to free school meals and second-hand clothes, to be ridiculed and pitied. But she certainly couldn't imagine sleeping with Geoff or Robbie, although she then did start to imagine it and had to lift up the toilet seat so that she could be sick again.

Rita certainly seemed keen, though, even if Geoff did have a way of looking at you, *really* looking at you, as if he could see everything, as if he could see every one of your darkest secrets, every drop of blood in your veins. He'd been married before, but nobody knew who to or for how long. And somebody once said that there was even a child, but nobody knew where the child might be either. People often thought the world small, but Stella had always thought it too big. There were too many corners, too many places for a person to hide.

Robbie was tapping on the toilet door as she was heaving, her stomach now bringing up nothing more than bile and phlegm simply to appease her.

'Stella, there's something wrong with one of the pumps.'

Christ, she couldn't have five minutes to herself to vomit.

'I'll be there in a minute.'

The 'minute' came out a little more aggressively than she intended.

Billy Yates was behind the bar when she came back.

'All sorted,' he told her.

'Didn't think bar pumps were your speciality, Billy.'

'One of my many talents.'

'Shame Robbie isn't quite so gifted.'

Robbie was currently leaning over the bar ogling Sonia Patterson's tattooed left breast.

'You'd better head back to your seat before Geoff sees you. He doesn't like anyone but me, Robbie and Faith behind the bar. And thanks.'

He smiled at her. She smiled back, the thought of sleeping with Billy Yates not nearly as repugnant as the thought of sleeping with Geoff or Robbie. It didn't make her feel nauseous at all. Perhaps this child could be his. He asked her if she'd like to see *Moonraker* at the Odeon later. Why not, she thought?

They had sex in the cinema toilets during the closing credits. She didn't usually sleep with a person so quickly, but the 'getting-to-know-you, getting-to-know-all-about-you' phase would have to come later. Not always a bad thing. Normally, the less you knew about a person the better. They were often hugely disappointing.

Five weeks later she told him that it wasn't a stomach bug she had; she was in fact pregnant. He seemed genuinely surprised – pleasantly so, thankfully – as if he'd never considered that he was capable of such a thing or realised the ease with which it could happen.

'We should get married,' he told her.

'There's no rush.' *Not now you've accepted that the child is yours.*

She didn't want to make it worse by actually marrying him. She was already beginning to feel increasingly guilty about deceiving him, about starting something that seemed to be gathering more and more pace until it was virtually impossible to step off the speeding train that she'd boarded.

She was no better than Faith, who had four children by four different men and yet still insisted that her husband was their biological father. Was doing a thing once as bad as doing a thing four times?

She was wondering whether to tell Billy the truth when Geoff approached her one morning with a pink envelope in his hand. It looked like a party invitation.

'Peggy Appleton claims you're responsible for Ed's death.'

Not an invitation, then; more of an accusation.

'That's ridiculous. I hardly knew him. She's just looking for someone to blame.'

She couldn't look at him. She studied the pink envelope instead: *To the landlord of The Swan.*

'I expect so.'

She could sense him trying to untangle her thoughts. He was part Six Million Dollar Man, part Bionic Woman and part Uri Geller, his eyes and ears stretching unfathomable distances, his thumbs bending silver spoons out of shape while predicting global disasters and celebrity deaths. She remembered her father once saying to her, 'You can be my eyes and ears,' and she'd wondered what was wrong with his own eyes and ears that he needed to enlist a second pair.

'You know what she's like. Everything's always everybody else's fault. Robbie saw her in Kwik Save last week arguing with someone over a loaf of Mother's Pride. She pushed the manager into a display of tinned mandarins when he tried to intervene.'

Stella picked up a pint glass and began polishing it vigorously. She'd never mentioned Peggy slapping her across the face outside WHSmith a few weeks earlier. I know *exactly* how it feels, she'd wanted to tell her, my child hasn't got a father now either, but Gail Harrison was already rushing into a nearby telephone box to call the police and the stinging slap had quickly escalated into a public brawl, Peggy pulling at her hair and calling her a whore, Stella trying to push her away. Stella insisted that she didn't want to press charges when a police officer came into The Swan later that afternoon to take a statement, managing to quickly usher him towards the door before Geoff got back from the bank.

Perhaps if she did marry Billy Yates then the accusations might stop. Peggy was hardly likely to harass a married barmaid in the same way, particular one who was pregnant.

'Maybe I'll just file it away instead of forwarding it to head office,' Geoff said, as if he was doing her a favour.

But if he'd really been doing her a favour he would have ripped it up and put it in the bin. She wondered if Geoff had seen her with Ed, heard her on the telephone. She'd always been careful, but sometimes being careful just wasn't being careful enough.

'Do what you need to do, but it's Peggy Appleton's word against mine and her word isn't worth the paper it's written on.'

She really didn't want to think about Ed or Peggy Appleton. And actually, Peggy's surname was Moon, not Appleton. She seemed to think that she could call herself whatever she liked and nobody would notice.

The wedding ceremony was held in a registry office, her stepfather's Parkinson's more pronounced and more incessant since only the previous night, it seemed, as he guided her unsteadily towards Billy. 'I wish you'd stop shaking,' she'd whispered in his ear. 'You're making everything a million times worse.' But her stepfather wasn't listening; he was alternating between port and starboard. She was starting to feel seasick.

He turned to smile at her, digging his nails into the sleeve of her peach dress as he did so.

She squeezed his hand. 'I'm sorry, I'm just nervous. And I look ridiculous.'

It was the only dress that she could fit into at such short notice, and she felt like the eponymous fruit in *James and the Giant Peach*.

Something peculiar is about to happen at any moment.

The drawback of a shotgun wedding, she supposed.

Or a sham one.

The clouds blackened the minute they stepped outside and the photographer cried, 'Gorgonzola,' their smiles as cheesy as the command. Clown smiles too much like smiles to be anything of the sort. A man in a panama hat, who Stella had never seen before, stood on the bottom step smiling back at them. She asked him what he'd been smiling at as she walked past. 'Why, you of course,' he replied.

The reception was held in one of The Swan's upstairs function rooms ('at a very competitive rate if I do say so myself,' Geoff had said. 'Consider it a gift.') and a local catering company prepared a menu of prawn cocktail, beef Wellington and sherry trifle for a curious assortment of guests.

Billy's sister's children were wearing identical satin-pink bridesmaid's dresses even though they weren't twins *or* bridesmaids; a middle-aged man with one arm and a glass eye, a friend of her stepfather's apparently, was attempting a Chuck Berry swivel on the dance floor, but looked like he was stubbing out a cigarette; and an elderly woman dressed in Italian black who they couldn't link to either side sat knitting.

Stella retrieved a Dean Martin cassette (*Welcome to My World*) from her clutch bag. She'd always had old-fashioned – or as her friend Donna liked to call it, 'really shitty' – taste in music, a legacy from her mother who liked to play the role of a fifties housewife and be serenaded by the likes of Perry Como and Andy Williams while doing household chores.

She passed it to the DJ (one of Geoff's cousins) but he didn't have a tape deck. He said that he might have some Frank Sinatra on vinyl though. She shook her head – no, that wouldn't do. That wouldn't do at all. Please don't play that, she begged him. He promised that he wouldn't, although 'New York, New York' always goes down a storm at the end of the evening, he told her, a bit like the *Titanic*. Disappointed, she slipped the cassette back into her clutch bag.

Months later Geoff could still recall the long-forgotten details of the wedding reception, having memorised them as studiously as a Shakespearian sonnet: the pink prawns, the bubblegum satin, his cousin Jim's one-liners. He asked her if she still liked Dean Martin. She did. She should have asked him what the woman in black lace was knitting and why a man with only one arm was stubbing out cigarettes on the dance floor, although she wasn't sure that she actually wanted to know.

'You should have been a detective instead of a pub landlord,' she told him.

'Who says I can't be both?' he answered, tapping the side of his nose. 'It's the perfect ruse, plying the clientele with drinks until a wealth of secrets start to spill. Of course, it's mostly gibberish coming from their lips.'

She wasn't sure whether he was being serious or not. And even when he laughed and told her that of course he wasn't an undercover police officer, she still wasn't sure. He just noticed the things that other people missed or didn't think important, he told her. It's a well-known fact that most people couldn't identify their neighbours in a police line-up. An eidetic or photographic memory, they call it, but I think it's more than a snapshot. It's a feeling. It's like I'm actually there. It used to horrify my mother that I could remember dates and entire conversations. I can still remember every line of dialogue in the film *Easy Rider* and I haven't seen it in years. She said that it wasn't normal and began to whisper so that I wouldn't be able to hear her. Nobody likes a smartarse, she'd say.

Stella's daughter, Marie, was born during a thunderstorm, the thunder so loud that nobody heard her arrival. She slipped into the world unnoticed.

Billy was in Cardiff, but Geoff was there smiling down at them both, absorbing it all like a sponge: the birthmark shaped like Italy on her scalp, the deep blue vein that flowed like a woodland stream across her forehead, all seven pounds three ounces of her.

And those early years were reasonably happy, or as happy as they could be considering she was married to a man who wasn't the father of her child and who'd been in Cardiff when that child was born.

But then, several years later, everything changed for the second time.

Marie was fidgeting in the seat next to her, tugging at her coat sleeve. She remembered her stepfather digging his nails into the sleeve of her peach wedding dress. She didn't want to go to ballet, could they fly kites instead? And then she wanted her to look at her new shoes: 'Mummy, Mummy, look at them,' she shrieked. 'Aren't they beautiful?' And then, 'Mummy, Mummy, watch that lady.' 'What lad—?' Her stepfather's nails were really hurting.

And then she was no longer inside the car, Marie tugging at her sleeve. She was lying on damp grass unable to move her legs. She tried to turn her head, tried to find Marie, but after what seemed like days, she hadn't moved at all – she was still pinned to a roundabout like a Post-it note, looking up at the sky. She called Marie's name, but it was swallowed up by sirens. And then she was moving, but not by herself.

'Where's Marie?' she mouthed, but nobody was listening or, if they were listening, then nobody could hear her.

She thought that she saw a white tutu beneath a car wheel, but she couldn't see Marie's new shoes. She'd be mad at her for not looking at them 'properly, Mummy, look at them *properly, both eyes*'.

When she woke up, Geoff was there instead of Billy. She wondered when they'd swapped places, when Billy had suddenly become Geoff. It seemed to have happened gradually. She wondered if Geoff should have been Marie's father and she'd got it all wrong.

'Where's Marie?'

He didn't say anything for such a long time that she thought she must be dead and this was the afterlife, but then a doctor stepped into the room.

'We couldn't save her. I'm so sorry.'

Save her? Why did she need saving?

He must have sensed her confusion.

'Your daughter, Marie – I'm afraid she didn't survive the crash.'

And then, a few days later, when Geoff had changed back into Billy, 'I'm afraid there's been extensive damage to the brainstem, more than we initially realised. It's unlikely that you'll ever walk again.'

Her daughter was dead and she would never walk again. Although it may have seemed a fitting sentence, being unable to get up and walk away from what she'd done, life without the possibility of parole, she wished that if anyone had had to die that day that it had been her, not Marie. Billy had looked at her as if he wished that it had been her too, and she wanted to scream at him that Marie wasn't even his child, what did it matter to him? She was hers to mourn, all hers. But hair-pulling and pinching wouldn't bring Marie back.

Nobody could make it right, even when they insisted that it wasn't anybody's fault, that it had been a tragic accident, so many other things building up to that moment, the Alfa Romeo two cars away that had paused at the traffic lights a second too long, the woman stepping off the pavement at that precise moment, the light rain that hadn't been forecast, if Marie hadn't been wearing the new shoes that she so wanted Stella to look at, or they'd taken a left turn and gone to the park instead.

And taking seven attempts to pass her driving test should have been impetus enough to stop driving. She was hardly a natural. Most people would have stopped at the second or third attempt. But no, not her. 'Perseverance is everything,' her mother had drummed into her from an early age. 'All things worth having come at a price.' How she wished now that she'd ignored her mother's trite sayings and spent the money on something more frivolous than driving lessons.

Every day sparked a new dilemma. What if Marie had been on the backseat? Does it matter where you sit? Is the difference between life and death, a full recovery and permanent disability, a passenger seat? Why didn't the seatbelt save her life? If she'd failed her test a seventh time, would Marie still be here? If she hadn't married Billy, if, if, if . . .

She was never the same again, a permanent scowl on her face, a snappy, inappropriate tongue, driven half mad with questions that nobody could answer. Geoff stopped calling because she wouldn't stop yelling at him and Billy was never home because she couldn't stop crying. She was certainly no phoenix 'rising from the ashes of despair'.

And her wheelchair, this monstrous contraption that she'd been burdened with, seemed to fill the entire house, like a lodger spilling out into rooms that weren't theirs, like a mountain that you could never see beyond. Or maybe she was the monster, not the wheelchair that carried her from room to room, that held her when she sobbed, kept her steady when she felt like collapsing, her emotions now painfully visible as if she'd been turned inside out or furiously shaken.

She asked Billy to leave, she hated him and wished that she'd never married him, but he told her that he wasn't going anywhere. It was just the two of them now, his continued presence a constant reminder that she was the cause of all of this, that she'd killed her own child. *And somebody else.*

She realised that she'd never given the other person a second thought, didn't even remember their name, there wasn't enough room in her heart to mourn two people, but Billy liked to mention it from time to time, liked to remind her that she stole two lives that day even though she wasn't legally responsible for either death. The brakes had failed, according to one official report, even though the brakes had recently been tested. It seemed that she'd suffered enough, enough for the technicalities of her daughter's death not to matter.

So many times she wanted to tell Billy that he was grieving somebody else's child; she wanted to be a single parent like the rest of her friends – albeit a bereaved single parent – but she really didn't have the energy to open up old wounds. There were too many other wounds to dress. And telling him he was shit at maths wasn't going to make those wounds heal any quicker.

She didn't leave the house for two years. She couldn't bear the thought of anyone seeing her, whispering about her, pointing at her, maybe even spitting at her. It felt like everybody knew what she'd done. Heaven knows what motivational clichés her mother would have spouted had she still been alive; 'Every cloud', probably, or 'Time is a great healer'.

It was the opposite of agoraphobia. It was being able to go out, but not daring to. It was being able to open the front door, but not wanting to. Outside there were no walls to contain her, no blinds to shield her. The world that she'd always thought too big was now far too small. So she wrote lists instead. Lists kept her world turning. They kept her structured and sane. Communicating with Billy was mostly done in writing, dependent upon an appearance on a well-considered list compiled with a swelling sense of pride and yet mostly received with an ambivalent, uninterested shrug.

And with more free time than she deserved, those hours were spent disinfecting and decluttering the house. No grease was allowed to congeal, no dust particles allowed to settle. And two years really wasn't long at all. Twenty-four months, one hundred and four weeks, seven hundred and thirty days. No time at all to remove every last speck of dirt.

Perhaps she need never go outside again, which for all its limitations was actually quite liberating – no sweating palms, no slight perspiration that quickly develops into a terrible clammy stickiness that can't be removed with soap and water, no gasping for breath. But more importantly, she wouldn't be able to hurt anybody else.

When she did finally open the front door two years later, the first two people she saw crossing the road were Peggy Appleton and her daughter, *her* daughter still very much alive. There was so much hate in her heart that she couldn't breathe. She spun the wheelchair around and went back inside. The fridge needed defrosting and there were the first silvery threads of a spider's web in the hallway.

Chapter Eight

The Calgary Winter Olympics

1988

Seven days later, Frankie felt brave enough to leave the flat again. And this time she took a writing pad and a pack of ten biros, essential stationery that she'd asked her grandmother to buy for her so that she could keep an accurate record of all the building's occupants.

Unfortunately, when she went down to the post room to compile a list of names and addresses, she discovered that the communal mailboxes were labelled by flat number only and an individual key was needed to gain access, so she had to improvise, asking her grandmother for a sketchpad and some new pencils so that she could sketch the residents as they were collecting their post.

Her grandmother helped with the names of two of the residents: Carrie, who she went to bingo with and Irene, who ran a market stall selling greetings cards. But her world was nearly as small as Frankie's. She'd recently traced her grandmother's limited itineraries on a local map that she'd found in the stairwell, carefully following the roads with a pencil so that she'd know where she was and how she'd got there (Frankie often worried that she might not come back) when she said, 'I'm off to bingo' or 'I'm heading to the market, do you need any more stationery?' or 'I've got a doctor's appointment, I shouldn't be long'. The pencil line stretched like an arm along Riverside Road, before forming a torso spanning the breadth of Church Gardens and then finally curving into a head on the southside of Selwyn Place. It looked like the chalked outline of a crime scene victim.

Frankie had to resort to codenames for the rest.

On Day One (although it was actually Day Eleven, if you started on the day she'd arrived at her grandmother's), she noted in her sketchpad that a bald man wearing a denim Led Zeppelin jacket ('Humpty Dumpty – see image below'), retrieved mail for Flat 60. A second man with a pierced eyebrow, a Chicago Bulls baseball cap and a straggly grey ponytail ('Sitting Bull – see image on next page') opened the Flat 59 mailbox. Neither was particularly friendly. Glaring at her, Humpty Dumpty had asked her what she thought she was doing. She told him that she was reading a magazine and that he was to pretend that she wasn't there.

When the Bishops, an elderly couple (Flat 6), came to collect a letter from their daughter in Canada they offered her a Polo mint and the Canadian stamp that was on the letter (a 1988 Calgary Winter Olympics figure skater) and told her the names of everybody on their floor, including a Nigerian prince named Emmanuel who worked in Boots. As a thank you, Frankie said that they could keep their sketches.

On Day Two a man with Debbie Harry hair ('Fab Five Freddy') and a woman with no lips ('Zippy') hesitated for a while before approaching the mailbox for Flat 88. It was difficult to determine their true colours because of the bold stripes and the colourful checks that they were wearing. Her grandmother tutted when she read what Frankie had written. 'That's Tom and Nancy Ellis. Nancy thinks she's Vivienne Westwood. Heaven knows who Tom thinks he is.' Frankie had no idea who Vivienne Westwood was, but she added the names Tom and Nancy Ellis to her notes. It seemed that her grandmother's knowledge loosened and tightened depending on the weather.

On Day Three she met Trevor Smith and Betty Rivers (Flats 49 and 31 respectively). They actually introduced themselves in full which she found particularly helpful, although the handshakes that followed were a little awkward. Trevor Smith was wearing sunglass-es indoors, as if he didn't want anyone, but especially Betty Rivers, to see his eyes or, more importantly, to see what it was that his eyes were looking at. They were looking at Betty Rivers' cleavage.

Unless he was blind, of course. But he didn't look blind. He certainly knew where Betty Rivers' breasts were, although locating them wasn't too challenging. They were disproportionately huge.

Betty Rivers was a young girl with yellow teeth and an old name. Frankie reached for a yellow pencil. She'd had to add coloured pencils to her growing list of stationery demands because there was more colour in the post room than she'd initially realised. And they were all starting to look like there were warrants out for their arrests.

A few minutes later Flat 26 exited the main doors with his Staffordshire pit bull, Vixen (she knew his dog's name because he was always yelling at it, but she didn't know his and, tired of inventing aliases, she'd started to refer to people by their flat number). They weren't supposed to have pets, but nobody dared report 26 because nobody dared do anything when you owned a pit bull and had a broken nose. Both he and his dog glared at her as they walked past. They even looked alike. It reminded Frankie of Ellie and Ringo Starr and how alike they were starting to look (Ellie had sent her a photograph of them both sitting outside the cricket pavilion) and she soon lost interest. She left Betty Rivers' teeth unfinished and went back up to the flat.

On Day Four she met Vinnie. She was in her usual spot on the post-room floor wondering how to rescue her drawing of a rotten crab apple that had been there since yesterday (she'd been struggling with 15's nose and 21's ears and needed a break from portraits). 26 had earlier squashed the crab apple with his foot before she'd finished (she thought that it might have been intentional), telling her that it was rude to stare. She told him that she wasn't staring, she was drawing, but she could feel her heart beating like a train. He growled like his dog as he was leaving.

'Aren't you cold sitting on the floor?'

A Chinese boy with a ruler-straight fringe was peering at her curiously.

'No.'

It must be Mr and Mrs Cheng's son (Flat 12), Frankie deduced by process of elimination. According to her grandmother, the Chengs owned a takeaway, a launderette *and* a travel agency. Proper entrepreneurs, her grandmother had said cuttingly on a day when she seemed to know everything about everybody.

'What are you drawing?'

'Nothing,' Frankie lied.

She covered the page with her sleeve. She didn't want him to see that she'd divided the page into squares. She liked to take a more mathematical approach to drawing sometimes. Unusual for a girl, her art teacher, Miss Sandown, had once commented, and she'd liked being unusual for a girl.

'Can I see?' he asked, gesturing at the drawing.

Perhaps she could allow him a quick peek; she'd barely started, the crab apple now as flat as her page.

'I've only just started, really,' she told him, lifting up her sleeve. 'There's not much to see.'

'You can buy graph paper, you know. You don't have to draw the squares yourself.'

'Well if that's all, I'd like to get back to my drawing, thank you.'

She turned over the page so that he couldn't see it any more. He took the hint.

'Happy sketching,' he bid her cheerfully before walking away.

'Don't step on that . . .' she began to say, but it was too late.

Dear Mum,

You'll be pleased to know that I'm a little less angry with you today, but that's only because I'm busy sketching people and I need to remain focused. As there are no gates here, I'm compiling a register of all the residents (currently 76 pages). It's taking forever waiting for people to collect their mail, though, and I think some of them might be dangerous, so I take a book now and pretend that I'm reading.

I started to draw a crab apple earlier today – I'm having trouble with earlobes and nostrils at the moment – but a scary man trod on it (deliberately) before I could finish it. And then a Chinese boy trod on it (accidentally) before I could stop him, so I picked it up and put it in the bin. Perhaps I should draw you, before you become so small that I can't see you any more. I think that very soon I'll be able to draw without using any squares at all, though. I'm practising a more freehand approach.

Grandma has been very kind (she buys all my stationery), apart from calling me Fiona sometimes. I forget that she's talking to me when she calls me that. But when I asked her if they'd found Stan yet, she didn't seem to know who Stan was, so I had to explain that he's the person who killed you. She just stared at me as if I was talking nonsense. It seems that everybody still thinks that you committed suicide. I'll have to investigate your death myself, I suppose – find out if the police ever spoke to him. I have a huge list of Important Things that I need to tell them.

I should warn you that I'll be writing a letter to my father at some point. I know that he doesn't know who I am, but I shall introduce myself first (light brown hair, or 'mousey' as you once called it when you'd been drinking – even mice wouldn't want to be 'mousey', you said – three feet nine inches tall, and unusual for a girl. He doesn't need to know about my hand).

According to Grandma, he was planning to build his own house and as I have similar, mainly gate-related goals, we have at least one thing in common. I hope you don't mind but I'm going to ask him to look for you because I think you have a lot to talk about after nine years.

I hope that he's able to find you. I also hope that you haven't run out of red lipstick. I know that you wouldn't want to meet him without first putting on some 'Revolution Red'.

F.

A few days later she was sitting on a wall by the garages, searching for something to draw that wasn't a person. She was tired of hair and chins and foreheads and whenever she thought that she'd identified everybody within a one-mile radius, another person who she'd never seen before would unlock a mailbox. Or a person who had been filed away weeks ago would be loading furniture into a removal van. It was a logistical nightmare.

She'd decided to boycott the cold flagstones on the post-room floor because it was starting to smell really fishy (she seemed to spend fifteen minutes most mornings picking up fish and chip wrappers and polystyrene boxes containing congealed curry sauce and pizza crusts) and sketching outside hadn't been nearly as traumatic as she'd thought it would be. She could still see the entrance from where she was sitting and the sky didn't feel nearly as big as it usually did. If she closed one of her eyes and squinted, it nestled comfortably between her finger and thumb.

A pigeon landed on the gravelled forecourt and since she spent hours staring at the birds on her bedroom wall, she thought that she might try sketching it, although when the boy with the fringe suddenly appeared alongside her, rolling a red and black football between his palms, it flew away.

'Is it a bird?' he asked her, pointing at her sketchpad.

It was until you came along, she thought.

'Does it look like a bird?' she replied.

'Yes.'

'Then it's a bird.'

They fell silent for several minutes, Frankie suddenly mesmerised by her pencil, the boy mesmerised by his feet.

Finally, 'You should do book illustrations,' he told her.

She couldn't tell if he was teasing her.

'I know – look, no squares,' she rallied, in case he *was* teasing her.

'I'm Vinnie, by the way,' he offered by way of a truce.

'That doesn't sound Chinese.'

'It isn't. I was born in Bournemouth.'

'I'm Frankie,' Frankie said.

'That's a boy's name.'

'It isn't.'

'Yes it is.'

Frankie sighed. She'd forgotten how annoying boys could be.

'What sort of name is Vinnie?'

'Short for Vincent, but everybody calls me Vinnie. What's Frankie short for?'

'Nothing, it's just Frankie.'

'Fair enough, Just Frankie. Can you play football?'

She hesitated before answering. It would be something to tell her mother, she supposed.

'I guess.'

She placed a stone on her sketchpad and tackled the ball from him.

'Not bad for a girl,' he whistled.

She liked being 'not bad for a girl'. It was almost as good as being 'unusual'.

'What happened to your hand?' Vinnie asked her.

She'd rolled up her sleeve, forgetting that it should always be rolled down. She rubbed the pink and puckered flesh thoughtfully. Like the sky, it assumed a range of different shades, although today it looked pinker than usual.

'It was an accident.'

'Does it hurt?'

'Not any more.'

'At least it wasn't your drawing hand.'

'It was.'

'Oh.'

Silence again.

'Which flat do you live in?' Vinnie asked her, breaking a silence that was tricky to break open cleanly.

'Flat 72, with my grandmother, Brenda.'

Frankie rolled down her sleeve, remembering how small children would tug on their mother's coat sleeve and point at her before starting to cry. She sat back down.

'Don't you live with your mum and dad?'

Frankie didn't know what to say. She wasn't used to so many wounds being opened up at once.

'They're somewhere else,' she said eventually, an element of truth in her response.

They fell silent again. But it wasn't an uncomfortable silence this time. It was more like a hyphen, a bridge to cross, the space between two breaths.

He glanced at the pigeon on Frankie's lap.

'Well, it was nice to meet you, Just Frankie. Happy birdwatching.'

Frankie would soon discover that Vinnie never said goodbye. He didn't like goodbyes, said they sounded too abrupt, too final ('farewells are best avoided'), so he would take his leave with a 'Happy Friday' or a 'Happy wandering' or some other 'happy' wish.

The pigeon reappeared as soon as he'd left, as if it had been waiting for him to go. She assumed that it was the same pigeon, although it didn't really matter, she supposed; they were all very similar. And this time it sat perfectly still while she finished the shading on its beak.

The third time she saw Vinnie, he was standing behind an oak tree in the residents' parking area, an index finger pressed vertically against his lips as he pointed to a rat that was scavenging inside a soggy cardboard box that had been left out in the rain. A skateboard was balanced against the tree, a red dragon breathing red fire onto black wood.

'You should draw that,' Vinnie whispered.

'I'd rather not, thank you,' she said, twirling a strand of mouse-coloured hair between her fingers.

'There's loads more wildlife up on the common. I could show you if you like.'

'Okay.'

The 'okay' came out a little quicker than expected. Since when had she started accepting random invitations?

'I'll meet you by the caretaker's storeroom tomorrow at ten. Happy exploring,' he wished her before jumping on his skateboard and speeding away, the dragon flames setting his trainers alight.

'Happy skateboarding,' Frankie called after him, although he was long gone by the time she'd thought of the unimaginative reply.

She'd been distracted by Trevor Smith, who was standing behind a parked car staring at her. He may have had his sunglasses on, but she knew that his eyes were focused solely on her.

Chapter Nine

Hungarian Wrestling

1981

Throughout January and February Peggy only left the flat to attend counselling sessions and to buy groceries. Mrs Shah, the owner of the corner shop, would coo at Frankie in her push-chair and produce a lollipop from her apron pocket as if she'd plucked it from thin air. It always made Frankie giggle. Peggy wondered when people stopped cooing at other people's children. Just once she would have liked somebody, besides Doctor Ingalls, who was paid to show an interest, to enquire about her welfare.

'She's so big now,' Mrs Shah would squeal, leaving a raspberry-pink thumbprint on each of Frankie's cheeks.

While Mrs Shah played peek-a-boo with Frankie, Peggy would read the notices in the shop window. She was always interested in what people were selling or missing or wanting to buy, and it was there that she saw an advertisement for the 'grand opening' of a new wine bar. She couldn't remember the last time that she'd been to a wine bar. Had she ever? She'd certainly never been to the grand opening of one before.

She thought about the leaflet frequently over the next few days, glancing disdainfully at Frankie whenever she did so, shackled by the burden of her, always the centre of everybody's attention. Doctor Ingalls *had* suggested that she broaden her horizons, meet new people – or was it more people? She wasn't sure which. What was it the doctor had said? 'Do you sometimes feel like you're the only person in the world?' Actually she did, but she certainly wasn't going to admit that to Doctor Ingalls, who was still writing down all the things that she wasn't saying.

It sounded ridiculous when the world was teeming with people, many of them similarly untethered and alone – although with a child constantly crying in the next room she was never truly alone, of course. Peggy had quickly changed the subject and asked her if she could recommend a good hairdresser. She was toying with the idea of a perm. Her Farrah Fawcett flick was taking too long in the mornings.

She was still thinking about the wine bar, which seemed to have taken up permanent residence in her brain and become her one singular thought, when she noticed Trina Kopylova, who lived across the landing with her mother, Magda, outside Littlewoods. She was watching two shop assistants undress a mannequin. She was clearly anorexic, her cheekbones jutting out like scaffolding, and she always wore skin-tight jeans that accentuated her malnourished frame even more, as if the results of such a restrictive regime were a water feature that the neighbours might also enjoy. Two black vipers hung loosely over her shoulders.

Polish, Peggy thought they were (the Kopylovas, not the vipers).

She crossed the road.

'Trina, may I have a word?'

Trina shrugged.

Peggy took that as a 'yes'.

'Would you be interested in earning some money?' Peggy asked her.

Trina studied her suspiciously, her eastern-green eyes narrowing as she flicked one of the vipers over her shoulder so that she could determine more clearly what this strange woman from across the hallway was saying to her. She no doubt wanted something from her. Most people did, especially the ones who yelled at her in the street to piss off back where she'd come from.

'Maybe.'

She clearly wasn't ready to commit just yet.

'Would you be able to babysit Frankie for me on Friday?'

Trina weighed up the implications of this request, squinting at Peggy warily through at least four coats of mascara. It seemed a reasonable enough request, her spidery eyelashes eventually surmised.

'Sure, Mrs Appleton. Let me know what time.'

Peggy was delighted. She could have asked Brenda, she supposed, but she now had a viral infection and she didn't think that she'd approve of her leaving Frankie at home while she went to a wine bar, her interest in Frankie far more sporadic now that she didn't bear such a striking family resemblance. In fact, Frankie looked like none of them. She could have belonged to anybody. At times, Peggy wondered if she really did belong to her at all or whether she'd been dispatched from the hospital to spy on her and stop her frequenting wine bars on Friday nights.

And she couldn't ask Jessica for any more favours. She already looked after Frankie on counselling days and if ever there was an emergency. She often gave her very little warning and Jessica had now had to hire a part-time assistant, sixteen-year-old Kelly Andrews, who was colour-blind and who had to check with customers that their dozen red roses were indeed red, but who was always available at a moment's notice.

On Friday, Trina arrived thirty minutes early, her black hair now sporting a vivid blue streak that ran like a river down her back.

'I can only pay you what we agreed,' Peggy reiterated.

'That's okay, Mrs Appleton. My mother is watching Hungarian wrestling and it's not, how you English say, "my cup of tea".'

'You look very nice this evening,' she added, casting an appraising eye over Peggy's black dress.

'Thank you, Trina. It's very kind of you to say so.'

She must look nice if Trina had bothered to mention it. She was practically mute. Or was the compliment simply a way of guaranteeing a little extra money, even though she'd specifically told her that the fee had already been negotiated? Perhaps it was the dress that Trina was admiring, intending to steal it at some later date. Peggy tried not to overanalyse the comment – in any case, the dress would have been two sizes too big for Trina (unless she planned to sell it) – but it continued to sit in the creases of her forehead, refusing to make room for any more rational thoughts.

'Frankie hasn't had her afternoon nap, so she shouldn't be too much trouble, and there's some cheesecake in the fridge if you get hungry.' Trina certainly looked hungry. 'Help yourself. I shouldn't be too late.'

There was a ridiculously long queue outside the wine bar, tantalising excerpts of what to expect escaping whenever the door swung open. She wished that it wasn't so hectic so that she could quietly slide onto a barstool unnoticed, but thankfully the queue dwindled quickly. By the time she'd unbuttoned her coat, an amaretto sour sat shimmering in front of her.

The man on the stool next to her leaned over.

'All alone?' he asked her.

She nodded.

She later tried to remember what happened next, but she couldn't recall the exact sequence of events – what came first and what came last. She remembered pastel umbrellas in *piña* coladas, chilli-flavoured breaths in her ear, fairy lights the colour of wine gums, a clammy hand on her knee, Michael Jackson's 'Don't Stop 'til You Get Enough', my name's Tony, Old Spice, new denim, I'll call a taxi, let me drive you, I insist.

And then she was in his car, on the backseat. She couldn't keep her eyes open. She couldn't tell him that she wanted to get out. When the car stopped, he crawled onto the backseat beside her. And then he was on top of her and she couldn't push him away. He was too strong. He unzipped his trousers and held a hand over her mouth. She couldn't breathe. She tried to wriggle free. But this only made things worse. And then he hit her across the cheek, just once, but it stung like a horsewhip.

After he'd finished, he pushed her out of the car and sped away. She had no idea where she was. She got up off the gravel, vomited twice by the roadside and limped towards a cluster of lights in the distance wearing only one boot, arriving home three hours later, her stockinged foot bloody and blistered, her black dress muddy and torn. She tapped on the flat door as quietly as she could. She had no keys and she couldn't remember when she'd last seen her handbag.

Trina opened the door, dishevelled and bleary-eyed. She stared at the bite mark on Peggy's neck, the palm print across her face, the broken heel on her one remaining boot, and waited for Peggy to compose herself before asking for her money.

'I'm sorry, Trina, I seem to have mislaid my handbag. Can I pay you tomorrow?'

'Okay, Mrs Appleton, just this once.'

Trina sounded pissed off. She couldn't really blame her. And she certainly wouldn't be interested in stealing her dress now. It was in shreds, like all those used tissues in Doctor Ingalls' litter bin.

The following morning she woke to the sound of Trina's incensed mother hammering on the front door, eager to lecture her about taking advantage of a fourteen-year-old girl. Peggy had thought that Trina was seventeen, that's what she'd told her, but she nodded politely as Trina's mother called her an absolute disgrace in English and other disparaging things in Polish. What could she say? It was probably all true, and when Trina's mother finally left, she felt as if she'd been slapped on the other cheek as well.

Chapter Ten

The Leopard-Print Murder Investigation

1988

The previous day's light splattering of rain had become a waterslide by the following morning. Frankie had spent the night praying for it to stop, even though her faith in the power of prayer had recently taken a few blows to the stomach. Praying hadn't made her mother any less dead. She was meeting Vinnie at ten, but the rain continued to pour as if it didn't know how to stop, as if it hadn't heard her fake prayers at all. Frankie remembered the last time that it had rained like this, the day that she'd found her mother hanging from the ceiling like a rag doll, staring at her slippers.

When she got out of bed she noticed a spot of blood on the bed sheet. The pit of her stomach shifted uncomfortably. Her mother had warned her many times of the torment to come, the price that women were expected to pay because they'd been born with a vagina *and* a uterus, 'while men can do what the fuck they want with no consequences whatsoever'.

She'd never heard her mother say 'vagina' before (she'd heard her say 'fuck' hundreds of time) and it didn't sound nearly as funny as it did when somebody else said it.

'And I was only nine when my periods started, still a child. It's a travesty, it really is – a child being able to conceive another child.'

She'd spend five or six days every month vomiting into the mop bucket, curled up with hot-water bottles and unable to communicate unless it was to screech at Frankie to 'fuck off and play'. You couldn't tell when one day ended and another began. And she'd make Frankie promise to always take precautions whenever she had sex because she really wouldn't want to get pregnant. It was the end of everything. Frankie tried not to take the latter part personally, but of course it was difficult not to, although her mother made 'having sex' sound like something that she'd never want to do anyway.

She spread four tissues along the gusset of her pants and went into the kitchen. She wondered if she was supposed to feel differently now, but nothing seemed to have changed, apart from the pain in her stomach, and she wondered if it was the same pain that had always been there. She wished that her mother was in the kitchen so that she could tell her about the blood and the pain, but of course it was her grandmother sitting at the kitchen table buttering toast. She decided to keep the news to herself.

She tapped the shell of her hardboiled egg with a teaspoon and scooped out the balled yolk, the only part she liked. It was like swallowing the sun in one go.

'What are you planning to do today?' her grandmother asked.

'I'm meeting Vinnie at ten,' Frankie told her. 'We're going up to the common.'

'In this weather?'

'I've got a hood and an umbrella. And it's only rain,' Frankie said. 'It can't hurt you.'

Sometimes it could, sometimes it was really painful.

When her grandmother had finished eating, she walked over to her knitting basket by the fireplace and returned with a second pair of hands.

'I finished these yesterday.'

She placed a pair of stripy mittens on the table beside Frankie's yolkless egg. Nobody had ever made anything for her before. Mrs Barlow often claimed to have 'just made cookies', but there was always a Maryland chocolate-chip-cookie wrapper on the kitchen counter, and they were never warm.

Frankie slipped her hands into the gloves and immediately both her hands felt and looked the same. It was the most perfect gift. You couldn't tell which hand was scarred and clenched like a fist and which hand wasn't.

'Thank you, Grandma. They're really lovely,' she told her.

And they really were.

After breakfast Frankie slid her sketchpad into her rucksack along with a five-pound note that her grandmother had given her, and made her way to the ground floor. The bleeding was getting heavier and the pain in her stomach was what she imagined seasickness to feel like. She'd padded her pants with several extra layers of toilet paper, and even though she was practically wearing a nappy, she didn't think that it would be enough. She'd have to purchase some sanitary towels when Vinnie wasn't looking.

By nine thirty-five she was outside the caretaker's storeroom. She was early for everything, far too early. She didn't like being late because people always noticed you more when you were late. They always remembered you, and Frankie didn't like being noticed or remembered. Whenever she *was* late, which was extremely rare and usually a result of somebody else's poor timekeeping, i.e. her mother's, her stomach would spin like a washing machine, the healthy palm would sweat and her heart would pound. She hated rushing, people waiting for her at the top of roads, at the bottom of steps, the blushes, the apologies, the centre of everybody's attention, everybody's restless feet. It made her feel sick.

She looked at her watch. Ten twenty. He wasn't coming. She waved at Clyde, the caretaker. He was painting over some graffiti on a concrete fence. He was seventy-eight, he'd told her when they first met, adding that he still had all his own teeth – well, five of them. He'd been especially helpful with the residents' register that she'd compiled and had offered to laminate the edited version.

Disappointed, she began walking towards the Asian supermarket.

As she was crossing the road, she heard a whistle.

'Sorry I'm late,' Vinnie panted breathlessly as he ran up beside her.

His long black fringe lay flat against his forehead like a swimming cap. Frankie was annoyed. She'd decided that when she did see him she wasn't going to speak to him at all, but then she said, 'I thought you weren't coming.'

'Dad wanted me to help him open up the launderette and when we got there there'd been a flood so we had to clean it up,' he explained.

Frankie offered to share her pink-rimmed dome umbrella, although she didn't think that two heads would fit inside it, but Vinnie waved her away.

'It's only rain. It dries soon enough,' he said.

She followed him past a Turkish barber's and a shop that looked closed but had a neon sign in the window that said 'Sex 247'. Then they turned left and then right along some terraced streets and began the steep climb uphill. She didn't know where the common was and she wondered whether it was wise to be following somebody who she'd only met three times, but it was too late to turn back now and her grandmother hadn't expressed any doubts at breakfast. Perhaps that's what people did around here, took dangerous risks and hoped that things worked out.

When she looked behind her she could see thin strips of the city between the buildings. She tried to determine which block of flats was theirs, but there were too many of them and, like pigeons, they all looked the same. When they'd gone as high as they could go she caught flashes of moss green and white netting in the distance.

'New gloves?' Vinnie asked her as he led her across the common.

She ignored him.

A group of teenage boys were sitting on the wet grass, smoking, and a black dog was circling them looking for a stick that they kept hiding. Frankie picked up another stick and threw that for the dog instead.

'What the fuck do you think you're doing?' one of the boys shouted.

Vinnie raised a hand apologetically and ushered Frankie past two girls in leather miniskirts eating fries by the toilets. 'There's over seven acres of common, although admittedly most of it's like a mud pit,' he told her. 'You have to watch what you're stepping in. There was an abandoned vacuum cleaner on one of the benches last week. I suppose it makes a change from Homeless Lenny. I'll introduce you if he's around.' Frankie wondered if he was as selfish as Selfish Brian.

'The council keep promising to develop it, build picnic areas and a playground and maybe some tennis courts,' he continued, 'but they never do.' Frankie couldn't envision what seven acres might look like. She'd have to draw them as squares on graph paper and even then she doubted whether using a standard OS 1:250 000 scale would provide an accurate representation.

In her last school report Mr Cassidy had written that her mathematical skills were 'exceptional', but perhaps he'd got her confused with someone who really was 'exceptional'. The two Jennys were always getting mixed up. The Jenny who was good at spelling was always being mistaken for the Jenny who could speak Welsh.

After sketching a pintail duckling and some ragged robin while Vinnie held the umbrella, her hand soon began to ache so they headed back for lunch. 'It's probably safer there,' Vinnie commented, glancing over his shoulder to check that they weren't being followed. Did she like noodles? She didn't know – she'd never had them. Did she like ribs? Definitely not, the smell of meat cooking always reminded her of the smell of her flesh burning, reminded her that she'd once put her hand in the fire to see how hot it was. She used to smear Vicks VapoRub beneath her nostrils or plug them with toilet paper when she cooked meat for her mother (as long it wasn't a leg or a thigh or anything that looked like it had once belonged to an animal).

She looked down at her mittens. It looked like she was wearing two oven gloves.

'I don't eat meat any more, but I don't mind other people eating it,' she told him.

It would be like eating her own hand.

'Bean sprouts it is, then.'

Vinnie's mother was one of the smallest adults that Frankie had ever seen, but she had the biggest smile and her face was perfectly round like the moon. Her mother had been a Moon too, but she hadn't been half as smiley.

As she was leaving Mrs Cheng, 'Call me Teresa', gave her a Tupperware container of spring rolls to take home and Vinnie wished her a 'Happy spring roll tasting day.' His goodbyes were getting longer. Frankie didn't know where to put her 'happy' – as usual she'd had no time to think – so she just said goodbye. She really should start making a list of appropriate responses.

Remembering that she needed sanitary towels, she ran back downstairs. She nearly tripped over Clyde who was on his hands and knees by the lifts looking for one of Betty Rivers' contact lenses. I'll help you look for it when I get back, Frankie told him.

As she was leaving the pharmacy she noticed a police station on the street corner opposite. A police car pulled up outside and two police officers walked into the building. Frankie followed them up the steps. There was nobody behind the desk when she went in and she wondered where the two police officers had gone.

She walked over to the desk and peered over the top of it. A woman with blue eyelids was sitting on the floor reading a magazine. She wondered if she was hiding from someone. She didn't look up, so Frankie spoke first.

'Excuse me, but I wonder if I could speak to the most important person here.'

The woman seemed offended, possibly wanting to say that they were all important, even her, but she said, 'May I ask what it's concerning?'

'I'd rather not say, if you don't mind. It's something to do with an investigation.'

'May I at least have your name?'

'I suppose that would be okay. My name's Frankie Appleton.'

'Very well, Miss Appleton, I'll see what I can do.'

The woman got up off the floor and disappeared through a side door. Frankie couldn't stay on her tiptoes any longer, it was hurting her ankles. They'd never been the same since she'd fallen off the park swings. Sometimes she wondered if her mother had deliberately ignored her pleas to stop pushing so that she could call for an ambulance – she was obsessed with hospitals, she even liked hospital food – but then she would chide herself for thinking such an awful thing. Her mother would never do that. She just wanted her to be as talented as Nadia Comăneci on the uneven bars and that required 'practice and dedication'.

Frankie had spent three months learning to do a cartwheel one summer, which was particularly challenging with only one good hand, but her mother said that it took more than a couple of unsteady cartwheels to become a champion gymnast.

The woman reappeared with an older man in a uniform. Frankie jumped up off the floor.

'Are you the most important person here?' Frankie asked him.

'It would appear so. Would you like to come this way?'

'Yes please.'

It took a long time for him to settle in his chair. Frankie had never seen anybody fidget so much. He pulled at his shirt collar, undid one of the buttons on his jacket, searched for something to write with in his desk drawer, then something to write on, re-buttoned the unbuttoned button and then he repeated the process again.

Finally, he remembered that there was somebody waiting.

'So, what can I help you with today?'

'I've come about Stan, the person who murdered my mother.'

He asked her fifteen questions about her mother – she wrote and numbered each one in her notebook. They included her name and address, when her mother had died, how she'd died, how old she'd been when she died (her mother, not her, she had to clarify that one) and whether she (Frankie) had any other living relatives; all questions that she knew the answers to, but when he asked her about Stan, she couldn't answer any of those questions in any kind of detail.

She didn't know his surname, or where he lived when he didn't live with them, or how old he was, or where he worked. But she did remember some of the registration number of the car that he drove and the leopard-print seat covers and the type of whiskey that he drank.

She pulled a sketch that she'd done of him from her rucksack and said that he could keep it if it would help. She hated looking at it anyway. He asked her where her father was, so she had to explain that he was dead too and that that was probably the reason why her mother was now dead because if he hadn't died then she would never have met Stan.

He asked her a few questions about her grandmother, writing down everything that she told him on lined yellow paper, and then she remembered that her mother's friend, Sylvia, might know where Stan was, so he wrote that down as well, although she couldn't remember the exact address, only the name of the road (Clare Street) the colour of the front door (winter green) and the type of gate (rusted metal).

'You will put him in prison when you find him, won't you?'

'We'll certainly want to question him.'

He offered to drive her home, but she told him that wouldn't be necessary, she didn't accept lifts from strangers, which wasn't strictly true. Uncle Stewart had been a stranger.

Later, she detailed all that had happened that day in a letter to her mother.

Dear Mum,

I started my period today, which I hadn't expected, but don't worry because I managed to deal with it without bothering Grandma. My stomach ached all morning, but because I've been so busy, I haven't really had time to think about it. At least I now know why you were always so angry. It's extremely frustrating when there are things that you need to do and you've got stomach cramps.

I went up to the common with Vinnie as we'd arranged, although he was late and I was really cross at first. And I did some sketching, even though it wasn't very green or particularly scenic and it was raining quite heavily. You had to look hard to find something worthwhile to sketch, which I liked. It's good to have to look hard at something sometimes.

We didn't stay long because I upset some boys who were being cruel to a dog and Vinnie said that they might have knives, but my hand was aching anyway so I didn't mind. I met Vinnie's mother, Teresa, who eats rice three times a day, and I've now got a comprehensive list of 'Goodbyes'. I also helped Clyde find Betty Rivers' contact lens, although I don't think she's going to be able to see out of that eye because it was really scratched.

But the most important news is that I've officially reported Stan. I didn't have as much useful information as I thought, but the police officer was very helpful and hopefully he'll be able to locate him from the sketch that I did. I'll let you know when he's been arrested.

F.

P.S. Grandma has knitted me a pair of stripy mittens that look like I'm about to take something out of the oven.

P.P.S. I've attached an updated list of my current Top Eight Favourite Garden Gates in case you're interested.

1. *Grape Vine*
2. *Green Hyacinth*
3. *Antique*
4. *Barrelled Archway*
5. *Moongate*
6. *Boarded Brabourne*
7. *Featherboard Concave*
8. *Swan Neck*

Chapter Eleven

Counting Stars

1981

Peggy tried to forget about Tony (if that was even his name) and the wine bar. But then she would think that she'd spotted him in the street and walk briskly towards him before realising that it couldn't possibly be him. Or could it? Even rapists buy milk and walk their dogs. Would he recognise her? Had he even looked at her? Would she recognise him? And if it *was* him, what would she say?

Something unspeakable had occurred between them, and yet she wasn't sure whether she would have recognised him if he'd stood next to her at the bus stop, if he'd asked her the time. Surely that wasn't possible. Surely she would just *know*.

And she didn't think that the police would be too sympathetic either, after learning that she'd left her child with a fourteen-year-old Polish girl who was slowly starving herself.

When she next saw Trina she paid her what she owed her, apologised for any inconvenience that she may have caused, and informed her that she wouldn't be requiring her services again. Trina looked at her oddly, no doubt wondering how a prostitute, because that's what she must have looked like last night, would cope without a babysitter, concluding that she would probably just close the bedroom door.

Trina thanked her for the money, which was more than they'd agreed, and left Peggy standing on the landing, biting her bottom lip. At least Trina's mother would be pacified. She was like a Rottweiler where money was concerned. She wasn't especially perturbed by Trina's timekeeping or the friends that she kept, but dare to defraud her and you saw actual teeth.

Peggy went back inside the flat and closed the door. The flat felt even more claustrophobic than usual. She couldn't breathe. It was like wearing a Victorian corset that couldn't be unlaced. She desperately needed somewhere with more light, more space, a place where she could take proper countryside breaths. She often wondered if Frankie was sitting on her while she slept and that was why she couldn't breathe. Had she punctured one of her lungs during the night?

Try counting down from ten whenever you feel anxious, Doctor Ingalls had suggested, but counting down only made her more anxious. It signalled the start of something, not the end.

She asked Jessica if she could watch Frankie while she took a bus into town to enquire about the possibility of moving, Jessica telling her that she'd be sorry to see them go. She'd grown extremely fond of Frankie. Peggy couldn't tell if she was being facetious or not. She often complained about Frankie's crying disturbing the customers (although recently Peggy was the one crying. Frankie rarely cried nowadays. She seemed to have realised that crying made little difference, unlike Peggy, who had yet to learn). And it would surely be a relief, not having to worry whether Peggy was alive or dead on the bathroom floor.

The clerk she spoke to at the housing office, a dour woman aged somewhere between forty and sixty (her age was difficult to gauge), claimed to have a plethora of fully furnished spacious accommodation just waiting to be leased and she didn't see why she couldn't move in immediately.

'Really? Immediately?' Peggy had failed to notice the sarcasm in her tone.

'No, not immediately. In case you haven't noticed, there's a housing crisis. A protest march is scheduled for this afternoon outside the Houses of Parliament, so unless you're the Queen of Sheba, then I'm afraid we can't help you.'

Peggy had no idea who the Queen of Sheba was, but she certainly wished that she was related to royalty so that she wouldn't have to be subjected to this woman's scathing tongue. Since when had council employees become so rude? She thought that this level of rudeness was the sole preserve of doctors' receptionists (How rude can you be? Very! Even when people are vulnerable and most need your help? Especially then. Then I'd be happy to offer you the position). She wondered if Prince Charles might know the Queen of Sheba. He'd just married Lady Diana Spencer and there were photographs of the 'happy couple' on the office walls.

A smile of bunting was still attached to the ceiling and April's 'Employee of the Month', according to the framed certificate on the desk (it must have been a particularly poor month), was sipping coffee from a commemorative mug.

'Excuse me, I'm so sorry to interrupt.'

Peggy spun round. A woman with curly black hair and crooked teeth was smiling at her. Peggy wondered whether she was another affronted customer indignant at the way Peggy was being treated or another ill-mannered council employee. Thankfully, she seemed to be the former.

'I couldn't help but overhear. I have a friend who's emigrating soon and he's hoping to lease his house. I've got a flyer somewhere,' the woman said, unzipping her handbag. 'Might you be interested?'

'I'm not sure . . . Maybe,' Peggy stuttered.

'Well if you are interested give me a call. The number's on the flyer. My name's Linda.'

Peggy took the flyer, leaving the open-mouthed housing assistant wondering if she had indeed just served the Queen of Sheba.

She arranged to view the property the following afternoon. If she could free herself from asphyxiating flats and the full body weight of deadly infants straddling her torso then perhaps she could begin to distance herself from all the other things that were slowly crushing her as well, things that she could never seem to slip from under.

She lifted Frankie out of her playpen and spun her around the kitchen until she started to cry. She wasn't used to being lifted and she was heavier than she looked, certainly heavy enough to break a rib if she *was* sitting on her late at night.

Two weeks later she was spinning Frankie around a new kitchen. A kitchen with exposed electrical wires and dripping taps, a kitchen that was really too dangerous to be spinning a child around in. A further tour of the property had showcased the rising damp, the single hinge on the front gate, a bathroom window that wouldn't close properly and the knee-high and deceptively thorny garden weeds. The two properties either side of it were in similar states of disrepair, as if dilapidation was contagious. But there were two good-sized bedrooms and a small backyard. And two floors were always better than one.

Linda, had handed her the keys and informed her that she would collect the rent monthly. She lived on the other (less dilapidated) side of town and was married to Tim, a man who Peggy never met. 'We don't have children of our own,' Linda shared before giving Frankie's arm an affectionate squeeze as she was leaving, implying that she might have children, but that they belonged to somebody else.

During the next few months Peggy attempted most of the minor renovations herself, but occasionally she would have to employ qualified plumbers or electricians and consider alternative methods of payment when she'd spent her family allowance on other less essential things.

Don Barlow, who could apparently 'fix *anything*', according to the newspaper advert, and who *had* been fixing anything since being contacted – the guttering, the fuse box, the windowsills, the leak in the bedroom and the boiler thermostat, becoming something of a fixture himself – had recently stopped taking her calls since sex had been added to an already lengthy list of demands, having suddenly developed a conscience. 'I don't think we should do this any more,' he'd told her, whatever 'this' was. So it was left to other people to fix things, people without newspaper adverts or a conscience.

And, mostly, they couldn't wait to leave once 'payment' had been received, often taking the stairs three at a time and slamming the front door shut behind them without bothering to say goodbye, which made her feel worse. Instead of it supposedly being by her rules and on her terms she began to feel as if she was the one being exploited, and all for a handful of unpaid invoices. She began to wish that she did have money in her purse to pay them because it was becoming sordid and insufferable and they never even washed their hands. At least Don Barlow rinsed his hands under a hot tap before heading upstairs.

And no amount of anaglypta wallpaper could paper over the other more serious cracks that had been developing since she'd stopped taking her medication. She'd decided that her medication was to blame for what had happened at the wine bar; that it had clouded her judgement, dulled her senses. And she'd been oblivious to the gradual decline in her mental health over the past few weeks, the way that she would stare at the ceiling without blinking, the way that tears would spill from her eyes while she was frying bacon, how she would stand in the backyard in the middle of the night counting stars. And then she would lose count and have to start again. Sometimes she would still be there in the morning, adding and subtracting stars that weren't there any more.

It was while she was staring through the window at a mural of bird droppings on the garden gate that the first accident occurred. She always referred to it as an accident, but she really couldn't be sure. One minute she was staring at splashes of white excrement, Frankie chewing a building block on the hearth rug, the next minute one of Frankie's hands was in the fire and lizard-tongued flames were hissing at it. There didn't seem to be anything in between, no reason why her hand would be there.

As she sat listening to the fire squeal it felt as if she was listening to her own squeals, but she knew that she wasn't the one squealing. The sensation of it lingered long after the squealing had stopped.

It was only when Frankie toppled backwards with a thud that Peggy's attention returned to the room and she was able to comprehend the seriousness of the situation. She immediately called for an ambulance and Frankie was rushed to the hospital burns unit. Peggy sat in the waiting room flicking through a magazine while she was being examined.

When the surgeon reappeared he looked utterly exhausted, the excessive hours that he was contracted to work and the surgical procedures that he was obliged to perform no doubt the cause of his exhaustion. Or perhaps he would have still been exhausted working for Radio Rentals.

Peggy had no idea how exhausting a full-time job could be. She'd only ever worked on the checkout at Fine Fare and then only ever part-time. And that had been tedious enough. Mostly, she'd survived on government benefits.

'Mrs Appleton?'

And just like that she was married to Ed again.

'Yes.'

'May I have a private word?'

'Yes, of course.'

She wondered if it was bad news, 'I'm afraid there were complications', or 'You can take her home now'.

Even though the waiting room was empty, he waved her into an empty consultation room just beyond it, a room with a vacant bed and a computer monitor and a button that would bring somebody running. He pointed to an olive-green chair in the corner.

She remained standing.

'Frankie's sleeping now, but you can look in on her before you leave. We've given her something for the pain, but we won't know the full extent of the damage until tomorrow. We'll consider the possibility of a skin graft then.'

Timely tears pricked her eyes. She was relieved. The role of the distressed parent didn't come easily to her.

She reached into her handbag for a tissue and dabbed at her nose.

'How did it happen?' he asked her.

'It all happened so quickly,' she sniffed. 'I went to get a glass of water from the kitchen and when I came back the fireguard was on the carpet and Frankie's hand was in the fire. I called for an ambulance straight away.'

Just as she'd rehearsed.

'Well, these things do happen – more often than you might imagine, sadly. We'll talk again tomorrow.'

He left her blowing into a tissue and returned to the wards.

Peggy tossed the dry tissue into a metal waste bin and, resisting the urge to climb into the empty bed, she went to find Frankie. Her burnt hand was wrapped in a fistful of bandages on top of the bed sheet, her other hand safely tucked away. She looked almost angelic. Only Peggy knew otherwise. She tiptoed over to her, kissed her softly on the forehead and then went home.

During the next six weeks Peggy visited the hospital daily. She would sit with Frankie until lunchtime and then in the afternoon she would stroke her hair while she cried 'Mummy, it hurts,' over and over again. Peggy often wondered whether she meant her burnt hand or the hair-stroking. She'd never seen so many tears flow from another person before. She was practically made of water. And how many times did you need to say something before the other person stopped listening? Twice, three times, four? She should ask Doctor Ingalls.

And then, disappointingly, and much earlier than anticipated, Frankie was discharged from full-time palliative care, having made 'excellent progress'. The good news, however, was that she would need several more operations over the coming months, and Peggy looked forward to those hospital appointments like other people looked forward to a day at the races or a night at the opera. Frankie would always cry. Unlike Peggy, she didn't like hospitals, and as soon as she arrived she would beg to go home. Peggy would have to shush her and assure her that there was absolutely nothing to be afraid of. Hospitals were like fairy-tale castles in enchanted forests that the outside world couldn't sully with its germs and its depravity. But of course she wasn't the one who'd been burned.

Frankie's hand never fully healed, despite her undergoing eleven operations and regular physiotherapy. Peggy could barely look at it. It didn't even look like a hand any more – would never look like a hand again, she supposed – but Frankie rarely complained. In fact she rarely mentioned it at all. And, sadly for Peggy, the physiotherapy department was a mile and a half away from the hospital and seemed more like a gym in an open-plan solicitor's office than the refuge she'd been hoping for, leaving her tense and restless.

She would pace around the living room like a boxer appraising his opponent. Sometimes she would sit outside the hospital watching taxis arrive, envious of the passengers disappearing inside. Carla, one of the nurses, spotted her once and came over, and the desire to hurt herself or somebody else briefly went away. Carla told her that she was starting a bookkeeping course in the autumn and that Catherine was engaged and for a short while Peggy felt normal again, happy even. She was able to forget about Frankie and the skipping ropes and the yoyos which, courtesy of Linda, had begun to appear in their lives.

Recently, she'd begun to feel unusual stirrings of jealousy whenever Frankie ran shrieking into Linda's open arms, wondering why Linda didn't have children of her own to buy yoyos and skipping ropes for, wanting to pry, but instead she watched her from afar, pondering what she wanted with *her* child. Perhaps she felt sorry for Frankie, the charred hand a permanent reminder of her mother's suspected neglect, or perhaps she genuinely wished to ease Peggy's burden.

She would never know. Linda disappeared a few months later. One day she was there, holding a pink balloon in the air, and the next day she wasn't, and Peggy never had to worry about her motives or the puzzling phrase 'We don't have children of our own' ever again. All future rental payments were to be paid into a Lloyds Bank account and the only thing that now preoccupied Peggy, apart from the hospital, was the billowing smoke and the squealing, although she could never remember which one of them had been squealing.

She would glance over at Frankie colouring in farmyard animals at the dining table and provisionally timetable an unscheduled hospital visit. The casualty department was always open. Did her hand hurt? Was she in a lot of pain? 'No, Mummy, my hand's fine now,' Frankie would say and Peggy would have to resist the urge to pinch it, to make it hurt.

While walking Frankie home from school one afternoon, thinking about something that one of her teachers had said, something about Frankie sitting in the toilets at lunchtime with her pencil case and refusing to come out, it started to rain, heavily. It was as if somebody was emptying jars of razor-sharp hardboiled sweets over her scalp, but she didn't loosen her grip.

'Mummy, you're hurting my hand,' she heard someone say.

Peggy looked down.

'Oh, pumpkin, I'm so sorry. I wasn't thinking.'

'It's okay, Mummy. It didn't hurt that much.'

'Why don't we play on the swings for a while?'

'But it's raining.'

'Rain can't hurt you.' It really could. 'Come on, it'll be fun. Put your hood up.'

'Okay,' Frankie agreed, uncertainly.

A man with no coat on was sheltering beneath a tree, calling for his dog. They both disappeared through the park gates a few minutes later, leaving Peggy and Frankie alone by the swings. Frankie sat down on one of the swings and Peggy began to push her, sleet and rain running like estuaries down their cheeks, their drenched clothes like extra layers of skin.

'When you're ready, straighten your legs, point your toes and then jump. Make sure you land on both feet. Remember, like a gymnast.'

Frankie giggled as she pushed her higher. Even when Peggy became distracted by something in the distance swimming towards her, she kept on pushing.

'Please stop, Mummy. I can't hold on any longer. My hand's slipping and I'm not ready,' someone was saying, but she had no idea who.

And then the thing that had been swimming towards Peggy suddenly vanished and it was her daughter sprawled across the concrete as if she'd been tossed out of the water, out of the vision. She was sobbing hysterically. Her burnt hand was bleeding and her ankle was twisted awkwardly beneath her. This was no gymnastic landing.

Peggy scanned the park for assistance, but there was nobody there. She didn't know whether to leave Frankie alone while she went to fetch help or wait until somebody passed by. She couldn't decide so she wrapped her arms around her instead.

'I'm so sorry . . . I'm so sorry,' she murmured, over and over again.

Eventually, she spotted a red umbrella by the bandstand which didn't seem to have been summoned by her imagination, and asked the owner to call for an ambulance.

When they arrived at the hospital Frankie's hand was cleaned and bandaged and her ankle X-rayed. It was fractured and would require a plaster cast but the doctor assured Peggy that there would be no lasting damage. He briefly consulted Frankie's notes and made a comment about Frankie's run of bad luck and then he left her in the care of the nurses.

It was a chaotic afternoon in Casualty so thankfully nobody had time to ask too many awkward questions. Peggy searched for Carla and Catherine, but she couldn't see either of them. The nurses here were more fraught. They didn't have time to show you bridal magazines or tell you about college courses. Peggy smiled at Frankie's grazed face. It still felt like home though, even when it wasn't quite as empathic or as sanitised as usual. And Frankie would soon see that she only wanted the best for her.

Chapter Twelve

Pearl's a Singer

1984

'That's it, I'm done, Linda.'

'What's that supposed to mean, "I'm done"? You're not a roast chicken.'

'It means I'm done – with this, with us, with you.'

Linda's husband, Tim, was gesticulating wildly, pointing at himself and then at her as if they were two peas in a pod when clearly he believed no such thing. He certainly looked done. His hair was moving in time with his hand gestures and his hair never moved. On a weekend break in Margate where the winds had been so strong that she'd nearly toppled off a cliff edge both his hair and his demeanour had remained unmoved as he'd unhurriedly guided her to safety.

He went upstairs to calm himself and his hair down, or so Linda had thought, but two minutes later he reappeared with a suitcase, his hair still flapping around his eyes and ears and no comb to tame it. He must have had the suitcase already packed because nobody could have packed that quickly, not even Tim, for whom packing consisted of throwing a pair of underpants and a toothbrush into a holdall.

Briefly, she wondered if it was some kind of test and if the suitcase was in fact empty – she'd done similar as a child, stomping along the avenue carrying an empty vanity case as her bemused mother watched from a neighbour's window. The sudden appearance of a suitcase by the front door should never be underestimated, but Tim didn't do anything rashly. He didn't play games. He didn't elicit a reaction, light a fuse and then run and hide. If he said he was done, then he was done. And if he said he was leaving, then he wouldn't be coming back.

That was five years ago and Linda had never admitted to anybody that he'd left, that he was 'done', 'with her', not even to the neighbours who must have had their suspicions. If anybody ever asked after him he was 'fine', 'working away' or 'working late'. And nobody ever seemed to miss him or be too concerned that he was never there any more. She hadn't even told her mother, who'd now stopped expecting him for Christmas lunch. It seemed that you could still give the impression that nothing had changed even when everything had, and if she wasn't perturbed by his absence then neither was anybody else.

She wasn't sure why she couldn't bring herself to tell anybody. She wasn't ashamed and she didn't feel guilty and she didn't particularly miss him – the house was much tidier without him in it. And marriages break down, couples drift apart, forever isn't always forever – rarely is it forever, in fact – often there's no justifiable reason ('irreconcilable differences', wasn't that the standard get-out-of-jail-free clause these days?) but it just seemed easier to pretend that he was still there, to keep making excuses for him.

More troubling was the fact that his absence had now derailed any hopes that she may have had of becoming a mother. She'd never been particularly maternal. As a child she'd preferred writing poems about Mexican-pink sunsets than playing with her Tiny Tears doll. Looking after another person had seemed like far too much responsibility – although her own mother regularly shirked such responsibilities, preferring to spend the majority of her time gossiping with Glenda Bates – and listening to newborn infants wail . . . well, patting Thor, Mrs Heath's aggressive Alsatian dog, was infinitely more appealing. But as soon as they decided to try for a baby, and the more difficult it became, the more obsessed she became as a result.

Now that she did actually want a child, she couldn't have one. She wondered if she'd spent so many years opposed to the idea that her body was now unable to adapt to this unexpected change of heart. And if Tim hadn't broached the idea of starting a family first, would it ever have mattered so much?

She thought that he would have moved in with someone much younger after being 'done with her' – a teenage girl who could get pregnant as easily as pulling on an Adidas sports sock, someone who was happy to have sex with him spontaneously, outside optimum ovulation windows – but he seemed to be spending his time with a woman who was almost as old as his mother, somebody who no doubt wouldn't want to spend twenty-four hours a day discussing their ovaries.

Twice, she'd seen him in town holding hands with a grey-haired woman in a white jumpsuit who looked like she'd just come from a crime scene. She'd forgotten how white his teeth were. She couldn't remember him ever smiling at her like that.

The birth of Louise Brown, the world's first test-tube baby, in 1978, hadn't helped either, spurring on childless couples like themselves, making the impossible seem possible when it was nothing of the sort. Sometimes things *are* impossible. Why else does the word exist? And her doctor was becoming increasingly concerned about the toll that the IVF appeared to be taking on her body as well as their relationship and their finances. They'd already had to remortgage the house twice.

While other couples looked forward to spending such amounts on their child's upbringing and education, they'd had to invest much of the money upfront and still had no child to show for it. It was turning out to be the world's most expensive offspring and the largest ever deposit.

Tim stopped attending hospital appointments midway through the sixth cycle. It seemed that she was doing more and more of the process alone, a single parent without the presence of an actual child. He began staying out later and later, his dinner on the table, then in the oven, then in the pedal bin and then no dinner at all because she got tired of cooking meals that were never eaten.

Often, he was only there when she was asleep and he didn't have to look at her, but even with her back turned and her eyes closed she could still sense his loathing, still feel his bitterness and disapproval for spending all of their savings on a child that obviously didn't want to be born, for thinking that she could play God and make it everything.

He stopped speaking to her completely for three months because she'd apparently become 'impossible to reason with' and she had to assume the role of primary decision-maker for those three months. She was thankful that they had enough sperm samples to complete two more IVF cycles because she wouldn't have wanted to ask a man who wasn't speaking to her any more for yet more of his sperm.

On the one occasion when he had needed to express himself out loud or risk putting his fist through the wall he'd become exasperated with her, demanding to know what was wrong with it just being the two of them, these things happen, people don't always get what they want. But it only made her feel worse. Many people got exactly what they wanted. Many people didn't deserve the things that they did get.

She'd seen plenty of teenage girls who should have been in school walking around council estates with two or more children under the age of five hanging from pram wheels like chimpanzees, barely alive heroin addicts asleep on deckchairs on patios while their children played with syringes, most of them more fertile than non-addicts, everybody more fertile than her, and she despised all of them.

Still she would not be deterred. She would never accept her reproductive failings. She spent hours preparing for the arrival of this medical wonder, this test-tube miracle, buying romper suits and denim dungarees in the January sales, crocheting bootees and matinee jackets in both pink and blue. She filled shoeboxes with photographs of babies torn from magazines, wrote the names of their future children on the lids of the shoeboxes (Josephine, Stephanie and Thomas) without any input from Tim – 'I'm not going to name something that doesn't exist' – and convinced herself that nobody could work this hard for something and not be rewarded in some shape or form.

In the unlikely event that it still didn't work, however, she was willing to consider other options – surrogacy, adoption – the widespread theory being that when another process is initiated, people often conceive naturally. She'd read of couples in the early stages of the adoption process receiving the news that they were expecting their first biological child, almost like a gentle threat to your firstborn: if you don't hurry then I'm afraid I'll be looking elsewhere.

It was while she was explaining the thinking behind this double bluff to Tim that he'd suddenly decided that he was 'done', that he wouldn't want her raising any child of his. Her name's Josephine, she'd muttered under her breath. She was obsessed with being a mother, he raged, and it wasn't healthy for either of them.

She had to cancel the weekend in Hove that she'd booked.

'Why don't you get away for a few days; relax, think about something else for a while,' her doctor had advised. 'It can help.'

Well, thanks to Tim, she now had no alternative but to think about something else.

She began to research single-parent adoption, but success rates were poor unless you were wealthy or adopting a child from a Third World country. She even had a preliminary interview with a social worker, who, having seen her collection of random baby photographs and crocheted socks described her as 'certainly enthusiastic about the prospect', but wondered if she was perhaps 'a little too enthusiastic'.

Linda tried to explain that wanting to be a mother was something that required considerable forethought and enthusiasm, surely, and to want something so badly that it hurt didn't necessarily mean that you shouldn't have it but, as the social worker was writing the words down, Linda realised their potential to be misconstrued, and wasn't entirely surprised to receive an official rejection letter a few days later.

Nonetheless, it still took her a whole weekend to recover, a whole weekend to realise that all she needed was healthy sperm, anyone's sperm would do. It didn't matter if it wasn't Tim's. It didn't matter where it came from. According to a survey that she'd recently read in the August edition of *Family Circle*, divorced childless couples who married new partners often fell pregnant within the first few months. Sometimes your egg and sperm are simply incompatible.

But she didn't have time to follow the more traditional route. She was already 'geriatric' in reproductive terms, and she'd found that men didn't particularly like being asked if they wanted children on the first date – it was hardly 'Would you like ketchup on those chips?' – so she embarked on the somewhat more reckless route of having several unprotected one-night stands in the hope of becoming pregnant naturally. She was convinced that it was Tim's lacklustre sperm that were the problem rather than her ovaries (she imagined her ovaries being nothing less than encouraging), sensing that his heart hadn't been in it at all.

In the first month she caught an STD and then a few weeks later she was given a cut lip, a bloody nose and her purse was stolen. She did not feel at all like the independent women she'd read about in magazines. It was hugely discouraging so she began to research the more controlled environment of sperm donor clinics instead, but soon grew tired of the time-consuming restraints imposed: the counselling and the legal advice, the blood tests and the lifestyle questionnaires. She wanted a child now. Not in nine months or two years.

And that's when she seriously began to consider taking a child away from someone who wasn't fit to be a parent, someone who had too many children and who would be grateful for one less child to care for, someone who mistreated their child, neglected them.

That's when she remembered Frankie.

In hindsight, the more sensible plan would have been to abduct a newborn infant from a pram left unattended outside the local Spar, slip the infant into her own empty pram and then wheel it away. The younger the child, the easier it would be to pretend that the child was hers, and the more easily it could be transported to another county, perhaps even another country. She didn't even care if it was a boy or a girl, Josephine *or* Thomas. It was a baby, that's all that mattered. Perhaps she'd steal more than one; two siblings, Stephanie as well as Josephine or Thomas. It certainly seemed possible, after years of seeming impossible.

Except the only child she was interested in was Frankie. She wasn't interested in the babies crying in pushchairs by the park swings, no adults nearby, or the babies in soiled nappies on dirty lilos in backyards, the parents smoking inside. She was only interested in

Frankie, sweet little Frankie with a hand so scarred that it didn't even look like a hand any more.

Linda suspected that Peggy was to blame, that she'd scarred her own daughter and made her believe that it was her fault. She hated the smell of alcohol on her breath and those blood-red lips, the parade of men and the 'I'm sorry but I'm a little short this week' most weeks, but mostly she hated the fact that Frankie didn't seem to matter. She was invisible. Peggy didn't deserve her. And somebody needed to rescue her before something happened to her other hand and she was unable to tie her shoelaces or count to five using her fingers ever again.

She hadn't yet finalised the precise details of her rescue mission, explored the technicalities of it, but it wasn't unusual for Linda to collect Frankie from school and invite her in for a glass of lemonade and a Club biscuit. She could break the news to her then that her mother had died and that it had been her dying wish that she live with Linda. She could tell her that children aren't allowed to attend cremations and then fill an urn with some ashes from the grate.

When she'd passed The Swan after Wednesday choir practice she'd seen Peggy linking the arm of a Puerto Rican man. She'd almost fallen into the road, she was so inebriated. She'd watched the man manoeuvre her into an adjacent alleyway garnished with fish bones and lager cans and she remembered wondering who was looking after Frankie.

Waiting outside Woodlands Primary School, she still couldn't believe that she was actually going to abduct her, although she preferred the term 'save'. She was there to save Frankie, she reminded herself. She'd signed a twelve-month lease on a crofter's cottage in the Scottish Highlands and had decided to change her name to Pearl. She'd been listening to an Elkie Brooks cassette in the car.

She even thought that like Elkie Brooks' Pearl, she could be a singer too. In fact she could be anything that she wanted to be in the Scottish Highlands. Nobody would ever know who she really was, who she'd been before. She'd managed to remain married to a man who didn't live with her any more so it shouldn't be too hard. She would encourage Frankie to pick a new name too, persuade her that new beginnings require new identities.

Ribbons of charcoal-grey fabric began to wrap themselves around the school gates and then disperse like ultraviolet rays. Linda stood watching from the bus shelter opposite. She didn't want to be seen, didn't want her own disappearance to be connected to Frankie's disappearance, heavily influenced by detective programmes such as *Cagney & Lacey* and *Columbo*, where witness sightings led to guilty verdicts.

She'd parked several streets away and told Frankie to meet her at the Esso petrol station where there would be a surprise waiting for her, and she must promise not to tell anybody. The surprise was her Tiny Tears doll and some sleeping tablets. They had a long journey ahead of them. Frankie had nodded earnestly, her eyes like saucers, as if it was terribly important that she pay attention.

Frankie was one of the last to leave. Fortunately, Ellie, her best friend, had chickenpox. Nobody stopped her as she was leaving, asked where her parents were. They simply let her walk away. Linda was both appalled and relieved. With her head down and the rucksack that she kept 'everything important' in on her back, Frankie made her way to the petrol station. The tree-lined avenue was quiet by then, most of the parked cars having collected their cargo and left. She looked as if she was counting her footsteps or trying not to step on the pavement cracks. Occasionally she would take a step backwards and start again.

A familiar fury spread through Linda, or rather Pearl (she should start using her new name, familiarise herself with how it sounded. She didn't want to forget to turn round when somebody shouted 'Pearl'). It was scandalous how Peggy treated her, palming her off like a half-eaten sandwich. She always had somewhere else that she needed to be, someone else who she needed to be with. Anything could happen to Frankie. Anybody could drive alongside her and pull her into the passenger seat of their car. She had to stop that from happening. She had to keep Frankie safe. It had to be her car, her passenger seat. She'd wanted a child for so long. She'd wanted this child for so long.

She'd been following Frankie for months now, to hospital appointments, to Ellie's house (where she took a particular interest in Don Barlow. She was sure that she'd seen Peggy in Don Barlow's van a couple of weeks earlier). She would sit in the car with a vanilla slice or a jam doughnut, watching Frankie chalk hopscotch squares on pavements, toss tennis balls against walls, flick through *Reader's Digest* DIY manuals on the front step while strange men stepped past her into the hallway.

She knew everything that there was to know about Frankie Appleton, knew exactly where to find her, although the surveillance and anxiety, but mainly the cream cakes, had added an extra stone and a half to her weight and she would have struggled to follow on foot if she'd needed to. She couldn't fasten the top button of her jeans any more and was out of breath going up the stairs.

There was a sharp pain in her head. She'd been having more headaches than usual recently. Pearl didn't appear to be quite as resilient as Linda. Ahead of her, Frankie paused in front of a gate. She held her breath, hoped that she wasn't going to lift the latch and walk away from her into somebody else's grasp. But she wrote something in a notepad and then walked on. It was starting to rain. The forecourt of the petrol station was just across the road. Frankie was almost there. And so was she.

The car seemed to come from nowhere, bringing with it an immobilising thud and a searing pain in her ribs, although initially she couldn't connect the three things. Or understand why she was lying on the tarmac with the upturned brake lights of a stationary car obscuring her view when there were over three hundred miles to cover.

Just ahead of her beneath a second set of car wheels she saw what looked like a cloud. Or was it a child's tutu? She couldn't be sure. But there was definitely a shoe, the shiniest shoe that she'd ever seen sitting in a puddle.

She wanted to tell Frankie that she was coming, that the car was just over there, but she couldn't find her, couldn't see her face among all the other faces now leaning over her. Where was she? Her head was spinning. She couldn't feel her legs. She couldn't lift her head. How would she ever be a mother if she couldn't lift her head? Can you tell me your name? someone asked her. My name's Pearl, she told them, and I'm a singer.

Part Two

Missing

Chapter Thirteen

A Dark Moon Rising

1985

Peggy decided that it might be best if she was less of a presence at the hospital. She wasn't sure whether this made her more or less culpable, the fact that she wasn't always by her daughter's side, but she didn't want Frankie to become an 'at risk' statistic on a child-protection register, someone who needed to be regularly supervised and monitored. She wanted to be a loving mother, an anonymous mother. She just wasn't sure that she knew how.

For a while now the nurses at the hospital had been taking more than a professional interest in Frankie every time she came in, peering at her a little more closely than they had before, checking her arms for bruising, forbidding Peggy to bring in non-hospital food items and, according to Frankie, asking her 'lots and lots of questions'.

Peggy would notice two or three nurses huddled in a quiet corner of the ward whispering, glancing intermittently at Peggy and then at Frankie, and it was obvious that they were starting to have their suspicions about Frankie, about her. Peggy wanted to march over and inform them that for their information they had been accidents, all of them. They had, hadn't they? And now Frankie had an ear infection. But that hadn't been anything to do with her. Frankie was being ill all by herself now.

To avoid further scrutiny, Peggy decided to book a holiday. She'd seen an offer in one of her magazines, six days in Torquay for the price of three, including coach travel, and, while pouring milk into Frankie's cereal bowl one morning, she broached the subject with her.

'So, what do you think, pumpkin?'

'But what about school?'

Frankie seemed horrified by the prospect. But she wasn't used to things being prearranged. Things were usually thrust upon her at a moment's notice. She wasn't familiar with the concept of holidaying, either. It wasn't something that they'd ever done.

'They'll manage without you for a few days, I'm sure. I'll call the school tomorrow and tell them that you're not well.'

'But I am well.'

'I know. We're just pretending that you aren't so they don't make a fuss.'

'But I don't want to be ill. I want to go to school. I like school.'

Frankie seemed scared. She wouldn't look at her.

'You'll like being on holiday too. It'll be fun, just the two of us.'

Frankie sighed, seemingly more nervous now that it would be 'just the two of them'.

They left during the early hours of the following morning. Peggy had booked the holiday three weeks earlier. Including Frankie in the decision-making process was nothing more than a formality; they were always going to go whether Frankie objected or not. One of the senior consultants at the hospital had recently approached Peggy in the canteen asking to have 'a quiet word' with her and she'd had to make some excuse about a parking ticket. And she'd lose the full amount if they cancelled, although Frankie was the one funding the trip, Peggy had used her child support allowance to pay for it.

Theirs were the last two seats. Frankie sat beside an elderly Scottish woman dressed in head-to-toe tartan who kept sprinkling talcum powder on her insoles, apparently to stop her feet from swelling up, she explained, while Peggy sat across the aisle from her beside a man with halitosis who insisted on leaning towards her even when he had nothing to say.

If Peggy's eyesight had been poorer she thought that she might have found him attractive in a 'holiday romance' kind of way, someone who could be tolerated for a week if the sun was shining. He was wearing a garish tie and his hair was slicked back with enough oil to fill a chip-pan, but he seemed to be relatively upbeat for three in the morning. Still, she imagined that the Yorkshire Ripper would have been similarly upbeat if he'd been going on holiday. She actually said this to the woman sitting behind her when he went 'to use the facilities'.

Frankie pulled a book out of her rucksack.

It was going to be a long week.

'Here we are in sunny Devon,' Peggy announced cheerfully when they arrived, as if she'd driven them there herself, although the 'sunny' was somewhat optimistic; it was barely even light. She watched the Scottish woman push a sticky sweet into Frankie's hand

and then the man with the greasiest hair in Torquay sauntered up behind her and slipped something into her own hand (his caravan details), holding it for far longer than she would have liked. She had to snatch her hand away in the end, letting the sweaty slip of paper zigzag to the ground.

The caravan site was virtually prehistoric, definitely pre-war. It may well have been a UNESCO Heritage Site, certainly of archaeological and historical interest to some organisation. Peggy queued with Frankie at the reception cabin and collected their caravan key from a man with no front teeth who was wearing a white string vest and a gold medallion engraved with the word 'Champ'. She unkindly wondered if 'Chump' or 'Chimp' may have been more apt.

Once inside the sparsely furnished caravan, Frankie sat on the threadbare bench seat while Peggy opened and closed cupboard doors, something that she did several times a day. Still dissatisfied, Peggy repeated the process twice more. Unsurprisingly, the cupboards were still empty the third time. There were so many empty cupboards that Peggy worried how she would ever fill them. Empty spaces made her nervous. Anything could crawl inside.

'Shall we go to the beach?' she eventually suggested, the obsessive cupboard-door-opening and the unsurprising lack of contents failing to ease her fraught nerves.

Frankie was hungry, her stomach rumbling wildly. Peggy never ate much during the day so she was unsympathetic to other people's 'three meals a day' dietary requirements, but Frankie rarely complained. If you asked her if she was hungry, she would say, 'Only an African child is ever hungry.' She'd then scavenge for something in private when she thought Peggy wasn't looking, hoping that she'd bothered to go shopping.

'Shall we buy fish and chips and eat them on the beach?'

'Okay.' Frankie didn't look too sure.

And it wasn't yet eight o'clock, so of course there were no fish and chip shops open at that time in the morning.

'Isn't this nice, just the two of us? It'll blow all the cobwebs away,' Peggy assured her as they sat shivering on the edge of the pier with two choc ices and a bottle of dandelion and burdock from a local newsagent.

Peggy pulled the flimsy cotton dress that she was wearing up over her knees and lifted her tearstained face towards the biting wind and rain. She wasn't sure why she was suddenly so obsessed with it being just the two of them – usually it was the more the merrier, as far as she was concerned. They spent the rest of the morning in cagoules, writing their names in the sand and combing the beach for seashells, Peggy rubbing her temples and periodically staring out to sea as if there was something out there that she would have liked to have taken a closer look at.

She continued to stare at the horizon long after the tide had washed away their names and then she declared that that was enough sea air for one day. They'd never get a brush through their hair if they stayed any longer. It was already twice its normal volume. They should flatten out the frizz with their fingers and go to the amusement arcade instead.

The clacks and dings of the pinball machines and the coins clattering noisily into the mouths of the one-armed bandits rekindled Peggy's earlier migraine. And a group of teenage boys were yelling so loudly by the racing-car steering wheels and the combat weapons that she thought they were being murdered in broad daylight. She quickly steered Frankie towards the hooks and the cuddly toys. Nobody was ever interested in those.

'Let's try and win that rabbit,' she said, pointing at a sleepy-eyed pink and white rabbit buried beneath all the other more awake soft toys at the back of a glass box.

She dropped a purse full of coins into the claw machine, but couldn't manoeuvre the hook properly because her hands were shaking so much. After thirty minutes she was exhausted and irritable.

'Sorry, pumpkin. It's harder than it looks. I'll buy you a stick of rock with your name running through it instead.'

Frankie looked devastated, although she was trying not to show it, until five minutes later when she did decide to show it and they were asked to leave by the arcade manager, which Peggy thought somewhat ironic considering a teenage boy was currently being pummelled into the floor just to the right of them. And then Frankie had insisted on banging the stick of rock, with the name Frank underscore rather than Frankie printed on it because the 'i' and the 'e' had run, repeatedly against her kneecaps all the way back to the caravan park.

Peggy didn't feel like speaking to anyone. Her head felt like a hand grenade about to explode. She wished that she could have sent Frankie to bed, but as the bed was only two feet away from her it wouldn't have made much difference, she'd still have heard her breathing, so Frankie, sensing her contempt, sat quietly reading while raindrops the size of fists pummelled the roof of the caravan and the wind whistled eerily through the vent.

Several hours later, unable to stand the boredom any longer, Peggy told Frankie that she wouldn't be long and locked her inside the caravan. It seemed that you didn't need anybody's caravan details after all. You saw the same familiar faces constantly, in the communal showers in flip-flops and Hawaiian shirts, on foldaway chairs burning Cumberland sausages on barbecues, in lengthy queues complaining to Chump/Chimp about the hot water (or lack thereof).

Peggy wondered what on earth they would do for the rest of the holiday. They'd done everything that she'd planned to do on the first day, and she wasn't sure that she liked it being just the two of them any more, but they rode on a miniature steam train along the promenade and pedalled a swan-shaped pedalo around the lake. They got lost in a maze, Peggy close to tears when she couldn't find her way out, spent thirty minutes on the park trampolines and visited the fairground twice. Peggy even took a few bites of pizza one lunchtime.

At one point she wondered whether to push Frankie into the duck pond so that she could call for an ambulance. Nobody would know them in Torquay. But it looked far too cold and she didn't want Frankie to get pneumonia. Or worse, drown. They'd never get home then.

The sixth and final day was spent in the amusement arcade sheltering from the rain, although Peggy had planned to be there at eleven anyway. She'd arranged to meet Greasy John, hoped that he'd be good with his hands, although he hadn't been so far. She really didn't want to leave Torquay without that rabbit.

'Look, there's Grea . . . John. Perhaps he'll have better luck hooking that rabbit.'

It looked like the last thing that Frankie wanted, particularly now that Greasy John was heading their way, feigning pantomime surprise. The manager of the arcade was also hovering nearby in the event of a repeat performance from earlier that week, even though Peggy was wearing oversized sunglasses and she'd pulled a woolly hat over Frankie's head.

Greasy John managed to hook the rabbit after twenty-five attempts and forty-five minutes of swearing, and he proudly presented it to Frankie. It wasn't pink and one of its ears was bigger than the other. It wasn't the same rabbit. Regardless, Peggy clapped enthusiastically and kissed him appreciatively on the cheek.

Say thank you, she told Frankie, but Frankie just stared at her and then pulled the woolly hat over her eyes, so Peggy had to thank him on her behalf. She invited him back to the caravan for a drink as a further thank you, but quickly lost interest. She was tired of saying thank you. And they had absolutely nothing in common. He didn't even like Roy Orbison and everybody liked Roy Orbison.

Before leaving, she opened the cupboard doors one last time and, as she hadn't filled them with anything since they arrived, unsurprisingly they were still empty – although there was now a dead/sleeping vole curled up in a corner that she hadn't noticed before. It made her wonder how many other things she'd failed to notice, how many cupboard doors needed to be opened before the truth finally emerged.

On the coach journey home she sat on her own and closed her eyes, exhausted.

It took seven hours to get home. There'd been an accident on the motorway earlier that day, a car hitting a crash barrier. She felt like crying.

'Go and watch television,' she told Frankie as she was unlocking the front door. 'I've got a migraine and I need to lie down.'

She'd spent the last six days trying to entertain Frankie, who'd been more sullen than usual even though she had a new toy rabbit that she'd almost forgotten to pack, and she'd tried to be pleasant to Greasy John, whose breath smelled of onions regardless of what he'd eaten and whose hair was as sticky as toffee, but nobody ever appreciated the effort that it took. She should have walked into the sea when she'd had the opportunity. The sea always welcomed her.

The bottle of antidepressants in her handbag was empty (she'd been foolish to think that she could cope without them). Glancing around the bedroom in desperation she spotted a pill on the carpet. It was stuck to the pile. She prised it free, wiped it on her pyjama bottoms and popped it into her mouth. She'd feel better after a nap.

Nights were always the most difficult, the darkness closing round her like fog, shadows slowly stirring. The gin bottles in the china cabinet would glisten like blue topaz, like beacons in stormy weather. And she would search for somebody to replace Ed, never realising that he was irreplaceable. But he needed to be replaced in some shape or form and preferably by someone who wanted to be with the real Peggy, the Peggy with no savings and nothing to steal apart from a child, not the Peggy that they'd rewritten inside their heads.

The longest that anyone had ever tolerated her for was two weeks (apart from Don Barlow, who she'd been sleeping with on and off for the past four years, when his conscience allowed it). Something would always scare them away, whether it was her reliance on painkillers and antidepressants, on gin, a secret that always spilled out, Frankie sitting on the kitchen floor poring over DIY manuals ('Jesus, is she deciding which power tool to kill me with?'), Ed, who they couldn't even see, or the fact that she was 'too needy' or 'too distant' or that they 'weren't ready for a serious relationship', 'it's not you, it's me' (it was always her). She'd heard them all.

Doctor's prescriptions barely scraped the surface any more and Ed wouldn't stop following her, his eyes in the porridge-thick layer of dust on the television screen, his smile in the cornflakes in her cereal bowl, his frown in the tears of the crying boy in the painting above the fireplace. He was nowhere and yet everywhere, his features never where they should be, like a Picasso painting.

Sometimes when she was lying in bed with the curtains drawn he would lie down beside her, other times she would suggest random, spontaneous things for her and Frankie to do and he would join them. Or they would leave Frankie at home so that it was just the two of them again, like before, which she preferred.

It seemed that Frankie and Ed had swapped places and it was Frankie who was now being forgotten.

Of course sometimes she wouldn't see him at all, his eyes wiped away with a duster, his breakfast smile scraped into the bin uneaten, the crying boy's tears just tears, and she would trip over wine bottles and fall off chairs trying to escape the clutches of Wine Bar Tony instead.

Chapter Fourteen

Two Choc Ices and a Runny Nose

1988

'Why are you always drawing gates?'

Vinnie had sneaked up behind Frankie as he was prone to do. She still hadn't got used to him not being there one minute and then being there the next.

'And why do you always sneak up on people?'

'You see more that way.'

That was true. You never saw anything of note when you announced your arrival. It really annoyed her when characters in films walked through buildings calling out names or shouting, 'Hello!' Surely it was more important to be stealthy if you wanted to catch a person red-handed, especially if you were a police officer. Why tell them that the area is surrounded or that you're armed? Where's the element of surprise in that?

'Gates are amazing. Every home should have a gate.'

'Not everyone can afford to live in a house with a gate.'

'A main gate for a block of flats wouldn't be too expensive if everybody contributed. And they're easy to make, you just need wood and springs and nails. It's not ideal when you're hemmed in like cattle of course, imprisoning yourself with hundreds of strangers, but it would stop more strangers coming in. I'm going to make a gate that people travel miles to see, like the Taj Mahal. Maybe I'll even be interviewed by a TV or newspaper reporter.'

'I'm not sure Harry Shaw from the *Gazette* will be interested unless you can build a gate *and* predict the next three Derby winners. Anyway, I came to tell you that we're going to Torquay for a few days tomorrow. Dad wants to borrow some money from one of his brothers who lives there.'

'I've been to Torquay and I didn't much care for it. Apparently, it's called the English Riviera but Mum said that it wasn't like any riviera that she'd ever seen.'

Vinnie said that he'd bring her back a stick of rock. She told him that she didn't like rock because it hurt her kneecaps and went back to her drawing, although she'd lost interest in gates now that she was thinking about Torquay. She wondered if it was still raining there.

She didn't hear him wish her a 'Happy gate-designing' as he was leaving.

And although she now had an alphabetical list of 'Happy' phrases in her rucksack, it was about thinking on your feet, she realised, matching the phrase with the occasion, and she wasn't very good at that.

When her mother had told her that they were going on holiday and that she would have to miss four school days, she'd had to pinch the back of her hand to stop herself crying, which was painful on account of both the pinching (normal) and the scarring (abnormal).

She would have liked to have pinched the healthy hand but she couldn't grip anything with the burnt one. And this had made her want to cry even more because she wanted to be able to pinch whichever hand she wanted to and it just wasn't fair. But as her mother was actually making breakfast for the first time in weeks, if you can call pouring semi-skimmed milk onto a Weetabix 'making breakfast', she'd said okay.

They'd left for Torquay in the middle of the night, causing Frankie to worry that they weren't coming back. Her mother had spent hours packing a suitcase as if it was the last thing that she was ever going to do and then she'd stood in front of the hall mirror and applied three coats of Revlon's 'Million Dollar Red' lipstick. It seemed that one coat wasn't going to be enough.

Frankie sat beside an elderly Scottish lady who smelled of talcum powder while her mother sat across the aisle beside a man with hair as black as the olives in her mother's martinis, and bad breath. His unbrushed breath drifted towards her whenever he turned to face her mother, which was practically all the time. He was going to have a sore neck.

He wore a tie decorated with colourful interlocking cubes and he was unusually cheerful. Everyone else couldn't stop yawning. When he excused himself to 'use the facilities' she heard her mother whisper to the woman behind her that she supposed the Yorkshire

Ripper would have been similarly upbeat if he was going on holiday. Frankie pulled *A Portfolio of Gates* from her rucksack.

It was going to be a long week.

'Here we are in sunny Devon,' her mother exclaimed brightly to the rest of the passengers when they finally arrived in Torquay, as if it was some sort of mystery tour.

Although 'sunny' was somewhat optimistic. It looked like it had been raining since Christmas. And even though it was eight o'clock in the morning it was at least ten shades darker than when they'd left. The Scottish lady pressed a warm peppermint into her good palm and then limped away while the man with olive-black hair and olive-black cufflinks whispered something in her mother's ear which made her mother throw back her head and give one of her fake laughs.

Frankie gave them both her best death stare. She hated it when her mother pretend-laughed. They then queued at the caravan park reception cabin and collected a key from a fat man in a white vest with no front teeth.

'Shall we buy fish and chips and eat them on the beach?' her mother suggested after she'd opened up every cupboard in the caravan at least twice and found that there was still nothing inside them.

What had she expected to find there? Or was she checking that they were empty? Frankie wondered whether to have a tantrum in Torquay, take advantage of the change of scenery, but she really didn't have the energy, so instead she just shrugged.

While her mother was in the caravan park toilets, she pulled the coffee flask out of her handbag and unscrewed the cap. As she suspected, it didn't smell of coffee.

Of course there were no fish and chip shops open that early in the morning so they had to be content with a couple of choc ices and a bottle of dandelion and burdock while they dangled their legs over the side of the pier, the waves crashing angrily beneath them and the clouds gathering menacingly above.

'Isn't this nice?' her mother said, lifting her lightweight cotton dress over her knees and angling her face towards the sky.

The wind was as sharp as pine needles.

Frankie didn't think she was expecting a response, she didn't even think that her mother was really talking to her, so she alternated between wiping her runny nose on her sleeve and licking her choc ice. This was time that could have been more wisely spent designing gates.

Her mother collected some seashells, the same seashells that she kept dropping and picking up again, insisting that they were 'better ones', and then they wrote their names in the sand with a piece of driftwood. Her mother sat on their names shortly afterwards, staring out to sea as if there was something out there that only she could see.

Frankie wondered if she was going to lift up her dress and paddle out to the thing that only she could see, maybe take Frankie too, but she continued to sit and stare into the distance until some seagulls squawked overhead and she suddenly announced that they were now going to the amusement arcade.

Frankie was mesmerised by the rainbow-coloured slot machines and the clattering coins. Her mother pulled her towards the cuddly toys in glass boxes, but she wanted to stay by the bright lights, even though they were hurting her eyes.

'Let's try and win that rabbit,' her mother said, pointing at a pathetic-looking creature with long floppy ears and sad eyes that all the better toys were trying to hide.

Frankie didn't want it – just looking at it made her want to unzip her pencil case and reach for her compass. Whenever she felt sad she would sit in the school toilets and stab at her burnt hand with a compass because she hated looking at it – but she patiently watched her mother flood the machine with coins, her hands trembling as she tried to press buttons and control the pincer at the same time. And when her mother said, 'Sorry, pumpkin, it's harder than it looks. I'll buy you a stick of rock with your name running through it instead,' Frankie suddenly decided that she did want the rabbit after all, it was the one thing that she wanted most in the world, and she wasn't leaving until it was hers.

'I don't want any rock. I want that rabbit.'

'Not here, Frankie, please.'

Why not here? Here was as good a place as any. The manager came over and asked them to leave just as Frankie was about to start rolling around on the floor – her screams were apparently disturbing the other customers' more arcade-friendly screams, but by then Frankie had run out of tears anyway and her mother had run out of coins.

She smacked the stick of rock that her mother had bought her in lieu of the rabbit against her kneecaps all the way back to the caravan park until they were red and sore. You couldn't read the 'i' or the 'e', so it said 'Frank' rather than 'Frankie'. It wasn't even for her. And her mother didn't speak to her for seven hours and twenty minutes (although even if she had been speaking to her, the torrential rain would have drowned out the sound of her words), until eight twenty when she locked Frankie inside the caravan and told her to 'be a good girl', she wouldn't be long.

She peered into the darkness, waiting for her mother to return, afraid that she wasn't coming back at all and that she would die in this grotty caravan without a crowbar to prise open the caravan door or defend herself against any would-be attackers, but she reappeared forty-eight minutes later, out of breath and with twigs in her hair.

Although Frankie was still feeling sulky the following morning, her mother was in much better spirits and had spent breakfast (a cola and a flapjack) scheduling several activities for them to do, some of which Frankie liked (the steam train, the trampolines, the pizza) and some of which she didn't (the pedalo, the ghost train, the diversions past the local hospital).

On the last day, as they were sheltering from the rain in the amusement arcade, with strict instructions from her mother to behave this time, her mother spotted the olive-haired man from the coach and called him over. She pretended that she hadn't seen him since they'd arrived, but Frankie was sure that he was the one responsible for the twigs in her mother's hair.

'Frankie,' – not 'pumpkin' any more, she noted – 'this is Grea . . . John. Shall we see if he has better luck?'

Frankie shrugged. She was too hot in the woolly hat that her mother had insisted she wear and she didn't want the rabbit any more, and what sort of name was Grea . . . John, but after twenty-five attempts (her mother had counted each one just to make him feel even more inadequate) and a string of swear words that she'd never heard before, not even from her mother, olive-haired John finally managed to hook the unwanted rabbit and bowed theatrically as he presented it to her.

She didn't say thank you (she didn't need to – her mother said it on her behalf, eighteen times in total) and dragged it along the pavement by its ears as she followed the two of them back to the caravan park. Her mother and olive-haired John played cards while she sat glaring at the rabbit that wasn't a gate. It was only then that she realised it wasn't even the same rabbit.

Roy Orbison was 'Crying' on the portable radio and she wanted to cry with him. 'Do you like Roy Orbison?' she heard her mother say, deflating like a balloon when olive-haired John said no, not really.

Frankie hid the rabbit behind the foldaway bed, but her mother noticed that she hadn't got it as they were leaving and made her go back and look for it. On the coach journey home she told Frankie to sit next to olive-haired John, who she was now calling Mr Collins, and whose breath still smelled like unwashed feet and who was now wearing a tie that was like a chessboard, while her mother sat on her own and refused to speak to any of them.

'Frankie, go and watch television. I've got a migraine and I need to lie down,' was the first thing her mother said to her when they arrived home and she'd decided to start speaking again. But Frankie didn't want to watch television; she wanted to draw. Her mother never knew what she wanted to do.

She overheard her mother on the telephone to Sylvia later saying something about a 'fucking rabbit' and 'a complete arse-wipe' and how she 'might as well have walked into the sea and never come back'. Frankie wondered if she'd have missed her if she had.

Now, three years on, she realised she'd actually be grateful for a last-minute holiday (though to somewhere that wasn't Torquay), ever since she'd overheard her grandmother tell Uncle Stewart that social services had called to discuss Frankie's 'educational needs'.

Frankie hadn't minded slipping through the system, hadn't minded being temporarily forgotten. She didn't want to go to a new school, didn't want to be subjected to the appalled stares and hurtful comments of spiteful strangers, at least not without the reassurance of a familiar face.

She remembered Linda walking her to school and then never seeing her again and nobody seemed to know why. The last time she'd seen Linda, she'd told her to meet her at the Esso petrol station. Pupils weren't supposed to leave the school grounds without an accompanying adult, but the teachers were always too distracted to notice whether you were with an adult or not, and, if you were with an adult, whether it was an actual parent. Her mother always said that teachers must have the patience of saints – looking after one child was difficult enough; God knows what it was like supervising thirty. They *are* paid to be observant, Frankie thought, but didn't say.

Linda said that it only took a fraction of a second to take something that wasn't yours to take, which turned out to be true. A boy from a neighbouring school had been strapped into a passing car by someone who wasn't a relative and never seen again. But Frankie would never see daylight if she waited for her mother to get out of bed and there were just too many gates that she still hadn't seen.

When Linda didn't arrive and a lorry driver filling up with petrol kept glancing across at her and then a police car and an ambulance sped past, Frankie had made her own way home. She never saw Linda again and she wondered if she was angry with her for not waiting.

When she asked her mother if this was the case, she told her that Linda had moved away, but when Frankie asked her where to, she didn't seem to know – said that she might have moved to Anglesey or the Isle of Man, she really couldn't be sure. We weren't what you'd call close, she told Frankie, but I'm sure she isn't angry with you.

If social services can kindly provide me with a copy of the school curriculum, I can teach myself, Frankie had informed her grandmother. She was extremely disciplined. When she had lived with her mother, she would often divide non-school days into achievable timetabled blocks whenever her mother's bedroom door was closed: one hour's fast walking around the backyard, two hours of reading (biographies on famous inventors predominantly), thirty minutes to eat a banana sandwich and a packet of cheese and onion crisps, three hours of pencil drawing, one hour for tea, usually beans on toast followed by a Penguin biscuit, and two hours of television – *Neighbours*, *Newsround*, documentaries on welding and wood carving, etc.

She'd often wondered why her life had to be so structured. Perhaps it was because her mother's wasn't. She'd only ever wanted to know the time when she was expecting a visitor. Otherwise she was asleep during the day and vacuuming at night. There was no pattern to her days and Frankie wondered if this unorthodox routine was one of the reasons why she wasn't able to function normally. It was only as she got older that she realised her mother wasn't like other mothers, who slept through the night and ate at regular mealtimes, who didn't unexpectedly announce that they were going on holiday in less than twenty-four hours.

When her suggestion was met with an 'Absolutely not, you can't possibly be trusted to manage your own education', she asked whether she could be homeschooled by Uncle Stewart. According to her grandmother, he had an O Level in chemistry (always useful when you're producing and selling crack, Vinnie had remarked when she'd told him, but when she'd asked him what 'crack' was he wouldn't expand further, only saying that she shouldn't worry, it was just a rumour).

This was also rejected, mainly by Uncle Stewart, who was 'too busy to give nine-year-olds spelling tests', hence why she was now vomiting behind a wall as the school bus was approaching dreading her first day. She showed the driver her bus pass, sat in the nearest empty seat and, pulling the sleeve of her blazer over her hand, she watched the buildings thin out alongside her. As they entered the school car park, the steady drip of blazers became a downpour. She hoped that the abundance of navy blue would mean that she was just another school blazer, just another pupil.

Mostly, she sat at the back of the class alongside boys who kept passing childish notes to each other and skimming the back of teacher's heads with paper aeroplanes, and at lunchtime she hid in doorways and alcoves, never in the toilets because that was where the mean girls congregated, trying not to make eye contact yet at the same time not wanting to extricate herself completely in case her aloofness backfired and catapulted her headfirst into the limelight.

She wished that she was invisible, like Marcel. She wished that she could intercept the paper aeroplanes and the stupid notes and tip up pencil cases and hit people with chalk without anyone knowing that it was her.

During double history, the end of the longest day that she'd ever known, she became distracted by a blackbird that flew onto the window ledge outside. Its eyes were like shirt buttons and its glossy black feathers glistened like liquorice. She thought of Torquay John and his olive-black hair and his olive-black cufflinks.

She began to sketch the bird in the back of her history book but Miss Dale noticed and made her sit at the front of the class where everyone could see her. She had to stare at the blackboard instead of the blackbird, trying not to cry. That's what everybody wanted and she wouldn't do it. She opened her eyes as wide as they would go and focused on the white chalk, the letters blurring like her name on a stick of rock.

At three fifteen she sprinted down the school steps and across the car park and as soon as she was alone again she cried the tears that she had refused to acknowledge earlier. How she'd held them in for so long she didn't know.

'And did you make any new friends?' her grandmother asked her later.

Frankie invented some girls' names that her grandmother would probably never remember.

She tried to navigate the school corridors undetected for the rest of the week, but some of the girls in her class had started to notice her in corners, especially after the history incident. They would pull at the hem of her blazer as they barged past, tug her rucksack off her shoulders, ridicule the way she spoke, the way she didn't speak, how she walked, her uniform (which was the same as everybody else's). They hadn't even seen her hand yet. She was being bullied about everything else first, the most ordinary things. She dreaded to think what would happen when they finally did see her hand, which until PE during the second week she'd managed to conceal completely.

Although some of the residual scarring had faded over the years, skin grafts had made the skin silky and taut in some places and black and mottled in others, the fingers fused together, the joints misshapen. It was nothing like a hand at all any more. And she really didn't want to remove her blazer. When she told Miss Curtis that she felt too ill to play hockey, Miss Curtis said nonsense, it would do her the world of good and unless she had a note from her mother (did it never end?) she was expected to participate.

The hockey field erupted into squeals of disgust and screams of 'Leper!' – all the usual ignorant responses that she'd heard a million times before, but which had never affected her as much as they did today.

'Elephant Man's got a daughter,' Lisa Newman shrieked.

Miss Curtis told them to be quiet, but even she seemed dubious about Frankie's hockey-playing abilities and whether the hand might be contagious, and she was made to sit on the reserve bench for the entire game, which made it all the more devastating. Nobody needed to have seen her hand at all, although if Miss Curtis had bothered to ask, Frankie would have told her that she was actually quite good at hockey and, no, her hand wasn't contagious. She imagined the whole school would know about her hand within the hour, their families too, and it re-affirmed how small the world was sometimes and how people who you'd never even met might now know things about you that you'd rather they didn't.

Later, she tore a page from her notepad while her grandmother was watching *EastEnders* and wrote:

Peggy,

I'm not sure whether you realise just how much I hate you. If you weren't already dead, I would wish that you were. That's how much I hate you. My new school is horrible, Vinnie is still in Torquay of all places, and apparently my hockey-playing skills are questionable and drawing blackbirds during history is very much frowned upon. I feel so angry with you that I don't think I can write to you any more.

She threw the pen down and told her grandmother that she was going to bed. At least tomorrow was Saturday. She lay awake all night pondering inspired ways to avoid ever attending school again, and the following morning she walked up to the common to think of a few more.

Her grandmother didn't like her walking so far on her own, but she always made sure that there were people or buildings either side of her, although both, she supposed, could be potentially dangerous. Perhaps it would have been safer to be out in the open, as far away from everybody as possible, so that if she did have to run then she'd at least have a head start.

But she'd been walking alone since she'd first started walking, slipping out of reins, letting go of hands, and she couldn't stop now. Her mother had said that she was always disappearing, always running up to gates, racing around supermarket aisles. She wouldn't keep still, wouldn't 'stay there'. It was exhausting. She was exhausting.

The sky was like the skin on a rice pudding and a low mist hung over the hedgerows. It was her favourite time of day, when only night-shift workers and morning birds were awake and the trees looked like paintings. She walked as far as the viewpoint and sat down on a bench. She studied her hand. 'You need eyes in the back of your head when you have children,' was all her mother would say, but how it had happened never really mattered because when they were in the ambulance on their way to hospital her mother would hug her so tightly that she felt that being ill was something that she could do for her.

Of course she'd overheard snippets of conversations that her mother had had with medical personnel over the years, some of them quite heated, but mostly Frankie remembered how serene her mother had seemed, chatting animatedly to the nurses, a smile as warm as summer on her face. She hardly ever smiled, usually only when a strange man stumbled downstairs in the morning. She'd always have her Million Dollar Red smile ready then as she was pouring him a coffee that he didn't have time to drink.

Frankie wondered what her mother would have been like if her father hadn't died. Maybe she would still have been unhappy, but they'd definitely have been living in a house built by her father, closing a gate that she'd helped design, a white elm gate with a stained-glass border that swung both ways. Maybe they'd have sailed a yacht around Greece every August, her mother in a wide-brimmed straw hat, her lips like bee stings, or taken skiing trips to Aspen in winter.

But her father *had* died, and her mother too. There would be no ski slopes or island yachts. And being called 'Elephant Man's Daughter' was nothing compared to that. They were just words. The letters weren't made out of axes or spears, even though they sometimes felt like they were. They couldn't hurt her any more than she'd already been hurt.

When she unlocked the door, the police officer who she'd spoken to about her mother's murder was sipping tea on her grandmother's sofa.

Chapter Fifteen

Clouds as Black as California Raisins

1987

Peggy squinted at the blade of sunlight inching its way across the duvet. Her head was throbbing and there was a stabbing pain at the back of her eyes. It felt as if somebody was sticking pins in her retinas, using them as pincushions. She'd barely slept. Checking her reflection in the dressing-table mirror before getting into bed, she'd had the strangest sensation that she was trapped inside the mirror and she'd sat there for hours trying to free herself from her own gaze, eventually sliding down onto the carpet and crawling away.

Normally, her anxiety was comprised of double- or triple-checking light switches and taps and being afraid to go outside because there was nothing to hold on to, but this felt different and it had unsettled her. She hadn't recognised the person caught inside the mirror and she wondered what would happen if she became trapped inside it permanently, if she became her own reflection. She'd thrown a pillowcase over the mirror in the end. She couldn't risk the possibility of that happening.

She sat on the edge of the bed, her head spinning like a tumble-dryer, and called out to Frankie. Her mouth was dry and her ribs were hurting. There was no reply so she stumbled across the room, snapped the curtains shut and got back into bed.

Ten minutes later she was disturbed again, this time by a pneumatic drill. At first she wondered if the drilling was coming from inside her head but then she heard what sounded like a cement mixer, rather than her thoughts being tossed around, and concluded that it must be coming from somewhere outside. Unable to get back to sleep, she got up. The throbbing in her head seemed worse than usual. She supposed being stuck inside a mirror all night hadn't helped. She drew back the curtains, temporarily blinded by the light, pulled on a clean T-shirt and went downstairs.

As she was pouring a thimbleful of whiskey into a black coffee and swallowing three aspirin, she noticed that Frankie's rucksack wasn't in its usual place behind the sofa. What day was it? She peered at the kitchen calendar, but still had no idea. It must be a school day, she eventually decided, the grid of numbers too complicated for her brain to decipher.

The house felt like bones without flesh when Frankie wasn't there. Sometimes it felt as small and as claustrophobic as a toilet cubicle and Peggy wanted to swing a hammer at the walls to let in the light. At other times it felt so palatial that she would have to cower in a corner until Frankie came home.

Avoiding all the mirrors she wandered aimlessly around a house that she didn't recognise, in a body that didn't feel like her own, looking for something, anything that might seem remotely familiar. Frankie had tidied up. Things were back where they belonged, neatly folded, perpendicular. She liked stacking things in boxes and sweeping things away. Peggy had no idea where anything lived any more.

She heard the washing machine stopping and starting in the utility room and back in the kitchen a packet of mince had been pulled out of the freezer to defrost, for her presumably. Frankie didn't eat meat, although she didn't mind cooking it for Peggy. You need to eat more protein, Frankie would tell her. It's an essential nutrient. In that case, you should be eating meat, too, Peggy would reply, well aware of the reason why she wasn't.

It was fortunate that Frankie liked cooking because they'd both have starved if it had been left to Peggy. A ring binder full of recipes torn from magazines lay by the egg basket, and the Victoria sponge that she'd made yesterday afternoon, which hadn't risen despite Frankie's meticulous calculations, was wrapped in cling film awaiting in-depth analysis: *'Please do not eat, further investigation necessary'*. Frankie's eyes always sparkled like sequins at the sight of a measuring utensil, and technical processes such as folding and creaming, caramelising and proving were as enthralling to her as logarithms, so she'd been hugely disappointed when two sponges as flat as pancakes emerged from the oven.

A note written in glittery pink nail polish sat beneath the garden gate fridge magnet: *'At Ellie's'*. It must be Saturday. Peggy wondered what they'd be doing now if Ed was still alive. Would they be throwing Frisbees in the park, eating hamburgers at McDonald's, waiting for Frankie's gymnastics class to end? What did families do on Saturdays?

She had no idea. Time seemed to move so much more slowly when you were listening to every second. And there were so many seconds to fill, so many minutes to live a life that she had no idea how to live. Why hadn't she done more, seen more, been more? Grieving was certainly not for the faint-hearted. It could last a lifetime. It was a thousand Saturday afternoons with nothing to do.

She remembered the red flecks in the whites of her eyes and the lilac thread veins on the apples of her cheeks in the mirror. When had white become red and pink become lilac? Her eyebrows had needed plucking and her roots had needed dyeing and there'd been constellations of pimples on her chin. Her face wasn't her face any more.

Resisting the urge to go back to bed, she waited for the washing machine to complete its spin cycle and hung out the washing. She stared at the wooden pegs left in the basket and thought about her mother.

'Peggy and her pegs' was a game that her mother once played with her when she was pegging out washing (on a day when she remembered how much she'd wanted a child). They had to clip as many pegs as they could to themselves while counting to twenty and the winner was the person covered in the most pegs. The one she clipped to her nose that made her voice more nasal always hurt the most, the ones in her hair she never felt at all.

In memory of her mother she sat on the back step and clipped the remaining pegs to her pyjama bottoms.

She should visit Ed's grave, she thought suddenly, jumping up. Tell him to his face what she thought of him. At his funeral it had taken two people to keep her vertical, each gripping an elbow and practically frogmarching her from the church doors to the graveside and then on to his mother's bungalow for salmon-paste sandwiches, mini pork pies and salted celery sticks in the conservatory.

The funeral had been postponed until she was well enough to attend, but she didn't know why. She'd told them that she wasn't going, but apparently she would 'regret not being there'. What nonsense. The thing she most regretted was buying a ticket to see Bob Dylan.

She brushed on some mascara, which was difficult without a mirror and which made her eyes water and her lashes clump together. She could feel the weight of them. And then she found the reddest lipstick that she owned, Revlon's Red Supreme, and, holding her hand steady, she pressed it firmly against her lips. Following her lip line wasn't easy, even though she'd done it a thousand times before and should have been able to do it blindfolded. She imagined the cold sores were even more noticeable now that she'd painted them red.

She pulled on her camel coat, a coat that hid so many things. Frankie never liked to touch it, would never pick it up if it fell onto the floor. She'd had to invent some ridiculous story about the camel dying of natural causes so that Frankie would stop crying whenever she wore it. And then she smoothed down her skirt, a little looser than it used to be despite Frankie trying to fatten her up with a range of calorific meals, and opened the front door. A car beeped its horn as she swayed unsteadily along the pavement in stiletto heels and she was briefly flattered until one of the passengers leaned out of one of the windows and called her a 'fucking embarrassment'.

She reached for the powder compact in her handbag – surely a mirror that small couldn't pull her inside – and checked her reflection. There was lipstick on her chin and mascara on her cheek. She wiped it away with a tissue, wondering why she was even bothering. It wasn't as if Ed could see her. She could just as easily tell him to fuck off and leave her alone right there at the bus stop and then toast him with a glass of brandy when she got home.

Peering through a café window while waiting for the bus, she wondered whether The Red Lion would be open. She'd gone to the effort of getting dressed and leaving the house. It would be a shame not to reward such effort. There was a man in the far corner of the café sitting alone reading a newspaper. She couldn't see him clearly because of the condensation, just splashes of him through a love heart that somebody had drawn on the window with their finger. Occasionally, he would flick back his shoulder-length hair as he turned a page, working backwards from the sports section.

He wasn't wearing a wedding ring, Peggy noticed, although that wasn't categorical proof that he wasn't married. She'd become particularly skilled in the art of detecting the almost undetectable band of lighter flesh, barely noticeable to the naked eye, on men's ring fingers. She would often watch them while they slept, inventing lives for them that she never got to see, examining hands that she never got to hold.

Feeling unusually bold, and because it was starting to rain, she walked into the café and sat down on the seat opposite him under the pretext of trying to avoid someone. He briefly glanced up from his newspaper, a fleeting glare of irritation transforming into a bewildered gaze before finally expanding into an absorbing appraisal. I hope you don't mind me sitting here, but I fear I may be being followed, she purred, angling her body away from the door and pressing a palm to her face to further emphasise her disinclination to be recognised. She was turning into Mae West.

'Be my guest.'

For once, it seemed, she'd managed to cultivate her own good fortune, 'taken the bull by the horns' and other such clichés. It had been a long time since she'd been an actual cliché. But she did later wonder if the person who she'd been hiding from that day was herself. He worked on construction sites, he told her, and she became further convinced that this orchestrated meeting was predestined. Ed had wanted to build his own house and now she was talking to somebody who'd already built so many things.

One of the waitresses had a tea towel draped across her shoulder, reminding Peggy that she'd left the washing out. Frankie didn't like having to do the same thing twice, even though she often drew at least ten identical sketches of the same gate. 'It's not the same gate,' she'd insist. 'Each one is microscopically different'.

She'd said the word 'microscopically' slowly, one syllable at a time.

Such a big word for something (and someone) so small.

I really should be going, Peggy would remind herself periodically, but then she'd remember something else, something that she'd seen and always wanted to tell somebody about, something that she'd heard and always wanted to share with somebody, things that she couldn't tell Doctor Ingalls now that she didn't see her any more. These things didn't include Ed, of course. He was buried so deeply that sometimes she imagined he was some mythical creature that had never been seen by anyone other than her. She didn't mention Frankie either.

And it wasn't as if the washing could get any wetter.

The coffee and the potpourri gave her a terrible headache for the rest of the day and the steam from the kitchen must have impaired her vision because she never noticed the dirt under his fingernails or the dried blood on his T-shirt, or realised that if she wasn't careful she might cut herself on him, until much later. She saw nothing but Maxwell House and a captive audience. She never saw *him*. And after writing down her telephone number in apple-red lipstick on a napkin, the clouds now as black as California raisins, she made her way to Sylvia's.

She'd first met Sylvia at church or, to be more exact, at an AA meeting held in a church. As the days had been merging into one, and she'd found that she couldn't remember the simplest of things, she'd decided to attend one of the meetings to see if it might provide her with some coping strategies.

She didn't want to stop drinking completely; it calmed her, made her more able to acclimatise in social situations. But if she could perhaps reduce the extent of it, the quantity of it, especially the solitary drinking, then maybe her long-term memory might improve because although there were plenty of things that she wanted to forget, there were some things that she would have liked to have been able to remember, such as the lyrics to 'Simple Twist of Fate' or 'Shelter from the Storm' (although it was getting increasingly painful to listen to Bob Dylan) or how old Frankie was. She was asked this so often, more than anything else, and Frankie wasn't always there to give her the answer.

Why were people so interested in birthdays and how old you were? What difference did it make to them?

Unfortunately, the minute she sat down on one of the unforgiving pews, she knew that she'd made a mistake. She wasn't sure exactly what she'd been expecting, but it wasn't this. It wasn't sitting in a draughty church sipping weak coffee and eating stale rich tea biscuits and introducing themselves in the most unflattering of terms. They were still people, although some of them did look like they'd vacated a perfectly good park bench to come here.

She just needed some proven practical techniques to stop her drinking excessively (of which there were none, she soon discovered – it was apparently 'all or nothing'), not tragic life stories and downward spirals. And she didn't like being so close to a god who was always elsewhere when all the 'bad shit' was happening.

Gazing up at the crumbling church ceiling and a Jesus with chipped shoulders, Peggy's focus returned to Gary, the motorcycle shop owner who she'd been shamelessly flirting with for the past two weeks, and what to wear on their first date. She was confident that there would be a first date. First dates were easy. It was the ones after, the second, third and fourth dates, that were more difficult to secure. She would have liked a new dress, but new dresses were expensive, although not as expensive as children, of course. It cost a lot to raise a child, in more ways than one.

As she was wondering about what she might wear, a scuffle was breaking out three pews away. The person chairing the meeting, a man wearing a knitted scarf and a tweed jacket with suede elbows, who seemed to lack any authoritative influence whatsoever, let it continue for quite some time before stepping in to advise them cautiously that this was perhaps not helpful.

One of the women sat down with a thump, which must have hurt because without cushions the pews were like granite. The other woman, meanwhile, punched suede elbows on the nose and stormed out of the church, calling everybody 'fuckwits' and slamming the huge oak door behind her as if it was made of plywood.

Peggy left Simon, she thought his name was, nursing a nosebleed and followed the woman out. She didn't want to be detained by the police. She'd taken two amphetamines before coming out, and she was sceptical about trusting a man who didn't have enough tweed to finish his jacket and who couldn't control a small group of sleepy, middle-aged alcoholics.

Once safely outside, she perched on the arm of a damp bench, lit a cigarette and stared into the night sky. Even the moon looked pink, like it too had a sore eye.

'Mind if I have one of those?' a voice asked.

Peggy spun round, expecting to see Jesus and his chipped shoulders, but it was the woman who'd just committed GBH.

'Sure.'

She held out a cigarette and her lighter.

'Quite a spectacle in there tonight – is it always like that?'

'Only when I'm here. I've got a filthy temper. Was there much blood?'

'Enough.'

'Christ, I'm definitely going to get arrested this time. I'm on my second police caution. But they're such arseholes.'

Peggy nodded.

'Do you fancy a drink? I'm Sylvia.'

And so Peggy had spent her first night of supposed sobriety drinking shots at The Pig and Whistle with Sylvia and they'd been inseparable ever since.

On her way to Sylvia's, Peggy called into British Home Stores to browse the clothes rails but the price tags were well outside her budget; even the sale items were ridiculously overpriced. Checking that nobody was looking, she slipped a green chiffon dress into her handbag.

'You're all dressed up today. What's the occasion?' Sylvia marvelled. 'There must be a man involved.'

Peggy said nothing. The man involved was Ed.

It was after midnight when Peggy arrived home. The house was lit up like a Christmas tree. She staggered along the path towards the front door, but before she could turn the key in the lock – it had taken a while to connect the two – Frankie swung open the front door and she fell into the hallway.

'Where've you been? I've been really worried. I asked all the neighbours, but nobody's seen you all day. There's a policewoman on the settee.'

'A policewoman?'

'She says that I'm too young to be left on my own, but I told her that I do all the cooking and I can change a light bulb if I use the big stepladders.'

'Christ, why did you call the police?' Peggy hissed at her. 'I was only at Sylvia's.'

'Well, there was no answer when I called and I didn't know where you were.'

Peggy's head hurt. She'd drunk far too much tequila.

She hauled herself up off the floor, pushing the chiffon dress further into her handbag and, carefully placing one foot in front of the other, entered the living room. Two extremely young police-women with swishing ponytails were sitting exactly where Frankie had said. Peggy waited for them to merge into one as she held on to the sideboard. It must be a quiet night if the police have got time to sit on people's sofas drinking tea, she heard herself slur. Where were her Polo mints?

'The name's PC Williams, Mrs Appleton, and might I remind you that leaving a young child alone is, most definitely, not a laughing matter.'

'She's very mature for her age.'

'That's as may be. She's been showing me the spaghetti Bolognese recipe that she was planning to cook this evening. But consider this a friendly [friendly?] warning. If anything like this happens again then I'll be speaking to my superior.'

Peggy noticed the wet towels draped over the clothes horse.

PC Williams stood up. 'Well, it's been nice meeting you, Frankie – and thank you for the tea.' She handed Frankie the empty mug.

And then turning to Peggy, who really needed the toilet, she said, 'And, Mrs Appleton, might I suggest that you keep the big stepladders out of reach in future. We don't want any more accidents.' The insinuation being that Frankie burning her hand hadn't been an accident at all.

'I'll see you out,' Peggy muttered.

Frankie followed them into the hallway with the empty mug.

When PC Williams had left Peggy confronted Frankie.

'Christ, Frankie. Social services will probably be on the doorstep tomorrow morning accusing me of being an unfit mother and you'll be sent to live with a foster family. Actually, maybe that's not such a bad thing. You can see how shit things can really get. Maybe I'll call them myself, hurry the process along a little.'

Tears welled up in Frankie's eyes.

'I thought something terrible had happened to you.'

It has.

You, Peggy almost said.

Instead she said, 'And turn these fucking lights off. I haven't paid the last electricity bill.'

Chapter Sixteen

Instructions on How to Make a Margarita

1988

'Hello, Frankie.'

'Have you found him?'

'No, I'm afraid not. I was just explaining the situation to your grandmother.'

'What about Sylvia? Have you asked her?'

'I'm afraid we haven't been able to locate her. We found a neighbour who remembered her, but she no longer lives at the same address. I'm sorry, but there's no evidence to suggest that your mother's death was anything other than suicide.'

'Well, you're wrong. He was there. His fingerprints would have been all over the house, all over the rope. He was always there. You obviously didn't look hard enough. Mum always said that you didn't know your arses from your elbows.'

'Frankie, there's no need to be rude.' Her grandmother frowned.

'There's every need. A serious crime has been committed and nobody cares. Close the door on your way out.'

Her mother always used to say that to her whenever she didn't want her in the bedroom any more, whenever she found something better to do with someone else. Close the door on your way out, Frankie.

She slammed the bedroom door shut, scaring the birds on the bedroom walls, and didn't speak to anyone for the rest of the weekend.

She was actually relieved when Monday arrived and she could go back to school, because refusing to talk to people was far more exhausting than actually talking to them, almost as exhausting as trying to make yourself invisible. She spent the morning studying the names etched into her school desk with a biro, sometimes the same name with only the first letter of their surname to distinguish them – Sarah C, Sarah K – and wondered if their attempts to become invisible had caused them to carve themselves into the wood and become part of the furniture instead. Some names were sharp and livid, Alex, Neil, Karl, others wriggled like worms, Sharon, Jennifer, Deborah, slack and limp. She wondered when she would be ready to add her name. Soon, she imagined.

Most days something would be missing from her locker, or something unpleasant left inside it, like rabbit droppings or cat food. Only yesterday another girl's purse had been found sandwiched between her PE shorts and an aetex T-shirt and she was due to see the headmaster later today. She didn't even know how they were getting into the locker, although many of the toilet-congregating girls had suddenly started wearing clips in their hair.

Vinnie still wasn't back from Torquay and Frankie wondered if he was ever coming back. Had his parents packed a suitcase as if it was the last thing they'd ever do? Why did everyone want to disappear to Torquay? He'd called her once and she'd spent the entire telephone call complaining about Lisa Newman. He told her that Lisa's father was serving a twenty-five-year prison sentence for stabbing and killing his business partner, and her brother had been arrested for having pornographic images on his computer, and he told her to tell Lisa to piss off, but she went one better and told her to 'fuck off' instead.

Her mother would have been proud. She could splutter at least eight different expletives in one sentence. The girl sitting next to her whispered forlornly, 'I wish I could say that,' and offered Frankie an Opal Fruit, a strawberry one.

'I can teach you,' Frankie said. 'It's easy. They're just words.'

'Really?'

'Really.'

'I'm Harry, short for Harriet,' the girl said, stretching out her hand.

Frankie liked that she called herself Harry for short and introduced herself with a handshake.

But as she was staring at the fragile, sparrow-like girl in the black Lycra headband chewing an Opal Fruit, another bird to pin to her bedroom wall, she wondered if teaching her how to swear with confidence was wise. Perhaps she wouldn't teach her the really offensive phrases, the ones that made people gasp.

Unfortunately for Frankie, swearing at Lisa Newman was why she was now scheduled to be introduced to the headmaster. Lisa hadn't 'fucked off' at all, but had instead stolen Alison Bentley's pink purse and hidden it inside Frankie's locker, but not before taking five pounds out of it. She wondered if the school operated fingerprinting analysis for incidents like this. The police didn't seem to bother. She also hoped that they hadn't called her grandmother, because Frankie still wasn't speaking to her.

Thankfully, the headmaster hadn't called her grandmother, but only because he didn't seem to have the correct number. He asked Frankie what the number was, but she said that she couldn't remember. She wasn't going to dig her own grave. He said that there'd been complaints about her swearing at fellow pupils, which she strenuously denied ('It was only one pupil, singular') and then he broached the discovery of the pink purse inside her locker, which she said had not been stolen by her and he was welcome to fingerprint her to prove it.

He told her that that wouldn't be necessary, but stressed that behaviour like this would not be tolerated at this school (as if it might be tolerated at a different school). He then added that it must be a difficult time for her, both her parents dying and then having to start a new school, and he understood that, which actually made it worse because she didn't want to be pitied. She knew how to stand up for herself. And he had no right to use her parents as some sort of emotional leverage. If she'd stolen the purse then she would have said so.

'I did swear at Lisa Newman – she deserved it,' she admitted. 'But I didn't steal Alison Bentley's purse and it's got nothing to do with my parents dying.'

It had everything to do with her parents dying, her mother especially.

He didn't say anything for what seemed like a whole episode of *Blue Peter*, and then he said, 'Very well – your punishment will be one hour's detention for the next fourteen days. Report to Mrs Wilcox in the assembly hall.'

'Thank you.'

She wasn't sure why she was thanking him for giving her detention, and she didn't know what she was going to say to her grandmother when she did start speaking to her again. She'd have to eventually, she supposed, although she was sure that she'd think of something. She usually did. In the end she told her that she was staying behind for extra singing tuition because they were rehearsing for a musical, *Bugsy Malone*, but she didn't like lying.

She was already best friends with six fictitious girls and only one real one, Harry, who wasn't particularly talkative, which Frankie supposed was a blessing. She didn't want her to get detention for swearing too, although she'd have welcomed an ally in the assembly hall. Mrs Wilcox's hearing was on a par with a horseshoe bat. Even Frankie's breathing was too loud for Mrs Wilcox.

While swapping sandwiches in the playground one lunchtime a few days later (Frankie, cheese and pickle, Harry, banana) Harry revealed that she was deaf in one ear, which was why she was sometimes quiet. Frankie had to guess which ear. She guessed the right one. It was the left. Harry said that background noise wrapped people's words up in bubble wrap and made them difficult to pop, but she was getting better at lip reading, which was the only type of reading that she was allowed to do at home.

Her mother didn't like her reading books because it 'gave her ideas and made her insolent', so she had to use the school library if she wanted to read, which she said she didn't mind because she really liked the librarian, Miss Johnson, who was from Antigua and who always said that 'you should never forget where you come from, no matter how far you travel'. Harry had asked her, 'Even if you came on the bus and it only took five minutes?' Even then.

Frankie hadn't corresponded with her own mother since practically disowning her with a curt, angry paragraph, the same curt, angry paragraph that stared up at her each time she opened the dressing-table drawer, and made her angry all over again, so she unzipped her pencil case and began to make amends.

Dear Mum,

I'm sorry about the tone of my last letter, but I was extremely angry with you. I'm still angry with you for dying, but not to such an 'extreme' extent. Being angry all the time is just too exhausting.

Vinnie's still my best friend even though he gives the worst advice, but when he's not around, which is a lot of the time, I sit with Harry (short for Harriet). Like me she has a physical disability, she's deaf in one ear, but she's nice too (she gave me a strawberry Opal Fruit when we first met), although her mother does have some very radical views on education.

You would have been very proud of the way I dealt with Lisa Newman, although it did backfire somewhat (thanks to Vinnie) and I now have to sit in the assembly hall with Mrs Wilcox, trying not to breathe. I used one of your favourite phrases, the one that you used to say to me all the time, although I know that you didn't mean it. It was the alcohol that made you say it.

Grandma said last week that I'd 'turned out well, considering . . .' 'Considering' what I don't know because she didn't finish the sentence, but it's always nice when people are pleased with you, particularly as I stopped speaking to her for nearly three weeks over the police handling of your case, which has been, as you always used to say, a 'travesty'. I'll be taking over the investigation now. I'm planning to break into our old house to collect evidence. Grandma doesn't know about the detention. Or the planned break-in. If I'm going to tell a lie I'd rather it was a Big Lie because small ones aren't worth telling. But I also tell the truth sometimes. It very much depends on the gravity of the situation.

Grandma has invited me to midnight Mass along with Uncle Stewart and his wife, Joyce, and although I no longer have any religious beliefs since your death, I shall probably attend, if only to light a candle in your memory so that you are never forgotten. I hope that my father has located your whereabouts. I'm sure that he'll try his absolute best, so you mustn't hide from him.

I drew a robin yesterday. It was sitting on a barbed-wire fence and must have been extremely uncomfortable, but I was very grateful for its patience and threw it a crumb that I found in my pocket. It flew off with the crumb in its beak. Maybe you saw it. I'm quite pleased with the sketch, as the robin was particularly fat and red. It would make the perfect Christmas card.

F.

The candle that Frankie lit, second row, third from the left, went out almost immediately when a latecomer slammed the church door shut, the flame flickering wildly and then sputtering pitifully before finally dying. She'd been staring at it until her eyes watered. She was mortified. She wanted to light another one, but the service was about to start and she was trapped between her grandmother and Joyce. *All rise.* She wished that she could rise. She really didn't want to be there. And she couldn't bring her hands together in prayer if she'd wanted to, the good hand wanting nothing whatsoever to do with the burnt one.

She did enjoy singing the carols, though, particularly 'O Little Town of Bethlehem' and 'Good King Wenceslas'. She knew all the words without having to consult the printed carol sheet, although she didn't know how she possibly could. She couldn't remember ever singing them before from start to finish, even during school carol concerts – she was always thinking about other things – but they were all there, inside her head; a legacy from her mother, perhaps, who sang along to the radio while she peeled carrots on Christmas morning.

Uncle Stewart and his wife Joyce joined them for Christmas lunch. Apparently, according to her grandmother, they had three children, but they never mentioned them, which seemed unusual, especially at Christmas. Who was cooking their Christmas lunch, watching them open their presents? Frankie tried to glean clues as to their names and their ages and why they weren't there, but all three of them were painstakingly tight-lipped about the other three. Perhaps all parents did that, pretend that they didn't have children.

She imagined that she had rarely been the topic of her mother's conversations either unless she was being derogatory about her, unlike Ellie who was all that Mrs Barlow could talk about. Even Mr Barlow got tired of discussing Ellie at the dinner table for hours at a time. He would tell Mrs Barlow to 'give it a rest' and accuse her of spoiling her and smothering her (Frankie didn't like picturing Mrs Barlow holding a pillow over Ellie's face), but as she always reminded him, it had taken them 'nine long years' to have a child and she could fucking well put her on a pedestal if she wanted to. Frankie would quickly turn her attention back to *Grange Hill*.

When Joyce took off her gloves Frankie noticed that she only had six fingers, the wedding ring finger on her left hand and the little finger on her right hand were missing. She wore her wedding ring on a chain around her neck. Frankie would have been grateful for any fingers on her burnt hand. She wondered how Joyce had lost the fingers and where they were now, but of course she wasn't going to ask. A person should be allowed to decide for themselves exactly how much or how little they wished to disclose about a subject.

She thought that Joyce might mention it in passing during lunch as she was grappling with her knife and fork, but she didn't. It had obviously lost its initial importance, no longer the freshly baked horror that it had once been. Frankie could certainly sympathise with that. And if Joyce wasn't going to discuss her children then it seemed unlikely that she would divulge the grisly circumstances surrounding her missing fingers.

Frankie didn't eat meat or other hard-to-cut-into food so thankfully had no need for a knife or a second hand. Using the back of her fork she pressed her peas into a firm green cowpat and then decorated the edge of her plate with Brussels sprouts.

Her grandmother had insisted that she was too young to be excluding meat from her diet, making such important, life-changing decisions while she was still a child. She'd turned to Uncle Stewart for moral support, but hadn't received any. *She'll grow out of it. It's just a phase. You worry too much. I'm sure it's all kosher* (very amusing). But of course her grandmother hadn't experienced the horror of smelling her own barbecued flesh burning like campfire chicken burgers.

As soon as Frankie was able to reach the oven dials she'd taught herself to cook. They'd have died of malnutrition if it had been left to her mother, and her mother needed a healthy diet to counteract her hedonistic lifestyle.

She found that she actually enjoyed shopping for ingredients and would carefully follow recipes that she'd torn from her mother's magazines, although she had to ask Mrs Barlow so many questions about techniques such as braising and poaching that she said she could choose one of her cookbooks to take home and keep.

After much procrastinating she selected *The Good Housekeeping Step-by-Step Cook Book*, enticed by the sliced strawberries that framed the front cover, spending most time on the baking chapter at the back because baking felt quite scientific, almost like calculating the dimensions of a timber ledge and brace, although most of what she cooked for her mother often ended up in the bin in favour of a gin and tonic.

At three o'clock it started snowing. Frankie carried her presents, a box of acrylic paints and a canvas (Vinnie), a red jumper with snowflakes on the sleeves (Uncle Stewart and Joyce) and a camera (her grandmother) into the bedroom. The camera excited her most. She was looking forward to taking a photograph of Stan and pinning it to a lamppost or sending it to a newspaper so that everybody would know who he was and what he'd done.

When she came back from her room, the adults were pouring themselves a celebratory sherry in the kitchen. Frankie was offered an orange juice and the bottle of sherry was locked away. They had no idea that she could recite the alcohol content of most types of alcohol, although she'd never tasted any of it. She could name six different types of whiskey, knew how to make a margarita, which sounded beautiful, but was in fact quite lethal in large doses, and she could determine whether a gin had been made with tonic or ice just by smelling it. She had often been given bartender duties when her mother could barely stand up: *pour some Baileys in this glass for me, pop a slice of lime in this tequila, more rum and less Coke next time*.

It was only as she got older that she realised what all these drinks that looked like glasses of blackcurrant squash and apple juice were doing to her mother, how they were making her worse, making her more spiteful, more argumentative, so she would top everything up with tap water and hope that her mother was too drunk to notice.

She would fill empty wine bottles with lemonade, replace full ones with soda, plead with her to stop, but her mother was unassailable. She was like a castle wall – a castle wall with a penchant for cheap corner-shop Lambrini when she couldn't afford the Moon Rivers and the dirty martinis, and the less expensive it was, the more of it she drank. And then there were the pills, which were much harder to find because they were so small and could fit into a handbag. And then there was Stan.

Maybe it was the sherry or the fact that she was celebrating Christmas without her mother, but Frankie suddenly felt unbearably sad. Why were the things that you loved most taken from you, as if you should never have had them in the first place? She desperately wanted to be alone. She *was* alone. She told her grandmother that she was going for a walk.

When she opened the door, a gust of icy air blew in from the corridor. She imagined her mother rushing inside to keep warm. She wondered what Vinnie was doing. He was in Birmingham, spending Christmas and New Year with another distant relative. She'd never known a family to stretch so far and wide. He had uncles all over the UK, he said, but none of them lived anywhere nice like Surrey. Frankie asked him if his father needed another loan. Probably, Vinnie said, I think he's gambling again. We go on lots of road trips when he's gambling.

Running down the stairs without holding on to anything – the stairs were dropping further and further down her list of fears, other things jumping ahead of them – she suddenly wondered if the sherry had been locked away because they thought she might be like her mother, and this made her even sadder because she did want to be like her mother, but not like that.

The courtyard was completely white and there was already enough snow to build a small snowman. Pearls of snow dripped from tree branches and telegraph wires and her footprints left a deep imprint as she walked across the courtyard. Somebody somewhere would know that she'd been there. Or that she'd been walking away from there. She wondered whether to walk in a circle to confuse them.

It was eerily quiet for a building where over a hundred people lived. They couldn't all be watching *The Living Daylights*. Perhaps someone was watching her from a window, her coat as bright as a button against the snow.

She walked towards the Asian supermarket and then turned left towards a small skateboard park barely larger than her bedroom where she lay on the snow and gazed up at the sky. It was disorientating. She could just as easily have been lying on the sky looking up at the earth because the snow and the sky were the exact same colour.

She wished that she'd brought the camera to capture the moment. *Frankie aged nine, lying on snow.* One day somebody would be sifting through a shoebox of old photographs and there she'd be. *'That's Frankie when she was nine, lying on the snow,'* somebody would say. She liked the thought of somebody finding her again after years of living in a shoebox. Unless there was no one to remember her, of course, and then she'd just be a girl that nobody knew lying on the snow. Did the camera have any film? She'd have to check.

A woman wheeling a shopping trolley with tiny pineapples on it came over to her and asked her if she was okay. She said yes thank you, I'm just resting, although she *was* starting to feel cold and it was beginning to grow dark.

Uncle Stewart and Joyce had gone by the time she got back, having walked across her footprints and turned them to slush. She ate three Roses, two purple and one red, and then watched television until she fell asleep. When she woke up her grandmother was watching *The Russ Abbot Christmas Show*, knitting. She didn't look down at her knitting once. Her fingers seemed to know exactly what to do without her having to check.

The days between Christmas and New Year crawled along at a caterpillar pace. Everywhere was closed, everything empty. It was as if the whole world had packed a suitcase and left. Even the robins had gone into hiding, all of them, even the scrawny ones with paler chests. They must have spied her armed with her camera, shooting anything and everything, a rolled-up bandage, a Toffee Crisp wrapper, an old man walking his Jack Russell, although she planned to dispose of that one once it was developed because she hadn't asked his permission – she wouldn't have wanted anyone taking a photograph of her without her knowledge – and she concentrated on what was on the pavement by her feet instead, although she didn't bother with the used condom and the splash of vomit. In fact she spent most of her time staring at the pavement. It was preferable to looking up and seeing what was really happening. She'd followed this particular route to the launderette at least a hundred times and each time she'd seen something that she'd never seen before – the ground was an Aladdin's cave of unexpected treasures that people trampled over every day.

She decided to save the last five frames for something extra-special, whatever that might be. Maybe it would be Stan from five different angles, being killed five different ways. Gavin, the assistant manager of Jessops, had demonstrated how to load film into the camera, a Canon AE-1 Program, when she'd tapped on the shop window on Boxing Day. He was on his hands and knees attaching sale price tags to tripods and flashguns.

Although they were closed he'd made her a hot chocolate and given her lots of useful information. He told her that because the camera automatically set both aperture and shutter speed, all she needed to do was focus the camera and shoot. He'd also advised her on lighting (to enhance luminosity and texture), and explained the rule of thirds (to create more interest), a photography technique that suited her analytical temperament.

She peered into the launderette window even though it was closed and Vinnie wouldn't have been there anyway. She thought she heard something rustling in the thistly undergrowth by the wall. She stood listening, her hand poised on her camera in case she was about to witness something extraordinary like a hedgehog covered in snow or a grass snake slithering around a twig like a helter-skelter, although she would have been terrified if it had been a snake. Or a hedgehog. She'd never seen one up close. And sometimes she was most afraid of the things that she didn't know.

Growing impatient, she walked over to the rustling and pushed back the undergrowth with the toe of her boot to take a closer look, but it was just an empty crisp packet, smoky bacon. Everything was always 'just' something else. Never had she felt so disappointed.

Just then a car pulled up beside her. She heard the window roll down and then a man's voice, but she pretended not to hear him, she didn't like it when drivers wound down their car windows, didn't like being beckoned over. Why would anyone want to ask a child anything? Nobody was ever interested in what they thought (except Mrs Barlow of course, who was always interested in her opinion, especially if it concerned Ellie) and Frankie had only lived in three places, so how was she expected to know where Edinburgh or Carlisle were unless she consulted a map and surely that was something they could do themselves.

She certainly wasn't going to admit that she'd memorised every footpath, every cycle trail and every public toilet within a five-mile radius so that she could keep track of her grandmother.

She slipped behind the launderette and ran towards the car park without glancing back.

Afterwards, she wondered if it might have been Stan, if she'd wanted to see him so badly that he'd miraculously appeared, and she vowed to be more observant in future, even if it meant paying attention to passing car drivers and other things that she was afraid of. He might have dyed his hair or shaved off his beard. He might not even look like Stan any more. So she needed to be vigilant.

Chapter Seventeen

A Spy Like My Father

1984

Reverend Ray Charles was making himself at home on Stella's sofa, his psalms and proverbs in a weathered leather briefcase by his feet.

Not *the* Ray Charles, of course.

This one was middle class and white.

But Stella did find herself wishing that it was the other Ray Charles 'unchaining her heart' on her sofa and wondered if he often disappointed people.

She poured them both a cup of tea.

'Perhaps you'd like to come to church on Sunday?'

She'd drifted away again, something that she did several times a day, although she was never quite sure exactly where it was that she went. There was never any sense of place, any identifying landmarks. Perhaps her mind simply wandered over to the bookshelf and back, where people put their feelings into longer, more articulate sentences. She didn't think that she'd have the stamina for any lengthier treks.

And for one blissful moment she'd forgotten that it was the wrong Ray Charles sitting on her sofa.

'I'm sorry? What were you saying?'

'It would be lovely to see you on Sunday.'

'I wouldn't hold your breath.'

'I understand how difficult it must be,' he replied (he had no idea). 'But being with likeminded souls can often help. The Lord will be your guide if you let him into your heart.'

'I don't want to appear rude, reverend, but quoting trite nonsense from the Bible is hugely insulting. And, rest assured, I will not be seeking solace in God – quite the opposite, in fact.'

'I apologise. I didn't mean to offend you. I spend so much time reciting biblical passages that they colour my everyday speech.'

'More tea?'

Despite her initial reluctance, however, and because Geoff had offered to accompany her, Stella wheeled herself to church four Sundays later in the hope that Christians were more Christian than she remembered and, more importantly, that she would be able to confront God in person. Because somebody needed to explain themselves.

Are You There, God? It's Me, Stella.

Judy Blume certainly knew the right questions to ask.

The service itself reminded Stella that nothing had really changed over the years as far as religion was concerned (an unusual unchanging commodity), but she did enjoy listening to the reverend's unhurried West Country vowels, even though she wished they affected her more deeply. Geoff had said that simply being there was enough, stepping through the church doors half the battle. And you can eat the sandwich without buying the sandwich shop, he told her. But she felt disappointed. She would have liked the Lord's Prayer and 'The Lord is my Shepherd' to have meant something. She would have liked to have felt something other than excruciating guilt, and to witness water being turned into wine.

Nonetheless she continued to seek forgiveness from a god who wasn't listening, a god who she'd now decided did exist so that He too could shoulder some of the blame, which at least offered her a shirt tail to hold on to.

A shirt tail that quickly became an elbow when she began to attend midweek services too, particularly if the church choir was scheduled to sing. It seemed that she'd grown tired of being imprisoned inside the four walls of her own home, preferring instead the four more ornate walls of St Giles. Billy didn't seem to mind her not being at home either, even if she was turning into 'a crazy choir-singing zealot', as he so eloquently phrased it. Praying won't bring Marie back, he warned her, or get you up out of that wheelchair, if you really can't walk.

He'd never been entirely convinced that she was paralysed, believing it to be an elaborate ploy to garner sympathy and avoid a custodial sentence for causing death by dangerous driving. He'd even stick drawing pins in her legs when he'd been drinking. 'Can you feel that? What about that? This?' No, she couldn't feel it. She couldn't feel anything. If she had been able to feel anything she'd have been elated. To have been able to feel the serrated edge of a razorblade slice into her wrist and watch the blood pour out would have been blissful. But all she felt was numb.

And faith was proving equally elusive too, unless it was in the more earthly form of Faith Goodman, who was far easier to locate. Since leaving The Swan she'd set up her own cleaning company and her leaflets were always littering the shopping precinct: 'Faith and Sound – No Home Too Dirty'. She'd asked Stella if she needed any help around the house – she'd recently recruited two new employees (her two youngest children) because business was 'booming'; 'at a reduced rate, of course,' she added, but Stella had politely declined: 'I think you'll find that my home *is* too dirty.'

It wasn't, of course. It was spotless.

The church choir were attempting to rehearse a little-known Scottish hymn, somewhat hampered by a flu virus that was being passed around like gossip. After fifteen minutes of coughing and sneezing and somebody almost fainting Phyllis abruptly brought the rehearsal to a halt and instructed the choir to go home and sip honey and lemon and to speak to no one which, as she was starting to lose her own voice, came across as vaguely menacing.

Further adding to the sense of menace, a man in a trench coat with a Russian accent (who, according to Phyllis, wasn't a KGB agent, he had family in Chichester) approached Stella as she was perusing the church noticeboard. She would regularly spend at least twenty minutes browsing the extracurricular church activities, noting down the coffee mornings, the bring and buys, the prayer meetings and any other church-related recreational pursuits advertised in the hope that she might one day meet the one person who might understand, who might be worth devoting more time to, who might smooth the way forward in a way that the church itself hadn't yet been able to.

She half expected the Russian man to pass her a coded message, the secret to spiritual enlightenment, or at the very least a vial of cyanide so that her heart would finally stop beating, but instead he produced a plain white business card with his wife's name printed on it in peacock purple: 'Rosa Chekhov – Spiritualist'.

'I hope you don't mind,' he told her, 'but she may be able to help.'

Stella thanked him and placed the card inside her notebook, a notebook that contained pages and pages of telephone numbers that she'd methodically written down over the past few months. For anything. For everything. Soon, she believed that she would have *the* number – the one number that she needed, the only number, the answer to everything, the number that Janine Martin had found. Janine had lived next door but one to Stella when she was growing up, and within the space of a year had gone from being a ten-year-old chatterbox to an uncommunicative eleven-year-old. She was taken to various specialists, psychiatrists, therapists, but nobody ever discovered why she couldn't, or wouldn't, talk.

Stella's mother hinted at disquiet in the Martin household and said that Janine must have her reasons for staying silent, and her sister had heard a rumour that Janine had witnessed something harrowing. Stella wasn't so sure. Whenever she passed Janine, she would smile at her enigmatically, like the Mona Lisa, as if she knew something that nobody else knew, had found the answer to something monumental. She remembered feeling so envious, without quite knowing why.

When the card fell out of her notebook a few days later she found herself dialling the number. What harm could it do? The worst had already happened. Geoff offered to come with her after ridiculing her for a full thirty minutes – 'Charlatan Hestons, the lot of them' – but she told him to go and annoy Robbie instead, who would appreciate his acerbic wit far more and who would be glad of the company now that Geoff had resigned and he was unemployed.

The new landlord of The Swan had told Robbie that Stevie Wonder could probably pour a pint better than he could, and he was blind. 'Who's Stevie Wonder?' Robbie had asked. He was dismissed without notice.

When she told Geoff the nationality of the spiritualist she was visiting, 'A Russian family moved next door to us when I was thirteen,' he said.

Stella was already intrigued. Geoff rarely spoke about his past. But he did like an audience.

'My mother was beside herself. She always gravitated towards people who were different, people who worshipped other gods, who wore turbans or burkas, kimonos or ponchos. They were always far more interesting than her own family. And she spent all afternoon baking peanut butter muffins. I was instructed to deliver the welcome gift and to not dawdle. I told her to deliver it herself if she was so desperate to meet them, but she said that I would feel the buckle of my father's belt if I didn't do as I was told, that same belt buckle the reason for her own reticence. She hadn't left the house in four days.' Geoff remembered the rhubarb graze beneath his mother's right eye that never seemed to fade.

Stella wanted to learn more about his father's belt buckle and why his mother hadn't left the house in four days. Those details sounded far more interesting, but Geoff dismissed her with a flick of the hand and, sitting back down, he continued:

'*We . . . welcome . . . you . . . with . . . peanut . . . butter . . . muffins*, I rehearsed as I crept along the path, as if the Chomskys had arrived fresh from another planet. I remember scanning the front garden for a spaceship, envisioning being greeted by a creature from Jupiter crafted from Bacofoil, a single aluminium antenna in the middle of its forehead and a huge spindly hand plucking me off the porch step and nobody ever seeing me again. Too many episodes of *The Twilight Zone*, I expect, but Russia seemed so far away then.'

'One of Marie's friends had a Russian doll that they always liked to play with,' Stella said. 'Marie once asked me if Russia was like a Russian doll, a small country inside a big country inside an even bigger country. I told her that it probably was.'

Stella rarely mentioned Marie. It was easier not to. While some people liked to talk about the dead as if they were still alive, beginning conversations with 'Do you remember when . . .?', Stella was happier pretending that they'd never been there to begin with, although Marie often made that difficult by talking to her, especially late at night, the weight of Stella's hands over her ears failing to silence her daughter's voice.

Geoff hesitated briefly, wondering whether to offer up one of his own memories of Marie in return, but he didn't like remembering Marie either, and returned to the relative safety of his own childhood.

'I wanted to leave the biscuit tin on the step and sprint home before I was seen, but the reprimand that I would receive from my mother – *I'll know if you left them on the doorstep and didn't knock* – and the thought of my father's belt buckle far outweighed my fear of the Chomskys, so I stood nervously waiting for an extraterrestrial being to fill the frosted glass and pull me inside.

'Eventually Mrs Chomsky materialised – with an expression was sour as lemon juice and a nose that was too big for her face. But she smiled when I handed her the biscuit tin. I remember how sharp and grey her teeth were. Inside the house, her son Andrei was lying by an unlit fire watching cartoons.

'The house was extremely cold, I remember, but it was sheer terror rather than the chill making my teeth chatter. It's strange how fear makes everything seem possible and yet when you're not afraid everything feels impossible. I wondered if they'd let me leave, but I said that my mother was expecting me straight back, and they did.'

Geoff reached into his trouser pocket for a handkerchief, and blew his nose. Stella noticed the initials 'SJ' embroidered in salmon pink in one of the corners – his mother's, his wife's? There'd been rumours of a wife, maybe even a daughter.

'At the door, Mrs Chomsky asked me what I wanted to be when I left school.

I told her I was going to be a scientist, unaware that I'd never see the inside of a science laboratory once I'd left school. "Andrei's going to be an astronaut," she replied, and I thought perhaps they really were from outer space.

'She told Andrei to walk me to the gate which he did, reluctantly. She called after me to thank my mother for the muffins, and at the gate, Andrei whispered, "I'm really going to be a spy like my father."

'Nobody was sure if Andrei's father *was* a spy because we rarely saw him, although we considered that to be one of the hallmarks of high-level espionage – being able to keep a low profile. According to my mother, though, the reason we never saw him wasn't because he was smoking cigars under street lamps, but because he was always propping up the bar at The Rose and Crown with his one good arm. She often heard him stumbling along the path singing Russian folk songs in the early hours. "So if he is a spy," she said, "then he isn't a particularly accomplished one." Her initial excitement had been replaced with indifference once she realised that the Chomskys were just like everybody else, and I decided that he couldn't possibly be a spy with only one arm. He'd be far too noticeable.'

Geoff put the crumpled handkerchief back in his pocket, adding, almost as a footnote, 'Andrei disappeared two years later. He was fourteen.'

Stella was riveted. The story had taken an unexpected twist. She waited for more – the circumstances of Andrei's disappearance, the reason why his father had only one arm – but annoyingly, Geoff was someone who could reveal a lot about very little, shying away from the more absorbing aspects, and he was suddenly in a hurry – 'I'd better go, Rita wants a lift to the hairdresser' – so she was left to pen her own ending. Did Andrei go back to Russia to be an astronaut or a spy? Did he assume a new identity? Was he murdered? Was it even true? Geoff could twist the truth into many different shapes.

At the Chekhovs', there was a pungent smell of boiled cabbage coming from the kitchen. It smelled like Billy's socks when he'd been running on the marsh, training for marathons that he never ran.

Rosa had drawn the curtains and switched off the light, so that all Stella could see was Rosa's illuminated face; it was as if she had no torso, was just a decapitated head dangling from the ceiling like a lampshade, or perched on an invisible stake like a flag. She flickered in soft focus, spelling out letters, telling Stella that there was somebody who wanted to speak to her. But it wasn't anybody that Stella knew.

She didn't think that she'd see the Chekhovs again, it had been a disappointing experience, but because there was nothing else to hold on to and because some things took time, two weeks later she found herself ringing their doorbell once again, wondering if today she might hear a name that she recognised. Rosa's head would rear forward and her eyes would roll back and Stella could see that Rosa was trying her best to channel something, anything, but maybe she was just trying too hard.

Ivan and Rosa had also had a child who'd died; Stella wasn't alone, even though at times it felt like she was. She'd overheard a conversation on the church steps while she was jotting down the details of a knitting circle and a book club, neither of which she had yet attended and probably never would. She'd grown tired of bitter coffee and mindless chats about the weather. She wondered if the Chekhovs had had better luck contacting their own child.

Natalia had been six, a year older than Marie, when she died, the sole casualty when the school bus that she'd been travelling on fell from a bridge.

Once again Stella was reminded of the consequences of sitting in the wrong seat.

Or, like Marie, of being the wrong daughter.

Chapter Eighteen

A Heart Can Always Beat Faster

1987

Peggy was waiting for Stan to call.

Frankie was bringing her homemade meals while she waited, cottage pie, pea risotto, quiche Lorraine.

Peggy would impatiently snap at her whenever she tried to talk to her, tried to move her into another room. She was waiting for a very important telephone call, she told her, a call that could change both their lives. Please stop bringing me food that I can't eat.

Earlier that day she'd told Frankie that she wasn't to waste any more money on expensive ingredients when a slice of something on toast was perfectly adequate, and Frankie had looked at her as if she'd just announced that they were going on holiday again, just the two of them, so she reluctantly relented and said that she could still cook at the weekend.

The 'very important telephone call' finally came at eleven minutes past seven, five days, six hours and eleven minutes later.

The sound of the phone made Peggy jolt, as if it was the last thing that she'd expected to hear, even though she'd spent the last five days waiting for it to ring. She patted her hair, coughed into the ball of her fist and lifted the receiver.

The conversation was brief. A table had been booked at Pierre's Bistro on Friday. More meals were being arranged without her. And after waiting so long, it now seemed to be happening too quickly. Her heart was thumping loudly inside her chest. She couldn't remember ever feeling this way before, but she was sure that she must have. Hearts can always beat faster.

Frankie was watching her closely, pretending to read. She still hadn't forgiven Peggy for threatening to call social services and for telling her that she could only cook at weekends.

'If you don't look up from those books every now and then you'll never meet the man of your dreams,' Peggy warned her.

'I don't care. I'm never getting married,' she announced, angrily flipping over a page.

'Don't be ridiculous. Everybody wants to get married.'

Ed hadn't even been her husband. She could never lawfully refer to him as her husband, her dead husband.

'Not everybody. And I'm only eight. I shouldn't be marrying anyone.'

'We all need to be loved.'

Frankie raised a scornful eyebrow.

'What you need and what you get are two *very* different things,' she told her mother haughtily, as if she was reciting an ancient proverb. 'And *you've* never been married.'

Peggy watched her stomp away, the majestic wrought-iron gate on the cover of *Garden Gates and Archways* clasped to her chest like a shield. She wasn't even reading a novel, entering a world where anything was possible, where a gate could be something other than a means of access (or, like theirs, lice-infested tongue-and-groove redwood timber that would put a bonfire out).

Like her father, Frankie was more interested in redevelopment potential rather than blindly accepting what was already there. Peggy would have been grateful for the most primitive version of something, no matter how it worked, although she *was* envious that Frankie was so like Ed. *She* didn't have his DNA. She had no biological connection to him whatsoever, and yet look how he'd made her suffer.

Frankie's jealousy was directed towards the men who Peggy invited into their home, men who she refused to speak to, which admittedly most were grateful for. They didn't have time to converse with Peggy, let alone an impertinent child who wouldn't answer the simplest of questions. Some even wondered if she might have a learning disability and even when Peggy said no, she's extremely bright for her age, they couldn't pull their trousers on quickly enough.

Peggy had long since given up asking her to at least be civil. Frankie said that they never stayed longer than five minutes so what was the point? 'There's every point,' Peggy had said, slapping her sharply across the face. After that, she told her to stay in her room whenever she was 'entertaining'.

By Friday morning Peggy felt sick with nerves. There was a small tear in the back of the green chiffon dress and, although she'd managed to conceal the majority of her facial blemishes beneath several layers of foundation, she later noticed that the dense covering had given her skin a strange yellow tinge, unless she'd always had yellow skin and the unflattering lighting in the restaurant toilets had simply heightened it. It looked like a yellow highlighter had been swept across her face and underneath all the yellow, still visible, were the dark shadows and the spots that she'd been desperately trying to hide.

She pecked Frankie on the cheek and told her that she could bake some cupcakes as a special treat. She still left Frankie unsupervised despite assuring PC Williams that it would never happen again. But Frankie was the sensible one. It was Peggy who should never be left unattended. And the threat of being placed with a foster family seemed to have dissuaded her from dialling 999 again if Peggy was ever late.

She couldn't remember whether Stan had said to go in or to wait for him outside. She'd lost count of the number of times that men had arranged to meet her and then never shown up, so it never really mattered where she waited. He finally arrived at eight fifteen. He apologised for being late, but didn't say what had made him late. She didn't ask. It was far too soon to be questioning his whereabouts.

He introduced himself as 'a table for two for Brown' and Philippe, their waiter, showed them to their table. *Brown*, like acorns and paper bags – she must remember that, she reminded herself. Sylvia had always stressed the importance of paying close attention to what people say because 'only then will they truly warm to you and confide in you'.

It made Peggy wonder what exactly it was that she needed to hear and why *she* should be the keeper of everybody's secrets. She had enough of her own to catalogue and archive. Unfortunately, she'd since discovered that what people said was not always what they meant. 'I'll call you' rarely meant 'I'll call you'. It tended to translate as 'I wouldn't call you if you were the last person on earth'. And until now, nobody but Ed had ever warmed to her. And nobody but Stan had ever called her.

When asked 'What wine will sir be drinking this evening?' Stan said that the house wine would be fine. He didn't consult Peggy, who was actually quite the aficionado when it came to wine, and while other women might have been offended by such misogynistic disregard, she admired his ability to make snap decisions. She unfolded her triptych menu and studied the extensive list of options. She felt fazed by the choice available. Jessica had been right: sometimes you can have too much choice. And surely it was better to cook a few things well than a variety of things badly.

She wasn't particularly hungry, Frankie was cooking her so many meals that she was still digesting the previous one as she was slicing into the next, even though she'd expressly told her that she was only to cook at the weekend. After several indecisive minutes she eventually settled on duck à l'orange. She'd never had duck before (Frankie preferred to cook meat that couldn't be anatomically linked to a specific animal – brisket, stewing steak, corned beef . . .). Of course the inclusion of Grand Marnier was an added incentive. Stan ordered a sirloin steak, medium rare.

He was still wearing his coat, a leather jacket that he never unzipped. Peggy wondered if he wasn't planning on staying long since he hadn't ordered a starter either. Perhaps he would get an urgent telephone call sometime during the meal and make his excuses, leaving her to pay the bill. People do that sometimes, Sylvia had said – flee at the earliest opportunity. In Peggy's experience things rarely got that far.

A yawning silence too sizeable to bridge then followed, Stan staring intently at the dessert board on the wall, Peggy glancing awkwardly around the room.

Perhaps he was shy. Perhaps dining with strangers wasn't something that he usually did. His eyes gave little away. They were dark and hooded.

Finally, encouraged by the wine, she said, 'It's lovely here. Have you been before?'

'No, never.'

'Well, that makes two of us then.'

Stan was staring at her lips. Had she put on too much lipstick? Was it too red? Talking seemed to have drawn attention to it.

'You look nice,' he told her.

She remembered Trina saying the same thing, remembered how that evening had ended. She blushed, she hoped endearingly, but she could feel tiny pearls of perspiration forming and no doubt glistening on her forehead. Her face must have been the colour of her lipstick.

When their meals finally arrived conversation thankfully became a little less tense. They were at least able to comment on the acceptability of each other's menu choices. 'How's the duck?', 'Delicious. How about the steak?', 'Good'. And no urgent telephone calls were received, which was fortunate, because Peggy only had three pounds and forty-two pence in her purse, she discovered later, as she was studying her mustard complexion in the restaurant toilet mirror.

And he was actually quite funny. At one point during the meal a champagne cork landed in a woman's cleavage and, as she was fishing it out with her Union Jack-painted fingernails, he whispered, 'What a corker.' Well, perhaps you had to be there. It didn't sound particularly funny on paper and she *had* actually been 'a corker', which kind of negated the punch line and made it seem like he'd rather have been sitting opposite her, but still. It was a start.

Until they opened the restaurant door to leave and the stifling silence that had afflicted the beginning of the evening regrettably returned to impede the end of it, the cold night air splashing over them like a bucket of sobering ice-cold water. They mostly walked in silence, Peggy replaying their dialogue, scene by scene, course by course, inside her head. And then at the roundabout at the end of the high street he left her to walk home alone.

She could feel the inkling of a headache in her temples. What was she doing wrong? She wished she knew. She wished that somebody would spell it out for her. She was tired of having to interpret another person's sentences, tired of being left to examine the structure of them alone. When she got home she collected a bottle of Merlot from the wine rack, rinsed a glass and, biting into a chocolate cupcake, sat watching repeats of *Terry and June*.

That awkward first date did however become a string of awkward second, third and fourth dates, despite Peggy's reservations, and the two of them soon settled into a companionable rhythm, not quite a ballroom foxtrot, more a stepping-on-each-other's-toes West Coast Swing. *PeggyandStan*. Not exactly *Terry and June*. But she liked how it sounded pushed together like that, like a film, a soundtrack, one never mentioned without the other, both part of the same breath.

She introduced him to Sylvia a few weeks later, which she regretted almost immediately when Sylvia labelled him 'a shifty bastard' when he went over to the bar to order their drinks.

'What do you mean, Syl?'

'What I say. There's something sneaky about him.'

Peggy tried to forget what Sylvia had said, but the words took hold of her by the collar and wouldn't loosen their grip. Yet to his face Sylvia couldn't have been sweeter, which made Peggy wonder if she was pretending to dislike him because she was interested in him herself.

She began noting every flirtatious comment and every clandestine glance that passed between them, which was exhausting and fed into her paranoia even further until she wasn't sure whether what she was hearing or seeing was a truthful representation of her suspicions or simply her own imaginings roaming wild. It became difficult to differentiate the two.

Frankie wasn't revealed until several months later. Sylvia's behaviour had unsettled Peggy and she couldn't risk any more setbacks, but she couldn't hide her daughter from him forever, as much as she would have liked to, or trust Sylvia not to mention her first. A couple of times she'd asked about Frankie and Peggy had had to steer the conversation in another direction, towards a different Frankie.

Before he'd even removed his coat, and before she could change her mind, she'd nudged Frankie towards him like a surprise gift. His face fell immediately. Neither of them had spoken about having children or not having children, wanting children or not wanting children, and Peggy could barely breathe she was so nervous.

'This is Frankie, my daughter,' she announced brightly, ignoring his obvious disappointment that it wasn't a Rolex watch or the keys to an Aston Martin. 'She's no trouble at all. I hardly know she's there most of the time. She makes a delicious lasagne.'

The lasagne comment seemed to startle Frankie. Her eyes flew open. But it *was* the first time that Peggy had ever said anything remotely complimentary about her cooking. And she'd meant it, even though she'd only managed to eat a few mouthfuls.

'Pleased to meet you,' Stan said, not seeming pleased at all, but by then Peggy had lost interest in analysing everybody's body language in microscopic detail and didn't always trust her own evaluation of a situation any more, so she chose to ignore her initial misgivings as Frankie shrugged and, to her horror, extended her burnt hand. She never introduced herself with the burnt one.

Nonetheless, despite the sudden appearance of a nine-year-old child with a severely burnt hand, a selection of men's shirts began to appear in Peggy's wardrobe a few days later, although as well as a rail of Ben Sherman shirts he also started bringing a different Stan back with him, a Stan who belittled her, a Stan who punched her in the mouth and chipped a front tooth after an argument about cucumber (it should be peeled and thinly sliced – 'What are you, a fucking animal?') a Stan who she saw whispering in Frankie's ear.

They'd moved away from each other a little too quickly and Peggy had wondered why they were whispering, or had it been Stan who'd been whispering, she couldn't be sure, but she couldn't pluck any possible hypotheses from inside her head. Her left eye was sore and she'd been unable to fully conceal the lilac and black streaks running round it like a racetrack. Frankie had looked at her oddly when she'd said that a door had slammed in her face, but she couldn't remember which door under interrogation. Had it been Stan? Frankie wondered. Of course not, why on earth would Stan hit her?

And then Frankie would bring Ed up, vomit him all over the living-room carpet and Peggy could never clean him up quickly enough. She would tell her to be quiet, ask her about lemon drizzle cake and lichgates, but Stan would insist on hearing all about the 'infamous Ed', that's what he always called him, as if he was a villainous historical character, like Jesse James or Al Capone, and the London fog inside her head would get denser still. And in the morning there would be another mauve bruise to disguise; so many shades of purple, so many racetracks.

She would retrieve Frankie's gifts from the dustbin, wondering why she kept throwing them away, but she didn't know what she was supposed to be looking at, what it all meant. She knew that she needed to drink less and to stop self-medicating, but Stan was always refilling her glass and replenishing her pills, rendering her helpless. And Sylvia never called any more. She vaguely remembered telling her never to call again, but she didn't know why she would say such a thing. Sylvia was her friend.

And then he told her that he'd be working away for a while. She was inconsolable. What would she do without him? She pleaded with him not to go. He called her 'pathetic', threw her onto the bed, and, pressing his elbow into her windpipe with such force that it still hurt to swallow days later, he explained how easy it would be to break each of her vertebrae, one by one.

Peggy wanted to ring Sylvia, but they were no longer speaking. She wanted to pack a suitcase and leave, but she couldn't move her legs. All she could do was hope that the mulberry bruises had faded by the time he returned and a roadmap of new ones hadn't been inflicted by the time he left.

Chapter Nineteen

The Thomas Crown Affair

1987

Following people in a wheelchair was certainly not easy, but over the past three years Stella had become surprisingly skilled at emergency braking and three-point turns now that she wasn't driving any more. She was able to manoeuvre her wheelchair into a less confrontational position with ease whenever Peggy or Frankie Appleton turned their heads. It would have been a far easier task if she'd been able to walk, but of course she wouldn't have been in this position if she'd been able to walk, stalking the Appletons day and night (was it still called stalking if you were in a wheelchair?) and wondering why it was her child who'd died while Frankie skipped merrily along the pavement, grazing garden gates with her fingers.

Sometimes she would see Ed's profile when Frankie turned to talk to her mother and her heart would tighten into a clenched fist that was difficult to loosen again without first applying lotion. But even though they occasionally glanced round, they never seemed at all curious as to why a woman in a wheelchair was always following them because although she was more noticeable than ever before, she'd never felt more invisible, more ignored or stepped around. Peggy Appleton didn't even seem to recognise her now that she wasn't serving drinks behind a bar. And if she wasn't being openly ignored, she was being pitied and given acres of room, which was somehow much worse.

Frankie was running her hand over a gate hinge while her mother impatiently tried to hurry her along. It was one of the rare occasions when the two of them were together. Frankie was usually holding the hand of another woman and Peggy was usually luring various men back to the house – although recently there appeared to be only one man – which made following them especially difficult because Stella could never decide which one of them to follow, which one of them she hated most.

While Frankie continued to scrutinise the gate hinge, Stella pretended to search for coins in her purse. When she looked up, she noticed Billy on the other side of the road walking away from her. Even he didn't appear to have seen her.

And he would have enjoyed watching her pursuit of the Appletons. Recently, he'd started accusing her of leaving gas rings on and not locking the front door when she went out. And he seemed to be hiding things. Every day there were more and more things that she couldn't find when she was sure that she'd put them safely away. She wished that she'd known how devious he was before she married him. Or maybe he'd only become devious since marrying her.

He certainly wasn't deeply religious or disapproved of divorce, so the only explanation for his reluctance to leave was presumably a desire to be like his father, who'd also stayed married to a woman who he only spoke to when absolutely necessary. It seemed that there were a lot of unhappily married people in the world, too lazy or too terrified to do anything about it. Stella wondered which category she fell into.

Since he'd suggested at her last hospital appointment that her symptoms might be psychosomatic ('it's not uncommon in cases of severe trauma, according to several peer-reviewed sources that I've consulted'), her doctor was now similarly baffled by her unresponsive limbs when he could see no logical reason why they shouldn't function normally. She wasn't sure when Billy had suddenly become an expert on unexplained paralysis and the ongoing challenges of caring for a 'disabled' wife. He could barely look at her most days.

But even she now thought that maybe she could walk if she really tried – seeds of doubt in her own mind. Maybe she just didn't want to, because nothing can be your fault if you have no muscle mass, if you can't walk towards it. And she now spent an hour each day trying to stand up, trying to wiggle a toe or flex an ankle, trying to prove them all right, now that there was apparently no evidence of the brainstem or spinal-cord damage that they'd initially diagnosed.

Some days she stared at her legs so intently that it looked like one of her toes *was* moving by itself or a calf muscle was twitching and then she blinked and her toe was flat and motionless on the footrest of the wheelchair, not raised a millimetre, not moving at all, the only moving part of her the perspiration dripping from her forehead and the tears in her eyes. And she was annoyed with herself for blinking and annoyed with Billy for sowing those seeds of doubt.

She started arguments with him just to feel less static, less invisible, but it was frustrating not being able to follow him upstairs without activating the stair-lift or chase after him once he'd slammed the front door shut, so she let him blacken her name and label her a fraud and threaten to burn the house down to 'see if that gets you up out of that fucking wheelchair'. She only wished her medical team could hear him ranting.

It was unusual for Billy not to have spotted her. Perhaps he wasn't used to her being outdoors where the walls were wider and the ceilings higher, although she didn't want him to think that she was following *him*. She didn't care where he went. He'd been even more arrogant and conceited since somebody had told him that he was the image of Steve McQueen in *The Thomas Crown Affair*. She really didn't see it, although she did concede that he'd be more than capable of orchestrating a bank heist.

She watched him turn the corner and disappear. Perhaps he had seen her and was pretending that he hadn't. She wished she could walk and was pretending that she couldn't.

As Peggy was forcibly peeling Frankie away from the gate, Stella gazed at Frankie's hand. It wasn't enough. More of her should be burnt. Should she set fire to their house, to the rest of her? Would killing them both be enough – *both eyes, Mummy*? Suddenly they both started running towards a waiting bus and Stella had to unexpectedly abandon her pursuit, resentful that her own legs couldn't sprint towards bus stops and hop on board waiting buses so she could continue her surveillance.

Not wanting to go home in case Billy was there, she turned left along Parklands Grove towards the library, a stately Georgian building with ten ridiculously steep entrance steps and no disabled access. She had to wait for a customer to inform one of the library assistants that she'd like to use the delivery entrance. It was either that or contact them by telephone and she didn't have ten pence.

She was then wheeled round to a side door hidden behind a wall of ivy and nettles and hurried inside as if it was a drug-trafficking operation and she was the drug being trafficked. One of the nettles stung her hand as she brushed past it and then she was squashed into the service lift with a trolley of paperbacks and a box of large-print novels on her lap. It was utterly degrading and surely a violation of her human rights.

Perhaps she should contact the local council, campaign for improved wheelchair access in public buildings. She'd embraced religion and that hadn't worked. Perhaps she should try something more proactive, something where the person in charge was flesh and blood and you could shake their hand. Perhaps she could attend committee meetings and rallies (ramps allowing) raising disability discrimination awareness. She was tired of rolling herself along empty pavements. And anything would be better than running over Billy's toes for her own personal enjoyment.

Once she'd been relieved of the box of large-print novels she settled in a quiet corner of the library and began to explore accidental fires, unexplained deaths, murders made to look like suicides and untraceable poisons (they wouldn't want to allow her access at all if they knew what she was researching). She then browsed the reference section for information on the Disabled Persons Act. She hadn't discounted something happening to Peggy and/or Frankie Appleton – although it was looking increasingly more likely that it would be Peggy – while she was in the process of drafting letters to her local MP.

Ed wouldn't want Stella to hurt his one remaining child. It was enough that she'd killed one of his daughters. And it looked like Frankie had been hurt enough. *She's my sister*, she heard Marie say. She wondered why she would ever have wanted to cover her ears and block out the sound of her own daughter. *I've always wanted a sister, Mummy. Can she live with us? I promise not to bite Annabelle Carter again and I'll remember to brush my teeth.* It was like the sun coming out, hearing Marie's voice again. She had been starting to forget the sound of her, although she'd rather not have been reminded about the biting incident. Annabelle's mother had threatened legal action, calling Marie 'feral'. She should air Marie's bedroom, wash her Sleeping Beauty duvet and pillowcase and her Snow White pyjamas. Frankie would need something to sleep in.

In her more lucid and rational moments she knew that she'd turned into something vengeful and bloodthirsty and slightly deranged, but she couldn't seem to let Marie's death go unanswered, no matter how hard she tried. Whenever Geoff was there she would try to wipe her mind clean so that he couldn't hear her thoughts, but she could never reach every membrane, never remove every stain, and she worried that he knew what she was planning to do, knew that she spent hours outside Peggy Appleton's house wondering how to kill her. And that it would have been so much easier if she'd been able to walk.

Fortunately for Peggy, Stella became temporarily consumed by something other than plotting her death when on 16 August a

Northwest Airlines flight crashed shortly after take-off, killing 148 of its 149 passengers. The sole survivor was a four-year-old girl, who Stella was desperate to locate, convinced that it was Marie and that they'd misreported her age and that this time she'd survived. It had happened the way that it was supposed to.

She began compiling a scrapbook of eyewitness statements, cockpit voice-recorder transcripts and crash-scene photographs gathered from newspaper articles, television documentaries and radio bulletins, hoping to see Marie's face or hear her voice (she hadn't spoken to Stella since informing her that Frankie was not to wear her Snow White pyjamas and she was to wash the Bambi ones instead), but there was no sign of her and no mention of the hospital where she'd been taken to or what injuries, if any, she'd sustained. Stella just knew that she was alive. And she was so grateful she was alive that for a while it didn't matter that the scrapbook was incomplete or that she couldn't walk or that Peggy Appleton wasn't dead yet.

But then she began to feel guilty because she wasn't by her daughter's bedside and yet nobody would tell her where she was. The airline hung up when she told them that she was her mother, as did all the hospitals in the Detroit area. She called the news desks of several national newspapers but they didn't appear to know where Marie was being treated either. Her identity was being closely guarded. But I'm her mother, surely I'm allowed to see her, she told the news editor of the *Daily Mirror*, who told her that pretending to be the child's mother was shameful. How dare you, she snapped, the child we buried is not my daughter and I *will* find the right number this time, with or without your help.

There was a light on in an upstairs bedroom. Stella could see silhouettes moving across the curtains, hear loud music playing. Or maybe it was raised voices. She stared at the window as intently as she stared at her toes, willing them to move.

'Remember, Mummy, both eyes, left *and* right.'

Chapter Twenty

The Yellow Tooth River

1989

Trevor Smith was smoking a cigarette by the incinerator, watching snowflakes land on car bonnets, when Frankie arrived back from The Peking Surprise. She'd been helping Vinnie's sister, Joanne, chop green peppers, oyster mushrooms and Spanish onions and coat fourteen slices of white bread with sesame seeds for an all-you-can-eat buffet for twenty-seven businessmen later that evening.

He was wearing his customary dark glasses and a new accessory, a cowboy hat. He tilted the brim of the hat as she walked past, like Clint Eastwood in *A Fistful of Dollars*. She almost expected him to say, 'Howdy, ma'am,' but he didn't say anything. He never said anything. She'd forgotten what his voice sounded like. It seemed that he didn't much care for conversation unless Betty Rivers was there. And she hadn't seen Betty Rivers since she'd thanked her for finding her contact lens.

Frankie had asked her if she could still see through it now that it was scratched and she'd told her that it had felt like her eye was being sliced open with a razorblade when she'd tried to put it in so she was managing with just the one for now. Frankie had been disappointed. It had taken ages to find it.

She wanted to turn round and ask Trevor Smith if he'd seen her, but she didn't really want him to start talking again because she wasn't sure what he might say. And he'd probably already turned round to stare at her because that's what he always did. Turn round and stare. She wondered whether to knock on the door of Betty Rivers' flat; she'd overheard a customer in the pharmacy say that baking soda was good for removing scratches on glass (perhaps Betty could use it on her discoloured teeth as well), but she already had Stan to look for, she really didn't have time to search for anybody else. And she'd probably turn up eventually. You couldn't hide in a block of flats forever. There was nowhere to go, no privacy at all.

Her grandmother was pacing back and forth when Frankie opened the door. She said that she'd lost something, but when Frankie asked her what she'd lost, she couldn't remember. It was like watching her mother opening cupboard drawers, looking for things that she could never find, although her grandmother did sometimes find the things that she was looking for: her pension book in the cutlery drawer, her door key in the fridge next to the butter, nothing where it should be. Frankie always had to check the rubbish before putting it out.

'Shall I help you look?' Frankie asked her.

'If you're not busy,' her grandmother replied.

And so they both searched the flat, neither of them knowing what it was that they were actually looking for.

'Have you seen Betty Rivers recently?' Frankie asked her grandmother as she was lifting up sofa cushions.

There was 60p down the side of the sofa and presenting the coins to her grandmother, she asked her if this was what she was looking for.

'I don't think so,' she told Frankie, repeatedly turning the light switch on and off.

Frankie wasn't sure whether she was referring to Betty Rivers or the 60p, and was about to ask when her grandmother said, 'Frankie, there you are. I'll put the kettle on,' and it all went back to normal.

She slipped the 60p into her pocket. Gavin had invited her to a portrait exhibition on 3 March and, although he'd said that it was his treat, she'd been saving up her pocket money to pay him back. The tickets had cost thirty pounds each. She was meeting him in the alleyway behind Jessops after school, the venue an hour's drive away. She hoped that he was going to keep his word, unlike Linda, although she still hadn't decided what she was going to tell her grandmother. Like Linda, Gavin had told her not to mention it to anyone 'in case they get the wrong idea', but the exhibition seemed like a good idea.

When Ellie rang later, she wanted to tell her about the photography exhibition – she didn't think that Gavin would mind her telling her best friend – but Ellie was in floods of tears. They didn't ring each very often because Ellie didn't like talking on telephones. They made her nervous and she always forgot to mention the thing that was most important, the reason why she'd called in the first place. She preferred to write. That way she could carefully construct her sentences and not leave anything out. And nobody could accuse her of not mentioning something. She took her correspondence very seriously.

But this was apparently too urgent to be left sitting in a postbox overnight. During one of her parents' many arguments, her father had stormed out of the house, trapping one of Ringo Starr's paws in the back door and breaking it and they'd had to take him to the vet which had cost 'an arm and a(nother) leg', her father having to sell his van to pay for treatment; although he'd been planning to sell it anyway – he'd already replaced the carpet and had the interior professionally cleaned.

Frankie remembered the perspiration from his moustache dripping onto his collar, the long silences, the hidden smile. Through hiccupping sobs, Ellie told her that the argument had been about Frankie's mother and Frankie asked her why they'd been arguing about her mother, but Ellie didn't know. She'd already moved on to Ringo Starr's bandaged paw and how much she hated her father and could Frankie please ask her grandmother if they could live with her?

The flat isn't much bigger than a cardboard box and, Vixen, the pit bull from Flat 26 will probably break Ringo Starr's other paws and then eat him for breakfast, Frankie teased, hoping to make Ellie laugh, but Ellie didn't appreciate her poorly judged attempt at humour and immediately began to wail, choking on the fizzy orange that she was sipping. Frankie said that of course he wouldn't eat him for breakfast (he *would* probably break his other paws, though), she was sure that they would be great friends, and she would definitely ask her grandmother if they could make some room.

Frankie could hear Mrs Barlow in the background telling Ellie to say goodbye, but she just kept crying and sniffing. Eventually, Mrs Barlow came on the line. I'm sorry about this, Frankie. She refuses to stop crying. How are you? Have you settled in? I'm fine, Mrs Barlow. Well, there's absolutely no need to worry about Ringo Starr. His injury isn't nearly as bad as Ellie would have you believe. His paw is a little bruised, that's all. You know how she likes to exaggerate. You must visit. I'll make peach scones and we'll eat them in the garden if it isn't raining. Ellie, go and wipe your nose and please calm down. I have to go. Take care, Frankie. I hope to see you soon.

When she called Ellie back a few days later to apologise for upsetting her, Ellie told her that Ringo Starr's paw was fully healed and they were all going to Norfolk for the weekend. I can't wait, she said. It's going to be spectacular. And, according to the hotel brochure, gourmet treats and dog chew toys are provided for your dog free of charge. Isn't that the best thing ever? I asked if you could come too, but Mum says maybe next time. It didn't look like there were going to be peach scones in the garden after all, and Frankie had been looking forward to sitting on Mrs Barlow's decking with a warm scone. She was being pushed towards the outer edges of people's lives and there was nothing she could do about it. They were both starting to forget her.

Vinnie appeared on the stairwell that same afternoon as she was heading to Betty Rivers' flat.

'How was Birmingham?'

'Dad had a massive argument with one of his cousins and we ended up staying in a hotel. I took these from the hotel room. I thought you might like them.'

He reached into his pocket and pulled out some headed hotel notepaper (The Britannia Hotel, Birmingham) and a matching pencil. She thanked him and zipped them into her rucksack.

'What are you up to?'

'I'm trying to find Betty Rivers. Nobody's seen her.'

'Perhaps she's on holiday.'

'That's what I'm going to find out.'

'I'll come with you if you like.'

Frankie knocked loudly on the door of Flat 31 but there was no answer and there was no letterbox to peer through, so she couldn't see if there was anyone inside. She noticed that the '3' on the door was a little loose. One of the screws had come out. She searched for it on the floor but couldn't see it. She pulled out her notepad and noted it down. Betty Rivers seemed to be in the habit of losing things. And now she was lost.

'Maybe she's just nipped out. I'm sure she's fine.'

'We don't know that. When you live alone it can take months for somebody to miss you. And where's the screw? It should be here. Did you know that Trevor Smith now wears a cowboy hat?'

'So?'

'Don't you think it's strange that he's replaced Betty Rivers with a cowboy hat?'

'Not really.'

'Well, I do. When people change their appearance it means that other things have changed as well, and you're not always part of those other changes.'

She regretted not finishing the sketch of Betty that she'd started, all those yellow teeth that she should have coloured in. She'd have to finish it from memory later. She didn't want a half-finished sketch to be the reason for her disappearance, only half of her existing. And she imagined some of the residents not knowing what she looked like, having no idea who was living a few floors above or below them. Perhaps you really could disappear in a crowded place.

'I wanted to tell her about baking soda. Did you hear that?'

'Hear what?'

She pressed an ear against the door.

'It sounded like a voice.'

'I didn't hear anything.'

'Does Clyde have spare keys?'

'I don't think so. And anyway, you can't go into people's homes without their permission.'

'I suppose. When did you last see her?'

'I don't know . . . a couple of weeks ago, maybe.'

'Did you know she wears contact lenses?'

'Does she?'

'I found the one that fell out. How do they fall out?'

'I've no idea. Perhaps they just do.'

'Should we call the police?'

'Because she lost a contact lens and isn't answering the door? What if she just doesn't want to speak to anyone or is visiting family or has just gone shopping? People like their privacy. They like hiding away sometimes. Why do you always think the worst?'

Because the worst often happens, she thought.

'I'll have to ask Trevor Smith then.'

He was the last person that she wanted to ask.

Vinnie sighed as he carried on down the stairs.

'If you want to come round later, we've rented *Crocodile Dundee II*.'

'What time later?'

'About eight.'

'Okay.'

'Happy sleuthing.'

She was too distracted to respond.

Two days later she spotted Trevor Smith coming out of the lift with a suitcase. It looked heavy. Annoyingly, he wasn't wearing the cowboy hat that she'd spent all morning drawing.

'Are you going somewhere?' she asked him.

He looked shocked, even glancing round to see if she was talking to someone else.

And then he nodded.

She was going to ask him where, but then decided that it didn't matter where. That wasn't why she'd stopped him.

'I was wondering if you'd seen Betty Rivers recently. I've been looking for her. I have something important to tell her.'

He seemed unsure how to answer. She wondered if he could talk. She really couldn't remember him ever saying anything. Had Betty Rivers introduced them both?

'No, I'm afraid not.'

He rolled his 'r's like Miss Curtis, who was Scottish.

'Do you have any idea where she might be?'

'No.'

'Where's your hat?'

'My hat?'

'Your cowboy hat.'

'At home.'

'Will you be wearing it in future?'

'Maybe. Why?'

'No reason.'

Should she remove the hat from the sketch? She wasn't sure. It was all very inconvenient. She liked consistency. You'd never find anyone if they kept changing their appearance.

'Is that everything?'

'I suppose so, for now. When you do see Betty Rivers, will you tell her that Frankie's looking for her?'

He nodded and walked towards his car. He seemed in a hurry, which was unusual as his eyes generally liked to linger on you for a lot longer. Still, she'd have to revisit Betty Rivers later. Stan was her current priority and she'd already decided that she would need to return to the scene of the crime, the place where it all began.

Chapter Twenty-One

Three Hail Marys

1987

Each time she heard footsteps along the path Peggy would run from room to room clearing things away and ushering Frankie upstairs if she was there, which was increasingly less often now that Stan was in her life. He would often arrive unannounced, hoping to catch her unawares, his hands momentarily full of things other than her, half a dozen half-price wilting red roses or a box of soon-to-expire Milk Tray that he'd purchased from a nearby petrol station.

And he would expect her to be waiting, even though she never knew when to expect him. It was like having to solve a riddle without any instructions. And on the one occasion when she hadn't been waiting (which could just as easily have been the thirteenth or twenty-second occasion), she'd suffered concussion. She was like a prisoner on death row, knowing that they were going to die but not knowing exactly when.

And each time he returned, his temper would be worse. He didn't even need a reason any more (or no reason that she understood) and he never apologised. He was never sorry like some people were, never promised that things would be different, that he could change. Because he couldn't.

She wondered if her right shoulder was fractured; she could barely lift it, the bloom of a bruise on her upper arm a hideous shade of Highland Thistle with a hint of Tuscan Yellow running through it. Her skin was the colour of a Dulux paint chart. Earlier that week he'd pinned her against the bathroom sink and hit her repeatedly with the shower head because she'd forgotten to switch on the immersion heater (she hadn't, and she wondered why he'd had to convince himself that she had).

She went into the bathroom and rubbed on some ointment, which made the bruise look worse, like a luminous lemon sorbet cycling towards her collarbone.

'His eyes are too close together' and 'He doesn't say much, does he?' Sylvia had once said when she'd stopped pretending to like him (or had already slept with him and decided that Peggy was welcome to him), just loud enough for him to hear, and Peggy was starting to notice that his eyes *were* too close together and it was his fists that seemed to do most of the talking, always looking for another part of her to argue with.

And she was now expected to wait for his telephone calls as well as his visits. He rang her several times a day until by the eighth or ninth call there was nothing left to say that hadn't already been said (or not said), just an angry static silence sitting between them. And whatever she did (or didn't) say was never what he wanted to hear. Tonight he'd said that he'd ring her at seven, but of course seven became eight and eight became nine and he still hadn't called. She now had to spend hours waiting for him to call. There was no escape. He seemed able to control her movements from any distance and in any manner.

She wondered if he was planning a surprise visit instead (his preferred type of visit) and stayed awake all night just in case, but he never called and he never arrived. She wondered if she'd misheard him and spent much of the following day on the bottom stair staring at the telephone, willing it to ring so that she could get on with her life, so that she could eat in the kitchen, while at the same time wishing that he'd never ring again.

At five fifteen the telephone rang. She reached it on the third ring (anything after that was 'inexcusable'). 'I'm here.'

'Mrs Appleton? It's Miss Sandown from Woodlands Primary School. I'm calling to see if you'll be attending the school's parents' evening tonight. We haven't seen you in a while and we're keen to discuss Frankie's progress with you. There'll be a display of some of the pupils' artwork in the foyer and some light refreshments, and we'd be thrilled to see you.'

Peggy didn't think that Frankie would be especially thrilled. When she'd once mentioned wanting to talk to the headmistress about some comments that had been made about her hand, Frankie had begged her not to, but she'd wondered at the time whether she was more concerned about her meeting the headmistress than any comments about her hand. Often, letters from the school would be pureed into a fine paste at the bottom of Frankie's waste bin, but she would notice the occasional heading that hadn't been torn into small enough pieces – 'recorder concert', 'award ceremony' – and she could only assume that Frankie was embarrassed by her, didn't want anyone to know that she was Peggy Appleton's daughter.

Fortunately, Frankie was at the Barlows so she didn't need her approval (or disapproval). Perhaps Stan wouldn't call either and he'd never know that she'd vacated the bottom stair and left the house without permission. She told Miss Sandown that she was on her way and went upstairs to get changed.

At the school gates she began to have second thoughts. She wasn't used to social situations any more and unsurprisingly she didn't recognise any of the other parents. Although she hadn't had anything to drink because she wanted to make a good impression, she wished that she had. She didn't know how to speak to people otherwise. And if Frankie found out that she'd been to her school she'd be furious. She'd spread butter on the soles of Stan's boots the last time she'd been upset about something and he'd skidded along the icy path, hitting his head on a rusty nail that was sticking out of the gate. Incensed, he'd broken Peggy's wrist with a hammer.

Just as she was about to turn round and go home, Barbara Barlow called to her from the school steps, Don Barlow standing behind her like an afterthought, although he moved away as Peggy approached, lighting up a cigarette by a parked car, leaving her alone with Barbara.

'I didn't know you were coming this evening,' Barbara said.

'No, it was very last minute.'

'Frankie *will* be pleased that you're showing such an interest.'

Peggy ignored the underlying (or was it blatant?) sarcasm. You couldn't always tell with Barbara. She sounded genuine, but her words implied otherwise.

'I'd really appreciate you not telling her that you've seen me. She prefers to keep her school and home life separate.'

Barbara was about to say something (probably something about Peggy being the last person to know what Frankie liked), but stopped herself, choosing another sentence instead.

'My sister's looking after the girls tonight while we discuss them in private. Ellie always demands to hear all the gory details when we get back, though.'

The irony wasn't lost on Peggy that Frankie was supposedly under Barbara's care this evening but was now being looked after by another person who wasn't her. Anybody who wasn't her own mother would suffice, it appeared. And what did Barbara mean by 'discuss *them*'? Was Barbara planning to discuss Frankie too – would teachers do that, would they tell a mother about another child's progress? – but she just nodded and went inside. Barbara no doubt already knew everything that there was to know about Frankie and the dates of any upcoming concerts or award ceremonies.

Miss Sandown was in the assembly hall behind one of the desks, her name handwritten on a piece of card (although somebody had added a 't' after the 'S' which seemed to have gone unnoticed). She was speaking to a smartly dressed couple in pinstripes and ruffles so Peggy grabbed a Viennese whirl from one of the trestle tables and went to view the artwork in the foyer while she waited.

A banner above the display read 'A Few of Our Favourite Things' in balloon-shaped lettering and there were paintings of a sleeping poodle, a pink sequinned ballgown, a Batman costume, a silver scooter and in the far corner, a small sketch with no splash of colour in it at all, more noticeable *because* of the lack of colour, but Peggy could tell even at that distance that it was her.

She felt a tear prick her eye. It didn't show any of the flawed parts of her: the bruises, the blotches, the broken blood vessel in her right eye that never seemed to heal, the things that she saw every morning; it was like she'd been wiped clean and redrawn. If only it was that simple. It was signed in the bottom right-hand corner but didn't have a title. When she returned to the hall to discuss Frankie's progress, Miss Sandown asked if she'd seen it.

'Isn't it wonderful? She wouldn't say who it was and of course that doesn't matter, we don't need to label everything, but Ellie told me that it was you and of course now that I've seen you I can see how extraordinary the sketch is.'

Miss Sandown continued with her effusive praise: 'She's such a pleasure to teach, academically and artistically gifted, punctual and principled,' and so many other accolades that Peggy didn't know what to do with that she left them on the desk. Frankie should have been the one hearing these things. She was everything that Peggy wasn't. Peggy wasn't even the person in the sketch. She wished that Frankie had drawn a more truthful version of her so that everybody could see what she was really like. She didn't want to be sugar-coated and condensed into a more acceptable format.

Before she left, she pointed out the amendment to Miss Sandown's name.

Miss Sandown shrugged. 'It's probably Mr Peters. I was recently made deputy head and he doesn't approve of the decision. He doesn't take rejection well.'

Does anyone, thought Peggy?

She noticed Barbara and Don having an animated conversation with a janitor outside the staff toilets as she was leaving. Unfortunately, Barbara spotted her as she was trying to slip by unnoticed and asked her if she'd like a lift home. It felt impolite to refuse, even though she'd planned to have a drink in The Red Lion to steady her nerves; her hands were still shaking.

In the car Barbara barely took a breath. She was one of those people who never stopped talking, who seemed afraid of a pause. Some people believe it to be a form of anxiety, but Peggy thought that Barbara just liked the sound of her own voice, liked to be the chief spokesperson in every conversation. Peggy was still thinking about Frankie's sketch and Miss Sandown's praise, but she did unintentionally catch the odd remark, which mostly seemed to concern Ellie. She talked about Ellie *a lot*; too much, really. It was a lot of pressure for a child to be the only interesting topic of conversation for her mother when she had so much to say. Ellie this and Ellie that. It made Peggy wonder what sort of life Ellie would get to live, if she wasn't allowed her own secrets, wasn't allowed to be more than her mother's expectations of her.

Don glanced at her a few times in the rear-view mirror and seemed to be raising an occasional eyebrow, but she might have been mistaken. You thought that he was thinking the same as you, but you'd discover later that he wasn't at all and it would seem like an embarrassing misunderstanding, like he didn't get the joke. And he only had a range of about four facial expressions, although 'Smiling Don' was his default, a person who you could never imagine doing anything remotely underhand.

He offered to let Barbara out at the end of their street but she said that she was happy to stay until 'the bitter end'. I don't see you very often any more, she added, and it's always nice to catch up. There it was again, the eyebrow. Unless that's what his eyebrows did nowadays. It had been a while since she'd been in a vehicle with him, sometimes not even going anywhere, just sitting in the van with the engine running.

He gave everybody lifts, it wasn't just her, stopping the van and whistling you over if there wasn't anyone else in the passenger seat as he drove from one job to the next. It was like having a free neighbourhood taxi service. Everybody knew Don Barlow. Everybody wanted him to pull over. Sometimes it was as if he knew exactly where you'd be, like you were the one doing him a favour by being exactly where you should be when he was driving past.

Although you could never open the passenger door from the inside, which for a man whose job it was to repair things (he was a qualified plumber and electrician) had been left like that for an unusually long time. There's a knack to it, he would always say, as if it didn't matter that you couldn't get out. But these days he tended to pass by without stopping, even if the passenger seat was empty. He preferred younger passengers nowadays.

He'd been the chauffeur in their relationship too, three Hail Marys and two Our Fathers conveniently cleansing him of guilt one minute and then paralysing panic and the search for atonement the next because 'someone might see us and tell Barbara'. She told him that he couldn't keep using the Catholic faith to absolve himself of his sins. You can't keep making the same mistakes and be repeatedly forgiven for those mistakes. You have to accept some responsibility, some punishment. But apparently you could.

Barbara was still trying to talk to her as they were pulling away, rolling down the car window to tell her that they were thinking about getting a dog. Frankie would never come home if the Barlows got a dog.

'I know we'd planned that Frankie stay with you until Wednesday, but I'll be picking her up from school tomorrow,' Peggy suddenly announced, praying that Stan wouldn't be there to object. She felt the need to reassert her status. She was Frankie's mother, not Barbara Barlow. She felt the need to reassert her status. S*he* was Frankie's mother, not Barbara Barlow.

But Barbara tried to dissuade her – 'Stop the car, Don' – telling her that Frankie had a maths test the following day that she needed to study for and wouldn't it be better not to disrupt her routine. Frankie's routine was continually disrupted. So much so that she could probably do her homework while balancing on one leg in the middle of the high street in rush hour traffic and still get an 'A'.

'She can study at home,' Peggy replied, wondering how Barbara was able to focus solely on Ellie if Frankie was there, how she must struggle to say everything that she wanted to say about her – unless Frankie's presence just meant that there were more people to listen.

Barbara rolled up the car window, clearly exasperated, and Peggy began walking towards the front door. When she opened the door Stan was standing at the bottom of the stairs. And it wouldn't matter that Barbara had been in the car as well. She'd been with another man and she'd missed his call.

Chapter Twenty-Two

The Butcher's Shop Doorway

1989

Frankie wished that there was somewhere nearby where she could mourn her mother, somewhere where she could sit and talk to her as if she was still alive, instead of writing letters to her that she would never read. The book on bereavement that she'd stolen from John Menzies had suggested she write her thoughts down, 'a restorative and therapeutic exercise designed to bring contentment and understanding', but for Frankie, saying things out loud felt more significant somehow, more powerful, like screaming in the middle of Dixons. You didn't have to labour over the words, correcting the grammar. You could just let it all out in one breath.

She wondered why people weren't allowed to bury loved ones in their back gardens like they did their pets. Wouldn't it be more practical to have them close by so that you could tend to the weeds and polish the headstone at midnight in your dressing gown if you wanted to? Although differentiating between official burials and homicides might be problematic, she supposed, if a murder victim has been buried beneath the garden patio by a murderous homeowner, which was apparently quite common, according to the news. And she wouldn't want just anybody opening the front gate to pay their respects. Of course, she currently didn't have access to a garden, just a small patch of yellow grass next to an incinerator, so for her it was purely speculative.

She wondered how different their lives would have been if her mother had never met Stan. He wasn't like the rest, the ones who ran down the stairs three at a time and couldn't wait to leave. He started leaving behind shirts and slippers, aftershave that smelled like vinegar, an atmosphere. She noticed the way that he sometimes looked at her mother, a look that stabbed at her flesh like an ice pick, changing the structure of her, shaping her into something else, something much smaller and darker. But her mother never seemed to notice that she was changing, shrinking. She just saw false glimmers of what she'd once had with Frankie's father.

She'd spied on many of her mother's male 'friends' over the years from the top of the stairs, but they never stayed long enough to become an issue, to warrant further examination closer to. She suspected that Stan, however, would be taking the stairs more slowly, his features becoming far more defined. He'd visibly recoiled when he first met her, his eyes unsmiling. Frankie un-smiled too, took the smile right off her face with a damp flannel.

She studied his stapled eyes, so narrow that it was difficult to see what colour they were (black, she guessed) or what their intent might be (evil, most definitely), and grudgingly raised her hand, the burnt one, as her mother continued to inch her forward with the back of her hand. Stan tried not to touch it, looked at it as if it might be contagious. If only it had been and then he wouldn't have been able to take her place beside her mother on the sofa.

Frankie wondered if her mother was blind. She wanted to raise her good hand and ask her mother how many fingers she was holding up. Instead, she was ordered to 'be nice' and to 'behave', and because she loved her mother, that's what she did (mostly) while she patiently waited for him to tire of her. They all did eventually, even though she'd met Bob Dylan and been a promising gymnast and was fluent in Spanish, but nobody would know these things about her because she kept them to herself, choosing to limit her talents to putting on lipstick, gin-drinking and being easy to bruise instead.

One Sunday afternoon when Frankie was in the kitchen peeling potatoes for a potato gratin, she heard the flip-flop sound of his slippers. Her mother's slippers made no sound at all. She drifted around the house as if she was three inches above the ground. Frankie tried to ignore him; she didn't have to be polite to him if her mother wasn't there, she didn't have to acknowledge him at all, but he began to follow her like a shadow, his breath as hot as the gas ring that she'd just turned on for the ratatouille.

As he leaned in closer her mother appeared in the doorway, the air unmoved by her presence. He quickly moved away when he saw her and, although he'd made Frankie feel flustered, she didn't understand why he'd moved away so quickly, why her mother wasn't supposed to see them together. Her mother said nothing, but she glared at Frankie as if it was her fault that he was in the kitchen with her when he should have been in the bedroom with her mother.

When she asked Marcel about it later he told her that people with beards couldn't be trusted and that they often hid their real thoughts behind their facial hair, and for a short while afterwards Stan maintained a more civilised distance while she was the one slipping in and out of rooms trying to avoid him, until a few weeks before her mother's death when she noticed how hot his breath was again.

She remembered Marcel's warning whenever she saw Stan staring at her, his eyes narrowed like he was guessing her weight, but she couldn't see *any* thoughts behind his beard. It was far too thick. And she didn't want to tell him how much she did weigh so that he'd stop staring at her in case he wasn't estimating her weight at all, but doing something much worse. At least Mr Barlow smiled when he stared at her.

Whenever he stayed overnight she would balance a chair against the bedroom doorknob because there was no lock, but she rarely slept. She would listen to them arguing, her mother's drunken accusations drifting across the landing, holding Frankie accountable too. She could hear things being thrown, heard them shatter and break, then muffled screams and doors slamming. And sometimes she thought that she could hear somebody breathing outside her bedroom door, a hand hovering over the doorknob.

She was too scared to open the door to see if there actually was anybody there and she'd sit in bed shivering, mainly because of the broken electric heater but also because of all the things she couldn't see, could only imagine, which was somehow much worse. She would clutch her knees tightly to her chest and press a pillow over her ears until it was over, when there would be an abrupt silence and she would think that one of them, hopefully Stan, was dead.

The next morning he'd be gone and her mother's eyes would be swollen and as red as her lipstick. She would have bruises on her arms and legs shaped like the continents in Frankie's *New World Atlas*, new bruises covering old bruises, new worlds hiding old worlds. And Frankie wanted to lock the front door so that he never came back. But he always came back, as if he'd started something that he needed to finish. And besides, as well as a new beard to hide behind, he now had a key.

She watched her mother turn into a person who she didn't recognise any more, a person with bald patches on their scalp and marbles for eyes. It was as if all the blood had been drained out of her and smeared across her lips. None of the others had ever done that to her, they'd left her more or less whole, but Stan tore strips of her flesh away each time he came. She was like the multicoloured plastic curtain in a butcher's shop doorway, Frankie now a choice that she would never make. *It's him or me.* It would always be him, particularly as he'd resorted to telling lies about Frankie, accusing her of things that she hadn't even done (or hadn't intended to do).

The damning evidence included:

A stolen bracelet (not in fact stolen, but given to her by her mother, who then later denied giving it to her).

Ten pounds taken from a wallet (his wallet and not taken, he'd said that she could have it).

Swearing (guilty as charged, but that was because he'd accused her of stealing).

Stealing his penknife (also guilty – she'd been scratching swear words on the fence in the backyard with it, combining both the alleged stealing and the swearing).

Violence (kicking a chair leg and a human shin – his, not accidentally) on two separate occasions.

Spreading butter on his boots (true) in the hope that he skidded along the icy paving slabs into the path of an oncoming lorry (her mother had a bandage on her wrist the next day and Frankie wondered why she was the one with the bandage on her wrist and not Stan).

And, finally, the decapitation and limb removal of a toy rabbit (most definitely true).

She visited Sylvia in the hope that she might be able to help. Aidan, her son, answered the door in his '*F**k the world and everyone in it*' T-shirt, tripped Frankie up as she walked past and then singed her burnt hand with the stub of the cigarette that he was holding. Even though Frankie's hand was coated in several layers of puckered skin, most of which didn't feel like they belonged to her and made her feel as if she was carrying around the scars of other people as well as her own, it still hurt.

Sylvia was sympathetic, although apparently Peggy wasn't speaking to her any more. They'd had 'words'. She didn't say which words. She poured Frankie a glass of lemonade and listened to her concerns, but sadly there was nothing that she was willing or able to do. Peggy makes her own choices now, sweetheart, she told her. You'd do well to distance yourself. Why don't you see if you can stay with Ellie permanently?

As much as Frankie liked staying at Ellie's – she was there most weekends and sometimes during the week now as well – she couldn't possibly leave her mother alone with Stan. Her mother couldn't see that he was the Devil, that the letter 'a' was the only thing between him and Satan.

She reread the last letter that she'd written to her mother.

Dear Mum,

I had a camera for Christmas, which must have cost Grandma most of her pension. I've told her that I'll cut back on stationery and Mr Kipling Cherry Bakewells as a thank you. I've already started to take photographs. Yesterday, I took one of an old man putting out his dustbin. Although I'd initially planned not to take photographs of people without their permission, I've now decided that it looks far more natural when they're not posing, so if they're in the distance and in profile then it's acceptable.

Gavin from Jessops has been teaching me about depth of field and composition. We drink hot chocolate in the storeroom and read old editions of Practical Photography. *He says that good photography requires practice and patience (like the balance beam) and he's taking me to a photography exhibition in March. We're stopping off for pizza on the way back.*

I wish that you weren't so far away. Sometimes I want to say things out loud, like how I wish Stan was dead instead of you (the butter on his boots didn't work) and how when I asked Sylvia to help she said that you were old enough to make your own decisions. She didn't know that your eyes were made of glass and that you had bald patches, but as we don't have a garden to bury you in I expect that I'd have had to keep your ashes on a shelf and I'm not sure how I'd feel about that, about you not being whole any more and being an ornament, and all of you being burnt.

And you really did give me that bracelet. I wasn't lying. You'd forgotten it was my birthday (again!) and the shops were closed, so you wrapped it in toilet paper and hid it inside the book that I was reading, Countryside Gates and Stiles *by Robert James, and then we went to The Best Plaice in Town and had fish, chips and mushy peas.*

I'm planning to catch a train home next week, although I've told Grandma that I'm going on a school field trip. I tell both Big and Small Lies now. But it's the only way to get to the truth, unless I'm talking to Vinnie of course. I'd rather say nothing at all than lie to him.

I'm still mostly vegetarian, although I do eat fish fingers sometimes. I pretend that it's mashed potato. I haven't felt like cooking since you died and Grandma's repertoire is somewhat limited (she often fills saucepans and then forgets about them and we spend ages scrubbing the bottom of pans with wire wool), but at least I can concentrate on other more pressing matters. Once I've located Stan, I shall be looking for Betty Rivers. She's been missing for six days now.

F.

P.S. I hope you've forgiven me for the Bad Thing I did.

Frankie hadn't wanted to write that last sentence down or explain what it was that she'd actually done, but it needed to be addressed because it had been the third worst day of her life after one, finding her mother's dead body and two, suffering third-degree burns.

It was the day she'd discovered a positive pregnancy test inside a tampon box.

Over the years she'd discovered various things hidden in unusual places, concealed inside the wrong packaging, ten packets of what looked like talcum powder inside the album sleeve of Pink Floyd's *Wish You Were Here*, something that smelled like mouthwash in a silver and blue glass decanter, a pair of West Midlands police issue handcuffs in a Fox's biscuit tin, and eight hundred pounds in rolled-up banknotes inside two pillowcases in the airing cupboard when her mother had insisted that she didn't have money for 'fucking icing sugar'.

Containers in their house didn't necessarily contain what they were supposed to contain, or what was written on the label. So it shouldn't have been a complete surprise to find something other than a tampon inside a tampon box. Except that this time it was.

Frankie removed the pregnancy test from its counterfeit box and studied the thin blue line running down the middle of it like a vein, carefully unfolding the instructions wrapped around it. *Positive.* Her mother was pregnant. The world went pin-drop quiet. Her good hand started to sweat. She sat on the toilet seat and tried to process what her mother being pregnant might mean, but all she saw was Stan staring back at her in the bathroom mirror, smiling. And she could see his smile clearly even through his beard, that's how pleased he was. He would never leave if her mother was pregnant. He would always be part of their lives.

And her mother couldn't look after another child; she couldn't look after the one she already had. Maybe Frankie would be expected to care for it and she was too young to be a mother, didn't want to be a mother, *ever*. Hadn't she already told her mother that she was never getting married? She pictured the child having a hand as deformed as her own, a child having Stan as a father. She couldn't possibly let either of those things happen.

She placed the 'bad news' back inside the tampon box, closed the bathroom cabinet door and went downstairs. Her mother was sitting at the kitchen table idly leafing through an old *Vogue* magazine that she'd stolen from the doctor's surgery. She didn't look pregnant.

Perhaps Frankie *would* be expected to move in with the Barlows permanently, like Sylvia had suggested, so that her mother could start again, and this child have a father. Among the rollercoaster of emotions that she was feeling, the one that she seemed to be feeling most acutely was jealousy. She was jealous of this child that hadn't yet been born, a child that would know its father, a child that her mother might even love, closer to her at that moment than Frankie would ever be.

She went back upstairs and closed the bedroom door. When she looked out of the bedroom window, even the sky was an envious apple green. Her burnt hand suddenly felt sore. All the hurt and anguish seemed to gather there in the dead tissue, a saucer of damaged nerve cells catching every drop of pain. She wished that it would drip onto the floor and seep into the carpet fibres so that she could stamp on it.

When she went into the bathroom for an ibuprofen, something on the back of the box – which hadn't been opened so did, unusually, seem to contain what it claimed – caught her eye: *consult a doctor before taking if less than six months pregnant.* Perhaps there was still time.

She couldn't rely on her mother taking the pills that Stan tipped into her open palm like Tic Tacs in the hope that they might do the task for her, because she seemed to be depending on them less and less. She'd even managed to distract him on a couple of occasions and spit them back out again when he wasn't looking. And, annoyingly, a glass of red wine would now last her all evening. She really seemed to want this baby, which made the erasing of it all the more urgent.

She briefly wondered if Stan might punch and kick the child out of her, so that she wouldn't have to stoop to such desperate measures herself, but she hated herself for thinking that it was acceptable to push her mother down the stairs or attack her with a wrench.

So she settled on the original, far less aggressive strategy and began stirring two crushed ibuprofen tablets into her mother's morning coffee, sweetening it with sugar. What choice did she have? Her mother couldn't possibly have Stan's child. She couldn't possibly stretch her arms around a third person. They just weren't long enough. Of course she never imagined that she would come home one day to find her mother hanging from the bedroom ceiling and not, as she'd hoped, having stomach cramps because she was losing the baby.

She should have devised a more foolproof plan for killing Stan instead and then her mother would still be alive.

When one of the police officers offered to get Frankie a glass of water, she'd wanted to explain then. She'd wanted to tell her everything, but the words sat in the pit of her stomach like stones on a riverbed and they wouldn't float to the surface. They wouldn't speak up. Nobody would understand why she'd done it. *Was it some form of revenge?* She looked at her hand, hesitated. No, of course not, it was an accident. I loved her. I did what I thought was best for everyone.

And surely they'd discover the truth for themselves, isn't that what autopsies were for? But they never did. They never suspected either of them, never even performed an autopsy. 'Suicide' was the official cause of death. There was no mention of a second casualty.

Frankie tried not to dwell on the third worst day of her life, but sometimes she couldn't help it. Something would stir in the corner of the room, something still waiting to be born. And it would all come flooding back. And she would wonder if a person could be convicted of killing something that wasn't able to breathe on its own.

She wished that she'd never discovered the pregnancy test. Or that she'd walked away and left it sitting in its substitute box in the bathroom cabinet undisturbed. She wished that she'd given her mother unsweetened coffee instead. She wished for so many things, but mostly she wished that her mother was still alive, her charm bracelet getting caught in her hair (always the genie's lamp and the platform boot because they had the sharpest edges), her painted nails flicking crumbs off the hospital bed sheet, a smile as big as the desert on her face.

But, like Stan, she was a murderer too. And sometimes it took the police years to solve cases, to find evidence, to elicit confessions. And sometimes like those riverbed stones the truth never surfaced at all. She wondered what it might be like to be locked inside a prison cell and didn't think that she'd like it at all. The lack of space would surely terrify her and not being able to open a door or a window, having nowhere for her breaths to go, she couldn't imagine how traumatic that would be – although not having to speak to anyone would be something of a relief. She was tired of explaining herself and defending her actions, even if it was only to Marcel, who sometimes stood at the foot of the bed late at night, frowning at her. He refused to tell her how he'd found her new address.

On the day of the school field trip she took a less direct route than usual to the train station to avoid being seen, along the canal towpath. She'd meticulously mapped out the journey the evening before in her notepad, noting down the relevant points of interest – the modern flats with floor-to-ceiling double-glazed sliding doors and steel balconies spacious enough to accommodate garden furniture (which all looked unoccupied, except at night when there'd be an eerily solitary sixth-floor light on), the abandoned flour mill dating back to 1890 with a wasp's nest outside one of the windows (you could hear them buzzing), the family of geese by the bow of the *Morning Mist*, a moored narrowboat selling tea and coffee, and finally the nine concrete steps to the left of the lock leading up to several soot-stained terraced streets that were almost identical. *Almost.*

What the hand-drawn map, and her notes, hadn't documented was the bevelled Persian pink rosewood gate with peony fretwork panelling on the corner of Mansfield Row and then, as she got closer, the two silver hinges glittering like tiaras. A black iron latch sat like a tick across the slats, the gateposts margins for further comment, 'Excellent Work', 'Congratulations'. Who would have thought that she'd find the perfect gate here along a littered and polluted street?

She took seventeen photographs of it from several different angles and then continued walking, wondering if she had time to call into Jessops on the way (as usual she was far too early) – Gavin was expecting a delivery of reflectors and light stands. The streets were deserted except for a white van that braked a few yards ahead of her on Victoria Parade but, just as she was preparing to say no, she didn't know where Sunderland or Plymouth were, or wherever else it was that they wanted to go, it sped away again. She wondered if it was Mr Barlow's van being driven by somebody else. Or Mr Barlow in a different white van.

A few minutes later another vehicle, or maybe the same vehicle, was slowing down beside her. She remembered seeing a car that was the same colour as Stan's parked across the road a little further back, remembered the leopard-print seat covers and the scratches. He could be driving a different car now of course, maybe even a white van. But whatever car he was currently driving she hoped that today was the day that she finally saw his stapled eyes staring back at her and reached for her camera.

Chapter Twenty-Three

The Wingspan of a Hawk

1989

Stella's running. Slowly at first, and then faster, much faster, gathering more and more pace, across cattle grids and zebra crossings, over footbridges and along bridle paths, her stride lengthening, her breaths quickening, her arms pointing forwards like arrows, displacing the air, slicing through the landscape. She doesn't know if she's running towards something or away from it.

'Mummy, Mummy, wait for me,' she hears, somewhere behind her.

She glances back. 'Marie?'

'Mummy, Mummy, I'm over here.'

Now the voice is in front of her.

She turns back around. There's no one there.

'Please run faster, Mummy, or you'll never catch me.'

'I'm running as fast as I can.'

'You're not trying,' the voice tells her.

'I am trying, I promise.'

'It's okay, Mummy, I believe you. I'll wait for you by that tree over there.'

She can't see any tree.

'Which tree?'

'You know which tree. That tree, the tree that nobody else can see.'

Her feet finally find a rhythm, one, two, one, two, her heart racing ahead of her, three, four, five, six, her breath trying to catch up, in, out, in, out.

And just as she thinks that she knows where the tree might be, she wakes up.

For one brief joyous moment Marie is still alive. The first few seconds after waking when she has yet to realise that Marie is dead are seconds that she wishes would never end. But they always do. And reliving her daughter's death over and over again is a torment that she can never outrun.

Her armpits were sticky with sweat and she was breathless. She felt as if she'd actually been running, which was impossible considering she couldn't even stand up. A cruel irony that she could sprint like Linford Christie in her dreams (or, more usually, her nightmares) and yet in reality her useless legs felt nothing, did nothing. How could she not stand up? Why wouldn't her legs hold her?

She threw back the duvet and willed her legs to move independently, but they didn't even spasm, didn't even pretend to be listening. She turned her head to the left, she wanted Billy to witness just how much effort she was making, but he wasn't there, the bed sheet stretched as tightly as his lips. It didn't look like he was ever there. And he seldom was.

They'd been living different lives in different parts of the same house for so long now, and since moving into a two-bedroom bungalow, the silence between them had been even more noticeable; there was no escaping it, no going upstairs to get away from it. Everything was levelled off and sandpapered down, too many right angles and not enough alcoves, too many tightropes and not enough bridges. A sigh in the kitchen could be heard in the bathroom. A nasty remark not meant to be heard at all could be heard from the garden. The house was too small. It underlined everything, put everything in capital letters, made everything that much harder to ignore.

Billy hadn't even been there when they (she) moved in. It was Geoff who hired the van, Geoff who filled four skips with all the things that she didn't want any more, which was practically everything. Her peach wedding dress had spilled out of one of the black bin liners, clinging to the back of the fourth skip as it turned right at the bottom of the road, already homesick. But Stella never wanted to see any of it ever again. She wasn't foolish enough to think that discarding it all was anything other than downsizing. It wasn't a new beginning, a fresh start. It was merely a continuation of what had come before but with less clutter and in more compact surroundings.

When she'd thrown Marie's new shoes into one of the skips because she couldn't bear to look at them, Geoff had fished them back out again. One day she might be able to look at them, might need to look at them, he told her, and then she would be devastated that they weren't there. Didn't he know that she was devastated because they were there and because Marie's feet weren't inside them?

He carefully wrapped them in tissue paper and placed them inside a cardboard box, as if they'd belonged to his dead child, along with the first tooth that she ever lost, her christening shawl, a red smudge with legs on a piece of card that was supposed to be a ladybird (*What do you call male ladybirds, Mummy?*), three photo albums and a diamond ring that Stella had one day hoped to give her. He stored the box in the loft where she couldn't reach it.

She knew that it was there though, just above her, those tiny shiny shoes tap dancing across the ceiling, that red smudge of blood dripping down on her while she slept. And all those photographs, all those memories of a five-year-old girl who would never be six.

Billy wasn't interested in hanging picture frames or the tiny tooth in a cardboard box in the loft. He didn't care where the screwdriver was or that the drawers were all empty (Stella had given up all hope of ever finding the numerical digits necessary to turn everything the right way round again). And he wasn't even jealous that Geoff was spending so much time there. In fact, he encouraged it. Call Geoff, he likes DIY. Call Geoff, he doesn't hate you as much as I do. She would catch Billy sometimes watching her from another room – rooms led into other rooms quickly here, a gaze could reach you in seconds – and she could sense his spite from several feet away, sometimes from behind two closed doors.

And recently she'd started to notice the smaller things too, probably because the bigger things were too easy to see: his lack of appetite ('I've already eaten'), the numerous bottles of aftershave on the bathroom shelf, the late-night whispering into the telephone (a 'wrong number' lasting twenty minutes; didn't he know that they were all wrong numbers?), the front door opening and closing as he disappeared for unaccounted-for periods of time, things that suggested there were other women, or maybe just the one woman – a woman who could walk, a woman who hadn't killed her own child.

She decided to confront him, even though she really didn't care what he was doing or who he was doing it with. She just felt like being quarrelsome, felt like pushing him further and further away until he didn't come home at all, until it was too far for him to travel. But it was followed by a stony 'it's none of your fucking business' silence and a more stringent containment of his hours and his possessions. A cheap shot, really. It's easy to keep things from the disabled, to place them on a higher shelf, to hide them in the loft.

The previous Christmas Eve he'd called her from a payphone to say that he'd be late, might not even make it back for Christmas. She was surprised that he'd bothered to call at all, unless his reason for calling was simply to establish an alibi: 'I was on the phone to my wife at the time. Check with the telephone company.' An argument sat simmering behind the suffocating silence and the heavy sighs. Fortunately, the pips beeped and the argument was put on hold, to be continued, like a two-part BBC Two costume drama.

He eventually arrived home on New Year's Eve, armed with excuses that he did not normally extend the courtesy of providing: the car had broken down in the middle of nowhere so he'd had to book into a nearby bed and breakfast and wait for a local repair garage to reopen. 'That'll teach me to let my AA breakdown cover lapse'. As she was studying a tiny bite mark on the back of his right hand, letting his lies wash over her, he handed her a rectangular box wrapped in a sheet of plain white paper. She wondered why he was giving her a pen and a sheet of paper – was it to keep a record of all these lies that he kept weaving? – but it was a silver bracelet. He fastened it to her wrist and she remembered wondering who it had belonged to and why he was fastening it around *her* wrist. She wasn't sure that she wanted to be his alibi when she had no idea what it was that he'd been doing.

She reached for her wheelchair and lifted herself into it. As she passed the spare bedroom she wondered whether to suggest he move his things in there. As much as he liked to disturb her by switching on all the lights and making as much noise as possible when he arrived home late, she was sure that he'd have preferred her to be in another room, or better still another galaxy, unless his only solace these days was lying awake beside her so that he'd be the first to notice when she did finally stop breathing.

She filled the kettle and crossed the hallway into the living room, a grid of rooms that she traversed in the same order each morning: bedroom, bathroom, kitchen, living room, kitchen, living room. There were tyre marks on the carpet where she'd rolled her wheelchair from one specially adapted wheelchair-accessible room into another. It was like the scene of an accident, the brakes failing over and over again.

The television was on and Billy was sitting in the armchair nearest the window. He would normally have left for work by now, or if it was the weekend he would have left for some other reason – fishing (although he owned no fishing tackle) or golf (although he owned no golf clubs), if he felt like divulging his (made-up) plans for the day.

'Do you want a coffee?'

He didn't answer, didn't even snort, which he was prone to do when she had the audacity to think that their lives were in any way normal and they could do something as ordinary as drink coffee.

'Are you watching this?'

He still didn't answer.

'I'll switch it off then.'

She'd spent so many years watching daytime television that she couldn't watch it any more, couldn't bear to hear the opening chords of *This Morning*. It was as if you'd failed somehow and it was aimed primarily at mothers and students, and she was neither. It certainly hadn't been easy extricating herself from its hooded presence in the corner of the room, the shallow breaths and the itchy palms as programmes started without her. She would have to force herself to do other things instead. Sometimes those other things involved staring at a magnolia wall or a smear on a windowpane or opening a book that she never read, but at least it was something else.

Billy still hadn't stirred. She hoped that he wasn't planning to spend the entire day watching television. There were several smears on the bay window that she was hoping to scrutinise later. She heard him slump forward as she was switching off the television, resisting the urge to find out more about a missing man who'd lived in a shed for nearly twenty years. She reversed and sat him back up. His skin was cold, one of his eyes half open as if he was still trying to keep an eye on her. She felt for a pulse, but couldn't find one. It looked like he'd been dead for some time, afforded the privilege of dying peacefully in his sleep, although he may well have been in agony. She wore earplugs most nights. He'd certainly be annoyed that he was dead and she wasn't.

Two out of three of them dead – was this her fault too? Was she being punished for the other secret that she'd carried alone all these years, a secret that was so heavy that she would have liked to have put it down occasionally or let someone else carry it for her? She studied him for a while. If she'd been able to draw she might even have sketched him, death drawing as opposed to life drawing. She doubted it would catch on.

She hadn't realised how old he looked, wrinkled in so many unusual places, behind his ears, below his nostrils, around his ankles, the skin bunched up like socks. He was in need of a good iron, although the iron had been thrown into one of the skips along with the ironing board, so she couldn't have removed the creases even if she'd wanted to. He certainly didn't look like Steve McQueen now. She looked away. She didn't think that he'd approve of her examining him in such detail when she'd barely been able to look at him when he'd been alive, so she wheeled herself back into the kitchen and made some toast.

She didn't contact anyone for eight hours, instead letting him enjoy a full day of 'golf'. If Marie hadn't died perhaps they'd have joined him.

At six o'clock she dialled 999. If her father had still been alive his car would have been pulling into the driveway as the clock on the mantelpiece chimed six. She often wondered if he sat waiting at the bottom of the road with the engine running if he was ever early.

Weekends are for spending time with family, was the only contractual clause he'd insisted upon when accepting the position of a pharmaceutical sales representative. Until the remains of a seven-year-old boy were found on the marsh. Medication had been found in the boy's system, medication that her father had access to, medication that had unfortunately been in the boot of his car at the time of his arrest.

Two police officers had stood on the porch step and asked her mother if they could speak to Mr Evans. Stella was sitting on the bottom stair, away from prying eyes, nervously wiping her fingers on her shorts. They'd been preparing tea, washing and readying themselves for their father and her fingers were stained with beetroot juice.

Her mother told them that he was due back at six and they were welcome to wait. Some motoring violation, I expect, her mother whispered to her in the kitchen later. Apparently, she'd noticed a parking ticket on his desk. The two police officers seemed unusually interested in their home (How recently had the front drive been paved? Is the garden shed usually locked?) and its occupants, asking where Gina, her older sister, was when her mother told them that they had two children (she was having a piano lesson next door but one).

Gina had repeatedly been warned to be on time; she often struggled with the 6 p.m. Friday curfew (she didn't like curfews, claiming they were draconian and militant). 'If I can get back from

Swindon by six o'clock then I'm sure you can walk the 200 yards from Mrs Hancock's front door in time to greet me.' If she was late today she would forfeit three months' pocket money. (See, militant!)

Finally, having ripped apart the foundations of the entire property and learned as much as they could about the Evans family, the two police officers walked over to the sofa, repositioned the cushions and sat with their helmets on their knees, declining offers of tea, squash and 'anything stronger'. The younger police officer seemed mesmerised by Stella's beetroot-coloured fingers. She sat on her hands and tried to hide them.

At five fifty-five Stella went upstairs to wash her hands again, scrubbing at her flesh furiously with a Brillo pad, but the burgundy blotches stubbornly refused to go white. She was worried that they'd think it was blood on her hands. When she went back downstairs her mother was unsuccessfully trying to glean further information on the reason for their presence, but the officers were refusing to elaborate.

At six fifteen her mother glanced anxiously at the mantelpiece clock. Gina wasn't back (surprise, surprise) and neither was her husband.

'He's *always* home by six on Fridays. Perhaps there's been an accident. Is that why you're here?'

'We're not at liberty to discuss why we need to speak to your husband, Mrs Evans, but we're unaware of any road traffic accidents.'

At six thirty the back door opened. Her mother breathed a sigh of relief, but it was Gina.

'Where's Dad? I made a special effort to be on time.'

'You're not on time. You're thirty minutes late.'

'Well, I'm more on time than him. Does this mean I still get my pocket money?'

Stella's fingers had never looked redder. She went back upstairs to wash them again and came back down wearing a pair of her mother's gardening gloves.

And then at seven o'clock, exactly one hour late, they heard a car pull into the driveway. Why her father had been so late was never ascertained. He was taken straight to the police station 'to help with their enquiries' and they were never alone with him again.

It's obviously a mistake, her mother insisted, when they formally arrested him, but as the trial progressed, the evidence against him began to mount. His car (or a car that looked like his car) had allegedly been seen parked in a lay-by alongside the northern edge of the marsh on more than one occasion, a witness had observed him talking to a young boy matching the victim's description a few days earlier, and medication was missing from his car.

Her mother refused to believe any of this 'poppycock' as she initially called it, when it had all seemed like a practical joke. 'The man I know did not do this,' she told a journalist who'd waited three weeks for a comment and who then misquoted her and turned him into a man who would do this. But what if he was a man who her mother didn't know, a man who she had never known? And they did only see him at weekends. There was a lot of him that they never saw, weekday pieces of him that were well beyond their reach.

And then as the practical joke that no longer seemed like a practical joke went on it became more serious than 'poppycock', it became a 'witch hunt', even when it transpired that her father was not always where he'd claimed to be, his mileage betraying him. Speeding tickets were produced placing him miles from his alleged destination and his employer confirmed that his sales area was not nearly as extensive as he would have the court believe, but her mother's faith in him never wavered. It was a case of mistaken identity. He was being framed, being made to confess to something that he hadn't done; she'd seen the injuries that he'd sustained while being 'interviewed'. He's not a stupid man. He wouldn't leave a trail of clues, wouldn't do their job for them, she told Stella.

On one particularly overwrought day, her mother had sat down beside her and said, 'I hope to God he's been having an affair and the woman comes forward soon.' It was certainly preferable to the alternative: that her husband had murdered a child. Stella had found her mother rifling through her father's desk twice in the past five days, presumably looking for evidence of this clandestine affair, carefully replacing things as she'd found them, unfolding and refolding sheets of paper, peering under the two Welsh snow globes – one a red dragon, the other a flock of sheep – that he used as paperweights, searching for keys to locked drawers.

Neighbours and friends began to distance themselves. Mrs Hancock was sorry but she couldn't continue with Gina's piano lessons 'under the circumstances'. Gina was thrilled. She said that Dad should get arrested more often. At one point Stella became prone to hysteria and wouldn't stop washing her hands, even though the beetroot stains had gone (it had taken four days and twenty-eight washes under a hot tap). Her doctor prescribed anti-anxiety pills. Her mother lost patience with her 'melodramatics'. How can we display a united front when you insist on howling at every possible opportunity? But she wasn't as accomplished an actress as Gina or her mother at pretending that whatever was happening was happening to somebody else – or, better still, not happening at all.

Her father pleaded not guilty and continued to protest his innocence. Stella wondered what the jurors made of him, this small, thin man in a grey suit, all sharp angles and hazardous protrusions. Auntie Jean had once called him 'a small, small man', as if he had no idea just how small he actually was or that being small could be deemed an insult. He wore thick-rimmed glasses and his hair was neatly parted. He certainly didn't look like a man who could do the things that he was being accused of. Or was his ordinariness the perfect disguise?

While outside the courtroom waiting for the verdict Auntie Jean, who'd spent all morning reading crossword clues out loud – 'gemstone, seven letters', 'the capital of Peru, four letters' – tried to distract Stella further by describing the tattoo of a hawk that she'd seen on a juror's left arm during the trial, but this only made Stella more anxious. She imagined it soaring into the air and attacking her father.

Before taking her seat, her mother had squeezed her hand and told her that justice would prevail, but if it didn't then she was to remain calm and she'd already almost rubbed a hole in her coat sleeve.

The courtroom door suddenly swung open.

'And you find the defendant?' the judge asked.

'Guilty.'

'Rot in hell, you fucking sick bastard!' somebody yelled.

Both she and Auntie Jean stood up and peered through the door just in time to see her mother collapse and her father disappear beneath their feet like a magic trick – so much for remaining calm. But her mother had no doubt assumed that he'd be home as normal on Friday. She couldn't possibly have thought that it would be her fault that a child had been murdered, that even though she only saw her husband at weekends, she should have known that he was a paedophile and a child killer (he strenuously denied being either).

Stella visited twice, the first time with her mother, after he'd been sentenced to life imprisonment.

While her mother discussed possible grounds of appeal, Stella sat rubbing her palms. He looked different when he wasn't wearing a shirt and tie, less like her father, which made it easier, she supposed. He could have been anybody. The second time was without her mother three days after her eighteenth birthday. Her mother wasn't well. He never asked how she was, but he did ask after Gina, who'd changed her name and severed all ties with them so it was anybody's guess how she was.

What do you even say to somebody who you only saw at weekends? Are they different at the weekend? Today was Tuesday. She couldn't remember ever seeing him on a Tuesday. For all they knew her father might have had a second family somewhere, a Monday to Thursday family, where he spent the majority of his time or, worse, had his best times with two less hysterical more punctual children and a woman with impossibly long legs and impossibly high heels, a woman who he would swear doesn't exist until you begin to wonder if it *was* your mother and not this other woman getting out of the car when she was supposed to be in the butcher's. Did they visit too? She left after fifteen minutes.

Ever optimistic of an appeal, her mother contacted the Home Secretary, the Right Honourable James Callaghan, numerous times, but each time he politely declined to intervene, so she decided to run a 'Malcolm Evans is Innocent' campaign from the kitchen table with seven other prison wives who also believed that their husbands were innocent (weren't they all?).

Her father, meanwhile, decided to represent himself. He could read. How difficult could it be? He was questioned about other unsolved cases involving children. It was never enough that he may have killed one child if there was the possibility of more. They were forever scratching at a blistered wound. *They're trying to pin other things on me and I won't be their pincushion. I've already lost nine years of my life.*

A few months later he was beaten to death in the prison yard by a distant relative of the murdered boy. Using the prison gym instead of the library might have equipped him better. Her mother remarried a year and a half later, a recently released inmate who'd been diagnosed with Parkinson's. He'd once killed someone, but now that he had Parkinson's he was considered far less of a threat to society. He can barely hold a pen steady, his probation officer had argued, so wielding a carving knife might prove somewhat challenging. And he was such a thoughtful, softly spoken man that it was hard to imagine him dismembering a woman in his garage.

The charity 'Find Me a Home' collected Billy's belongings a few days later. They even offered to climb into the loft to see if there was anything else that they could relieve her of and threw down a couple of cardboard boxes. She remembered the shoes and the tooth. One of the boxes burst open as it landed and she almost expected Marie to fall out of it with her one tooth and her shiny shoes, but a silver chain, a school blazer and a child's lunchbox flew across the carpet. She didn't recognise any of it and didn't know why it was in the loft. Had the previous owner left it there? Geoff had never mentioned there being other things up there, other cardboard boxes that nobody wanted to look inside.

She unfolded the piece of paper that was in the pocket of the blazer, looking for a name and address. But it was a crayoned drawing of a woman with no hair and a barefoot child standing outside a house with a blue door and no downstairs windows. She couldn't remember Marie drawing it. She placed it back inside the pocket of the blazer and went to find the Sellotape.

Part Three

Saved

Chapter Twenty-Four

Listening to Hear Where You Are

1989

Vinnie was about to knock on Frankie's front door when it flew open.

'I heard footsteps and thought it might be Fiona. She isn't home yet,' Frankie's grandma explained, visibly disappointed that he wasn't Frankie.

Or Fiona. She often called Frankie Fiona. He didn't know why, unless she had a middle name that she'd never mentioned. He never understood why children were given a middle name that was never referred to again. Wasn't a name there to be used? Wasn't that the point? Although people often called you every name but the one you were born with, pet names, pen names, nicknames, insulting names, so none of it really mattered, he supposed. Sometimes people even renamed themselves. He'd never liked Vincent. It was an old person's name. It didn't suit him at all.

'I'm sure she'll be home soon, Mrs Appleton. She's probably taking a photograph of something.'

Frankie was always taking a photograph of something, or someone, pausing mid-conversation to photograph you before you had time to protest. *Click.* She'd even started wearing her camera on a leather strap around her neck for easier access. Having been adamant that she would never take a photograph without a subject's permission, he'd seen her do just that on several separate occasions. She had a number of unflattering shots of him picking his nose and squeezing his spots.

The gate that he'd been hoping to surprise Frankie with was beginning to get heavy, so he balanced it against his left leg.

'Did you see her at school today?'

'No, Mrs Appleton, I haven't seen her all day. I was on a field trip. Lyme Regis.'

'Didn't she go with you? She said she was really looking forward to it.'

'No, she didn't go. I wondered if she might be sick.'

'She was fine when she left this morning. And I've been at my friend Carrie's all day so if the school did ring I would have missed their call. I've tried contacting the school secretary but there's no answer. Perhaps I should telephone the police.'

She left Vinnie and his gate in the doorway while she did just that. He didn't know what to do with the gate. It seemed inappropriate to be standing outside Mrs Appleton's front door with a gate that he'd crafted out of driftwood. He repositioned it against his other leg while he waited. She returned a few minutes later.

'Someone will be here shortly. I'm going to wait for them downstairs.'

'I'll wait with you. I just need to drop this off first.'

She was too distracted to ask him why he was carrying a garden gate and he didn't want to leave it for Frankie in such unusual circumstances. Besides, he wanted to be there when she saw it. He'd spent weeks sourcing materials, Tee hinges, self-closing springs, weatherproof wood stain. He'd even carved Frankie's initials onto the latch and stencilled a Mr Kipling Cherry Bakewell in the left-hand corner of the lower panel (she was obsessed with Mr Kipling Cherry Bakewells).

He'd never realised before that a gate could be anything you wanted it to be, something that you could personalise and put your own creative stamp on. There didn't seem to be any of the legal constraints or red tape that hindered other construction projects. Mr Samson, his woodwork teacher, had let him borrow a spirit level and a plane, and shown him how to hammer in a nail without losing a finger. He'd wanted to have it sandpapered by Christmas, but it had taken far longer than expected. He'd missed several important football matches and an Under-12s skateboarding competition. And now she wasn't even there to see it.

Where was she? And why hadn't she gone on the field trip? When he'd asked her if she was going, she'd quickly changed the subject. Lying didn't come easily to her. When cornered, she would often say nothing at all rather than invent something entirely plausible. His father was never quite so considerate. Vinnie had learned all about 'What Not to Do When Lying' from his father, who was a habitual liar but not a particularly accomplished one.

Perhaps something had happened to her on the way to school. Was Lisa Newman involved? Before boarding the minibus that morning he'd hidden twelve three-week-old prawns inside Lisa's locker as payback for the pink purse incident. Apparently, the locker still smelled fishy hours later, Gary Jacobs ran over to tell him as he was getting off the minibus, even though the offending prawns had been double-wrapped and transferred to the outside bins and the locker disinfected with bleach. The headmaster had told Lisa that there were no spare lockers so she'd have to put up with the smell for now – hang an air freshener in there or something, improvise. She liked drama, didn't she?

Or maybe it had something to do with the school bus driver, whose timekeeping Frankie liked to question. As soon as the bell rang she would sprint onto the school bus, sit in the seat directly behind the driver and repeatedly ask him the time. She kept a log of all his departure times. '*I've already got one boss, I certainly don't need another.*' '*A second pair of eyes can be hugely beneficial.*' Maybe he'd taken her somewhere where she couldn't ask questions, couldn't keep a record of how long it took him to smoke a cigarette (eight minutes) or eat a Twix (four and a half minutes) or flirt with one of his passengers (twelve minutes).

He'd recently stopped answering her, said that he'd no longer be telling her the time and that she would need to buy a watch, but she told him that she'd got a watch, see, it's got Roman numerals and a pink face like you, she just didn't see why they had to wait around in the school car park when everybody was on the bus and he obviously needed to be reminded of that fact. Was his watch working properly? Did it lose time? Is that why he was always late leaving?

He'd ignored her, said that it was protocol and that she should take it up with his boss at the depot if it bothered her that much. He then reached under the seat for his Walkman. She told him that Protocol needed to be informed that it was ridiculous and could she please have the depot address, but he wasn't listening, his headphones already muting the sound of her voice.

In her travel journal she wrote, 'Driver listening to Bon Jovi while driving, highly irregular and potentially hazardous, closer examination of wristwatch necessary, six minutes late leaving today and refusing to say why (NB. Have recently discovered that driver's watch belonged to his grandfather, who was decapitated in World War I, so that might explain the erratic minute hand). Perhaps Protocol will explain further when contacted.' She probably should have added her own name to the journal: 'Person directly behind driver often to blame for late departure. Too many questions asked.'

He was certainly the slowest bus driver that Vinnie had ever encountered, though. He crawled along like he'd never seen a bus timetable before, and he was only twenty-four, Vinnie had once overheard him tell Claire Cole, a fifth-former who apparently didn't wear any knickers. She always wore a pink bra, though. You could see the straps through her school shirt. He would ask Claire Cole where the bus driver lived. She seemed to know a lot about him.

He wondered at what point he'd suddenly decided that something sinister had happened to Frankie, that Lisa Newman or the school bus driver might be responsible for her not being there. She could be miles away. The thought alarmed him, even though he'd earlier been miles away in Lyme Regis, searching for fossils. He wished that her grandma had kept a closer eye on her, stopped her from venturing out alone. She'd now got a taste for it and she didn't know the area like he did, like all the other residents did. They knew how to look after themselves. They knew where they could go, who they could trust, who to question. And it would soon be too dark to see anything, let alone find anything. What on earth could she be photographing in the dark?

A police car finally pulled into the forecourt and Vinnie was grateful for the distraction. He didn't know what to say to Mrs Appleton now that his thoughts had taken a more sombre turn. Unfortunately, it took the two police officers another fifteen minutes to actually emerge from the parked police car and stride slowly towards them. They didn't seem to be in any rush whatsoever, even though it seemed to be a 'rushing' type of situation.

Vinnie turned to Mrs Appleton and tried to reassure her. We'll soon find her now, he told her, but she was already crying. He felt guilty for blaming her for Frankie's absence and for calling Frankie Fiona (he had to correct her twice when she was explaining the situation to the police officers, in case they started looking for someone else). She was too old to be following Frankie around when she would never keep still, had to keep moving to 'stop bad things from happening'.

One of the police officers was particularly overweight and Vinnie wondered how he'd be able to find anyone, he was wheezing just talking to them. They asked a range of questions – what had Frankie been wearing that morning and what time had she left for school and was there anything troubling her? – and the answers were written down in a tiny black notebook that looked like two questions would have filled it. Even when Mrs Appleton couldn't answer a question, they still wrote something down.

They asked Vinnie his name and he told them that he was Vinnie, Frankie's friend, and they seemed satisfied with this response, not bothering to note it down, but you can't always tell. Sometimes they suspect you of something but they don't always tell you straight away. They like to keep you guessing, watch what you do next.

When there'd been a fire at the takeaway they'd seemed very concerned about his dad's well-being and the amount of smoke inhalation that he'd suffered, but then a few days later they charged him with arson so they couldn't have been too concerned.

It was completely dark by the time they'd moved on to a selection of questions that there were no definitive answers to, such as how tall Frankie was (about this high) and whether she might have had a change of clothes with her (possibly). Frankie doesn't have many clothes, but I can't tell if there's anything missing, she told them. It didn't sound as if she knew Frankie at all *or* spent any money on her, which happened a lot around there sadly. Weekly child support was often spent on Panasonic television sets or Sony Walkmans rather than on the actual child. They loved their electrical devices far more.

He did learn that both her parents were dead, though. Frankie rarely mentioned them and he'd wondered if they were still alive so it was useful to receive confirmation that they weren't. The two police officers (PC Brooks and PC Hillman) asked Mrs Appleton if they could search Frankie's bedroom to see if there might be any clues in there as to her possible whereabouts. She nodded, and they followed her back up the staircase (in the time that it had taken for the police car to arrive, the lifts had stopped working, but at least the overweight police officer would be getting fifteen floors' worth of much-needed exercise), Vinnie trailing closely behind. He didn't want to leave until Frankie had been found.

The overweight police officer, or Tubbs as Vinnie had re-christened him (his current favourite detective show was *Miami Vice*), kept glancing across at him as if he was wondering why he was still there. Hadn't he already told them that he was Frankie's friend, that he was fully authorised to be there? He sat on the sofa next to Mrs Appleton while they searched Frankie's room, wondering if they'd written his name down in their notebook and would be arresting him later.

They reappeared clutching a handful of letters that they said would need to be taken away for further analysis. When asked if she might be aware of anything else that could help, something unusual that may have happened in the weeks leading up to her disappearance – an argument perhaps, a frightening incident? – Mrs Appleton told them that Frankie had recently contacted the police. She believes that her mother was murdered and that a man named Sam, no . . . not Sam, Stan – yes, Stan, that's it, killed her. I'm afraid I don't know his surname. He was violent, apparently. The police officer she spoke to investigated her allegation, but found no evidence to suggest that it was anything other than suicide, even though her body was covered in bruises and there was broken glass by the back door.

Vinnie was learning far more about Frankie than he ever had when he'd been in the same room as her. He made a mental note of the third suspect, a man named Stan. Well, he hoped his name was Stan. With Frankie's grandma you couldn't always be sure. Tubbs said that they would try and locate the report after a cursory search of the immediate area had been completed and then he asked for her mother's address and if she knew anyone named Gavin, but she shook her head. Vinnie didn't know any Gavin either.

Mrs Appleton reached for her coat, but they advised her to stay by the telephone in case Frankie or somebody ringing with news of Frankie called. They never said who the 'somebody with news' might be or whether the news would be good or bad. And the 'in case' didn't sound particularly encouraging either. Vinnie wondered if people often didn't come back from wherever they'd been, the news received mostly bad.

While the two police officers were circling the flats, Vinnie ran home to ask his mother and sister to help with the search. His father wasn't in, but he was never any use in a crisis. He had a habit of making things worse by setting them alight. They searched the skateboard park, the Asian supermarket where Frankie would gaze forlornly at the brightly coloured spices – she said that chilli powder was the colour of her mother's lips and paprika the colour of her hair – and up on the common where they could barely see their own hands. He didn't know where else she might be.

Three hours later he was searching the bins behind the flats, which wasn't something that he'd ever thought he would one day be doing, looking for someone, or something belonging to that someone, in other people's rubbish. He was extremely relieved not to find her there, but he wished that she hadn't gone missing in January because it was so much harder to find someone in the dark.

There were now five police cars and several more police officers in the vicinity and residents were being asked to unlock garages, the assumption being that Frankie had never actually left. One of her sweatshirts was pressed against the noses of two police dogs in the hope that they might be able to track her scent. Vinnie wondered whether to mention the owner of the black dog, who Frankie had upset, the one with the hunting knife in his pocket. Vinnie had noticed the glint of metal as the man was snarling at her, although he hadn't told Frankie this, merely suggested that he might have a knife, so it was always best to be cautious. He decided to say nothing. He was sure that she'd be back soon.

He envisioned Barry Michaels in Flat 11 frantically flushing cocaine down the toilet, terrified that the torches and the dogs were for him, which then made him wonder if someone *was* holding her captive inside one of the flats, a fifth suspect who he hadn't yet identified, but he couldn't think who. There were a few suspicious occupants like Trevor Smith who stood outside school playgrounds with bags of gobstoppers, and Leonard Watkins who was always putting bulging black bin liners into the boot of his car, although he worked in refuse so nobody thought anything of it, and several residents had criminal records, but there was nobody who particularly stood out.

As soon as it was light Vinnie joined the rest of the residents gathered in the forecourt. Even Tammy Salt was there on her crutches and she was allergic to the police. She said they brought her out in a rash. But that was probably because she'd found the crutches outside a betting shop and was now fraudulently claiming disability benefit. She said she could smell 'The Filth', as she liked to call the police (often from an open window) from three shop tills away and she'd limped outside to investigate. She was already starting to feel itchy, apparently.

Only last week Vinnie had seen her jogging along the canal towpath with two handbags. She was repeatedly being chased along the high street by bearded security men in uniforms and she could run pretty well for someone with 'limited leg mobility'.

She was regularly sent appointments requesting further medical assessment and follow-up social security reviews which she failed to attend because a) she 'couldn't fucking walk' and b) she didn't have money for buses and taxis. And when they suggested a home visit, she told them that she probably wouldn't be able to walk over to the door to let them in. Some days she could barely get out of bed. Pretending you can't walk is easy, she told Barry Michaels. You just don't walk. What can they do? They can't prove otherwise. You can make up any old shit. Best day of my life finding those crutches. They've been a fucking goldmine.

He heard her quietly murmur, 'Oink, Oink,' behind a police officer's back and push her nostrils into the air.

Vinnie was surprised not to see Stewart Appleton, Frankie's uncle, there. Surely he would want to help find his niece, regardless of his affiliation with Barry Michaels (he was his cocaine supplier). He wondered whether to add Stewart's name to the growing list of suspects, although, according to an article in the November issue of his sister's *True Crime* magazine, the perpetrators of crimes generally liked to 'join search parties and participate in televised interviews', so Frankie's abductor, if she had been abducted, was most likely distributing flyers, handing out biscuits or offering condolences. He decided to keep a close eye on everyone. He still hadn't seen Betty Rivers.

The search party had been divided into four groups and a description of Frankie handed to each group leader. Nobody had a recent photograph. Or even an old photograph. There was no evidence to prove that she'd ever existed. Vinnie had no idea how the groups had been decided or the group leaders selected, but was disappointed that he'd not been given the role of a group leader.

Someone said, 'Remember that she has a burnt hand,' which he found deeply insulting. Why did they think she wore those stripy mittens? Because she wanted to be known as something other than a girl with a burnt hand. But they were trying to make her easier to find, he understood that; make her stand out, be easier to see. Still he couldn't help himself.

'Her hair is light brown and her eyes are green.'

They all turned to look at him and an inappropriately overdressed Nancy Ellis, who'd obviously ignored the 'waterproofs only' memo in favour of orange corduroy trousers, a daffodil-yellow blouse and green clogs, noted it down. As nobody seemed particularly interested in which group Vinnie should join, he decided to follow the group heading up to the common. There was extensive ground to cover up there and his knowledge of the area might prove useful.

Forming rows of twelve they combed the common from left to right and back again like lawnmowers, examining every dropped tissue and every cigarette stub in case it was of evidentiary value, the end of a piece of thread leading them to Frankie.

They stood for a while looking at the pond, wondering if she might have fallen in, but the water was only ankle-high. Vinnie had jumped in after a football once and it had barely reached his calves.

'You can drown in a thimbleful of water,' someone said.

They all ignored him and moved on.

And however solemn their faces might have been, however serious their thoughts, Vinnie still expected to find her. He still expected to see her face, and *in colour*, not in black and white newspaper print (if they ever did find a photograph).

Walking past a police car, he overheard the fat breathless police officer tell a colleague that there'd been nobody at the address they'd been given and it was looking doubtful that she would be found alive. He'd had a bad feeling about it from the start, he said. Vinnie wanted to punch him in the stomach.

But it was as if she'd been swallowed up by a yawn. There were already whispers of a possible connection with the abduction and murder of nine-year-old Charlotte West and the attempted abduction of twelve-year-old Amy Foster, which Vinnie tried not to listen to in their entirety, although he could scarcely avoid the headlines, all presuming the worst, when he went into the newsagent for a Turkish Delight. And he wasn't ready for that yet. It was far too early to be comparing her to dead people. It had only been two days.

He glanced at the driftwood gate that he'd propped against the wardrobe door. Like the niggling thought at the back of his mind ('what if she really is dead?'), he didn't know what to do with it. It was of no practical use to him, or to Frankie's grandma, but he asked Mrs Appleton if she would keep it for him, keep it for Frankie 'in case' she came back. Even he was starting to doubt that she'd ever return. Like the overweight police officer who'd feared the worst from the very beginning, he realised that hope can only last so long.

Chapter Twenty-Five

Face Down, Looking Up

1987

Peggy was lying on the kitchen floor, slowly regaining consciousness. The neighbours on the left side, Graham and Judy Lloyd she thought their names were, had decided to walk round to the back of the house after failing to get an answer at the front. Why on earth they would want to introduce themselves now, after three years, when her head was spinning like a car wheel, Peggy had no idea. Unless they'd come to complain about the noise. That seemed more likely.

She registered their footsteps as they walked along the perimeter of the property, even thought that she could hear them breathing. And then they were peering through the kitchen window at her. She wished that she'd thought to hang blinds or a net curtain at the kitchen window. She really didn't feel like speaking to anybody. She even tried to convince herself that they hadn't actually seen her, the 'if I'm not moving then you can't see me' school of thought, but they were staring straight at her with such a look of horror on their faces that she had no alternative but to scramble to her feet and limp towards the back door in the hope that it wasn't locked from the outside.

The bruising on her ribcage made progress slow and she thought that her right ankle may have been broken. She couldn't put any weight on it. Thankfully, the key was in the door. She clearly looked a fright closer to, so much so that both Graham and Judy took a step back, and the only thing that she could do to make herself look more presentable at such short notice was to scrape back her hair with her fingers. She could feel dried blood on her scalp.

'We just came to give you this letter. It was delivered to us by mistake,' Judy said.

As she was saying it, she must have realised that it was the feeblest of pretexts. They could easily have dropped it through the letterbox, but that obviously wasn't going to give them the information they required.

'Thank you.'

'Is everything all right?' Graham asked.

He looked ready to roll up his shirtsleeves if the answer was no.

'I'm fine. *Really*. I suddenly felt lightheaded and hit the corner of the kitchen table as I fell. I'm so sorry about all the noise last night.'

She thought it best to address the issue head-on like her head had supposedly addressed the corner of the kitchen table. She wondered if they could smell alcohol on her breath.

'We were going to call the police—' Judy began.

'Not now, Judy – can't you see she's bleeding? She needs to go to hospital. A doctor should take a look at her,' Graham interjected.

They were discussing her as if she wasn't there. And why would anybody want to take a look at her in this condition, she wondered? She was beginning to wish that she was back on the kitchen floor, concussed and undisturbed, somewhere quiet and peaceful, where it didn't matter if her head was bleeding and her ankle was broken. A few years earlier she would have jumped at the offer of a lift to hospital, but not now, not when there were so many things wrong with her. But they wouldn't let her close the door and go back inside.

At the hospital a young Indian doctor, Doctor Patel, examined her. Her left eye was virtually sealed shut and her top lip felt four times its usual size. He obligingly gave her a comprehensive list of her ailments that read like the menu on the door of the local Chinese takeaway. Two cracked ribs, one ruptured spleen (this one didn't sound particularly appetising), two black eyes, one swollen lip, one torn tendon, 'And a partridge in a pear tree,' she wanted to add, but didn't because she felt like crying and it wasn't Christmas. She hoped that he hadn't missed anything. Strangely, the thing that hurt most, her ankle, was fine.

'I think we'll keep you in overnight for observation, Mrs . . .'

'Appleton.'

'See if we can't get to the bottom of these fainting episodes.'

He may as well have used air quotes for the term 'fainting episodes' because he was clearly dubious. Peggy rang Ellie's mother Barbara to ask if Frankie could stay a few more days while she was in hospital having 'routine tests'. She told her that she wasn't allowed visitors. She didn't want anybody else to see her like this.

She heard Barbara breathe a sigh of relief. She told her to wish Frankie luck in her maths test and hung up.

As she lay on a metal trolley in a hospital corridor waiting for a vacant bed, she wondered how she'd managed to acquire all the trappings of a marriage without an actual marriage proposal, an H. Samuel 'it's definitely *not* an engagement ring' on her finger that she'd tried to remove on numerous occasions with MeadowLea margarine spread, but hadn't been able to manoeuvre past her knuckle. It was like a noose around her neck rather than her finger, a constant reminder of her gullibility in giving a man who she didn't really like very much a house key and some coat hangers.

Stan wasn't there when she arrived back from the hospital the following morning, but sometime later she heard clattering and banging downstairs. She wondered if he was assembling her coffin on the kitchen table so that she could try it out for size. Nobody would ever see her alive again. She'd be like one of those people who suddenly vanish and are never found, people like Suzy Lamplugh, people who are remembered for disappearing rather than for being there. She hoped that it was a burglar who'd come to steal her jewellery and the VCR, rather than Stan brandishing a hammer and a chisel, and held her breath.

The bedroom door squeaked open (everything in the house squeaked, even her, but never the gate, which she wished squeaked loudest). It wasn't the cat burglar who she'd invented minutes earlier coming to steal her 'it's definitely *not* an engagement ring', a tall man wearing black leather gloves and a balaclava. It was someone much shorter and far more familiar. He moved stealthily across the room towards her, his feet making no sound. There was a mug in his outstretched hand, something that she couldn't remember him ever doing before, even when they'd first met and he was pretending to be normal.

She took the mug from him, briefly wondering whether the contents might be laced with arsenic and, erring on the side of caution, she placed it a safe distance away on the bedside table.

'How are you feeling?' Stan asked her, as if he'd played no part in her injuries.

'Much better,' she replied tentatively, even though she felt like she'd been hit by a train, a train that had then braked and reversed back over her.

She gripped the duvet. She felt adrift and helpless and uncertain. Had it been the right response? She hoped that she was disfigured enough, that he wouldn't want to add to her injuries. He continued to stare at her, neither of them seeming to know how best to proceed, and then his lips curled upwards, the tension lifting slightly. No teeth, but better than the alternative, she supposed. She exhaled. But it wasn't over yet, it seemed. He was still standing there, a strange non-smile on his face.

'I've got a surprise for you,' he teased.

She hadn't noticed that his right arm was behind his back, hiding something – roses perhaps, although the kind of surprises that Stan liked to deliver were far less sweet-scented or chocolate-coated, and she wouldn't be fooled a second, third, fourth or fifteenth time. She pictured a small mallet in his right hand, a compact wooden mallet for just such an occasion. She closed her eyes and waited for him to smash it against her skull. He'd be cleaning brain matter and blood splatter from the walls for the rest of the week. But instead of swinging a wooden mallet in the direction of her left temple, he produced something much flimsier and began waving it in the air like a flag of surrender, a temporary ceasefire.

'I've booked a week in Scarborough. Hotel, half board. We leave tomorrow. Frankie can stay with Ellie.'

Frankie was always staying with Ellie. She was at Ellie's more than she was at home – 'for her own safety', Barbara had once told Peggy over the telephone. When she next saw Frankie she asked her what she'd been saying, but Frankie promised that she hadn't said anything; everybody just knows, she told her. Knows what? About the bruises. They think he might start bruising me. I would never let him hurt you. You know that, don't you? Frankie had nodded. But she hadn't looked entirely convinced.

Peggy didn't know what to say. It seemed such a *normal* thing to suggest and yet the normality of the suggestion perturbed her and she wasn't sure that she liked the speed of the booking. She sympathised with how Frankie must have felt when she'd forced Torquay upon her without warning, although maybe this time things would be different, maybe this time she wouldn't come home at all.

'That sounds lovely,' she lied.

He nodded and went back downstairs. She reached for the mug. He was hardly going to poison her if he'd just spent money on hotel reservations. But the tea did taste like rainwater.

She didn't see him again that night as thankfully he slept on the sofa. He probably couldn't trust himself not to colour in the few remaining parts of her that were still white. But she still heard every cough and every yawn as he lay mulling over the meticulously laid plan that he was so obviously devising. She never did discover why he'd been making so much noise the day before.

He was washing the car when she drew back the curtains the next morning. An AA roadmap and a thermos flask were on the path. She'd woken up not wanting to go, not wanting to be alone with him. She wished that he'd stopped breathing during the night. Most days she wished that she was dead, but today she would have liked it to have been him. She watched him for ten minutes; if she really concentrated then perhaps it would happen, perhaps he would have a heart attack right there in the middle of the road but, much to her dismay, he carried on washing the car as if nobody was wishing him dead. She could even hear him whistling. She was ashamed that she'd allowed things to get this far and now they were going even further.

She sighed and reluctantly began to pack, which took considerable effort with sore ribs and a painful shoulder, and then she applied several layers of foundation in an attempt to conceal the varying shades and textures on her face. She didn't think that she even owned enough foundation to mask Stan's artwork, and she had thirteen tubes. She decided against lipstick because it drew too much attention to the rest of her face.

She pulled on some unflattering jeans and a black polo neck sweater and sat on the sofa waiting for him to finish whatever it was that was taking him so long. Finally his car was clean enough. He made some comment about her wearing far too much makeup these days, which was ironic, *considering.* And then he had the audacity to suggest that her jeans were a little on the tight side when a black leather belt was the only thing keeping them up.

It was a long and tiresome journey, particularly in the company of someone who she wished had a congenital heart condition, and the leopard-print seat covers started to get increasingly itchy north of Manchester.

There was an ELO tape on the dashboard which she slipped into the cassette player. She should have asked him if he minded her playing it, she belatedly realised; he liked to be asked, even when it didn't concern him, and when he turned to smile at her, a smile that *almost* reached his eyes, she was immediately worried and annoyed with herself for momentarily forgetting that 'actions have consequences'.

As they were skirting the desolate Yorkshire Moors, she hoped that he wasn't going to suggest a stroll among the heather and the shallow graves to 'teach her a lesson'. But his fingers were tapping along to 'Mr Blue Sky' and it didn't look as if he was planning an alternative, more remote, route. She gazed out of the window at the blues and greens rushing by like bruises, the pencil-grey trees stabbing at the earth like spears. When had she started to become so afraid of him?

Arriving in Scarborough with all her limbs thankfully intact, they checked into the Grand Hotel, an imposing, majestic building that had obviously been grand back in the day, but which now merely dominated much of the Scarborough skyline and blocked out the midday sun. There was a watercolour on the wall behind the reception desk, a lilac landscape that resembled the bruise on her upper thigh. She noticed Stan looking at it and hoped that he wasn't planning to replicate it on the other thigh.

After they'd unpacked, they ate lunch in the hotel restaurant (chicken Kiev and crinkle-cut oven chips followed by Black Forest gateau) and then spent the rest of the afternoon in the hotel bar listening to substandard piano renditions of Elton John songs ('Rocket Man', 'Daniel' and 'Goodbye Yellow Brick Road'). On the second day they strolled around the castle and visited the Italian Gardens and by the fourth day her ribs and shoulder felt far less sore and it took only four layers of foundation to hide the bruising. She was sorry that they'd not booked for longer. The change of scenery seemed to be generating other more meaningful changes.

And Stan would often disappear for a few hours after lunch, so there was still a chance that he might get hit by a car as he was crossing the road.

She wasn't going to count her chickens just yet, of course. He'd been like this before, lulling her into a false sense of security and then pulling the tablecloth away unexpectedly.

Unfortunately, as she did mistakenly begin to count her chickens during breakfast on the seventh day (reaching a total of one hundred and twenty-five while prodding five anaemic-looking grapefruit segments and a bullet-like glacé cherry), his mood grew more sombre and subdued, and she knew enough of the signs to realise that she should melt into the background as soon as possible, there wasn't time to collect anything. But she felt too exposed. There was too much sky and it was everywhere.

He suggested a walk to North Riding Forest Park, even held her hand. She wished that she'd put gloves on. She didn't like the feel of his flesh against her bare skin. She tried to listen to what he was saying, he was unusually talkative, but she couldn't help wondering if there was a freshly dug grave waiting for her in North Riding Forest Park. Fortunately, he was map-reading at the same time so he didn't notice that she'd stopped listening back in Scalby. He hated it when she didn't listen, or pretended to listen, or even worse admitted that she wasn't listening, because there was nothing more important than his opinion. She should know that by now.

Two hours later they were lost. He rotated the map clockwise and then anticlockwise, held it up to the light as if that might help, but whichever way he held it, they still seemed to be heading back towards Scarborough. He blamed the cartographer, the hotel receptionist who'd given him the map, the rain that had smudged the print on the map. He even blamed her for not checking where they were going. She could read, couldn't she? She told him that she hadn't seen a way marker since Scalby (the point at which she'd stopped listening).

Perhaps we should do a coastal walk instead, he said. It should be easy enough to follow the sea. I need to change first, though. What into, Peggy didn't ask. She squinted at the horizon ahead of her. One push and nobody would ever see her again. There'd be no need to dig holes in secluded wooded areas. She'd be buried at sea. And who would miss her? Frankie certainly wouldn't – the Barlows would see to that. He'd say that they'd had an argument and she'd left. Or that she'd met somebody else and left with them. He could say anything. And who would question it? She was hardly Mother Teresa.

When they eventually found their way back to the hotel, having asked a dog walker for directions, all the staff and guests were gathered on the pavement outside waiting for the fire brigade to allow them back in – somebody had apparently been smoking in the lift, so the coastal walk was postponed, her death rescheduled. And anyway Stan was tired, his feet were blistered. He was going for a drink instead. She shouldn't wait up.

As they were packing the next morning she wondered if she should make one last bid for freedom, head for the hotel exit and keep running. But he never took his eyes off her the entire time and she didn't think that slipping ELO into the car cassette player on the journey home would save her a second time.

He didn't say a word to her all the way home. When they stopped to use the toilets at the motorway services it was performed in complete silence. It was as if the sound had been muted on the television, her volume turned down. And she couldn't help thinking that she'd escaped another round of bullets. Just how many lives had she got left?

Chapter Twenty-Six

The Quarry

1979

Stella had told Ed that she'd meet him at the quarry. Her shift didn't start until lunchtime. He tried to dissuade her, insisting that Peggy would be there. She'd almost laughed. Peggy wouldn't be there. She was never there. And of course she wasn't. He'd frowned when he'd first spotted her climbing over a stile and heading towards him, but Peggy's notable absence and his enthusiasm for the building project soon dispelled any reservations that he might have had regarding her unwelcome presence.

They discussed how many bedrooms the house would have (four, maybe five, depending on planning permission), the sloping skylight and fitted wardrobes proposed for the en-suite master bedroom, and the double-glazed conservatory with under-floor heating that would overlook the buttercup paddock (south-facing, wicker-furnished).

'You'll ripen like tomatoes,' she'd sneered.

He ignored her and walked over to the buttercup paddock, a yellow sea of thankful lucky stars that almost reached the dual carriageway. As she listened to the crickets in the bracken she imagined herself lying beneath the sloping skylight of the en-suite master bedroom, ripening like a cherry tomato in the midday sun.

A small green bird sat on a neighbouring fencepost, watching her. And then the crickets fell silent and the bird flew away and he told her that he couldn't live like this any more, he loved Peggy. He wasn't normally so deceitful. He wasn't like that.

But he obviously was like that. He was a walking cliché. *I've never done anything like this before . . . my wife/fiancée/girlfriend is not the woman I married/met . . . we don't even sleep in the same bed any more . . . maybe when the children are older . . .* She'd have respected him far more if he'd been honest with her from the beginning.

Her eyes trailed a chalk-blue butterfly dipping in and out of the quarry. She wanted to tell him that she was pregnant, that he couldn't just wash his hands of her that easily, that their child would need a bedroom too, but she wasn't a teenage girl trying to trick a wayward boyfriend into marrying her.

Or perhaps she was. She searched in her handbag for the ultrasound scan, finding instead an unsigned letter addressed to Peggy. She hadn't been able to decide whether posting it would open the door to his four-/five-bedroom house or close it. Would he know that it was her? Would news of his unfaithfulness draw him and Peggy closer? The prospect of losing something often made a person realise just how much they wanted to hold on to it.

She'd hoped that it wouldn't come to this, enticing him with baby scans and anonymous letters, hoped that Peggy would sabotage the relationship without any outside intervention whatsoever, but sometimes you had to nudge things along a little or nothing would ever change.

Before she could locate the scan (where on earth was it?), Ed had retrieved a small maroon box from his jacket pocket. She knew immediately what it contained without him even opening it, but he still opened it, and it was like he'd slapped her. It was like she meant nothing to him at all. Why was he showing her this? It wasn't her who he wanted to marry, although to anyone watching it would have appeared otherwise, he was showing her a ring that he was intending to give to somebody else, asking for her opinion. How dare he? Did she mean that little to him?

His palm closed around the velvet box like a clam while she wrestled with this new development. But they weren't married yet. Peggy might say no. She would probably say, 'I'm not sure, leave it with me.' Peggy was someone who couldn't make snap decisions. Stella had once seen her in Boots staring at hairbrushes for so long that an assistant had walked over and asked her if she was okay. And even if she did say yes, marriage was hardly the lifelong commitment that it had once been. Despite all this, Stella was furious. And she couldn't hide it.

She snatched the box out of Ed's hand and hurled it into the open-mouthed quarry. It was impossible to see where it landed.

'There's something you need to know . . .' she began.

He needed to know that she was pregnant, that leaving her wouldn't be as straightforward as he imagined.

But he wasn't listening.

'For fuck's sake, Stella,' he yelled. 'That ring cost me ten months' wages. And why are you even here? Go home. It's over.'

Fuming, he threw down his jacket and began rolling up his shirtsleeves, intending to climb down after it.

She pictured him finding the ring and placing it on Peggy's finger. She pictured him nervously waiting at the altar, Peggy gliding towards him like a chiffon swan. She couldn't let either of those things happen.

As he was searching for the best route down, already off-balance, she walked up behind him and pushed him, hard.

She thought that he'd stumble down the shale like a stammer or maybe head over heels unrolling like a carpet, but he tumbled down at such speed that he seemed to almost be flying. It all happened so quickly, in the space of a gasp, the sound that his body made when it hit the quarry floor like a gunshot.

When she looked down, he was the tiniest black speck at the bottom of the quarry, like a dead bug on a hot windscreen, and he wasn't moving. He didn't even look like a person. She quickly looked away, glancing down at her feet. The ring was glistening on the sandstone to the right of her.

She still wears it sometimes, imagines that it was *her* future husband who cracked his skull open trying to retrieve an empty maroon box.

Did she mean to kill him?

She really isn't sure, which sounds like something that Peggy might say, but it's the truth.

And she couldn't possibly have known that his death would result in the death of their daughter five years later. Or perhaps their daughter was always destined to die whether Ed survived or not. There are plenty of other ways to kill a child.

Chapter Twenty-Seven

Made Only of Cuts and Bruises

1988

Peggy dreaded the jangle of Stan's key in the lock, the detailed account of her movements that he always demanded before removing his jacket. Something as innocent as going to the corner shop required the syncing of both their watches and if she wasn't back by the prearranged time, she would have to be taught the sacred art of timekeeping. She felt like a Swiss train. She was surprised that he didn't keep her locked up permanently, something that he currently only did when Frankie was at Ellie's.

Sometimes, she even felt sorry for him – she often thought that she would test the Pope's patience. Or maybe it was pity that she felt; it was difficult to tell. Her emotions were often bewildering, even to her. If she smiled it didn't necessarily mean that she was happy and if she cried it didn't inevitably mean that she was sad, but she didn't know whether it could be attributed to the alcohol, the pills, Frankie or Stan. Perhaps it was all four of them doing this to her. She began to wish more and more that it was just her, that she was everything.

When Stan spat at her after she'd asked him where he'd been all day, she decided that she couldn't live like this any longer. She couldn't live with these four extra things in her life. Her life was intolerable. It wasn't any sane person's definition of a life; it wasn't even a half-life. It was insufferable. And exhausting, trying to hide the bruises and the broken bones. For the first time in a long time she felt herself smiling and it seemed to be genuine. She could just walk away.

She pulled on a raincoat and walked into town still wearing her slippers, nervously glancing behind her to check that Stan wasn't following her (she'd twice noticed him admiring his reflection in Woolworths already that week), but then she remembered Frankie, the third stone in her shoe. And she couldn't do it. He would kill them both. Hadn't he said as much? So she turned back.

And then an alternative solution arose, one that she hadn't considered before. Or perhaps it was the final nail in her coffin. She couldn't decide which. Was she too old to have another child? She was younger than her mother had been. Would Stan be thrilled at the prospect of fatherhood or utterly distraught? She wasn't sure. They never discussed children. They certainly never discussed Frankie. But he never stayed longer than a few days at a time now and the words would grow stale in her throat, impossible to coax out in such a short space of time.

Perhaps she should write them down, those two life-changing words. Who's pregnant? *I'm* pregnant. She'd never said that before, not even to Ed, never watched someone jump for joy or look as if their life was about to end.

Of course when she did finally say it out loud, she wished that she hadn't, because he didn't want a (had he said 'another' child? She must have misheard him) fucking child and he definitely didn't want a fucking child with her (she didn't mishear that part). *Get rid of it. Or else*, he told her, as if it was nothing more than a piece of chewing gum stuck to the sole of his shoe. But she didn't want to 'get rid of it'. She wanted to keep it, wanted him to have a reason to keep coming back. She wanted them to be a family.

Although his toothbrush was still in the toothbrush holder, she counted only two shirts in the wardrobe. There seemed to be physically less of him and yet psychologically more of him. Was he really working in Sheffield or was he living two streets away with somebody else, the father of another family? Was he sleeping with Sylvia? Is that why she never called? Did Peggy even want him to keep coming back? Didn't she want to be left alone? She felt so confused.

She tipped the last of the pills out of the soap dispenser, wondering why she went to such lengths to hide them. It was the world's worst-kept secret, written all over her face: the dilated pupils, the chronic insomnia, the severe mood swings. And then she remembered what had led her here. Ed had sent her tumbling down this rabbit hole, Frankie guiding her into the warren's darker burrows and now Stan was ensuring that she stayed there. A fourth person would surely fill in the hole permanently.

If only she'd died instead of Ed, left Frankie with her father so that they could build things together, not tear things apart. A few decades earlier and the probability of her dying during childbirth would have been much greater, although in many respects part of her did die that day, her adaptability. As a child her life had been a never-ending game of musical chairs, and yet now she could barely cope with a change in the weather.

There were only three pills left. She swallowed all three, casting her mind back to two days earlier when she'd been waiting to end a life that hadn't yet begun . . .

Everything had been still, apart from the occasional quiet rustling of paper. Peggy uncrossed her legs and reached for a magazine, 'Woman's' something on the front cover – weekly, monthly, something that didn't need to be read daily. There was a desert-dry plant on the windowsill, its khaki fronds brittle through lack of water or too much water, through being unloved or loved too much.

The receptionist called her name (still 'Mrs Appleton' after all these years), and the unread magazine fell from her lap when she stood up. She picked it up off the floor, placed it back on the coffee table for somebody else to not read and followed the receptionist along a dark narrow corridor without windows where nobody could see her and know that she was there.

Doctor Daniels seemed angry with her, his features squashed spitefully into the middle of his face. He barely spoke, his gloved hands impatiently pointing and circling like a vengeful mime artist. She supposed the thought of killing a perfectly healthy foetus had rendered him speechless. Although, maybe he should walk in her shoes for a while, see how much they pinch and squeeze.

She looked up at the ice-white ceiling and tried to step back into the room that she'd just left, the room with the four sunlit walls and the hushed shadows and the magazines that nobody ever read, but she couldn't feel the sun on her arms any more. Somewhere along the corridor the memory had grown colder.

She tried picturing Ed's face instead, but even he was getting more and more distant; still recognisable, but blurrier than before. Was he finally leaving? She didn't know if she was ready for that. She wished that she could remember him in more detail, the things that he'd done, the things that he'd said, but only echoes of those things remained and she wasn't sure if those echoes were an accurate representation of him or not. Why hadn't she kept a journal, recorded those things? It was more important than ever now that he wasn't there to ask.

She concentrated on a black speck on the ceiling – was it a spider? She couldn't see any legs – and willed him back into focus, but he wouldn't come back the way she remembered him and there were two screaming mouths where his eyes should have been.

Afterwards she thought that she would feel differently, as if something was missing, lost even, which of course it now was, but she felt exactly the same as she always did, which was hugely disappointing. She expected it to matter. What would it take for something to matter?

Before going home, she sat for a while on a bench by the river, the bronze plaque on the backrest of the seat dedicated to Norman Pearson, 'a devoted husband', and watched sheep grazing in the field opposite. She counted seventeen white sheep, one black sheep and one sheep that looked dead. She wondered if she should tell the farmer. She should cross the river and let him know. She wondered how deep the water was. She slipped off her shoes and walked down to the riverbank. A sheep was bleating loudly.

As she was dipping a toe into the water, a voice yelled at her to step back. 'Can't you see the sign? "No Swimming, Deep Water".' When she turned round, a man with a fishing rod was glowering at her. He was wearing a red hat and had a silver beard. He looked like a garden gnome and she wondered if he was real. She eventually decided that he must be real when he was still standing there after several purposeful blinks. She wanted to ask him what business it was of his if she wanted to cross the river, but she obediently returned to Norman Pearson and slipped her shoes back on.

'There's a dead sheep in the field opposite. I was looking for the farmer,' she offered by way of explanation. It sounded odd, even to her. She tried smiling instead, but it didn't feel at all like she was smiling. It felt more like a grimace.

He still seemed unsure. 'Unless you can walk on water then I'd suggest you use the footbridge like everybody else – it's a couple of hundred yards that way.'

She nodded and he walked on. She made a mental note to revisit the river at a later date now that she knew it was deep enough, and spent the rest of the afternoon staring out of the bedroom window where there was no danger of her being seen.

She liked watching people from the bedroom window, liked having a bird's-eye view of everything. It felt safer somehow, from above. And she particularly liked watching people who had no idea that they were being watched. You saw so much more. She'd once seen Evelyn Banks slap her son so hard that she'd sent him spinning into the road, and she'd seen a man following Jenny Stanton. She should have probably reported both incidents, but she didn't want to antagonise Evelyn Banks, who was rumoured to be married to a Portuguese hitman, or the man following Jenny Stanton. He looked more than capable of snapping both Jenny's neck and hers.

Two council workmen had earlier started painting the front doors of the council houses opposite, alternating between mustard and forest green, but now it was raining they were no doubt reading Page Three Girl Stacey from Liverpool's views on the economic recession and asking the homeowners to put the kettle on.

Peggy wished that she lived in a council house where everything was done for you (when it wasn't raining, of course) and it didn't cost you anything, where you didn't have to choose colour schemes or paint, where you dialled a number and all your prayers (or repairs) were answered. She would have liked a bathroom suite that wasn't avocado and a gate that closed properly. Mustard was an unusual colour for a front door, though. It made her think of roast beef rather than interior design.

Tired of watching painters not painting, she went over to the dressing table to put on some lipstick. She always enjoyed the ritual of opening a lipstick and running it across her lips, the turtle-shell casing, the ski-sloped tip and then the splash of glossy-fingered colour, the way that it transformed her face, made her seem invincible when she felt invisible. This lipstick unfortunately was like putty, sticky and misshapen. Frankie often sneaked into her room when she wasn't there. She'd seen several red lips that weren't hers on discarded tissues.

She pressed the clammy lipstick onto her dry, chapped lips. It was getting harder and harder to apply and yet somehow more necessary. When she glanced at herself in the dressing-table mirror the two reddened lips didn't look like they belonged to her at all. It was as if she'd stolen somebody else's lips or applied lipstick to her reflection, drawn lips on the mirror. Her reflection might have been wearing lipstick, but was she? She remembered getting trapped inside a mirror once before and quickly turned away. She threw the lipstick in the waste bin and went downstairs. All that mustard had made her hungry.

The following morning she found Frankie in the kitchen wrapping Ellie's birthday gifts, a Beatles *Abbey Road* cassette (featuring 'Octopus's Garden', written by Ringo Starr, side one, track five), and some signed drumsticks. Frankie had joined the Beatles fan club specifically to source Ringo Starr merchandise for Ellie.

She was carefully folding the edges of the *Sgt Pepper's Lonely Hearts Club Band* wrapping paper into neat triangles, holding each one down with an elbow while she cut a length of Sellotape. Peggy saw her own hand pushing Frankie's hand into the fire, holding it there until she was screaming so loudly that she had to let go and cover her ears. She blinked the image away and went over to her, kissing her tenderly on the cheek, her lipstick leaving a dirty smudge that looked like dried blood. She felt Frankie flinch awkwardly.

There was a mug of lukewarm coffee by the kettle. Frankie made her endless cups of coffee each day. Most of them she poured away. There was only so much coffee that she could bear and none of it made her feel any more awake. She picked up the ironically titled 'World's Best Mum' mug and sat down beside her. Frankie was now rolling wrapping paper around the drumsticks.

While Peggy preferred Christmas, Frankie could barely sleep the day before a birthday, and she looked forward to other people's birthdays far more than her own, probably because her own birthday often passed by unnoticed. Being born on the same day that a person dies is not the happiest of birthdays. For Peggy it was little cause for celebration. She could only think of Ed. She should have unofficially changed the date of Frankie's birthday, she belatedly realised. What did a few days either side matter unless you were applying for a passport?

How can you not like birthdays? Frankie would ask her. A whole day devoted just to you and they're always different (except Frankie's birthdays of course, which were the same, if not worse, than any other day). Christmas is celebrated by everybody and it's always the same, she complained. Not everybody, Peggy argued, thinking of Mrs Shah who always opened on Christmas Day, but that's what makes it special, the fact that it's always the same: the satsuma in a Christmas stocking, the sixpence in a Christmas pudding, the advent calendar counting down the days. And the presents are always different (they weren't. Perfume, slippers, socks. They may have been a different colour or a different scent or a different style, but the gift was still the same).

And anyway you hate being the centre of attention, Peggy reminded her before walking away. I like Christmas when it's just the two of us, Peggy heard Frankie murmur.

The day after celebrating one birthday Frankie would begin planning the next, collecting lost buttons and autumn leaves and spending her pocket money on lipstick-red food colouring to pour into cake batter.

She couldn't have wished for a more perfect daughter now and she so wanted to tell Frankie that she did love her that she'd always loved her, but she doubted that she'd believe her. So instead she told her not to eat too much birthday cake – she didn't have time to take her to the dentist for another filling.

As soon as Frankie left, the walls closed in and the thoughts in her head became too loud. She tidied away the scissors and the Sellotape and switched on the radio. The front door opened and closed during Belinda Carlisle's 'Heaven Is a Place on Earth'. She wondered if Frankie had forgotten something but it was Stan who walked into the kitchen as if it was his kitchen, even though he was never there.

Usually, she let him think that this was where he lived, with her and Frankie, but mostly with her because Frankie was never there either – but not today. Yesterday she'd erased their child as if it was nothing more than a broken nail. She'd let what happened to Ed affect everything that happened afterwards. Belinda Carlisle had left her earthly heaven and Bill Withers was now forecasting a 'Lovely Day'. She switched off the radio. She didn't want to spoil a lovely day.

She started slowly, but soon gained momentum. Where had he been? Why was he never there? Who was he sleeping with? Was it Sylvia? Why was he always staring at Frankie? *So many questions that neither of them really wanted answers to.* She wasn't even aware that she'd noticed these things, but they were all there in the waiting room inside her head, queuing up to be heard, and her head felt so much lighter without all those questions inside it, without all those occupied seats.

The argument began to escalate and change direction, weaving in and out of the past: the provocative way she dressed, the condescending way she spoke to him, the embarrassing way she behaved, until it was no longer about Sylvia or Frankie or the embryo that she'd just aborted and not even mentioned, but about something else entirely. It became all about her. And not everything was about her, although it may have seemed otherwise. She heard herself screeching and then she was crying and she didn't know if she was crying because she was angry or because she was heartbroken. Perhaps she was both. She'd been heartbroken for a long time.

As she was leaning against the sink trying to compose herself, he punched her with such force that she fell to the floor and while she was lying there he kicked her, eight times in total (she counted each one, like a breath), as if she deserved every kick, as if she'd earned all eight. She was so tired of being kicked in the stomach and punched in the face, tired of his feet and his fists voicing all his concerns. They were now starting to form actual sentences. But before she could tell him just how tired she was, the back door slammed shut and she was alone, again.

She remembered the river, how she wasn't supposed to swim in it. She remembered the dead sheep, how she hadn't told the farmer. She noticed the broken coffee mug by the fridge door. No longer the 'World's Best Mum' – the 'Mum' was missing – she wondered what she was now: 'World's Best Punchbag'? 'World's Best Worst Mum'?

Using a stool for leverage, she slowly pulled herself up off the floor. There were shards of glass by the back door from a glass panel that Stan had smashed as he was leaving. She searched for the dustpan and brush in the cupboard under the sink but bending over made her head spin and she had to sit down again. Perhaps she should ask one of the council workers to paint her mustard if it wasn't raining, disguise her as a roast dinner. She should get the locks changed first though.

She called the Barlows.

'Don? It's Peggy. I need the locks changing. Any chance you could come over this morning?'

'Not really, I'm in the middle of setting up the trampoline. It's Ellie's birthday, in case you'd forgotten. Can't it wait?'

'*Please*, I wouldn't ask if it wasn't urgent. And bring some glass to replace a panel in the back door.'

He arrived thirty minutes later and he wasn't happy. Unlike Peggy, his expression determined exactly how he was feeling. He wore it like cologne and today he was wearing Furious Don. Peggy was tired of being judged, tired of people adopting the expressions that she should have been able to adopt. He studied her swollen face, the way she was cradling her right arm as if it was a newborn baby.

'Why do you let him do this to you? Call the police, have him arrested.'

He'd already lost patience.

She watched him drop his tool bag on the floor and pull out a screwdriver. The front-door lock was difficult to disengage, but he eventually managed to wriggle it free.

Peggy switched on the kettle and spooned coffee into two mugs while he searched in his bag for a lock that might fit.

'Top-up?'

She was waving a bottle of whiskey in the air. He shook his head. She poured whiskey into both mugs.

'Frankie shouldn't have to witness this.'

'Me putting whiskey in my coffee?'

'No, you giving any Tom, Dick and Harry a front-door key.'

'His name's Stan and in case you haven't noticed, Frankie isn't here. She's never here. She's always at your house eating Marks and Spencer's macaroni cheese, and jam and coconut sponge cake.'

This was courtesy of Barbara, who'd recently discovered the wonders of the ready meal. Frankie had still looked incredulous the next day when she was explaining to Peggy that dinner had only taken six minutes to cook.

Don screwed the lock in place and tossed the key onto the kitchen table.

'She's always at our house because it's not safe for her here. She'd be much happier living with us permanently. And it would certainly make your life a lot easier not having her around.'

How dare he assume that she would like nothing more than to abandon her own daughter?

'I know what you're trying to do, but it won't work. You can't have her, she's mine. I'm her mother and she belongs with me. I won't let you take her. I'd rather die than let her live with you.'

She was shaking. Without Frankie, she'd be nothing. She'd be like a plant without water. He seemed to sense that it was more about her own survival than Frankie's.

'Always thinking about yourself as usual, never about what might be best for Frankie. You're not the first person to ever lose somebody and you won't be the last. It's been nine years since Ed died. Get a fucking grip. Five miscarriages and a stillbirth, Barb's had to go through, but do you see her wallowing? No, you fucking don't.'

While she was tired of Stan's fists, Don Barlow was tired of her excuses.

'Maybe I should tell Barbara where you really go on Tuesday nights when you're supposed to be having a quick pint after work, Mister I'm-so-fucking-perfect. She might do some wallowing then. Maybe I should call her now. She might also be interested to hear about what *we* used to get up to behind her back.'

He ignored her, pulling a piece of glass from his tool bag and holding it up to the back door, but it was too small. It seemed like the last straw, this too-small piece of glass. He put it back in his tool bag.

'I'm going. Get someone else to do your dirty work.'

'You can't go. What about the back door?'

'I've got a trampoline to put up.'

As he turned to leave, Peggy picked up the whiskey bottle and threw it at him. It hit his left cheek and knocked out a tooth. She watched the tooth fall from his mouth and roll under the kitchen table. He clutched the side of his face. Blood was dripping down his chin.

'What the fuck? You're a fucking psychopath.'

'I told you not to go.'

She'd never seen 'Furious Don' this furious. He bent down to retrieve the tooth and then began striding towards her.

She ran into the hallway and picked up the telephone, balancing it against her left ear like a violin while she dialled the number. She could barely move her right arm.

'Who are you calling?'

She wondered whether she should be calling the police. His tone was icy.

'I'm calling Barbara. She should know the truth.'

'Put the phone down.'

'No. She's trying to steal my child.'

'I'm warning you. Put the phone down.'

She ignored him and continued to dial. She felt dizzy. She was obviously dialling the wrong number, there were far too many digits, but Don was too livid to notice. He was breathing heavily, his pupils dark and still, his gum bleeding. He looked like a vampire.

Her head was swimming.

'Shall I tell her how you like to . . .' she taunted.

She couldn't seem to stop. Was she mad at Stan or was she mad at Don? She couldn't decide. Maybe her fury was directed towards all men. Although she suspected that Ed was the one who she was really mad at.

She never finished the sentence, slumping to the floor and knocking the telephone off the stand. She wanted to close her eyes. Just for a few minutes. But the telephone wire had somehow become wrapped around her neck. She couldn't breathe, couldn't see, but she could hear a faraway voice, the same words over and over again,

'You fucking bitch, you fucking, fucking bitch . . .' Who were they calling a 'bitch'?

She tried to speak, is that Barbara?, but the line was engaged, the space between breaths too long. Still, it was nothing that she hadn't dealt with before. She waited for another breath, but the telephone wire was still wrapped around her throat, being pulled tighter and tighter, and nothing could squeeze through. She desperately tried to find another breath, tried to tell the faraway voice that she couldn't breathe, but the line was dead and being wiped down with a cloth.

And then she was upstairs on the bed, but she couldn't remember how she'd got there. There was a gap between the hallway and the stairs. Had she walked or been carried? There was a rope attached to the light fitting on the ceiling, a chair left beneath it like somebody had changed a light bulb and forgotten to remove it. Surely the rope wasn't for her, the light fitting would never hold her, although she seemed to weigh so little now and be made only of cuts and bruises.

She noticed that her slippers were on the wrong feet as the rope was being placed over her head. She would have liked to have told somebody, but she was making no sound at all. It was as if she was slowly dissolving and when she next opened her eyes she'd be nothing but a bloodstain on Frankie's cheek. Where was Frankie? She needed to tell her that she loved her and that she was sorry. *For everything.* The chair toppled backwards. Ed, is that you?

Chapter Twenty-Eight

The Ballad of an Invisible Man

1989

Most days Geoff wished that he'd never left The Swan.

And today was no exception.

A factory conveyor belt had sliced off Kevin Armstrong's index finger during a senior management meeting and he was now in casualty cradling the finger inside a packet of Birds Eye frozen peas, while assuring Kevin that as factory foreman he would be ensuring that heads rolled if they were deemed in any way responsible.

Fingers were certainly rolling, quick-thinking Neil Williams thankfully managing to rescue the detached finger before it rolled into a vat of hot oil. But God knows why Geoff was making such bold promises; nobody ever listened.

It was the fourth accident in as many months, the other three fortunately requiring nothing more than a bandage, a splash of brandy in a teacup and a promise to not breathe a word '*to anybody*'. But the accidents were getting progressively worse. What would be next – an eye, a leg, an actual fatality? They wouldn't be able to conceal a death on the premises quite so easily. And he should know. He'd tried to dispose of a body there once before, but the entire place was like a flimsy amateur theatre set so he'd had to move it to somewhere more secure.

He'd had several heated conversations with Cyril Johnson, the supposed health and safety manager who knew next to nothing about health or safety and who didn't particularly want to know about the hazards of ordering heavily discounted Czechoslovakian machinery and how it was impossible to eat a ham sandwich and an apple in ten minutes, but he always had the impression that he wasn't even listening. He never even politely nodded his head like most people who didn't give a shit would. He just said, 'Is that everything?' which was a whole other conversation. No, it wasn't everything. It was barely the first bite.

And, sadly, he didn't think that the loss of Kevin Armstrong's index finger would change that. He wasn't even sure that somebody actually dying would change that either. He suspected that Cyril would just sweep the body aside and tell everybody to get back to work, '*pronto*'. It saddened him that a workforce was so willing to tolerate such shoddy workplace practices, rising unemployment making turning a blind eye inevitable – if you still had an eye to turn, that is.

Kevin was groaning beside him. Geoff wondered if a splash of brandy and an extra ten pounds in his wage packet would be enough this time. They hadn't been able to reattach the finger and Geoff wondered if fingers could ever be reattached, no matter how cold you kept them. Somebody somewhere probably had jars full of odd fingers. Maybe they'd even managed to fashion a complete pair of hands.

Between groans, Kevin asked him how Rita was. Fine, Geoff told him. She wasn't. She'd stormed straight past him this morning without a word. At the beginning of the week she'd at least been able to mutter a 'yes' or a 'no' or an 'I don't know', and, while brushing her teeth one night, an 'I really don't care', but now there was nothing but the sound of a door closing behind her. And it made him nervous. He didn't like her being so unreachable, didn't like second-guessing her.

A few days earlier she'd found a silver necklace inside a balled-up pair of socks in his sock drawer and he couldn't help wondering if she'd found anything else in there that she wasn't yet mentioning, something that he hadn't hidden carefully enough, something that she might 'later rely on in court' when she did start speaking to him again.

She didn't say anything about it at all for a couple of days ('I found *this* a couple of days ago'), letting the discovery linger and ferment until it was all that she could think about and had quadrupled in size. She'd no doubt spent the past couple of days imagining every worst-case scenario, her imagination creating more and more absurd reasons for it being there, although none of those reasons would have remotely resembled the truth, he imagined – the girl in the Disney T-shirt skipping over the remains of the stationmaster's house by the railway track, the hissing pocket of liquid rage inside him eventually settling into something more solid, more manageable.

She'd been even dirtier up close and her hair smelled of Benson & Hedges cigarettes and brown ale. She'd stood there, chiselled from stone, frozen like ice, barely blinking, a silver letter 'E' around her neck – 'E' for 'Everything', or in this case 'The End of Everything'. Her name was Emily Rogers, he later discovered.

He wished that he hadn't removed the necklace from Stella's loft, but he'd wanted to have access to something that he didn't have to keep climbing into Stella's loft to see. Even though he remembered every victim, every last breath, in cinematic wide-screen, maybe one day due to some cruel degenerative twist of fate he wouldn't be able to remember the blue of their eyes or the sound of their screams and he'd be grateful for something to hold on to, something to remind him.

And sometimes memories alone weren't enough, no matter how convincing they might seem. He liked the feel of a thing in his hands, liked to roll it back and forth between his fingers. It was a shame that her name hadn't been Rachel or Rose.

Somewhat predictably, Rita had accused him of having an affair, Stella often the source of her suspicions because he spent so much time there. I'm not sleeping with Stella, he told her. I found it at work inside a crate. Nobody's claimed it yet, but I thought I'd hang onto it just in case. It might be of sentimental value. I'll take it into work if it upsets you so much. But nothing he said pacified her. He wished that he'd kept it in an office drawer. He wished that he'd never married her at all.

He needed privacy. He needed to come and go as he pleased, undetected, an invisible family man with a wife and child, somebody who was quickly glossed over, although that child (Robbie) was quickly becoming a liability, recently arrested for breaking and entering and possession of a Class B drug, drawing more unwanted attention to the outwardly ordinary Jenkins family.

As soon as Kevin's girlfriend, Nina, arrived at the hospital, threatening 'a hailstorm of shit like you've never seen', Geoff left. He took a taxi back to his car and telling June, his secretary, that he wasn't feeling well, he headed home. Peter Degg, the trade union rep, would be more than a match for Nina. He was a friend of Cyril and didn't mind how much shit was on his shoes.

Not wanting to go home to Rita's cold shoulder and Robbie's light fingers he drove around aimlessly for a while, left and then right and then left again, far too many turns for someone who just wanted to accelerate. If he'd lived in the Midwest or the Australian outback he'd have been able to drive in a straight line for days, only stopping for gas, but he didn't particularly want to sit in rush-hour traffic on a dual carriageway.

He decided to head to Stella's house to 'check the loft insulation' or tell her that he'd heard scratching when he was last there and had forgotten to mention it. He wanted to put the silver chain back in the loft and check that the other items hadn't been tampered with: the school tie that had been wrapped around Stephen Spooner's head and then his neck, the lunchbox in the shape of a red sports car, the tiny fists of paper and broken crayons, the exercise book with twenty red crosses and a 'see me' and the small dinosaur wallet containing a few loose coins. He'd taken everything from Stephen Spooner.

Afterwards, he'd flattened out one of the paper fists, a crayoned drawing of a triangular woman with no hair and a spherical boy with full stops for eyes standing outside a house with a smoking chimney. There was a dog in an upstairs window that looked like a horse and a red flower by the blue front door that looked like a sock.

He thought of his daughter, the daughter that he'd once had and now didn't, the father that he'd once been and now wasn't, all the unfinished drawings that would never be finished. And he didn't want to be reminded of that. Except that perhaps he did. Perhaps this was one drawing that needed to be finished. He tried to unclench his balled fists, but they were keeping a tight hold of his rage.

Stella's father, Malcolm Evans, was convicted of the murder of Stephen Spooner. He remembered Stella sitting outside the courtroom during the trial beside a woman with a beehive reading out crossword clues, Stella repeatedly wiping her hands on her coat. He'd recognised her immediately when she'd walked into The Swan asking if they had any bar staff vacancies. She'd barely changed. She was still rubbing at some invisible stain.

He told her that an employee had recently resigned and fired Colleen, who'd worked there for nearly ten years, the next day. Faith told him that he should be ashamed of himself. Bert, Colleen's husband, had only recently lost his job at LKT Mechanics. But Geoff was unrepentant. Stella was a different type of victim, a different kind of itch, a daily reminder that you really can get away with murder.

When Stella opened the door, Geoff noticed a scratch under her left eye. He briefly wondered if Billy was responsible, but didn't think that he cared enough to assault her, unlike his father who stretched into every corner of the house until there was no room for anything else, no room to gather up your thoughts before he sat on them, his mother always the one apologising. He didn't mean it. It won't happen again. He didn't trust her.

When his father wasn't there she would slip on her Sunday coat, the one with the lizard brooch, and disappear for hours. He'd followed her once, watched her walk into another house a few streets away. And that's when he realised that no amount of apologising would change anything. Even his mother had had to find somewhere else to keep her thoughts.

He stepped inside. The house was bitterly cold.

'Is the heating not working?' he asked Stella. 'Need me to take a look?'

'No, it's fine. I prefer it cold. It kills all the germs that I can't reach.'

He should have been used to Stella's eccentricities. She kept a duster and a bottle of Dettol in a carrier bag on one of the wheelchair handgrips for easy access.

'Coffee?'

He nodded, his thoughts returning to his father and the moment when everything changed, when something happened that he couldn't quite grasp and hold in his hands and examine properly, his father with another boy, a boy of about eight or nine.

They were in a quiet corner of a derelict silk mill, two walls meeting, two worlds colliding, and he was jealous. Of all the things that he should have been feeling he couldn't believe that jealousy was one of them, but it was like two hands altering the shape of his heart, the realisation that he was now too old and yet it was still too late and it had all been for nothing.

His father handed something to the boy and then the boy rode away on his bike. He could hear a faint sound – an engine perhaps; a woodpecker; his own breathing.

A young girl stood watching him.

'What are you doing?' she asked him.

She had short brown hair and was wearing a beige turtleneck jumper and brown corduroy trousers. She looked like a boy.

'What are *you* doing?'

'I asked you first.'

Jesus, she was worse than his brother. Daddy, why is the moon round? Daddy, why is the sky blue? Who gives a fuck, he wanted to say? You colour it in with whatever crayons you've got in your pencil case. More often than not his skies were green and his moon was square.

'Nothing.'

'But what were you doing before you were doing nothing?'

'For fuck's sake, why all the questions?'

He didn't realise that he was the one now asking questions, about questions, didn't realise how angry he was, how devastated he felt. He wished that she would go away. He could make her go away.

'It's rude to swear. And I was only asking. What's that over there?'

She was pointing at what looked like a dead fox beside a fence.

Did she never stop?

'Do you want to see?'

Finally, questions that led somewhere else.

'Okay.'

She followed him over to the fence, staring at the dead fox that was actually a dead cat. Maggots were wriggling around inside its belly.

'Do you think it tickles having all those maggots wriggling around inside you?' she asked him.

He picked up a piece of copper piping that was lying by his feet and as she bent over to take a closer look at the maggots he smashed it against her skull.

'I doubt it, it's fucking dead.'

He unthreaded one of her shoelaces and put it in his pocket. That was the first time he killed someone. He was surprised at how easily one thing became another, how you could be reshaping your heart one minute and then sculpting it into a hardened mass of granite the next, although not everyone who crossed paths with him necessarily suffered at his hands. And rarely were his actions premeditated; his father, his brother Dennis (although Dennis was already dying, so that didn't really count), a couple of prostitutes who stole from him (Candice with the rose tattoo and Angela from Queensland), Stephen Spooner and Damian Shaw.

But he hadn't planned to kill the girl dressed like a boy or Emily Rogers or Shelley (buried north of the M6) or Andrei Chomsky or hitchhikers Faye and Shirley (buried in a Yorkshire field while on vacation) or his first wife. He hadn't meant to do any of it.

He wondered how different his life would have been if there'd been no boy on a bike and no girl dressed like a boy.

As Stella was tearing open a packet of chocolate digestive biscuits, Geoff wondered if the ring she was wearing was the same ring, the ring from the quarry, the day when everything changed for Stella. It seemed that the people who disappointed you most were often to blame for the poor decisions that you subsequently made. He'd known for some time that she was sleeping with Ed Appleton, of course. She'd tried to be discreet, but being childishly infatuated had made her careless. And he saw everything, remembered everything. He'd told her that on numerous occasions, warned her that walls have ears. And so he'd followed her.

After she'd picked up the ring and left, he'd peered into the quarry. Ed was still moving. He was crawling along the quarry floor like a wounded soldier. Geoff couldn't tell if he was still searching for the ring or simply trying to stand up. He picked up a rock by his foot and threw it into the quarry. He didn't expect it to hit Ed, but it hit his outstretched arm. He picked up a bigger rock. It hit one of Ed's legs. The third rock hit Ed's head and he finally stopped moving.

Geoff had hoped that his and Stella's relationship might develop into something more meaningful after that, particularly as she was pregnant – he would have liked to have been a father again – but before he could lend a sympathetic ear or wipe away her vomit she was walking down the aisle with Billy Yates, a marriage that had put Stella in a wheelchair and her daughter in a morgue drawer. He didn't want to remember Marie. It hurt too much. He hoped that it hurt because he missed her and not because he'd wanted to strangle her. Sometimes it was difficult to differentiate the two, thanks to his father. And now all he had was the ultrasound scan that he'd stolen from Stella's handbag, the only evidence that there'd ever been a child.

'You're bleeding.'

Geoff glanced down. The sharp edges of the silver 'E' had pierced his skin. Stella tore off some kitchen roll to wipe the blood away and then dabbed at the drops of blood on the kitchen table with some disinfectant. He slipped the necklace in his pocket.

'It's nothing,' he told her, pressing the kitchen roll against his palm. 'By the way, I forgot to tell you: I heard scratching last time I was here. It seemed to be coming from the loft. I'll just go and check it out while the kettle's boiling.'

He sat in the loft for a while, sifting through the contents of two cardboard boxes, and then he climbed back down. Stella was eating a biscuit at the kitchen table, staring at a starling on the bird table, unaware that she was now the unwitting custodian of all the lives that he'd stolen.

'Anything up there?' she asked him.

He stared at her blankly.

'The scratching?'

'Oh, that. No, all good.'

Stella poured them both a coffee and they chatted about Rita ('She's fine'), Robbie ('Mixing with the wrong crowd') and Kevin Armstrong's finger ('He's lucky it was only one of his fingers'). As she was smoothing a plaster onto his hand, he asked her how the campaigning was going. She told him that she'd grown tired of canvassing for improved disabled access, it only emphasised the fact that she couldn't walk (wasn't that the point?), so she'd moved on to Scientology. It's fascinating, she told him. It really makes you question how we . . . Geoff wasn't listening. He was back in the loft, knotting shoelaces and zipping up wallets.

As with Stephen Spooner, he'd taken everything from Stella too, her father, Ed Appleton, her twelve-week scan photo.

There were roadworks at the bottom of Stella's road so he took a detour along some quieter backstreets by the canal. Turning into Mansfield Row he noticed a schoolgirl in a navy blue blazer taking multiple photographs of an ornate pink garden gate. She was wearing a brightly striped woollen mitten. Mostly, people walked around staring at their feet. They didn't stand outside people's homes photographing garden gates. But it *was* a very unusual gate. Rarely were they the colour of a pink carnation.

His curiosity piqued, he parked across the road and watched her for a while. She didn't seem to be in any particular hurry. Perhaps the photographs were for a school project. He looked at his watch. It was two fifteen. As she lay sprawled on the pavement looking through the viewfinder, he imagined her on the other side of the gate, sandwiched between the slats, sawn in half and then half again. He liked imagining her divided up like that, broken into smaller, more digestible pieces, an earlobe, a collarbone, an elbow, rather than swallowed whole.

She suddenly jumped up off the pavement and spun round. For several seconds she stood completely still as if she'd realised that she was being watched, had sensed a curious gaze rolling up behind her, catching her by surprise. It was *too* quiet, far too quiet for the number of parked cars lining the street. He sank down further as she was glancing across at him and, although she stared at the car as if she might have recognised it, she didn't seem to notice him hiding behind the steering wheel, his own face sliced in three.

He could have left then – there was still time, it wasn't too late – but now that he'd glimpsed her face, that seemed less and less likely. He needed to take a closer look. He needed another thing that wasn't his. He rehearsed what he was going to say. *There's been an accident* (today there was an element of truth in the statement). She would respond with a name, which he would confirm: *Yes, that's right, get in. I'll give you a lift to the hospital. [Insert name here] is asking for you. I'm Geoff, by the way, Geoff Jenkins.* No – not his real name, he should be someone else this time, a new character. A real name always guaranteed a particular ending. And he liked surprises.

Sometimes he had to improvise. It didn't always go smoothly. But she was young, impressionable. She could be manipulated. Splashing a thimbleful of aftershave on his chin he pulled the teddy bear with the red heart from the glovebox and placed it on the passenger seat. He then waited a while before switching on the engine to give her a head start, an opportunity to be rescued, to go somewhere where he couldn't follow her (a white van had already slowed down a few yards down the road and then sped away without her), and when this didn't happen, he drew up alongside her.

He thought of his dead daughter, why she was dead and this girl wasn't; he thought of Marie, not a scratch on her new shoes; and then he wound down the car window.

Chapter Twenty-Nine

The Lifesaving Features of Gates

1989

The car drew to a halt alongside her. Or maybe it was the van that she'd seen earlier, circling the neighbourhood. Please be Stan, please be Stan, Frankie repeated to herself as the car/van window whirred open. Her camera strap was around her neck so it would take only a matter of seconds to obtain photographic evidence of the man who'd murdered her mother. But then instead of the man's voice that she'd been expecting, she heard a woman's voice, 'Excuse me, excuse me,' a woman who wasn't in a vehicle but who was at that precise moment sprinting along the pavement towards her, waving a familiar stripy mitten in the air.

'Excuse me. I think you dropped this,' she puffed, crimson-faced and breathless.

Before Frankie could turn back around and photograph the car driver (it *was* a car, unassuming, charcoal grey) the car window had snapped shut and the car had joined a queue of traffic turning right. She wanted to follow it or at the very least record the registration number, but she felt obliged to take the dropped mitten being offered, snatching it roughly from the woman's hand, annoyed that she'd been distracted, although she was of course grateful that her mitten had been recovered and so swiftly returned. She wouldn't have wanted to tell her grandmother that she'd lost one of them so soon after she'd knitted them, even though one mitten was all she actually needed. Her burnt hand was never cold.

'Thank you,' she snapped angrily, thrusting her mitten-less hand into the mitten and stomping away.

If it *had* been Stan, then he'd escaped again, like a cat with nine lives. If not, then the driver would have to ask someone else for directions.

When she arrived at the train station, an earlier train was waiting at the platform so she decided to catch that. It was scheduled to arrive at 3.50 p.m. and then it was a short walk home. She still thought of it as home.

When she turned the corner and saw that the front gate had been repaired she felt like crying, partly because it should have been repaired much sooner but mainly because it was exactly as she'd imagined it would be, an imposing hardwood gate that didn't look like just anybody could walk through it. If only she'd had the money to repair it herself. Perhaps they'd still be living there.

When she walked along the path this time, she imagined her mother waiting to greet her, wanting to hear all about Ellie's birthday party, not hanging from the bedroom ceiling examining her slippers. And while part of Frankie wanted to believe that when the front door opened it would turn out differently, the other part of her wondered if she'd find her mother dead for a second time. She was nervous. It would be painful stepping into her mother's bedroom, revisiting the story of her death, remembering the stitches of a tapestry that she'd been trying hard to forget.

But as she was scrutinising the outside of the house she realised that it didn't even look like their house any more, so her mother wouldn't have been there anyway. There were scalloped lace nets at the windows and the front door was now a glossy sage green instead of a weathered streaky-bacon brown. It was like they'd never lived there at all, every trace of them wiped away, the house having forgotten *them*.

She took a deep breath (some things didn't change), lifted the gate thumb latch and rang the brass doorbell (also new). She'd planned to slip through an open window without anybody noticing but instead hoped that whoever lived there now would let her inside voluntarily without a police warrant so that she could quietly gather the evidence against Stan that she'd come to collect (she had a roll of cling film in her rucksack to wrap it in). Providing they hadn't painted over that in sage green as well of course. But nobody answered the door. She walked round to the back of the house, which her mother always said was extremely rude. If someone doesn't answer the front door then they're out or they don't want to see you. Knocking on the back door isn't going to change that. But she'd come all this way and told so many lies that she couldn't give up now. She couldn't not try every door.

There was now a shed in the backyard on top of the yellow bird's grave. The lollipop cross must have been thrown away or flattened.

It was unlocked. Frankie decided to go inside and wait for the new owners there, even though she was now officially trespassing.

Trying to find somewhere to sit that wasn't like sitting on a guillotine took considerable effort. There were dozens of garden tools in the shed even though the garden was no bigger than a postage stamp. A trowel, a pair of shears and a yard brush were pretty much all you needed. There wasn't much room for anything else, certainly not a full-grown person. Thankfully, she was only half grown.

She placed a deflated paddling pool that was hanging on a hook inside the wheelbarrow and climbed in. It was actually more comfortable than it looked. In fact she could have lived in the shed quite happily if the contents were removed and she kept the door open. Perhaps she *should* be living in a shed in someone's garden if she couldn't live in the house that her father was supposed to have built. How much would the rent be, she wondered?

She unzipped her rucksack, which contained everything that she currently considered most important, and pulled out a Mars bar and her torch. It was beginning to get dark. She opened David Miller's book and read the chapter on 'What We Look For in a Gate' while she ate a cheese sandwich, and then she reread the letter that she'd written to him while she ate a packet of Quavers. She noticed three spelling mistakes that she hadn't noticed before. No wonder she'd received no reply.

According to her watch it was now seven thirty. She clambered out of the wheelbarrow, accidentally standing on the prongs of a rake which hit her in the face and elicited a 'Shitting hellfire!' and, rubbing her forehead, peered through the shed window, but there were no lights on inside the house. Perhaps she could scale one of the drainpipes with the help of one of the stepladders in the shed (not easy with only one fully functioning hand) or smash a ground-floor windowpane with one of the spades. She would have preferred to have been granted lawful entry, but her grandmother would be worried. She thought that she might have been on her way back by now, having discovered a crucial piece of evidence, or Stan himself sitting on the sofa.

She wished that she'd told her grandmother that she was staying at a friend's house overnight. Perhaps she should find a telephone box and call her, explain the situation. Might she have contacted the police? Or would she be relieved that Frankie had gone, pray that she never came back? Stationery wasn't cheap. She should find Selfish Brian and ask him where she should sleep. But first she needed to find that all-important incriminating fingerprint. She searched for the rope that he'd tied around her mother's neck, but there was only netting and twine and it didn't look nearly strong enough.

She was starting to feel tired. Investigating crimes on your own was exhausting. No wonder the police always patrolled in twos. She put David Miller away and curled up inside the wheelbarrow, using her mittens as a pillow and her blazer as a blanket. Just a few minutes' rest, that's all she needed, and then she would log the entire contents of the shed, remove the rake, which had given her a headache, and consult her notes again. She'd written a list of everything that Stan had touched and hoped that at least some of those things were still there and that they'd not all been wiped clean or painted over. Most things he touched ended up bruised.

When she next opened her eyes, it was light outside. She looked at her watch. It was eleven thirty in the morning. She'd slept for nearly sixteen hours and for much of that time Stan had been trying to drown her in a giant paddling pool. She pulled herself out of the wheelbarrow, checking for spikes and blades. Everything ached. She wasn't sure that living outdoors would suit her after all, if this was how you felt when you woke up. There was a minefield of hidden dangers to contend with and no mattress to sleep on.

She glanced across at the house. It still looked empty. She walked over to the back door in case she was mistaken and knocked again. Again there was no answer. She peered through the kitchen window, but she couldn't see anything through the lace net. She contemplated breaking the kitchen window with the brick that was balanced on top of the bin, but she didn't want to be arrested. She'd never find the incriminating piece of evidence then. She just wanted somebody to open the door and let her inside.

While she waited she did twenty laps around the garden and twenty-five star jumps, and then urinated on some 'EverRed' Chinese Witch Hazel (a care guide label was planted in the soil) that looked like crepe paper. It didn't mention watering with urine. Hopefully, she hadn't killed it. She'd have preferred not to have urinated in somebody's back garden, but she really couldn't hold it in any longer.

She lay on the grass for a while looking up at the clouds and then she ate a banana which had turned black inside her rucksack and was deeply unpleasant. She'd only packed enough supplies for one night, so things were already starting to look bleak. She pictured packets of Nesquik and jars of lemon curd in the kitchen cupboards, Dairylea Triangles and strawberry yoghurts in the fridge, just beyond her reach. She was salivating just thinking about what might be on the other side of the wall, but she didn't want to venture to the corner shop to satisfy her chronic hunger in case somebody saw her. Mrs Shah would surely recognise her. She'd hoped to find time to visit her mother's grave while she was there but that was looking more and more doubtful.

Rummaging in her rucksack she decided to save the egg yolk roll and the second Mars bar for later and sipped half a bottle of water instead. She needed to urinate again soon after, but this time she went behind the shed. She wrote eight short stories, including one about a shoemaker whose shoes made people do terrible things when they wore them, and compiled the contents list that she'd planned to do the evening before, together with a health and safety audit. Occupying herself while she waited required an advanced level of creativity (or repetition when there wasn't much to work with).

She did twenty more laps of the garden and then tackled some weeding by the back fence, which she thought would be appreciated and made her feel slightly better about killing the witch hazel, by which time it was four forty-five and already dark. She settled in the wheelbarrow, daydreamed for a while and then closed her eyes. But she wasn't tired and it was colder than it had been the day before. She wrapped some tarpaulin around her and pulled the door to.

She didn't sleep at all the second night. She heard every creak, every groan. She expected a madman wielding an axe to open the shed door at any moment and chop her into tiny bite-sized pieces and she was so hungry that her stomach hurt. She couldn't read or write because the torch wasn't working and she spent the entire night cowering beneath tarpaulin. She couldn't possibly spend another night in this shed no matter how much she wanted Stan to be punished for what he'd done. It was too terrifying.

As soon as it was light, she gathered her things together and, after finishing the weeding and touching her toes thirty-three times, she decided to visit the next-door neighbour's house. She would ask Graham and Judy Lloyd where the new owners were, if they still lived there. They did. The front gate was as ugly as it had always been. The same coarse wood, the same oversized rusted screws and hinges; it was like the entrance to a medieval dungeon.

Judy opened the door in her dressing gown. There were toothpaste stains down the front of it. She looked surprised to see her. Frankie didn't know why – she knew who she was.

'Frankie, is everything all right?'

'Hello, Mrs Lloyd. Are you ill? I'm terribly sorry to disturb you, but there's something in our old house that I need to retrieve and there's no one in. Do you know when the new owners will be back? I don't have a key any more.'

'I think they've gone to Weymouth to visit relatives. Come in. I'll see if I've got a contact number for them.'

She pulled the belt on her dressing gown tighter. She didn't look ill.

'I suppose I could spare a few minutes. I do need to use the toilet if you don't mind.'

She didn't want to spend another night sleeping in a wheelbarrow, and a telephone number would help establish when the owners would be back, so that she could make alternative arrangements. Perhaps she could stay in a hotel. And then she remembered that she'd only got ten pounds.

'Of course not. I'll go and get dressed and then I'll check my address book. Would you like something to eat?'

'It's okay, Mrs Lloyd. I don't need anything to eat. I've got a second Mars bar and an egg yolk roll in my rucksack. I always carry supplies.'

Judy went upstairs. Frankie thought that she could hear her talking to somebody, but when she asked her who she'd been talking to when she came back down, she said nobody. Graham's at work, she told her. Perhaps it was the radio. I often sing along when I'm doing chores.

'But weren't you getting dressed?'

'Perhaps I sing then too.'

'May I use the toilet then, Mrs Lloyd?'

'Of course. I'll get that number.'

Judy and Graham's house was like a show home. Everything sparkled like champagne. Everything shone. Except Judy, who looked like a second-hand armchair. She was wearing an old dog-eared fleece and a pair of elasticated trousers that were no longer quite as elasticated. She had to keep pulling them up.

Their twenty-year-old cat Cilla had just died, she told Frankie, when she came back from the toilet. She had cancer and she was blind in one eye and she was just skin and bone towards the end and riddled with lice, so it was a blessing really. And she'd lasted longer than most marriages. But I don't think I'll ever get used to her not being here. Her ashes are in that mahogany box on the windowsill, the one with the gold-plated paw print. She used to spend hours watching birds.

Frankie pictured her mother in a wooden box on the windowsill.

'Did you find the number, Mrs Lloyd?'

She'd stopped looking through the sideboard drawers and was gazing at the bird table outside.

'I can't seem to find my address book, but it probably wouldn't have been in there anyway. We don't really have much to do with them. Nice family, though – two teenage children, a boy and a girl. They had to convert the second bedroom into two smaller bedrooms.'

Frankie pictured her bedroom sliced in two. Instead of moving to somewhere more spacious they'd decided to make what little room they had even smaller.

'How's your grandmother?'

'She's fine, thank you.'

'Have you heard that the Barlows are moving away?'

'Moving away?'

'Yes, Barbara's pregnant and they're moving to Norfolk.'

Ellie had mentioned something about Norfolk when she last spoke to her, but she had no idea where Norfolk was. Nobody had ever asked her the way there. And at the time she had been thinking about the peach scones that she still hadn't had.

'No, I hadn't heard.'

She couldn't think about that now, about Ellie being in Norfolk and Mrs Barlow being pregnant. She'd address it later. She was about to interview an important witness.

She opened her notebook.

'Do you remember Stan?'

'Not really.'

'Did you never see him?'

She wanted a neutral party to confirm that he'd existed, that she hadn't made him up as a way of dealing with her mother's death.

'Rarely; like your mother, he kept himself to himself. I don't know that I ever spoke to him.'

'Did you see Stan on the day she died?'

'No. But there was a van parked outside the house that morning.'

'What type of van?'

'It was a white van, like the one Don Barlow drives. I didn't see anyone inside it, though.'

'Do you remember the registration number of the van?'

'I'm afraid not. I didn't think it was important.'

'Everything's important in an investigation, Mrs Lloyd. Did you mention it to the police?'

'They never asked.'

'You were never interviewed by the police?'

'No, but why would we have been?'

'I have reason to believe that my mother was murdered, which is why I'll be taking over the investigation. That's all I'm at liberty to disclose at the moment.'

'Murdered? Surely not.'

'I'm afraid so, Mrs Lloyd.'

She'd stolen the last sentence from her notebook. It was number two on her 'Things to Say When Trying to Sound Official' list.

Suddenly, Frankie wondered if the deceit stretched further than Stan. What if people who were (or who had been) serving police officers were protecting him? How would she ever be able to bring him to justice then? She would have to consider more carefully who to trust. Or better still, trust no one. Perhaps she should call her grandmother to tell her that she was safe (for now), but then she'd be forced to go back and 'let the police do their job' and it was becoming very apparent that they weren't doing it very well, that police corruption was far more widespread than even her mother had realised.

The doorbell rang as Frankie was adding footnotes to her interrogation transcript. Judy got up and answered the door.

'She's in there,' Frankie heard her say.

'Hello, Frankie,' a police officer said. 'We've been looking for you. You gave us quite a scare.'

She certainly had. She was getting closer to the truth. She just knew it. And this proved it.

'Are you here to arrest me?'

'No, I'm here to take you home.'

'Very well.'

She closed her notepad so that he couldn't read what she'd written and zipped it inside her rucksack. There was no point resisting. She needed to remain calm.

It appeared that Judy Lloyd was part of the conspiracy as well, claiming that she'd never spoken to Stan when Frankie had seen them with her own eyes having a conversation over the hedge, she'd recognised Judy's sandals, the white criss-cross ones, and now she'd called the police to stop Frankie discovering anything further. There was no white van. There was only Stan.

'You've been very helpful, Mrs Lloyd,' Frankie assured her. 'I'll be in touch if I need to speak to you further.'

She deliberately left the gate open as she was leaving.

As Frankie was about to get into the police car she noticed something glistening beneath the hedge that divided their house and the Lloyds house. She walked over to the hedge while the police officer was speaking into the car radio. It was a silver lipstick buried in the dirt. Frankie picked it up and wiped off the dirt with her blazer sleeve. She studied the label.

Angel Red.

Like her mother.

If there was red lipstick then there was still hope.

Special thanks to:

Ajda Vucicevic for being so encouraging and for championing this book.

Everyone at Mirror Books who played a part in its publication.

Amber Burlinson for copyediting the novel.

And Mike for his endless support.